Ada Hoffmann

THE FALLEN

ANGRY ROBOT

ANGRY ROBOT
An imprint of Watkins Media Ltd

Unit 11, Shepperton House
89-93 Shepperton Road
London N1 3DF
UK

angryrobotbooks.com
twitter.com/angryrobotbooks
From the Outside in

An Angry Robot paperback original, 2021

Cover by Lee Gibbons
Set in Meridien

ISBN 978 0 85766 868 4
Ebook ISBN 978 0 85766 871 4

Printed and bound in the United Kingdom by TJ Books Limited

9 8 7 6 5 4 3 2 1

PRAISE FOR ADA HOFFMANN

"*The Fallen* explores solidarity and cooperation in extreme situations with thoughtfulness and poise, weaving together a breathtaking array of themes from cosmic horror to superpowers. Ada Hoffmann's second novel brings action, excitement, and kindness surfacing in the strangest places. It warmed my tentacular heart!"

Bogi Takács, Hugo and Lambda Award-winning author

"*The Fallen* takes a look at what it means for something to be truly changed. Splintered and fragmented. The characters have been fundamentally altered, and the novel does a beautiful job of showing how and, more importantly, what the characters are going to do about it... It's a complex and intricately woven tale of people finding and building community and being vulnerable to the right people in order to be unstoppable together. A sweeping sequel that builds on the first book and leaves me hungry for more!"

Charles Payseur, Hugo-nominated author of Quick Sip Reviews

"The worldbuilding continues, fascinating and compelling. *The Fallen* is a complex, nuanced book which engages thoughtfully with the costs, consequences, and decisions around resistance and rebuilding."

Juliet Kemp, author of The Deep and Shining Dark

"*The Outside* is a fantastic debut. I can't wait to see what Hoffmann does next."

Locus

"Hoffmann confidently layers morality and disability rights into a breezily told adventure that bursts with sheer fun... This beautifully smart, uncynical space opera will charm fans of Charles Stross and Lois McMaster Bujold."

Publishers Weekly

"With a boffo combination of hard science fiction, cosmic Lovecraftian horror, both cyber-and-god-punk, some ridiculously charismatic aliens, and a fascinating female protagonist somewhere on the autism spectrum, Ada Hoffmann's *The Outside* feels like it was made to order for us."

Skiffy and Fanty

"*The Outside* is a gripping examination of the battle between good and evil on a grand scale."

The Guardian

"*The Outside* starts with a bang and ratchets everything up from there, giving us gods, angels, machines, mayhem, casual queerness, delicious ambiguities, and note-perfect character moments."

Sarah Pinsker, Nebula Award-winning author
of Our Lady of the Open Road

"There awaits wonders and horrors alike, wrapped in delicious prose and unforgettable imagery. And no matter how far into these fantastic and weird worlds we delve, there always remains a solid, comforting sense that we are not alone."

A. Merc Rustad, Nebula Award finalist and author
of So You Want to be a Robot

For Virgo

To Citizenship Lake; to Nic Lysosy Grej, Nana Gao, and Simplicity Bird; to Temperance, Persistence, and Tact Hunt; and to everyone else who loves me and might need to hear this:

I'm sorry.

I'm sorry I had to leave so quickly. I know how it feels to be left this way, and I would have said goodbye in person if I'd been given the choice. Angels took me; you can guess why. I'm not with them anymore, which is why I am able to write this now. But I can't come home yet. It wouldn't be safe, and there's something else I need to do first.

Please understand that I love you all, individually, unreservedly. All of you loved me even when it was difficult, when I was grieving and saying things that didn't make sense. I'll remember that always. None of what's happened to me is your fault.

To Ship – especially, to Ship – I'm so sorry. We meant well, but we were trying to make a future by denying the present and past. I hope I will see you again someday, not as your lover, but as your friend.

Please understand that I am doing what I need to do. I am doing what I believe in. It won't be safe, and I won't be able to write often. But please, if you understand nothing else in this letter, trust that I know what's right. My heart is where it always was, and I'm following it.

I am hoping with all the hope in me that we will meet again, in better times, and that you will be proud.

With love forever,
– Productivity Hunt

CHAPTER 1
Now
(Six Months after the Plague)

The familiar door of Yonne Qun's house stood tall in its doorway. If Tiv Hunt looked straight at it and not to the right or the left, it almost looked normal. Wooden and rectangular and solid, in a gray brick wall, set with the button of a doorbell – non-functioning now – a tin knob, a tin knocker. A mail slot near the bottom, a ramp running up to the threshold. Extremely normal, except for the way the mail slot curved, like a metal mouth, grinning or frowning or smacking its lips by turns.

If Tiv turned her head, of course, she'd see the garden, a mess of surreal plants that often moved of their own volition. The street the house stood on, with a surface that twisted and rippled, was walkable but no longer suitable for bicycles or electric cars. The houses next to Qun's stood in various states of disrepair: one blasted long ago into a pile of picked-over rubble; one twisted into an impassable, un-houselike spiral; one intact, but somehow pink and dripping; a few others, like Qun's, livable with their various blemishes and clumsy repairs. This was one of the better streets. It had been six months since the Plague, and Tiv still wasn't entirely used to things looking this way. Maybe no one ever would be.

She raised a hand, shifting the heavy pack on her shoulder,

and knocked. Three quick taps, a pause, and two more.

A moment passed, and the door swung open. Yonne Qun stood there: a middle-aged Riayin man, thin and lined, with medium-brown skin, very fine black hair, prominent cheekbones, and a quick, nervous smile.

"Leader," he murmured in Riayin, giving a short bow. "Come in. Come in, please."

Tiv bowed back clumsily, stepping over the threshold. She *really* wished people wouldn't bow to her. Yasira had told her it was normal in parts of Riayin, like shaking hands. But in Tiv's home culture, bowing meant submission, and combined with the "Leader" title, it creeped her out.

She'd learned not to protest about the title. Months ago, she and Yasira and their team had started calling each other by code names, in ways that she initially thought were a joke, but the names had proved meaningful in some weird ways, and more difficult to let go of than expected. Especially once the rest of the people in the Chaos Zone started calling them those names, too. But that didn't mean the names were accurate.

Tiv didn't actually lead anything. She organized more and showed her face more than the others on the team because the others had severe mental health issues and weren't up to it as often, but the team itself wasn't for the purpose of leading anything. Just connecting people. Helping them.

She shut the door and let her eyes adjust to the candlelit gloom. Like most of the Chaos Zone, Qun's house hadn't had electricity in six months. A large sitting room was still in reasonable repair, with armchairs and couches around the edges, boxes and piles of supplies stacked in the corners, and a central coffee table on which the candles and lamps gave their dim radiance. There was a small television in the corner which, incongruously, worked; the Gods had put a high priority on making sure people could watch their announcements every day. It was powered by some kind of God-built battery Tiv didn't understand. Qun, like in most households Tiv saw, had thrown a blanket over it and ignored its presence.

"Thank you for having me," said Tiv in polite Riayin. She was getting much better at speaking the language. She still felt self-conscious about her accent, but the people who called her "Leader" never seemed to care. She swung her pack off her shoulder and sat down in one of the armchairs, stacking up the pack's contents as she listed each one. "I've got most of what you asked for. These are the water filters, the batteries, the baby food, the insulin." She fished deeper, and brought out a pile of neatly folded, wrapped papers. "And these are the messages. From Babec, Küangge, Cheilu, Zhuon, Büata, Bolu, Lanne, Molu, Hunne. And Huang-Bo."

The supplies were useful, but if supplies were all Tiv knew how to give, she wouldn't have been called "Leader". Angels distributed supplies in places like this, too, often in greater amounts. Tiv's team just filled in the gaps. Many of the items were supplied by other survivors, in other cities, who had a surplus and were able to share. Others were stolen goods, palmed from warehouses and stockpiles elsewhere in the galaxy. That part still gave Tiv a guilty pause. It bothered her how easily she'd grown to embrace *stealing*, even to fill a desperate need.

The messages were what people like Qun really wanted. Communications in the Chaos Zone were patchy and heavily monitored. Travel by portal was prohibited, and overland travel could be deadly. Groups who weren't completely in lockstep with what the Gods wanted didn't have a safe way to find other such groups, to coordinate. That was where Tiv's team stepped in. They kept tabs on things and held the lines of communication open. The messages in Tiv's pile contained supply requests and offers, but also news of the kind angels didn't want shared. Updates on a group's efforts to resist the angels' regulations, or to develop the heretical magical abilities that had arrived with the Plague. Stories of the angels' atrocities. Essays and arguments about what it all meant, many diverging sharply from the dogma everyone here had been taught their whole lives.

Tiv didn't know how to lead a resistance, but she knew how to keep one alive.

Qun picked up the sheaf of messages, cradled them to his chest in the gloom. "I'll read these," he promised. Some he would share with his community, as he did the supplies. Some, the most sensitive, he would memorize and burn. "Thank you."

"Thank *you*," Tiv insisted. People like Qun were the ones who lived in the Chaos Zone full-time, steadfastly holding up their communities. Tiv's team had no meaning without them. She often wondered, late at night, what it would have been like if it was just her and Yasira, alone against the Gods. Without the needs and lives of people like Qun to ground them.

Shuffling across the room, Qun put the messages down on an unused chair, presumably to look through as soon as Tiv left. He unlocked a small drawer and pulled out another sheaf of papers, each carefully folded and sealed, each with the name of a destination printed on it. "Here are Renglu's messages. For Babec, Küangge, Cheilu–" He looked embarrassed. "Well, you can read it on them. But I had one more thing to ask."

Tiv looked at him warily. When community leaders like

Qun looked at her that way, with that hesitant, frustrated hope, it meant only one thing.

"Of course," she said. "Ask."

"We need weapons."

Just what she'd thought. She looked in Qun's eyes, feeling sympathy for the request even though she disagreed. He was a man under enormous pressure, trying his best to keep his community together under colossal threat.

She smiled sadly. "You know I have the same answer I always do. If you want to ask for weapons from the other communities, I'll pass that message along. I'm not judging you. But my team doesn't steal or make weapons. My team doesn't fight."

"Please, Leader," said Qun. He didn't look desperate so much as determined. He moved to the chair next to Tiv's and sat, taking one of her hands in both of his. "Listen to me."

Tiv looked at him doubtfully. Qun didn't mean any harm. But there was nothing like sudden physical contact to remind her what she really was – an unassuming twenty-seven year-old woman, traveling alone through dangerous territory. Untrained. And without the uncanny abilities the rest of her team had, to protect her, if anything awful occurred.

"This is in the messages, but I need to tell it straight to you," said Qun. "I need to know you understand me. You know we're near the border here."

"Yes," Tiv said, uncertainly. The border of the Chaos Zone was guarded fiercely; angels believed that the surreal state of things here was contagious, and, thus, it was officially all under quarantine.

"This week," said Qun, "a group of kids made a break for it. All orphans, none of them over twenty, Leader. The youngest, five. Across one of the unfenced stretches of forest. We all told them not to, but they were hungry and afraid and gambled that they could make it to safer territory. The angels gunned them down. Children, Leader. Do you understand?"

Tiv looked into his eyes and bit her lip. These were the eyes of a man who *knew* those children, who'd seen them playing in the creepy surreal streets and fighting over scraps, who remembered their faces and names. Who'd been trying to help them when he could, and who'd been powerless to save them. It wasn't the first time she'd seen eyes like that.

"I'm so sorry," she said.

Qun held her gaze. "There's word that a crackdown's going to start on the use of heretical abilities to grow food. As if they weren't being harsh enough about that already. *I* know how to keep those things private, but so many of the young people here don't. My own daughter has a talent for growing plants we can eat, and so many like her are tired of hiding what they do to survive. We need weapons, Leader. What else is your endgame if it isn't a fight? You're helping us survive, but it won't be enough in the end. Not unless we can fight *back*."

Tiv looked down, gently tugging her hand out of his grasp. "It's not that simple, Mr Qun. Even if my team was in favor of violent rebellion, we don't *have* any weapons that would stand a chance against an organized force of angels. Nothing we own now would do that, nothing we know how to make or steal, not even our powers."

"I don't believe that," Qun insisted. "*Ask* your team, Leader. That's all I'm demanding of you. Ask Savior."

"Savior's–" Tiv started, and then she bit down the words. *Savior's not a magic-dispensing machine.*

Once, Yasira had radically altered the very structure of

the Chaos Zone. It had been even worse before. People like Qun, for the most part, were only alive because of what Yasira had done. If they saw the toll it had taken on her, they wouldn't have been so quick to demand it again.

But they hadn't, and they were, and there was nothing Tiv could do about that.

"I'll mention it," she said.

There were six cities on Tiv's itinerary for today, scattered across the vastness of the Chaos Zone.

Tiv didn't have any magical powers. In the Chaos Zone, that made her something of an exception. Among random civilian survivors like Qun, about a third of them had low-level abilities of some sort. To grow edible food, like Qun's daughter, to repel monsters, to do a hundred other tiny things that helped keep them safe. There were other, stranger groups in the Chaos Zone, groups that the survivors called "gone people" because they couldn't talk or live in houses, and those groups had similar powers in a heightened form that nobody fully understood. And the other people on Tiv's team had special powers, too. It was a result of their special connection with Yasira, a linking across time and space that Tiv didn't quite understand. Yasira and the rest of the team had been Dr Evianna Talirr's students once; they'd all been indirectly exposed to Outside ideas long before the Plague happened, and at the time Yasira needed extra power for her miracle, they'd been primed to give it. It hadn't been possible to include Tiv in that linking, and sometimes she suspected that Yasira wouldn't have included her even if it was. She would have seen it as something Tiv needed to be protected from.

Yasira herself was, obviously, special. But Tiv was just a

normal person. She sometimes thought they'd called her "Leader" as a pity title; she might as well organize, since there wasn't much else she could do.

She pushed her bangs out of her eyes, tired and sweating after her sixth meeting. Shouldering her pack, she looked right and left for observers, then pulled open the door to a half-broken storefront that no longer sold anything.

She stepped through, not into the thoroughly looted wasteland of shelves that actually lay within, but into an airlock. A clean steel space, rectangular and bare, like a closet. The door swung shut behind her. She exhaled carefully: this place carried the same underlying Outside eeriness as the Chaos Zone, a prickle below her skin that had become as familiar as sore feet, but the feeling here wasn't as strong as on Jai.

The people that the Seven worked with knew they got around this way, but it was best to be careful. It was best to make sure that the angels, in particular, couldn't see them doing it.

Dr Evianna Talirr had built this airlock. One of her many accomplishments was the construction of portals allowing instantaneous travel across space. Most of Dr Talirr's portals resembled the ones that the Gods built, although the underlying mechanisms were stranger. But this airlock was her masterwork, a *meta*-portal. One end of it connected to Dr Talirr's abandoned lair. The other would synchronize with any mundane door in any place the user visualized – or as close to what they intended as it could – and it would stay there, opening only to them and the people they willingly brought with them, until they returned.

The airlock was how Tiv and her team traveled so quickly between dozens of cities, across a wide and dangerous fifth of a planet with its infrastructure in tatters. The airlock, much more than any magic, was Tiv's power.

The inner door opened, and Tiv walked through into the lair. No longer Dr Talirr's lair, but theirs now. It was a cavernous, windowless space, and it had once been full of Dr Talirr's half-finished projects, machinery and equipment strewn every which way. It really was *every* which way, even the walls and ceiling; gravity worked oddly here.

In six months of living here, Tiv and her team had remodeled a bit. They'd replaced the harsh, bluish lights that once washed out the room with warm, full-spectrum, dimmable ones. The tangles of incomprehensible wiring had been carefully packed away. A few devices, the ones that actually worked, sat cleaned and polished in their own nooks: an ansible, an old-fashioned non-sentient supercomputer, and the power generation and life-support machines that hummed under the floor. Plus one odd broken thing at the very far end of the room, a twisted metal *something* on a dais. Yasira called that device a prayer machine, designed to facilitate communication with Outside, and she had broken it herself, early on, before Tiv could work up the courage to use it.

In the remaining open spaces, Tiv and her team had made a home. A few private rooms, cubicle-like and clumsily decorated, dotted the lair at odd angles. But most of the team, traumatized from long isolation, had elected to sleep in the open instead. A central area, not far from the airlock, held their nest of ragged blankets and beanbags, hammocks and futons and cushions, a riot of softness and color and mess. Beyond it stood the working area where they organized. The team had started calling that area the "war room", even though they were opposed to war – it was half a joke, and half maybe some suppressed frustration on their part. Tiv strode towards it, ready to record her activities for the day.

Five of the team were still out making their rounds. Daeis Jalonevar – a pale, squat, quiet Anetaian who went by the code name of "Keeper" – had been indisposed today. They sat more or less where Tiv had left them this morning, holding silent court in a pile of blankets with an armful of the squirrel-sized, bug-like Outside creatures who infested the space. Daeis had difficulty talking much, but they had a special affinity for Outside monsters, and could communicate with them mentally on levels unparalleled by anyone but Yasira herself. In turn, the smaller and more common of the monsters had become Daeis's friends, and Tiv knew that they were now attempting to comfort them.

Splió spi Munu – code name "Watcher" – had made partial rounds but had returned early to care for Daeis, and he sat there now with a lethargic hand on their shoulder. Splió was a Gioti man with tousled hair and a cynical grin, who was usually seen around Daeis when not out working or sulking by himself. He looked up as Tiv walked into the space, and hauled himself up on his feet to greet her.

"Hey," she said with an attempt at a smile. Tiv usually had more energy than most, but she was tired today.

"Hey, Leader. That bad, huh?"

"The usual. Everyone's trying the best they can."

That was a platitude Tiv had begun using often. No one needed the hanging *buts* spelled out: everyone in the Chaos Zone was trying their best, *but* conditions were awful. The Gods' relief efforts weren't keeping up with their needs, *but* any attempt to meet those needs in another way was punished severely. Everyone on Tiv's team was trying their best, *but* they were only nine people, eight of whom were mentally ill enough that it affected the kind of resistance they could run. Even their heretical abilities were no match for what was out there.

It had been even worse when the Plague was new. In those first few terrifying weeks, it had just been Yasira and Tiv, alone against the world, and Yasira had been so ill that it sometimes felt like Tiv was on her own. The other seven, shambling into the lair one by one during the latter half of the Plague's first month, had been a surprise. They were former students of Dr Talirr's, like Yasira; they'd been captured by angels, just like Yasira, and they'd languished in captivity until Yasira's magic set them free. Yasira had meant for them to go home to their families, but all of them, through some mysterious Outside homing sense, had instead found their way to her doorstep. All of them had offered their loyalty and their help.

Tiv could use all the help she could get, honestly.

"They asked you for weapons again," said Splió. "You've got that look."

Tiv abruptly started walking again, towards the war room, and Splió followed. Daeis seemed content for Splió to leave; they quickly turned their attention back to their Outside pets with a small smile. "We don't do weapons. We are a non-violent resistance movement. We agreed."

"Yeah, I know." Though some had agreed more than others. Splió had been on the fence. Tiv had been the one who put her foot down, who'd refused to consider any other option. She might be a heretic now, but she wasn't *that* far gone.

The war room was neither a room nor a place for planning war. There would not be a war if Tiv could help it.

What the war room did have, once Tiv passed the living nest and crossed the makeshift barrier dividing the two areas, was a large table and a set of even larger whiteboards and easels on which the team's plans could be coordinated. Schedules, maps, lists of needed supplies. Incident lists. Tiv took a black whiteboard marker and methodically checked off her six cities. Then she moved to the incident list and hesitated, reluctant to write down what Qun had told her.

She lowered the marker and sighed, looking at the floor. Splió was still watching.

"The angels are shooting children," she said without looking up. "At the border."

"Eh, well, it's not like arming the children's gonna help."

Splió's primary mental health symptom, during his captivity, had been depression. He'd perked up a bit once he was free, but he still carried a lethargic cynicism which sometimes annoyed Tiv. Other times – like now – she found it strangely comforting. She gave him a warning look; she didn't want him getting *too* morbid. "They wanted arms for the adults, not the children, obviously. It's still..." She sighed shortly. "Fighting any way they understand isn't going to help them, and they know it."

Splió raised an eyebrow. "Then why'd they ask?"

Tiv looked back down at the table, squaring her shoulders. "Mr Qun asked me to ask Yasira."

Splió gave a long whistle out through his teeth. "Good luck with that."

People were always asking after Yasira, clamoring for another miracle. Tiv usually rebuffed them. Yasira had so little ability to deal with the world right now. There was no sense bothering her with wasteful or greedy or impossible requests. She'd say no to those, if Tiv gave her the choice, and then stew in guilt about it for weeks. It was rare for Tiv to actually pass a message along – much less a violent one.

She didn't know why she'd said yes this time. She was stewing in guilt, too, maybe.

Splió shifted, leaning against a small partition strewn with tacked-up maps and notes. "Well, let all of us know how it goes, Leader."

Tiv wasn't sure if what she saw in Splió's expression was resentment or frustrated hope. Some of the students were raring for a fight.

"I'll let you know," she said.

He detached himself from the wall and wandered back to check on Daeis. Tiv raised the marker, refocusing on the incident list, and jotted down a quick recounting of what Qun had told her. The list was already long, a thick easel pad with most of its pages used up and flipped over. Someday soon, she and Grid and Picket would have to go back through it and find a better way to organize the information.

She capped the marker and set it down, then tidied up a bit to steady her nerves. Realigned stacks of paper, wiped away jots on the whiteboards that were no longer needed.

Then she took a breath and walked up the lair's wall, halfway around its radius, to a private chamber that hung upside down relative to the war room, enclosed and dark. The door was barely decorated in spite of Tiv's best efforts, just a blank wooden slab with a knob. She knocked, and when there was no answer, she quietly eased it open and slipped into the small room where Dr Yasira Shien, the visionary heretic and miracle-worker called "Savior" by most of Jai's Chaos Zone, lay in her rumpled bed, unmoving.

"Hey," said Tiv in the darkness, and Yasira stirred. She didn't look up, but she moved a hand spasmodically to push against the bedspread, as if she was thinking about it.

This was one of the bad days, then.

Tiv probably wasn't going to ask about weapons today.

Yasira was a Riayin woman Tiv's age, with the same fine dark hair and petite features as Qun and most of the other survivors. She'd never been large, but she was thinner now than when Tiv had first known her, the result of months lying around with an angry mental illness and no appetite. She was pretty in an unstudied, uncared-for way. Her narrow face wasn't visible in her present position, pressed against the pillows as she lay flopped on her belly, with her long hair spreading everywhere in a careless tangle.

Tiv walked forward and knelt beside the bed, leaning her head against the bedspread. She ached to touch Yasira, pull her in close and cuddle her, like they'd used to before any of this Outside stuff started. But touching Yasira, especially without a warning, wasn't always helpful anymore. Tiv mostly did things like this instead, making herself unthreateningly present and soft.

"Eat anything good while I was out?" she asked.

"Mmph," said Yasira, which meant *no*.

"Yeah, I didn't think so. Drink anything?"

Yasira made a more equivocal noise at that one. She'd probably had a few sips of water at some point, then gotten annoyed with having a body and stopped.

"All right," said Tiv, "I'm getting you a glass of water and a pile of toast, 'cause you're going to feel better after you eat. You want anything special? Jam? I think we've still got some chocolate butter left, unless Weaver ate it."

"Not hungry," Yasira mumbled into the bedspread.

"Yeah, that's what you always say, and then you feel better after you eat. Genius brains need food. What else is going to fuel all those gears turning?"

"'m not a genius anymore."

"Nuh-uh. None of that. You know exactly what's wrong with you, and it's not a lack of brains. Stay here, okay? I'm gonna be right back."

She heard a resigned groan behind her as she slipped back out of the room. Pouring water and making toast was the work of only a minute; it required shimmying up a rickety ladder to the odd upside-down space that served for a kitchen in the lair, with a Bunsen burner for a stove and entirely too little fridge space for nine people. They were always filling up that fridge and the pantry next to it, then running out in a day or two and having to make yet more errands from the airlock for groceries, most of which were stolen like the rest of their supplies. Or paid for with stolen credit chits, which was ethically the same.

When she made it back into the bedroom, Yasira hadn't stirred any further.

"Hey, I got the food," Tiv announced. "You want to eat?"

"No," Yasira mumbled, face down.

"Well, too bad, 'cause you can't get out of it that easily. I'm just gonna sit here and watch you until you eat the toast. You know how this works."

Yasira did, and so did Tiv. It was another twenty minutes of coaxing before she had Yasira sitting up in bed, her hair falling over her face, tentatively reaching for the plate of food. The first bite was like pushing a pair of repelling magnets together, but after that Yasira calmed somewhat, as usual. She gradually started to chew and swallow in more of a rhythm.

"I'm sorry," she murmured between bites. "I shouldn't be so difficult. I mean– I'm glad you're here." She looked up and her gaze briefly flicked against Tiv's. Yasira had always been autistic, and her capacity for eye contact was limited;

she'd never stared into people's faces soulfully the way some did. But she'd liked looking at Tiv, back before the Plague, in the ways that were easy for her. The briefness of the glance was comforting, familiar.

What wasn't as comforting was the way Yasira stiffened, a second afterwards, and seemed to change her mind again. That had been happening too much lately, a seeming disorganization of thought. Yasira's speech definitely hadn't skipped around this way, before the Plague. "I don't know what I'd do without you. I mean–" She set the plate down with a clunk, half-emptied. "You shouldn't be here. You shouldn't be fucking weighed *down* with me, Tiv, you need–"

She cut off again, and Tiv tapped the plate, handing it back to her to finish. "Don't cuss. And don't pretend I don't want you here with me, okay? We've talked about this."

They had talked about it endlessly, in circles, every day. There were only so many ways Tiv could tell Yasira that she still loved her. She'd spent fourteen months, before the Plague, thinking Yasira was dead. Being together and alive was *miles* better, no contest at all. What the Gods did to Yasira had broken Tiv's faith, but Tiv still believed in something.

Yasira picked up the last piece of toast and reluctantly started chewing again.

Tiv knew that Yasira needed therapy from a professional. But there wasn't exactly a place to get that when you were a heretic on the run. Tiv had done what research she could, had resolved to do her best, but she knew it was only going to feel like treading water sometimes.

But she wasn't here out of pity, as Yasira sometimes sulkily implied, or out of some misplaced nostalgia for what they'd had. Tiv had hero-worshipped Yasira ever since they met. During the Plague, Yasira had saved a whole fifth of a planet. She'd known – she *must* have known – that what she did for the people of the Chaos Zone would break her. And she'd done it anyway.

People in the Chaos Zone clung to Yasira's story like a scrap of hope. And when Tiv looked at the woman she loved, she felt a little of that, also. She, too, felt not pity but awe.

Here is the official story of the Chaos Zone, the one that the Gods tell and the angels repeat:

Once upon a time there was a heretic.

Her name was Dr Evianna Talirr. She hated the Gods and loved chaos. So she made contact with Outside, a realm of unknowable chaos and madness. She summoned a part of Outside into the planet Jai and created an area contaminated with Outside's very essence. One-fifth of the planet's surface. More than half of the prosperous country of Riayin, and a tenth of its sister nation, Slijon.

Within this Chaos Zone, all the laws of reality were suspended. Physical matter could not be counted on to retain its shape. Horrific monsters stalked the streets. Millions died. Millions more were stressed to the point of madness. Some lost their identities altogether and took to roaming like the monsters, becoming what we now call the gone people. And many tens of millions were tempted into heresy, attempting to manipulate the Outside effects of the Chaos Zone themselves.

Through the immense hard work and sacrifice of many angels, we have contained the Chaos Zone. We have quarantined it, stopped its growth, and achieved a reduction in the lethality of its effects. We continue to provide aid to those affected and to work towards further improvement.

The Chaos Zone's existence is the worst affront to humanity since the Morlock War. When we have caught Dr Talirr, she will suffer retribution proportionate to her crimes. In the meantime, we beg the citizens of Jai to remain calm and to hold on to hope. Do not give in to heresy. Dr Talirr wants you to reject the Gods. Do not give her the satisfaction. Do not share in her punishment.

CHAPTER 2
Five Months Ago

Elu Ariehmu, no longer of Nemesis, looked down at Akavi Averis nervously as the other angel stirred on the operating table, beginning to open his eyes.

Akavi was in his true form, that of a Vaurian shapeshifter, delicate and androgynous, with translucent, vaguely metallic-looking skin. His hair was a soft gray-white that had nothing to do with age. His eyes, when they fluttered half-consciously open, were pale, and the lashes around them paler. He had a white blanket draped over him for modesty, and bandages around his forehead where the medical bots had reached in to modify the neural circuitry that made him more than human. He was very beautiful, and even though he was not quite awake, he already looked faintly annoyed.

"How are you feeling, sir?" Elu asked. The bots had indicated that everything went according to plan, but they weren't sentient, and this wasn't a surgery in the official angelic repertoire. The principle was simple enough, but if Elu had misprogrammed something or forgotten a crucial detail, he might not know until the telltale symptoms of a mistake appeared.

Akavi made a small *nngh* sound. The microexpression software in Elu's visual cortex dutifully logged his emotions: exhausted, in pain, dismayed by his own vulnerability. A second later Akavi collected himself, squared his jaw, and said, "I have no complaints." His syllables came out slow, slurred with the aftereffects of anesthesia.

Elu smiled fondly. Akavi never would admit weakness, not even at a time like this.

"Can you feel your ansible uplink?"

"I– hm." His brow furrowed again, and he was lost in thought for six and a half seconds, long enough that Elu started to wonder if he'd fallen back asleep. "No. It's not just dormant but gone. Cleanly, it seems."

Elu let out about half of a relieved breath. "Are you feeling well enough to run diagnostics? Are any other systems affected?"

"Stand by." A longer pause this time. Fifteen seconds. Twenty. "No, everything else appears normal." The corner of Akavi's mouth quirked, something that might have been a smile if he'd had more energy. "You are competent, as ever."

Elu sighed out the rest of his breath.

It had been several weeks since the Plague. For most of that time they'd been on the run from the Gods in a stolen God-built spaceship. The Gods had expected Akavi to prevent the Plague, then They'd expected him to solve it, and then They'd ordered him terminated for failing at both. It had been Elu's idea, not Akavi's, to escape.

A stray bit of magic from an encounter with Evianna Talirr had given them the head start they needed. She'd meant to hide Akavi from the Gods long enough to reckon with him herself. But that attempt had failed, and, when she left, her magic stayed behind. For an unknown period they'd been hidden from all the Gods' sensors. And they'd used that time to run.

It was anyone's guess how long that magic would hold

up. So Elu, who had some facility with cybernetics, had been making his own arrangements. He'd removed and disabled everything that connected the *Talon* to the ansible nets, and all the failsafes that might allow the Gods to override its controls. He'd used bots and printers to modify the ship's exterior so that it resembled a small civilian transport, not the sleek God-built marvel that remained within. And he'd planned, painstakingly, a neurosurgery that would make the corresponding modifications to him and Akavi. The ansible connections in their brains would be removed, leaving them crippled by the standards of angels, cut off from the network where they'd stored so much of their knowledge and community, but safely anonymous for that very reason. They could go where they wanted to, once they'd recovered from a surgery like that.

Well, almost. The titanium plates at Elu's forehead, marking where his circuitry went in, would still be there. Even aside from being an angel, Elu looked distinctive – frozen by angelic anti-aging treatments at nineteen, when most angels joined the corps in their thirties or forties. With an order out for his and Akavi's arrest, that would be the first thing everyone would know to look for. He'd have to stay on the ship or hide his face completely. Akavi was luckier, but he'd still have to watch that his shapeshifting abilities and his more-than-mortal intelligence didn't give him away.

Elu had wanted to go under first. If there was a bug in the software, let it be him who suffered the consequences and not Akavi. But Akavi, uncharacteristically, had insisted otherwise. Elu was the one who understood medical software; he needed to watch the first surgery with all his faculties intact. That way, if something did go wrong, he'd have a fighting chance at setting it right.

The surgery had mostly involved the inorganic part of Akavi's brain, but recovery from such a procedure could be nearly as complicated as the organic version, as mind and soul struggled to accommodate the changed shape they inhabited. Exhaustion, confusion and incredible headaches could be expected for the next several weeks. And, for the next few hours, there'd still be the leftovers from general anesthesia.

"Let me get you some water," Elu said. Akavi murmured something in acknowledgment. It was the work of only a few seconds to grab a glass of clear, pure water from the food printer. By the time Elu returned with it, Akavi had already fallen back asleep.

"I want revenge," Akavi said to Elu later. He was sitting up now, looking out the *Talon's* window at the stars. They were in his quarters. Akavi sat on a chair that had been folded out into a stretcher and covered with a sterile sheet. There was no bed. Angels rarely needed to sleep; they had other means of maintaining neurological homeostasis. It was only when profoundly exhausted, in the wake of surgery, illness, or injury, that the biological version overcame them.

"I know, sir," said Elu. They'd talked about it before.

"Yasira betrayed me. Irimiru betrayed me. *Nemesis* betrayed me." He hissed out that last name: the name of a God. It was blasphemous to speak a God's name in anger this way, but Akavi was already slated for termination and damnation. He could say whatever he liked. "The guilty must be punished, and that is our nature."

Elu tugged nervously at his long black hair, which he kept carefully brushed out of his face. He understood

Akavi's argument. He was hardly going to object on moral grounds; he and Akavi had done many things more terrible than seeking revenge. It was just...

He'd had a vague hope, maybe, that life on the run would be different. They'd find some different things to do, on their own terms.

But he wanted to be with Akavi much more than he wanted those vague, half-formed things. Elu had happily followed Akavi's orders for fifty years.

"I don't know how you can punish a God," said Elu.

Akavi frowned slightly. His gaze was still glassily fixed on the stars. He hadn't recovered from the anesthetic yet, but with his straight spine and sharp words, he was trying very hard to pretend he had. "No, I haven't found a promising avenue yet. We'll start with Yasira; she's an easier target. A broken heretic on the run, without support."

Elu would have quibbled about the *without support* part. Yasira had taken her girlfriend with her when she escaped. And she had Outside abilities whose precise nature remained unknown. But he knew what Akavi meant. Irimiru was a powerful, high-ranking angel protected by a massive divine apparatus, and Nemesis Herself was even more so. Yasira didn't have those things. Like him and Akavi, she was making do as best she could.

"What about Talirr?" Elu asked carefully. "Did she betray us?"

He liked the idea of keeping up the search for Talirr, much more than he wanted to hunt Yasira down. He wasn't sure *how* they'd do it; they'd tried before, with the full resources of an Inquisitor in good standing, and still failed. He knew they couldn't work their way back into Nemesis' good graces. Forgiveness wasn't what Nemesis *did*. But Talirr had hurt hundreds of millions of people, and making her pay for those crimes still felt like a good thing to do. The right thing to do.

Elu had seen what serving Nemesis, the God of punishment, was really about. But there was still a childish part of him, deep down, that just wanted to catch all the bad guys and make the world safe.

Akavi flicked a hand. "We'll add her to the list with Irimiru, if you like. We'll – ugh." His face contorted slightly. Elu rummaged in his supplies for another painkiller. "What did you say was the estimated recovery time for this procedure?"

"It's hard to say, sir," Elu replied, as he found the appropriate bottle and shook out two small tablets. It still felt natural to call Akavi *sir*, but should he? Akavi wasn't technically his commanding officer anymore. They were outside that whole structure, but that didn't make them equals. Maybe he should ask.

He didn't quite want to, though. Not while Akavi was still in recovery. The question was too big, too connected to too many other things.

"My simulations indicated a few days to basic functionality," he continued, refocusing. Akavi took the tablets and the glass of water by his bed and easily swallowed them. "A couple more weeks for any lingering pain, mental unease, or disorientation. But we won't really know until we're through it. A slower recovery isn't necessarily a warning sign. What would be more worrying is if you display any symptoms that aren't on the predicted list, so we'll be monitoring that carefully."

Akavi made a small *hmph* sound, looking away from him.

"Where do you think Yasira is?" Elu asked. "We won't need a full recovery just to start looking."

"She'll be on Jai. Or near it. That much is obvious."

"Is it? I almost think she'd run off and hide somewhere. Have a bit of a rest." Yasira had been traumatized and exhausted the last time Elu saw her. And the Chaos Zone of Jai wasn't going to be a restful place for anyone.

Akavi gave him a contemptuous glance. "Of course she'll rest at first. But Yasira Shien rebelled against us precisely because of her desire to *help*. She'll keep that desire, no matter how exhausted. That's doubly true if her lover is with her. When we're sufficiently recovered, we'll go to the Chaos Zone. We'll take stock of the current situation and of who's being helped, in mysterious ways, against the Gods' orders. That's where we'll find Yasira, rest assured. And when we find her, then the fun begins."

Elu gave him a doubtful look. "Fun, sir?"

Akavi smiled sharply; his gaze had already returned, out the window, to the stars. "That's when we destroy her."

A line of warrior angels, wearing the red-and-black active-duty livery of Nemesis and the bronze-and-white uniform of Arete, stood at attention in front of Enga Afonbataw Konum, marshal of Nemesis. Most held God-built firearms, sleek and heavy, in their hands; a few, like Enga, were modified so heavily that they did not need them. Some dragged larger weapons behind them in the training field, a rectangular area of short dry grass not far from the angels' encampment. Border Camp 342-6J, this was called, one of an irritatingly long line of makeshift stops all around the edge of the Chaos Zone. All devoted to the same purposes: to keep the Plague-ridden area from expanding, and to serve as a home base for missions further in.

Enga stood as straight as the rest of the warriors, with the alien Spider known as Sispirinithas waiting at her side, and an ungainly makeshift target just behind her. Enga was a distinctive-looking angel, easily picked out even if she hadn't worn the elaborate piping of her recent promotion. Enga was tall, muscular, dark-skinned, and silent. Where most angels had arms, Enga sported the most elaborate customized prosthetics in the angelic corps, a tangle of muzzles and manipulators sprouting from her shoulders, which compactly contained dozens of deadly weapons along with nearly any other tool she might require.

Her new rank of marshal was as high as she could go without vaulting all the way into administration: as prestigious, in its way, as the rank of Inquisitor. She'd been racking up commendations for decades, and her performance during the Plague, combined with her previous supervisor's failure, had finally pushed her all the way up here. She had been the first angel to demonstrate that Jai's largest monsters could be killed. She had been one of a very small number to survive field placement in the Chaos Zone at all, back when it was still cut off from off-planet communication and support, and she'd directly saved the lives of half a dozen other angels on the return journey. Now that the Chaos Zone was opened, she'd been given the role of training the rest of the infantry who served here.

Enga did not feel proud, the way she had a right to feel, being granted all these honors. Enga felt lonely and bored. She could see all the angels in front of her, not only with her eyes, but with her circuitry, which picked them all out as bright points of light in the surrounding network, living nodes temporarily suborned to hers. But grunts were just grunts. Enga didn't like any of them. She was lonely for something else.

She wanted Elu and Akavi, but they were gone, and they were never coming back except as corpses.

READY, she text-sent to the line of infantry, and she watched them shoulder their weapons with precise efficiency. No one form of weapon could be guaranteed to work on every Outside monster. Each was unique. A heavy armor-piercing missile would do the job in a pinch, but those were cumbersome to carry around, and they were in many cases overkill.

AIM, she text-sent, and the angels pointed their weapons in unison at the practice target. Just a black circle cobbled together from scraps, at about the height of one of the medium-large Outside monsters. It bobbed slowly in the air, imitating movement patterns that had been extracted from Enga's own sensory videos.

She paced the ranks, examining the way each angel scoped out the target, the way they kept their eyes half-averted. She paused meaningfully by one, a curly-haired man in Nemesis' colors, who was staring too directly at the stupid black circle, too focused. She telescoped an appendage out to grab that one by the chin.

DO NOT LOOK DIRECTLY AT THEM, IT CAN FUCK UP YOUR VISUAL CIRCUITS, she instructed.

"Yes, sir. Sorry, sir," said the recruit.

Enga let go, and watched him snap back to attention, nearly losing his balance. *TEN,* she ordered, before walking away down the line.

The man obligingly dropped to the ground and began a short set of pushups.

Enga didn't care about honors and ranks, but there was something satisfying about being addressed as "sir" in that frightened way. Getting to dole out punishments, even in these small ways, as she saw fit.

"Sir," said another of the angels, also of Nemesis, a woman

almost as large and strong as Enga. Enga could have looked up her name on the network if she'd wanted to. "Question."

MAKE IT GOOD, said Enga, who did not like being questioned. Long ago, before she was an angel, Enga had worked as a fitness instructor. There was enough of her old self left that she faintly remembered what that was like, and why responding to questions was important. But she didn't enjoy the process anymore. Being an angel wasn't like doing martial arts for fun. When you were an angel, it was safer to obey without thinking.

"Sir, why are we bothering to do it like this, to go out into enemy territory and pick off the monsters one by one? Why bother shooting carefully at what we think is their head? We have the weaponry to do better. We could burn out a whole district at once, the monsters and the heretics alike."

Enga glowered, because she actually agreed. She would much rather bomb the whole place into oblivion. Not long ago, Nemesis had come very close to doing it Herself: orbiting the planet with a convoy of Ha-Mashhit-class warships and melting every square foot of affected land back to magma. Starting again clean.

But there were reasons why She hadn't gone through with it. Gods relied on human worship. They consumed human souls to keep Themselves alive; without that process, They would only be very advanced machines. They could do it without individual humans' consent, but if humans ever did rebel – if they started a second Morlock War – they could force the Gods to destroy them in Their own defense. And the Gods would be diminished afterwards, with only a remnant of the human population to give them sustenance. It would take hundreds of years to recover.

So the Gods could only use Their power in certain ways.

The most brutal acts were done in secret – or to targets that could be painstakingly justified. Worse than any individual heretic going unpunished was the risk of crossing some moral line and becoming, in mortal humanity's eyes, an enemy.

Some of the Gods, like Nemesis, restrained Themselves for that reason alone. Other Gods had more complicated feelings. Arete, who fought so often at Nemesis' side, didn't like to dirty Her hands; Arete genuinely wanted to be a benevolent master. Enga could see some of Arete's angels in the group, shifting slightly, giving uncomfortable looks to the angel who'd asked.

So bombing out whole cities at once, in the Chaos Zone, was something the Gods had decided They couldn't do. But Enga wasn't impressed. Everybody in the Chaos Zone was a heretic, right? The Gods were already busy elsewhere, carefully crafting propaganda vids that showed why the Chaos Zone couldn't be saved. They were either building up to a large-scale bombing eventually, or They were stupid. And in the meantime, angels like Enga were having to waste their time pretending that individual fights with monsters even mattered. Enga did not like wasting time.

Another problem was that Nemesis' forces were spread thin. The Keres, the Gods' ancient enemy, had scented blood here. She was beginning to make Her own forays into the area. Nemesis' forces on the ground often had to shrink their own efforts because personnel were needed to fend the Keres off.

But Enga didn't like that argument either. Personnel would be less of an issue with a different approach; it didn't take a lot of angels to just bomb the shit out of something. It did take a lot of angels to do what she was doing – recruit and train endless troops to patrol an area, dealing with threats one at a time.

But the third argument, the one Enga was least able to dispute, was that bombing the shit out of the Chaos Zone wouldn't solve anything. Not until they'd found Evianna Talirr. She was the one who'd done this to the planet. And she could do it again. Clean up Jai's Chaos Zone too quickly and neatly, and Talirr would only make another one somewhere else. There were only a few dozen populated planets in human space; pretty soon they'd start to run out. The Gods had to find Talirr, along with Yasira Shien, who was capable of something similar. *Then*, maybe, They could bomb what remained.

But that meant that Enga and the troops in her care were only buying time. Spinning their wheels uselessly until some other part of the angelic corps got its act together. Pretending what they did here, until then, mattered.

Enga *hated* feeling useless. And she hated having to explain things she hated to subordinates who hated them as much as she did. Having to pretend – because protocol demanded it – that she thought those things were good.

WE ARE KEEPING ORDER IN THE CHAOS ZONE, Enga replied, *NOT BURNING IT. THAT IS NEMESIS' COMMAND.*

But the junior angels could probably feel the frustrated rage under her text-sending. She couldn't help it; she'd never learned to filter her feelings out completely, as the most skilled angels could. And that was going to make everyone question more, not less. She was fucking it up.

NO MORE QUESTIONS, said Enga, and she turned on her heel and walked away.

She heard Sispirinithas, behind her, picking up the slack by diving into a lecture. "The maddening quality of Outside monsters isn't solely conveyed through the visual system," said the characteristic whispery voice from his translator.

Sispirinithas was an alien, one of the vanishingly rare non-humans who worked for human Gods. He wasn't literally a giant spider, but he looked like one, with ten spindly legs radiating from a rounded, many-eyed, heavy-jawed body. "If you don't have sensory filters installed – hm, raise your hand if you don't have sensory filters installed? No one? Good. You might notice those filters apply to all your senses. That's because you can be driven mad with any of them. Even species who don't share any specific human sensory faculties can be driven mad by Outside. The filters prevent that, but if you focus too intently on the worst kinds of Outside monster, the filters' processing capabilities can overload and glitch, causing a general loss of vision or of whatever other sense. By the way, I believe the field commander is asking for a short break."

Enga had asked for no such thing, but Sispirinithas knew how to pick up on her patterns. They'd worked together a long time. When Enga was promoted, Irimiru had some concerns about how she would fare in her new rank, given her neurological oddities, so she'd assigned Sispirinithas to her as a minder. It was an unusual assignment, especially since Sispirinithas wasn't a military expert. He was a folklorist with some minor background in cross-species linguistics. But Enga didn't like to talk much, even over text, and Sispirinithas was happy to take over the talking when necessary.

Now he pranced back and forth with his ten-legged gait, while Enga stood in the corner of the field, trying to pull herself together. Occasionally he veered too close to a recruit, mandibles clacking, as if by accident. Sispirinithas found it very funny when humans – mortal or angelic – flinched.

"Anyway," he said, "as the marshal was saying, you shouldn't look too closely at Outside monsters, and your sensory filters will block you from seeing anything useful if you try. You might think that this puts you at a disadvantage, not being able to tell one part of their anatomy from another. Where's the head, for instance? Where are the vital organs? What you've got to remember is that no one else can answer that question either. Outside monsters don't *have* a sensible anatomy. That's why you can't be too clever with your aim. Just hit them with the biggest thing available, as close to the center as you can. I have a very informative slideshow prepared to illustrate this point. Let's go indoors a bit, shall we, morsels?"

The grunts followed him, and even Enga, standing in the corner, did not miss the looks they gave each other. Sispirinithas was happy to cover for Enga as much as she liked, but even his skills were beginning to slip. Enga was ninety-five percent sure he'd shown them this slideshow before. If she'd bothered to search through her sensory recordings, she could have checked and made it a hundred. If she actually cared.

She began to hit her head, lightly and rhythmically, against the makeshift wall.

The loss of Akavi and Elu reverberated in her like a hollow-point bullet, but that wasn't the only reason why Enga was failing. There was something about teaching that did not suit Enga anymore, even on days when her mood was good. She could wade through a hellscape of enemy fire and mud, she could fight as long and as hard as she had to; that was a stress her body understood. She couldn't always face all these able-bodied angels in a peaceful field, looking at her skeptically and expectantly, like they wanted her to prove what the marshal's livery implied. To make them strong.

Enga was alone. She was too stupid to do the job she'd been assigned, and too swayed by useless emotions to focus. She hit her head harder, twice, against the wall. She couldn't even pull herself together.

Attention, said a pop-up notification inside her brain. *Minor self-inflicted bruising detected. Please desist before incurring further injury, or your Overseer will be informed.*

Enga paused, and then pushed herself away from the wall with a venomous, directionless *FINE.*

When Enga had still been in training, she'd had an off switch. Akavi had installed a restraint program in her because of her neurodivergence and the heavy, deadly weaponry she carried around. If she had a meltdown like this, if she was about to be violent to herself or others, then the restraint program would have detected it automatically, frozen her body, and numbed her senses to the point of blindness until she calmed down. Enga had always hated that program, and she was glad not to have it anymore. Her systems still monitored her, like any angel's, but they couldn't shut her down that way. They could only give warnings like these, both to her and, if necessary, to her superiors. Enga's superiors placed a lot of trust in her, giving her authority and violent power.

She had a feeling she was going to make them regret it.

Enga sent a request in Irimiru's direction and then stalked through the field, past the building where Sispirinithas was helpfully showing his stupid slides. Past everything, through the portal at the heart of Border Encampment 342-6J, and into the throne room on a spaceship millions of miles away.

Irimiru Kaule, Overseer of Nemesis, was a Vaurian shapeshifter like Akavi. At the moment Irimiru looked like a tall, gaunt woman with long twists of black hair hanging down her ragged body. She had been taking forms like this more often since the Plague, forms with off-putting or sinister features, as if to better express a general displeasure with everything. She sat on a throne of twisted metal, and her metal-plated fingertips danced up and down its arms, coursing visibly with electricity as unfathomable amounts of information passed into and out of her organizing mind. A swarm of tiny, flying bots, like bees, filled the air around her, carrying auxiliary processing space between them.

Just as Enga's body was altered to make her better at her job, overseers were altered in their minds. Overseers' souls no longer resided solely within their skulls, but in an interplay of thought distributed through the network: the throne, the bots, the face-bearing body almost an afterthought. The promotion process to Overseer, in which the soul was coaxed to adjust to this state, was correspondingly excruciating. Enga didn't want that one yet.

Overseers still had physical bodies, unlike the ranks above them. And so Irimiru was able to glare directly at Enga in greeting.

MY LADY, said Enga, genuflecting. *I WANT TO BE DEMOTED.*

Irimiru crossed one leg over the other and leaned back, becoming a languid, bearded man, the kind who might lounge around in an old-fashioned fiefdom listening to the peasants' disputes. "That's the thirteenth time you've asked in the past three weeks. The answer is still no. You know what is required of you."

WHAT IS REQUIRED OF ME IS STUPID AND I AM FAILING. DEMOTE ME. OR KILL ME FOR FAILING. OR PUT ME ON THE NEMESIS-DAMNED SEARCH FOR AKAVI AND ELU WHERE I BELONG.

She had, in fact, asked this basic question twelve times before, but not as strongly. This version was suicidal for several reasons, not just the "kill me" part. The blasphemy was unacceptable. The word "fail" was *never* said aloud, by an angel of Nemesis, in reference to themselves. It was a show of weakness, and it would inevitably lead to whatever punishment one's superiors thought was funny at the time.

Unless, of course, one's superiors thought it was funniest to keep one right where one was.

Irimiru raised one hand from the buzzing arm of the throne and examined his metal-plated nails with seeming idleness. "After Akavi's failure, it took a good deal of work to keep the punishments contained to him and not to literally everyone else on my team. Your good performance helped. You are an asset to me, and I need to be seen using you as your accomplishments demand. Putting you on yet another search team, all signals analysis and no shooting, would waste you. Then my superiors would ask why I am wasting you. The assignment that you have been given is prestigious, and will lead to yet more honors and awards for you as soon as you stop pouting and actually *do* it."

I CANNOT DO IT, I AM STUPID, said Enga.

Irimiru raised his eyebrows, and, with a smooth shift, he became the type of person who might have taught kindergarten on Enga's home planet; dark-skinned, soft and somehow motherly-looking despite an indeterminate gender. Their penetrating gaze didn't soften to match.

"I'm not going to make soothing sounds," they said, "and tell you that you can do whatever you put your mind to. Maybe you can't. You are brain-damaged, after all. But, based on the video files I've reviewed, you haven't actually *tried*. You've done a passable job for an hour or two at a time, and then stormed off and had your little sulks. That's not incapability. It's insubordination."

THEN TERMINATE ME, said Enga.

She half-meant it. She really wanted Akavi and Elu, not death. But right now everything felt gray and heavy and intolerable. She wanted to shoot and destroy everything, anything she could, even herself.

Irimiru sighed out some odd, wistful emotion, bringing their free hand to their mouth. "You know I love to hear my subordinates begging for death. But I'll refer you to what I just said. The archangels want to know that I'm handling my part of this competently. If an angel of your talents is not playing a leading role in our development of Chaos Zone-appropriate skills for our infantry, they're going to ask me why."

Enga, against her own better judgment, took a step towards Irimiru. She let her arms whir a little, slightly unfolding and resettling themselves into a different configuration, the way she did when she wanted to unsettle mortals.

Akavi and Elu had always described Irimiru as somehow terrifying, which was very funny to Enga. Elu was afraid of everything anyway, and Akavi normally preferred to be the one who terrified everyone else. But Enga wasn't afraid. Maybe because she wasn't good at reading faces and bodies the way the two of them were. She could turn on programs to help her interpret them, but, maybe on some visceral level, Irimiru's intimidation tactics were based on little facial and vocal signs that went right over Enga's head.

Or maybe it was something much simpler. She'd often suspected that Irimiru had a soft spot for angry women. Maybe Irimiru saw that in Enga and liked her.

YOU MEAN YOU NEED ME, she said.

Irimiru narrowed their eyes. "Hardly."

But the damage had been done; they'd said it. They'd told Enga that Enga's good performance was one of the things keeping Irimiru safe.

GIVE ME WHAT I WANT, said Enga. *PUT ME ON THE SEARCH FOR AKAVI AND ELU. OR TERMINATE ME. OR ELSE I WILL GO BACK TO THE BORDER ENCAMPMENT, SHOOT EVERY OTHER ANGEL IN RANGE, DESTROY THE ENTIRE FACILITY AND LET THE MONSTERS OUT. AND THEN YOU CAN EXPLAIN TO THE ARCHANGELS WHY THAT HAPPENED.*

She was half-convinced Irimiru would terminate her for real for making such a threat. Instead, Irimiru paused, then let out a long, low, appreciative laugh.

"You're feisty," they said. "But it wouldn't work. All I'd have to say is that you were tragically driven mad by all your close encounters with those Outside monsters." They sat up a little straighter, regarding her carefully. "I'm going to throw you a bone, though. Only because I like you. And because I really would like you to actually train my infantry rather than having increasingly vivid fantasies of murdering them, or delegating the work to an unqualified Spider. I'm going to tell the team tracking Akavi and Elu that, when we locate them – and not an instant sooner – you'll have the first crack at bringing them in. That's as much as I can offer."

Enga heaved a sigh and squared her shoulders. This was not as much of a relief as it should have been. She still itched to shoot something that wasn't a dummy made of scraps. *THANK YOU, MY LADY.*

Irimiru shifted again, becoming an eerily exact likeness of Elu. The long hair, the gangly limbs, the soft facial expression. Even his eyes looked gentle and kind like Elu's.

Only the voice – Elu's in timbre, but Irimiru's in tone, sharp, mocking – gave it away.

"Go, then," he said. "But I've made my offer. And if you don't quickly begin to do your actual work, I can take it away."

Four Months Ago

Akavi's recovery had gone rougher than expected. The effects on his soul, from an alteration as simple as removing an ansible uplink, should have been mild. But there were aspects of angelic medicine, key details about how the connection between brain and soul and circuitry functioned, that were hidden even from angels like Elu. To discourage exactly this kind of illicit tampering, no doubt.

It didn't surprise him, then, when Akavi periodically doubled over with cluster headaches, strong enough to crack even the former Inquisitor's careful control. Or when he slept, exhausted by pain and medicine, only to wake in a night terror. Elu knew it would pass, the way the symptoms of their long-ago ascensions had gradually passed. But he didn't know how long that would take. All he could do was treat the symptoms and wait. Analgesics, nerve agonists, anxiolytics, sedatives.

He steered the *Talon* closer to the surface of Jai. Now that the ship was disguised it was not difficult to fall into the civilian transport lanes, to print the kinds of identification codes that would get them waved through Jai's local portals as traveling merchants. And, from there, to surreptitiously take sensor readings of the area. He studied the Chaos Zone's current state and the movements of its populace, and drew up charts, which Akavi examined, on his good days, with a thoughtful frown. Eventually he found a place for the ship to settle – a calm and out-of-the-way area, not far from the city of Büata, where it could hide among mossy crags. On a suitable day, when it was foggy and the sky was aurora-filled enough to confuse the Gods' sensors, he navigated down there and landed.

Akavi was doing better by now, active and impatient, only occasionally falling into his spasms of pain. And the Outside magic – as far as Elu could tell – was beginning to flicker. The protective aura around the *Talon*'s sensors and transmitters had been faintly visible to him, a black mist that activated his sensory filters, and he could see it gradually thinning and shifting as the days wore on.

"Do you think you can handle it?" he asked Akavi, indicating the medical setup. The bots, equipped with Elu's program, would do the most delicate work on their own, but it still took mental focus and emotional fortitude to supervise. To wait and make sure Elu woke up properly, to check his symptoms and do all the other small tasks of recovery.

Akavi gave the bots and the stretcher an unimpressed look. "I can, but do you believe it's wise? You haven't worked out how to correct for the side effects."

Elu sighed. He'd been trying. But he had yet to come up with a change to his procedure that he felt confident about. And if he dithered much longer, their protection would fail.

"It's our only option at this point anyway," he said. "I'll live."

He came out of anesthesia in a haze of blue; he'd decorated his personal quarters in light, cool colors, and that was the first thing he was able to focus on, the sky-blue of the ceiling. The subtle copper filigree that ran across it, in an abstract pattern like a rippling stream over smooth stones. He liked the color. His vision swam; his head pounded with something that wasn't quite pain yet, only a disorienting pressure, a sense that something wasn't right.

He felt the surgery's wrongness deep in his bones, on a level no anesthesia could touch. The same way he'd felt it, so many decades ago, after his ascension. Something about him had been irrevocably changed, and some part of him even deeper than his physical body wanted to fight it.

Akavi said something, but that felt wrong, too. He didn't know what was wrong, how a voice that had been his anchor for over half a century could feel harsh and unwelcome in his ears. He was so preoccupied trying to figure it out that he missed the actual words. By the time he thought to ask Akavi to repeat himself, he'd fallen back asleep.

When he woke up again, Akavi's form had changed. She was a Riayin woman now. Average height, average build. Elegant and poised, like most of Akavi's forms, but without any specific qualities to make her stand out from a crowd. Her clothes were the kind of shabby that suggested once-well-made garments subjected to months of harrowing strain.

This was the kind of body Akavi would use for undercover work down here. Which meant–

Which meant Akavi was leaving. Soon.

Elu tried to form a question, but it came out as a vague groan. Akavi turned and looked down at him with a calm, disinterested expression. "You're awake."

Elu *nngh*ed in agreement. He liked the way Akavi looked, no matter what form she was in. He always liked it. He probably shouldn't stare up admiringly like this, but he was very tired and fuzzy-headed, and he could either focus on this or fall back into the pain that was rapidly growing behind his eyes. Real pain now, oh dear. He didn't suppose it would wear off any quicker for him than it had for Akavi.

"I've been monitoring your vital signs," said Akavi. "So far you're recovering at about the same rate I did. I've ensured the bots are equipped with all the fluids and medicines you might require. I believe they can take it from here."

Elu tried to thrash upright, and immediately regretted it, as a wracking pain bloomed all down his head and neck. Was she leaving? She couldn't leave. He wasn't even well enough to move or speak yet.

Akavi sighed slightly, looking down at him. "I'm sorry, Elu, but we've wasted enough time already. Yasira is still out there, doing Gods know what to this planet, while we sit and do *nothing*. I need to be out there. Scouting, making contacts, lining up the kinds of resources I can use. The longer I wait, the more we'll both fall behind. I'll be back later and keep you updated, I promise. And you'll be safe here."

Elu lay back on his pillows, hating himself. Akavi was a proper angel of Nemesis, even now. Akavi could not tolerate weakness, and Elu was being weak. Clinging like a child, wanting to be fussed over and cared for, when there was nothing medical Akavi could do for him that the bots couldn't.

The mission came first. Elu had vaguely hoped that would be different now, but why should it? Akavi didn't owe him anything. She was here with him because that had been the available option: run away with him, or stay behind and be terminated. She had never been the kind of person who valued other people romantically, or even as respected friends. That wasn't going to change, and neither was her need for activity, for some overriding goal to drive her onward. Even without their ansible uplinks, they both were what they were.

Akavi hesitated over him a moment longer. Something in her face looked uncertain. As if she was weighing up several difficult options.

Then, with swift decisiveness, she leaned down and kissed him lightly on the lips.

She'd *never* done that. Akavi could be seductive towards mortals when a mission required it, but she had barely ever laid a hand on Elu, even in the most unromantic, practical ways, in all of their half-century together.

He was too exhausted to try to work out what it meant.

"Be good," she said, shouldering her pack. The *Talon*'s airlock slid shut behind her before Elu could formulate a response.

The local greenery rustled under Akavi's feet as she walked away from the *Talon*. One enterprising shrub curled around her ankle, tugging like an attention-hungry child, and she shook it off.

They'd landed in a rustic little hole in the ground, all mossy boulders and winding trees. The *Talon* would be well-covered and the land here wasn't especially corrupted by the Chaos Zone's standards. The undergrowth that wound around Akavi's feet was still mostly green, and had recognizable parts like leaves and stems, even if sometimes the leaves verged to blue or red or spiraled into strange patterns. The air was humid but not unpleasantly warm, and the sounds that buzzed and hissed around her were at least vaguely the right timbre to be insects and birds. If Akavi had installed any naturalist software she could have analyzed the sounds, classified those that matched known wild creatures and flagged those that were unfamiliar. She lacked that, but there were small animal paths here just as there'd be in an ordinary forest, and she had enough map-reading and positioning software to be able to follow one in an appropriate direction.

She had about an hour of walking to do before she reached inhabited areas. That gave her time to think, which was not necessarily ideal. She was not at all sure that kissing Elu had been the correct choice.

Elu had been, for fifty years, a known quantity. He had been a loyal assistant, attached to her by the angelic corps' usual hierarchy. Intelligent in many ways; weak in others. Constantly and pathetically in love with her. *Loyal,* though. She'd valued Elu's loyalty above almost anything else. Most angels of Elu's rank were hungry for promotion and power, even to the point of betraying their superiors. Elu was different. Elu was that rarest of creatures, an angel she could trust.

But Elu had worked for Akavi because they were part of something bigger. They had a hierarchy, and Elu was attached to Akavi by that hierarchy, not merely by his own emotions.

And the structure that the hierarchy provided was gone now. No Overseer was here to hand down assignments and check that they functioned correctly as a team. Elu and Akavi had nothing now but themselves and a vaguely adequate spaceship. Elu couldn't realistically go anywhere, but there was no external force in place to make him follow Akavi's orders now. Nothing forced him to agree to her plans, to call her *sir* as he'd done, with that new uncertainty. Nothing but Akavi's will and Elu's old habit.

It was only a matter of time before Elu figured that out.

Twigs snapped under Akavi's feet as she pressed on. The forest wasn't dark; sunlight filtered easy and bright through the leaves. But she saw branches curling in her direction, warding or beckoning. Once or twice one reached and touched her shoulder, and she batted it away. Mortals would not enjoy entering this area at night, she suspected. So much the better.

Akavi did not love Elu, but she valued him. So she had acted, despite misgivings, to give him a reason to obey a little longer.

That tactic wouldn't be effective forever. Human hearts were fickle things, and she couldn't count on the effect to be permanent, no matter how far she took it and how well Elu was fooled. Sooner or later he would need–

She didn't know, and that made her uneasy. It wasn't just sex, or even a facsimile of love. He would need something as unshakable as the whole angelic hierarchy, as dear to his heart as the God he'd followed, and even Akavi didn't know where to get a thing like that.

She resented having to think about it. Having it turn over and over in her mind, when she should have been strategizing, all through the long walk to Büata.

Here is the unofficial story of the Chaos Zone: the one seen in dreams by the Chaos Zone's newly minted mystics, repeated in hushed tones, scribbled on heretical broadsheets. To speak the story this way, in the hearing of angels, is to die:

Once there was a woman named Destroyer.

(That was not her birth name. She was known to the Gods as Dr Evianna Talirr. She never called herself Destroyer, and neither did They. But stories simplify, even when they are true; in a story, sometimes the best name for a person is a simple truth that they deny.)

Destroyer was born unlike other people, and the Gods tried to destroy her for it. True to her name, she tried to destroy Them back. But Gods are not so easy to destroy. What fell into her crosshairs instead, as an opening gambit, was our world. She uprooted the life that we knew, killed us in the millions and took apart our homes. She sent the Plague to Jai and created the Chaos Zone, on our world which had once been so orderly and simple.

But Destroyer, no matter how powerful, was human. And Destroyer was lonely.

Once there was a woman named Savior. She was a student of Destroyer's, and Destroyer summoned her, wanting friendship, wanting help. But Savior had been born on Jai, and she loved her world as Destroyer did not.

"Help me," said Destroyer. "For we are born more powerful than other people, and the world will never do anything but hate us. Together, let us take the hateful world between our hands and tear it open."

"I will not," said Savior.

*So the Gods took up Savior instead, into their immaculate ships,
at the helms of their most fearsome weapons.*

*"Help Us," said the Gods. "For We are more powerful than any
human, but we are not infinite. We must rip out threats by their
roots – threats to humans, and threats to Ourselves – and a threat
like Destroyer is difficult even for Us. You have some of her power.
Use it with Us, to destroy the Chaos Zone entirely, to murder every
human who survives there."*

"I will not," said Savior.

*So Savior was thrown into Outside, the place that breaks the
sanity of anyone who sees it, where she and Destroyer and the Chaos
Zone all had their terrible origins. The Gods meant to break her.*

"Help me," said Savior.

And Outside turned, in its terrible ineffable might, and saw her.

*Outside joined its own incomprehensible power to Savior's.
Savior joined her own desperate, compassionate soul to Outside's.
There was no longer any true separation between them. Savior was
Outside made manifest. But Savior remembered her will.*

*Savior reached down, into the heart of the Chaos Zone of Jai,
and did what she could.*

*Nothing that is done can be fully undone, even Outside. Savior
could not erase what Destroyer had done. But she could alter it.
She turned the Chaos Zone's roaming monsters less deadly, its
disruptions to the shape of things less violent. She stopped its border
from further expanding. And, most merciful of all, she made a
change to a third of the people who lived here. She gave us powers
of our own, small echoes of hers. Power to bring forth fruit from the
strange ground, to see the truth in dreams, to protect our loved ones
and survive.*

Then, exhausted from her struggle, Savior went far away.

*"We have stopped the growth of the Chaos Zone," said the Gods.
"We have made its effects less deadly. You may stand by for further*

improvements." But They had nothing to do with what Savior had done. They did not even understand it. Their angels walk the Chaos Zone now, making Their paltry attempts at help and control, but it will win Them nothing.

Destroyer walks the planet now in disguise, a lone woman speaking to no one. Shamed by Savior's courage, she seeks now to remember her humanity and to learn what she can. One day she will return, perhaps to earn something other than her name.

Savior hides now, half-awake, licking the wounds she incurred for our sake. A small group walks the planet in her stead, gifted with fragments of her power, helping where they can. It will not be enough, but it will keep us alive, in spite of all the Gods' efforts otherwise.

One day Savior, too, will return, and save us fully.

CHAPTER 3
Now

Yonne Qun had asked Tiv for weapons yesterday, her hand clasped in both of his, his eyes grief-stricken and desperate. She had promised him she'd ask Yasira about it. And then she'd chickened out. All that night, as Yasira sulked and mumbled, she'd wondered if she should ask. But Yasira could barely get in the shower without Tiv's help on nights like this; there was no way she'd be up for a talk about actual violence. About a desperate populace that would always want miracles from her, not knowing or caring the toll it had already taken.

The morning hadn't been much better. Tiv had delivered breakfast but she hadn't been able to drag Yasira out of bed in time for the weekly planning meeting. So Tiv and the Seven had assembled in the war room without her. Everyone but Yasira sat hunched over in their chairs or their beanbag nests; eager, wan, tired or anxious as their individual needs dictated, all looking to Tiv to direct them.

A thin, light-skinned, short-haired thirty year-old stood next to Tiv, arranging and rearranging their various notes. Ulutrujcy Unaczysy Jasl, code name "Grid," was one of the more organized of the Seven, and the most useful when preparing for meetings like these. Something like a team secretary, although nobody here used that title. They'd spread the reports out and arranged them by category: modest piles of notes about monsters, food shortages, inadequate God-built supplies. A small pile of violent incidents between competing groups of survivors; the bands of raiders and other criminals which had inevitably arisen; clashes between normal survivors and gone people, who were a law to themselves. A medium-sized pile of the survivors' own reports about their growing abilities, their newly developing heretical ethics and metaphysics, which had led to its own series of clashes. And a much larger pile of violent incidents involving angels.

Angels who'd shot mortals on sight for using their newfound magic. Angels who'd shot mortals for trying to cross the border, or for entering other areas unauthorized. Angels who'd injured mortals, under the guise of crowd control, when there was a shortage at a relief station. Angels who'd captured mortals and made them disappear, to be interrogated or punished or whatever else the angels had in store.

Not long ago, most mortals in the Chaos Zone had trusted angels completely. It had taken only a few months of such violence for that trust to fall away.

Tiv, sitting in a cheap folding chair, tapped a small gavel on the table. It was an item one of the Seven had stolen for her as a joke, calling her "Leader" with an amused grin, back in the early days when their code names hadn't felt quite so settled. Tiv wasn't leading much of anything, but getting the Seven to do something could be like herding cats, and Tiv seemed to have a knack for it, gently pulling distracted people back to their tasks. So the gavel had been given to her, and the ability to set agendas and start votes.

"Well, good morning," Tiv said. Some of the Seven were still eating breakfast; she'd already had hers while trying to wake up Yasira. "Thanks for showing up. Does anybody have anything urgent to say before we dive into the agenda?"

"Just the weapons," said a sardonic alto voice from across the table. This was "Blur" – also called Luellae Nyrath, an Anetaian woman even paler than Grid, short and round and with a habit of being unamused by everything. She'd finished her breakfast long before the meeting and was now leaning back in her chair, arms crossed. "But I'm guessing that's on there already."

"Yeah, that's... most of the agenda." Requests for support with forms of violent rebellion had been increasing from all sides, not just Yonne Qun's. Luellae herself had been fielding more than her fair share, and the rest of the Seven hadn't been immune. Even if Yasira wasn't up to discussing it, this was still a problem needing attention from all of them. "Want to get started?"

There were general nods and attentive looks, and Grid made their way back to a beanbag seat at their own side of the table. Three of the other students reached for them, leaning on each other and holding hands as their group of four was reunited.

Years ago, Luellae, Splió, and Daeis had each been captured individually by Akavi's team, and they'd spent the long years before Yasira's arrival in isolation. Only the occasional visit from Akavi for interrogation, or Elu to check up on them, or a sell-soul psychiatrist to study their deterioration in detail. The other four students had been captured all together and locked in a four-bedroom suite: an apparent attempt, on Akavi's part, to disambiguate the mental strains of solitary confinement from the mental strains of Outside. It still made Tiv angry when she thought of it, the way the angels had treated whole lives and souls as nothing but data.

The Four – as they now called themselves – had developed a bond even stronger than that between the rest of the Seven. It wasn't romantic, not like Yasira and Tiv's relationship, or Daeis and Splió's. But it was still a bond that had them looking eerily like a collective of gone people at times, moving in unison, responding to each other without a visible prompt. The Four used their code names more than their real names, which somehow accentuated the effect. Four aspects of one entity. Grid, thin and serious, constantly organizing and rearranging. Prophet, anxious and childlike, often distracted by images even the other three couldn't see. Weaver, petite and vibrating with energy; she was sitting in the pile of beanbags with her groupmates for now, steadied by their presence, but it was a rare team meeting that didn't eventually see Weaver rocketing up, pacing or running about the room. And Picket, pale and sickly, frowning into empty space as he listened.

"Okay," said Tiv, tapping her gavel again. "First item on the agenda is: weapons. We're coordinating a peaceful resistance, but people on the ground want guns. We need a better way of handling that, because it's only getting worse. Thoughts?"

Splió raised a hand. "It's not guns they want, you know."

Tiv sighed shortly. It was somehow easier if she called it guns. Guns were concrete, and she knew how she felt about them. "Okay, Yonne Qun asked for Yasira, not guns. Let's see if we're all on the same page about this. How many requests for actual guns have we been getting, and how many for magic?"

"Me," said Weaver immediately. Weaver had messy hair that flopped down into her eyes, and she was bouncing up and down in her seat. "They ask me for magic. But my magic is for healing, so it's a little different, I guess – but they ask me for that. And guns. And Savior. All three."

Splió waved a desultory hand. "Most of mine don't ask

for Savior. Not directly. Magic, though. More than half want magic. They start with guns, and when I tell them why guns won't work, they ramp it up. If they don't want Yasira, they want *some* of us, at least."

Picket leaned forward, a wistful frown on his pale face. Picket was chubby and shy, and he'd liked video games, back in the days when life was more mundane. War games, which were an odd, nostalgic genre, since humans very rarely made war against each other anymore. He had a corresponding odd, game-theoretic way of picking through advantages and disadvantages in any conflict.

"I don't think they really understand the way our powers work," said Picket. "I could use my powers in a fight, maybe. It'd hurt both sides and be pretty imprecise, but I *theoretically* could. Daeis could. Blur might, sort of, I guess. And then Yasira's in whatever league of her own that she's in. But the rest of us? Nah. We've got specific things we can do that most people can't, but it's healing like Weaver said or it's recon stuff. We're not some kind of battle team."

"You can't call it recon if we're not a battle team," Weaver shot back, fidgeting by picking at the backs of her hands. "Recon's a battle word."

"It's a *military* word," Grid corrected, gently guiding Weaver's fingers away from the spots where they might do damage.

"Military schmilitary. You all know what I meant."

Each member of the Seven had a smattering of the modest magics that were common in the Chaos Zone, plus a specific power of their own, something that had blossomed in them as a specific result of how they'd been connected to Yasira when she performed her miracle. As near as Tiv could understand it, each of them had lent their mental strength in a slightly different way, something that made sense for that individual based on how their mind worked, and some part of Outside now lived in that part of each of them, both maddening and empowering.

Picket's power was precisely adjusting the level of Outside contamination around him, from horrifying eye-crossing surrealism to seeming normality, or whatever in-between point he liked. Using that ability to hurt people *might* be possible, with the right kind of cruel creativity, but it wouldn't be straightforward. Weaver's powers were purely about healing and repair. Grid could sense the presence of angels and God-built technology, through a second sight which detected the shape of the local ansible net. It was very useful; it had stopped Vaurian angels from infiltrating their group in the past. But in a battle, unless someone tried to sneak up on them, it was nothing.

"Okay," said Tiv, redirecting them to the original question. "Who else has been getting requests for magic?"

"Me," said Luellae, her arms crossed over her chest as she hunched in one of the folding chairs. Luellae was the most standoffish of all the Seven. Her power was moving from place to place, in slantwise ways that filled the gaps in what the airlock itself could accomplish. She didn't fidget like Weaver did, but it seemed to Tiv that Luellae was always preparing to move like that. To flee or slink away from the rest of the Seven if she needed to. "But you knew that; I've told you before. And mine do ask for Savior."

Prophet raised a hand, hesitant, still staring off into space. "Mine don't. Not magic, very often. Never Yasira."

"That's because you're a meek little waif," Luellae countered. "And your powers are no good in a fight. They don't look at you and see someone who can protect them. No offense."

Grid shifted, moving ever so slightly in front of Prophet;

Picket and Weaver, as usual, followed. Prophet gave them all a strange look, as if she wasn't quite sure what she needed to be defended from. "Offense taken, Blur," said Grid. "There's more than one way to protect something."

"I said what I said."

Tiv redirected them back to the actual question again, and they went around the table like that, trying to count up numbers of people on each teammate's daily rounds who did and didn't want violence. Grid went back to taking notes, trying to tally up vague figures from seven perspectives into something that made sense.

While watching the other six, Tiv remembered to keep half an eye on Daeis. Given their trouble with talking, Daeis's opinion could get lost in rowdy meetings like these. If they had something very urgent to say, they could gesture for attention, or grab at a piece of paper and scrawl a word or two – but none of those methods would work unless people like Tiv were paying enough attention to notice them.

Daeis seemed content to let the others handle this for now, though. When Tiv called on them, they made a gesture and whispered to Splió, who translated it as, "Not many asking for weapons on their end." But apart from that they only sat back and observed, with one hand petting a small, sea-slug-like being in their lap.

"You know there will be battles regardless, don't you?" Prophet murmured.

There were noises of agreement and noises of doubt. Prophet's predictions were always worth listening to, but most of them were ambiguous, and it usually wasn't clear exactly what to do about them. It could be that the Seven would be inevitably drawn into violent conflict despite their best efforts. Or battles could happen that had nothing to do with them at all. Prophet had made this prediction before, but she'd never figured out how big the future battles were, widespread or localized, key to the Chaos Zone's freedom or costly distraction.

Eventually, after trying and failing to make the figures line up one too many times, Grid dropped their pencil and pushed away from the table.

"This isn't working," they announced. "We're better than this. I don't mean better at plotting violence. I mean we've all got advanced degrees in science but we're talking about a convenient sample of people who were brave enough to broach a topic like it means something. Are we saying the people in the Chaos Zone should vote on it? Because if we are, then we need to figure out how to hold a vote. And if we're not then comparing the numbers is pointless." They looked around the table, meeting eyes with Tiv and with each of the rest of the Seven in turn. "Do *we* want to fight the Gods?"

Tiv bit her tongue. She knew *her* answer was "no." But sometimes being Leader meant speaking last, so she didn't intimidate everyone else into compliance.

Luellae tossed her head. "Of course we do. We're already fighting the Gods. You heard what Prophet said. We're just doing it piecemeal with little heretical deliveries instead of going on the offensive."

"Yeah, but is piecemeal better?" Weaver countered. "That's the question."

Picket leaned forward. "Better question. Wars have strategic and tactical objectives. What's our objective? Or, if all we do is arm the people who want to fight, what's theirs?"

There were murmurs around the table at that – uncertain, speculative murmurs, vague words like *defense*. Grid snatched another piece of paper in reflex, as if they could start writing all the possible reasons down.

"If we don't know," Tiv said, pitching her voice to carry over the other murmurs, "then why don't we ask them? Next time they ask, we start asking them questions right back. Let's make *them* build the case."

There were several nods.

"Sounds like passing the buck," said Splió, "but I'm in."

"They'll already have a case," Luellae countered, a dark expression in her eyes. "They're not stupid. And when they see us asking, they'll know that means they have a chance. There's no going back once we start asking that."

"But we'll be getting better asks," Picket countered. "With more info."

Tiv chewed her lip. Luellae had a point. But people like Yonne Qun were going to keep asking and asking anyway. Tiv didn't like it, and she didn't want to arm them, but she needed to start listening more to their reasons. Their needs. Maybe Tiv's team could meet those needs another way.

"Then we'll deal with that when it happens," she said firmly. "All in favor?"

It was unanimous except for Daeis, who often abstained anyway. They moved on to the next orders of business: scheduling concerns, sorting out who was bringing which items where. Tiv focused on sketching out a proper plan for the week, and she tried not to imagine what would happen the next time Yonne Qun asked her for something.

Three Months Ago

"I'm not sure if these are any good," said Akavi, meekly upending a sack of potentially edible fungi onto Yonne Qun's coffee table for inspection, "but I feel like I'm getting the hang of it. Practice makes perfect, right? I'm sorry it's not more."

Akavi was, of course, in disguise. This was one of half a dozen stable cover identities she'd established in recent months, a woman in her early twenties with a supposed gift for food production, matching that of Qun's daughter, Genne. She'd been charmingly inept following Genne through the fields and trying to copy her techniques, and then before her next visit she'd brought a few of Genne's own creations back to Elu on the *Talon*, instructing him to analyze them on a molecular level and to print something similar with minor cosmetic changes.

She and Elu had fallen into a useful rhythm. Akavi did the fieldwork and Elu was logistical support, creating clothes and items and whatever else she required. Aside from the fact that they'd started to kiss each other now and then, it was just like working together on any normal mission. Elu was used to Akavi's long absences for fieldwork, and to focusing on his own work without her, and after a bit of awkwardness the two of them had simply fallen back into that rhythm for now. He'd done a good job with the fungi; they looked very real.

"These are amazing," said Genne, bending her broad-cheeked head down to inspect them. They were nodules, mostly, blue and violet with a spongy mushroom-like texture, mottled with jaguar spots. "Where'd you get so many?"

Akavi focused on the blood vessels in her face until a slight blush appeared, and she covered her mouth, looking abashed by the praise. "I guess it works better when I'm alone. Want to try?"

Pathetic, the way both of them nodded, their microexpressions displaying easy acceptance and trust. Once one of the Chaos Zone's loosely organized miniature societies accepted you, you were *accepted:* trusted without question, no matter how erratic your behavior, so long as you contributed something, didn't steal, and weren't violent. Helped without question, if help was possible to give. Some individual groups had stricter rules, and of course there were a few bandit gangs that had chosen to roam and raid. But, by a large margin, most survivors had avoided that life, instead choosing mutual trust and aid. Most people knew it was the only way they'd truly survive.

It made Akavi's job astonishingly easy – and, no doubt, the jobs of other Vaurian angels who'd been assigned to this mess. It was a wonder such angels hadn't rounded everyone up already. Akavi suspected that it was an issue of scale. Unquestionably there *were* other Vaurians around, on similar trajectories to her own. But given that there were literally millions of heretics on this planet, those spies were better spent on monitoring and influencing their chosen groups than on capture.

She picked up one of the mushrooms and took a bite. Yonne Qun's collective believed in *that* rule, at least: those who grew the food were responsible for sharing in any unwanted effects. The mushroom wasn't bad. On the squishy side, but hearty and sweet; dried, it would likely improve. Yonne and Genne followed suit, and Akavi watched their smiles of pleased surprise. She made a mental note to mention this to Elu.

"Look," said Genne, "if it works better when you're alone, go ahead and be alone as much as you want. These are great. Do you think you can make more?"

"As much as you want," said Akavi. That, too, was how people in the Chaos Zone did things now. Money was only for certain situations, such as trade between communities. For everyday necessities, one gave as much as one could and took as much as was offered. "As long as some monster doesn't get me, I guess." She scowled; that kind of bleak humor was how people here did things, as well. "Or an angel."

Genne leaned forward. "Do you think the angels will really crack down? On people like us?"

"I'm positive," said Akavi, who knew no such thing. "I hear whispers about it all the time. Where else do you hit a group like us but by going after the food? Where it hurts."

"I just can't believe they'd be that cruel."

Spreading rumors like these wasn't the most important part of Akavi's plan, but she knew it would be the modus operandi for other Vaurian agents like her. The Chaos Zone was already in disarray. Its citizens could be dissuaded from the useful kind of organizing by keeping them paranoid, dividing cells from each other and pushing them to reckless acts – for which they could be further punished or, in the best case, destroyed.

Of course, Akavi couldn't spread enough rumors to turn the tide of Jai's nascent rebellion by herself. Her true plan was far beyond anything the Quns would have access to. She needed revenge against Yasira, but Yasira wasn't easy to access. She didn't make the rounds talking to survivors in person the way Tiv Hunt and the Seven did; she seemed to have gone into hiding completely. And the Seven seemed to have some ability that detected and rooted out Vaurian angels when they got too close.

So Akavi wasn't trying to get into the lair. Not directly. Instead, she had suborned one of the Seven in another way. She spent her time, when that contact wasn't available, practicing her skills in places like this. Doing as the rest of the Vaurians did. That would be useful for many reasons;

in particular, it would keep Akavi informed about the development of a very complicated, volatile situation. But Akavi's true plan was to apply those skills to the Seven themselves. The Seven were the key to how all of Jai's multitude of rebellions coordinated across distances. If *they* could be turned against each other – full of distrust, competing for power – it would all fall apart very neatly.

And then, without the little support network that she'd so blithely assembled, Yasira would be forced to come out and meet Akavi herself.

She'd have her revenge. It would only take time.

"I hope you're right," said Akavi, hugging herself pensively. Genne was an optimist, a girl young enough to believe that if her heart was in the right place, then the Gods might turn a blind eye to her heresies forever. Her father knew better. It was Yonne – at whom Akavi was careful not to glance directly – who would absorb this message, frightened for his daughter as only a father could be.

These people meant nothing to Akavi. The revenge that she craved was for sins vastly larger than the Quns' petty heresies. But it was still satisfying, until such time as she could see her contact among the Seven again, to manipulate them in such little, plausible increments to their own destruction.

Now

On her first assignment of the day, Tiv found herself creeping through a disused train tunnel near the heart of the city of Dasz, alongside a man named Sedajegy Utridzysy

Akiujal, one of the few community leaders whose trust she'd earned from the Stijonan part of the Chaos Zone. Akiujal was a gray-haired man with stooped shoulders and a stern, intense demeanor who occasionally broke into an unexpected wry giggle. He'd mentioned weapons – on the day's very first stop; Tiv was really *not* having any luck at this – and she'd asked, nervously, the question her team had decided on. "What do you want them for?"

Akiujal had scowled across his living room table at her. "Defense, of course. Weren't you listening?"

Tiv had leaned in. Her Stijonan was terrible and he didn't know any Arinnan or Riayin, so they'd been speaking Earth Creole, both with atrocious accents and frequent misunderstandings. "No, I mean, what are your *objectives*? I'm going to be honest with you, Mr Akiujal, people have been asking us for weapons more and more and we're starting to want to know why. I know that you fear for your safety, but that's not enough reason by itself. What are you planning to defend – a location? A group of people? A team while they do a specific task? My team does not fight and my team does not give out weapons. But maybe there is some other way we can help you, and we won't know that unless we know your objectives."

Akiujal's scowl had deepened, and then he had abruptly straightened, gesturing to her. "Come with me."

"It's dangerous–"

"No. *Come*. I will show you something."

Which was how they had ended up in the train tunnel, peering through a mouse-sized crack in the wall at one of the angelic relief stations in the center of Dasz.

It was dangerous for Tiv to be anywhere near here. She and Yasira and the Seven were the nine most wanted people on all of Jai. She could hide her face to a degree – as she'd done now, in fact, with one of the thick scarves that were becoming the fashion around here. But if any angel caught a glimpse of her directly, their facial recognition programs would blare an alert, and she would immediately be chased with all the forces at that angel's disposal. She'd had a few narrow escapes like that already. This far from Akiujal's house, discovery was a probable death sentence: Dr Talirr's airlock only worked if she could get back to the door she'd arrived by.

Tiv peered through the crack at the long line of civilians standing out in the hot sun, queued blocks deep for the rations that the angels were handing out. Simple bottles of water, tiny protein bars, thin blankets. Tiv had seen this before. She had been an angel's prisoner, though not for long, and she knew angels could print feasts' worth of any food supply they liked. Any clothing, any medicine, any *anything*, within reason. If their offerings were meager now, that was a deliberate choice. A thing they were doing to put the Chaos Zone's population in its place. Or maybe, knowing Nemesis, for a darker goal. To keep the people desperate. To provoke them into actions they wouldn't otherwise have taken – robbery, heresy, violence – and prove to the galaxy that they weren't worthy of help after all.

She'd thought about this a lot already. It was one of the reasons why she didn't want to give out weapons.

"*You* see," Akiujal insisted beside her. "How it is never enough."

"They know it's not enough," Tiv murmured back. "They want to see what you'll do when you don't have enough. They want to provoke you. And you know why the Gods would want that, don't you? They want to crack down harder, and They're looking for an excuse."

Akiujal chuckled darkly. "What, then, is the virtuous thing to do when we don't have enough? Give up? Starve? Sustain ourselves through heresy, which will be punished just as viciously as violence? Or we could try to collaborate with the gone people; they've been gathering more often recently. They're up to something, I'm sure. But that wouldn't be your style either, would it, Leader? The gone people might fight. They might use blood, or something else you disapprove of, and we can't have *that.*"

Tiv bit into her cheek, refusing to be baited.

"Watch," said Akiujal. "I know you have somewhere safe to go at night. Watch more closely those of us who don't."

Tiv stared out through the crack. She watched the expressions of the people in that long, long queue. Some haunted and nakedly desperate; some tired and bored; some greedy; some resentful. A middle-aged woman reached the front of the line. An angel of Arete, expressionless, handed her the same small rations bundle as everyone else, and the woman suddenly exploded into a rage. Tiv couldn't catch most of the words in the verbal torrent, not at this distance and in Stijonan, but she thought she heard the words *five children.*

A pair of angel bodyguards, one in bronze-and-white livery and one in Nemesis' black-and-blood-red, stepped forward. As expressionless as the one doling out the supplies, they took the woman by the arms and hauled her, struggling, away.

"There was an organized protest here not long ago," said Akiujal in Tiv's ear. "You can guess what happened."

"An illegal protest," Tiv clarified, which earned a snort. Peaceful protest against a mortal government was legal throughout human space, as long as everyone had the appropriate permits and followed the rules. Arete's priests even encouraged it. But protest against the Gods was, by definition, heresy. The Chaos Zone no longer had any government; just these groups of angels, doing less than the barest minimum.

"As illegal as everything else we do to keep ourselves alive. The Gods mowed them down, of course. Not only did They shoot the protesters, but as further punishment, They have reduced rations to the city's full population. That is why this relief station is so pitiful, even compared to what it was before."

"I'm sorry," said Tiv, gritting her teeth.

If she didn't want violence or heresy to solve this, then what did she want? People had been asking her this more frequently, and she didn't have an answer.

"You want an objective? Here's an objective. The angels have a printer with which they produce these supplies. An angel printer can produce almost anything. Imagine if we stormed them. Took them by surprise, pressed into that prim little building, and liberated the printer for our own use. Just one printer. No angel lives lost. Imagine the good we could do with that, if we were armed enough to do so."

Tiv ran her fingers down the tunnel's rust-caked interior, next to the crack she was looking through. She and Akiujal could both see that the angel bodyguards had guns of their own. Not just better weapons than anything Tiv's team knew how to source, but better training, better reflexes, better tactics, better aim.

"What would be 'enough', Mr Akiujal? Even with guns, you wouldn't win that fight. It would be a massacre." And the surviving population would be punished again, even worse than they'd been punished for the protest.

"For this, I am not asking for guns. You know what I am asking for, Leader. The same thing everyone else is."

Tiv did know. She was determined to be polite to people like Mr Akiujal, to be kind; they were all so desperate and so brave, and it wasn't their fault that they needed what she couldn't give. But she felt the uncomfortable sting of rust under her nails, against the metal, as she involuntarily made a fist.

Three Months Ago

When Akavi was finished with the Quns she wandered out of Renglu, looking determined to magically grow some more fungi for the good of the community. She was about to do no such thing, of course; that was Elu's job. Instead she walked into the surrounding wilderness until she was alone, and then she shifted into another body, a Riayin woman of about forty, older and more authoritative than the body she wore with the Quns. Finding some privacy between the trees, she dug in her pack and changed into clothes that better suited this new form. A knee-length skirt, a simple blouse, classic shapes that must have once looked elegant before the harsh conditions of the Chaos Zone wore them down. Now they were a little worse for wear, but with their holes carefully darned and their stains scrubbed out to near-invisibility. This was the garb of an intelligent, upper-class woman, someone whose educated opinion was to be trusted, someone who still clung to reason and respectability even after a disaster that had all but erased them.

In that body, she set out for the spot just outside of town where she had arranged to meet Luellae Nyrath.

Luellae was Akavi's contact among the Seven. Meeting

her, in the first few weeks after his and Elu's landing, had been a stroke of luck – or as close as Akavi ever got to luck. She'd already set the stage by ingratiating herself with the more resistance-oriented pockets of the nearest communities, making herself useful, proving herself devoted and loyal to the cause. She'd worked out where and when the Quns met with members of the Seven, and she'd finagled her way, using the identity under which the Quns knew her, into observing one of those meetings. And when she saw Luellae, she'd known that she was even more fortunate than she'd planned. Luellae had unique weaknesses, and she would be even easier to control than the rest.

Back in the days when Yasira and the Seven studied with Evianna Talirr, Luellae had been a perpetual student. Quiet and observant and a bit of a perfectionist, toiling away at a doctoral project that kept getting delayed. A more conscientious mentor might have guided her to reduce the scope of her work, but Talirr wasn't interested in reducing the scope of *anything*. She'd been entirely blasé about letting Luellae stretch out her studies to five years, six, seven, ten. Luellae had worked diligently despite an inability to finish, and she'd attended social functions with punctilious consistency; she'd gotten to know each of the other students, polite enough in her standoffish way, watching and learning.

Luellae's research hadn't been heretical, and for a long time Akavi had ignored her in favor of other prisoners with more insight into the forbidden parts of Dr Talirr's work. But eventually, reaching an impasse with the other six, Akavi had ordered Luellae brought in as well. He'd put her through a different set of interrogations. Less about Dr Talirr – though that was in there – and more about her interpersonal observations. She'd watched each of Akavi's other prisoners at their work for years on end. What were their weaknesses? What distressed them most? What could be used to guilt or coerce them into continuing?

The other students didn't know that Luellae had betrayed them in these ways, making each of their torments a little bit worse so as to avoid torments of her own. Akavi's cover identity had no way of knowing that either, but she wouldn't have been a proper Vaurian angel if she didn't know how to capitalize on it indirectly, to befriend her knowing those mental weak spots and slowly exploit them.

For Luellae, Akavi presented herself as a scholar – not a physicist, Akavi didn't have enough specialist knowledge to fake expertise in Luellae's own field, but a professor of political science and law. Universities weren't really a thing anymore in the Chaos Zone, although survivors passed books and tracts of thought to each other when they could. Law wasn't really a thing either, without the infrastructure for mortals to enforce it; serious crimes were dealt with informally by the community, and the rest were ignored.

But this woman Akavi pretended to be had not given up on her gifts. Instead she was using them in something parallel to the way the Seven used them. This imaginary woman knew how revolutions worked, and how the groundwork had to be laid for them, in ways a mere physicist never could. And with her own research, her own network of contacts, she claimed to be patiently putting that groundwork in place.

Today, she'd asked Luellae along to help her observe the gone people. And after their usual brief greetings and one of Luellae's lightning-fast bursts of motion across the miles, that was where they went. Akavi lay carefully, mindful of further damage to her outfit, in a field of yellowish, corkscrew-bladed grass. Luellae, sprawling more casually, lent her a pair of simple binoculars.

"They've been doing this more and more," she said now, as Akavi watched the gone people milling in the field about a hundred feet away. "Gathering for a purpose we don't understand. Before, we saw them doing spiritual rituals together, but this is different."

The gone people had lived through the onset of Jai's plague, just like the people who got to be called survivors; they still looked human, dressed in tattered rags that had once been casual wear or business suits. They were humans of all ages and types, old and young and in-between, male and female and other genders, Riayin and Stijonan and the smattering of other ethnicities that the Chaos Zone possessed. They were also no longer people in any sense that mattered to Akavi. They did not speak. They lived in nests like animals, constructed out of strange Outside materials; they ate only the Outside plants and animals that naturally occurred here. They appeared to lack individuality. They could explore and survive on their own, but when they gathered, they moved in synchrony, appearing to share their minds on levels even angels couldn't match.

Even the Seven had difficulty connecting to the gone people. Some people had a rudimentary ability to communicate with Outside monsters: Daeis, a member of the Seven Akavi hadn't met yet, had a particularly advanced form of that ability. Such people could get across simple concepts to the gone people, things like *danger* or *come here* or *stay back*. But the gone people's more complex group mind was inaccessible even with magic. Whatever their heretical ceremonies felt like to them, however they saw the world and whatever perverse beliefs they cherished, nobody knew.

The things that the gone people were best-known for, of course, were heretical rites. They involved bloodletting and the summoning of formless Outside energies. But the gone people in this field weren't doing that. Instead, they crouched together in small shifting subgroups. They weren't speaking, but every so often they made strange gestures that looked more explanatory than ritualistic. As if giving directions, mapping something out on the grass below them.

"Curious," Akavi said, keeping the binoculars fixed to his eyes. "They look like they're planning something."

"They do, don't they? But I wish we knew *what*."

Akavi shook her head. "Everyone worth knowing in the Chaos Zone is planning the same thing, of course. Revolution. The only question is how they intend to achieve that aim." She passed the binoculars back to Luellae. "Do you see how they're gesturing? As if they need to illustrate something visually to get their plan across. I'd always assumed a group mind wouldn't need that."

"Yeah, it's weird," Luellae agreed. "They only started doing this a week or two ago."

"Has your team discussed it?"

"A little. Nothing useful. Mostly it's the same debates over and over again. Circular. They're a bunch of physicists; they work with numbers; they don't have *insight*." Luellae rested her chin in her hand, frowning as she watched. Luellae was a physicist too, of course, but she had been a careful observer of people even before Akavi misused her for that end. It would frustrate her, naturally, that the Seven seemed more interested in debating abstract ethics than in figuring out the motives of the most odd and crucial creatures on the planet.

"But surely you have people who could try to open communications," Akavi pressed. "You have Daeis–"

"We tried Daeis. They did a better job than the rest of us would have. But they don't have the kind of rapport with the gone people that they do with monsters. They got impressions, feelings, things we could use if we were writing an anthropological study on what gone people are like, but they couldn't get *plans*."

Akavi hesitated delicately. "What about Savior?"

Luellae tossed the binoculars down and flopped her head into the grass. "Savior won't get off her ass. And Tiv keeps her there."

It was a point of small satisfaction to Akavi, that Luellae had never once in her presence called Tiv Hunt "Leader".

Akavi sighed. "I wish your group listened to you more. It's not your fault none of you were trained for this, but you have such resources. It's a waste."

"Tiv's so concerned about not hurting anybody." Luellae looked up at Akavi mutinously. Luellae was such a naturally suspicious person anyway, after what she'd been through; she'd been primed for these conclusions, and it had been so easy, pleasant and effortless to lead her to them as if they were her own idea. "But we're already in a war. Even some of the others are starting to see that. Every time she tries to shield someone from harm it only splashes the harm out to everyone else. She tries protecting Savior, and Savior just stays lying there depressed in her safe little room, and she suffers, and everyone who needs her help suffers. She tries to say we're not fighting a war, because she doesn't like that people get hurt in a war, and that's why we're going to *lose* the war. Because we can't see it for what it is."

Akavi looked at her, understanding and calm. "But you can."

Eventually, Luellae's frustration with the Seven and

with Tiv in particular would grow to the point where she could be induced to make her own bid for power. When that moment arrived, Akavi would encourage her to openly rebel against Tiv and to wrest control of the whole Jai resistance from her hands. By doing so, she would either destroy it, or would forge it into a newer, crueler, more reckless entity – a group even easier for Akavi to exploit. A group from which the elusive Yasira Shien could finally be pulled – because Luellae, at least, would not let her hide from the world forever.

Akavi could feel that moment coming, perhaps in the next few months, and oh, how she savored it.

Luellae flopped back down in the grass again. She spent much of her time with Akavi acting petulant like this. Childish, really; but with Akavi, Luellae knew that her petulance would meet a sympathetic ear. "They don't listen to me."

Akavi reached out and clasped Luellae's shoulder, warm and reassuring. "But they will."

They call me Destroyer, but I am not sure what I am supposed to have destroyed.

Infrastructure? Perhaps. Lives? Of course. Sanity? That was always a lie. Angelic hegemony over Jai as a planet? That is what I meant to destroy, but it is still here, if in an altered form.

I walk these streets, trying to understand what I have done, and how I could have done it better. I feel regret, if only because I have failed Yasira Shien. I meant to make her understand the Truth, and she did understand it, but she did not like how I looked to her in its light. She saw the Truth, and still held on to something like morality, and in her eyes I was found wanting. I am still chewing over that in my mind, as I look at the houses ruined and repaired, the common people adjusting to their new lives, these strange fruits of my labor and hers.

I am not prepared to apologize. If you are reading this, you already know what the Gods did to me. I still intend to pay them back. I meant for this, the Jai Plague, to be the first true strike in a war over the cosmos themselves.

And it will be.

– From the diaries of Dr Evianna Talirr

CHAPTER 4
Now

Tiv and Akiujal were nearly home again, all the way back to the small suburb where Akiujal had his apartment. They'd crept through the disused tunnels and back up to the surface, and it was only a block further. It had been dangerous to strike out so far from one of the team's known safe places, away from the airlock that would bring her safely home. And Tiv hadn't learned from it any of what she'd hoped she'd learn. The problem of weapons was no more tractable than before. Akiujal and everyone like him still wanted the impossible from her. And, more importantly, from Yasira.

Even if Yasira had been in perfect health, glowing and eager and determined to help in the fullness of her power, it might still not have been enough. She'd miraculously changed the landscape once, but that didn't mean she could pop into every location where people needed her. It didn't mean she could fight the angels in each of those places and emerge unscathed. Yasira had given the Chaos Zone its miracle, and now everybody thought of her as a miracle and not as a person. Not a person whose abilities might be finite. Not a person who might, themselves, be harmed.

Let alone a person who was desperately ill.

Stijonan architecture was slightly different from Riayin. More curlicues, flatter roofs, drabber colors. Akiujal's apartment wasn't in the busiest center of Dasz, but its neighborhood was fairly tightly packed, in places where the Plague hadn't made it unusable. Tenements and townhouses crowded side by side, jagged like teeth at their tops, where some of the apartments had vanished and others were arbitrarily left intact. The survivors in this neighborhood were good at making do with what they had. The building next to Akiujal's had partially melted when the Plague hit, fonts of liquefied brick and stucco frozen on its walls like tear-streaked makeup. It was inhabited anyway, by a gaggle of ordinary determined people who'd used both magic and masonry to tidy it back into a vaguely livable state. The small gardens in front of the houses were inhabited too, with groups of people determinedly coaxing vegetables from their plots of soil. Ordinary vegetables, not heretical ones: nobody here was bold enough to use food-growing powers in the open.

It was absurdly dangerous to walk out exposed like this, and Tiv had worn a partial disguise. Not enough to fool God-built technology, but enough that these random people in their gardens wouldn't immediately identify her as Leader. A wrap around her head and shoulders, of a type that was common here for keeping out the sun. A bit of makeup, applied by Akiujal's wife, to slightly distort her Arinnan features.

"Freeze," said an electronically amplified voice from the other end of the block. An angel's voice.

"Fire!" Akiujal bellowed at the same time, nearly as loudly as the angel. "The gas main's about to burst! Run!"

The people at work in the gardens scrambled in every direction. In the confusion, Akiujal shoved Tiv toward the building they'd been walking towards – his own apartment building, as streaked and stuccoed and uneven as the rest. "Run, Leader. You'll make it. Remember what you saw here."

Too panicked to question, Tiv ran.

"You are harboring a fugitive from Nemesis Herself," the angel's voice called out behind her. "Freeze, or I will fire."

There was further shouting and hubbub, and the people around her ran aimlessly. Tiv rushed to the apartment entrance. She heard gunshots behind her. She wasn't sure why they didn't hit; an angel's aim was supposed to be good. Shouldn't she be stopping to check if the other people here were okay? But she couldn't stop running.

She reached the door and ran in, slamming it behind her. She could still hear the chaos outside, more shouting, more shots. The apartment building's anteroom was dim and dingy, the lights that once illuminated its brownish tiles and potted plants having long ago lost their power. She turned.

She had come into this building this morning, using the meta-portal, through the main front door. If she focused, her motion through the portal would reverse the process and return her to the lair.

There was another series of shots and screams behind the door. Tiv had a wild urge to open it again the normal way, face the chaos like a warrior. But she knew she couldn't hesitate. As soon as the angel finished plowing through the crowd, it would open the door itself.

She pictured the lair, yanked the door open, and stumbled through.

The sounds immediately ceased. The feeling of the Chaos Zone around her lightened. She was in the airlock's interior, a bare metal closet-like space. She sank to the ground there and shook, unwilling to go further.

Tiv had never had an escape this narrow before. She'd

known the dangers; she'd known she was the second most wanted person on Jai, and she'd had smaller scares. A few others on the team had been shot at like this before. Luellae had experienced it several times. Luellae's abilities let her flit from place to place in ways even the airlock didn't allow, so she'd scouted and risked herself more than the others.

Tiv hadn't stopped to think about it in her panic, but now that she had a moment to breathe, she understood what had happened. Akiujal had stirred the whole neighborhood into a panic so that Tiv could slip away in the confusion. She'd seen that technique in vids. Popcorn action movies, silly things Tiv had used to enjoy, because their kind of violence didn't seem real. The line about the gas main had been almost too obvious to believe; the neighbors might not have listened, if not for the fact that Akiujal was well-respected, a leader in his community. He'd had their loyalty. And he'd used it to–

To sacrifice them all, in the blink of an eye. To put his neighbors in the line of fire between the angel and Tiv.

And the angel *had* fired.

Tiv felt her stomach clench, and she leaned forward, suppressing a dry heave. As soon as the worst of it was over, she hauled herself up. She had to understand this. She had to know for sure.

She stepped towards the airlock's inner doors, which parted for her automatically, and into the warm confusion of the lair.

Splió was sitting just inside, doing something in a notebook. He startled as he saw her and put the book down, striding towards her. "Tiv, are you–" She could see the word "okay" die on his lips; obviously she was not. "What happened?"

"Angels, with–" Tiv was shaking harder than she'd thought. She wasn't usually the type who lost verbal speech under stress. But she'd never had *this* kind of stress before.

Not when the angels had briefly captured her, before she was Leader, as leverage against Yasira; not even in the *Pride of Jai* disaster, when she'd watched the lifeboat's doors shut behind her even as another handful of doomed crew ran towards them. Those things had been horrific, but they hadn't been about *her*. "They– shot–"

Splió's eyes widened even further. "Are you hurt?"

"No, I–"

She nearly doubled over again as her stomach twisted. She wasn't hurt. Because she was called Leader, and the people on the ground thought that *meant* something. She faffed around delivering packages and wringing her hands about weapons. She was connected to Yasira. And Akiujal had sacrificed a whole crowd of people to save her. Just for that.

She straightened herself as best she could and faced Splió, still shaking. "I need you to look at something for me."

She didn't like using Splió like this, but he was the only one who could safely do it. Splió's code name was Watcher. Anyone could use the airlock to move themselves, but Splió could use it in other ways. Splió could use it to *see*.

"Anything, Leader," Splió said gravely, and there was no irony in his voice this time as he used the title. Tiv wanted to crumple up the word "Leader" and throw it far away forever.

"I just came from Sedajegy Utridzysy Akiujal's house in Dasz. Angels came, and Mr Akiujal created a diversion, and I ran. I couldn't look back. I need you to look there. I need you to tell me if… How bad it is."

Splió nodded and stepped to the airlock. Splió liked being useful in this way, which didn't make Tiv stop feeling guilty about it; she was asking him to peer into horrors that were hers to contend with, not his. Splió looked higher-functioning than Daeis on the surface, able to talk lucidly and be charming in his cynical way, but he still couldn't muster the energy to make his rounds most days. Some of the time he spent with Daeis, who needed individual care, and some he spent listlessly reading or staring at the wall. Sometimes he went on long jags cursing himself and his lack of ability. Using his powers to help, even in painful ways, helped him feel better about himself. That didn't make it right.

Nothing about this team or this planet would ever be right.

Splió raised a hand to the metal door, but instead of going through, he leaned on it, contemplative. He closed his eyes, and Tiv watched the twitching under his eyelids, as if in the throes of a dream. After a moment she heard him gasp, just a short, chagrined intake of breath. Nothing more dramatic than that.

"They're dead," he informed her flatly. "The angel's gone. About… a dozen people shot, it looks like."

"Mr Akiujal?"

"I don't see him. Probably means he got away, but I can't tell for sure." His eyelids twitched a little more, and then his shoulders relaxed and he pulled away. "Sorry."

"I'm the one who should be sorry."

Splió opened his eyes and looked at her flatly. "Yeah, how dare you wade out there and shoot all those people?"

Tiv's breath was coming faster. She'd thought knowing would make it better, but of course it didn't. "They died because of me. I took a stupid risk and they all died covering my escape." All those human beings, snuffed out. Because someone – because *Akiujal* had decided Tiv was worth more than that number of ordinary lives.

"Yeah? Did you ask them to do that?"

"You know why they did it," Tiv snapped, her voice raw. "You *know* why."

She'd known she was taking a risk, but she'd thought *she* was the one taking it. She hadn't been thinking at all.

Splió sighed softly. "Hey. I'm sorry. I'm shitty at this part. Come here." He opened his arms, hesitantly, offering a hug. "Or do you want to be with Yasira? I think she's awake."

Tiv bit her lip. She *should* want to be with Yasira. If only she could collapse in Yasira's arms and cry on her shoulder. If only they could whisper to each other that it would be okay. But Yasira wasn't well. Yasira had been too distraught to even get out of bed this morning. Tiv hadn't even told her yet that people were asking for weapons. How could she explain what had happened *now?* Yasira couldn't handle this.

She flopped forward and let Splió hold her. He rubbed her back. "Hey, you're safe. It's okay. I mean, it's not *okay,* but – this all just sucks, and we're doing what we can. It's not your fault. You're trying. You're good. You're brave."

A second pair of arms wrapped hesitantly around her from the side. Daeis, pale and quiet as always, had entered unnoticed. They didn't have Splió's platitudes, but they were warm and soft, and between them and Splió it felt like being carried. The two of them, in concert, could almost hold the weight of her.

Tiv leaned against them and dissolved into loud, howling sobs.

Yasira had been dozing, too groggy and listless to do anything but not quite unconscious. Sometimes she lay awake and let the dozens of conflicting thoughts in her head argue it out; sometimes she dreamed, formless dreams that transcended any waking concept. Outside dreams.

Yasira was mostly Outside these days. Very little of her,

on the inside, resembled the mental shape she'd once had. She had told Tiv most of the bad things that had happened to her, but she had never told her the last and worst.

After her miracle, six months ago, Outside had offered to destroy Yasira's soul. Alive, she was likely to be captured and tortured again; dead, her soul would be in Nemesis' clutches, which was even worse. But if her soul did not exist, if there was nothing left capable of feeling or understanding enough to suffer, then she would be safe.

Yasira had, in the core of her mind, said *yes.*

She'd felt herself starting to crumble. And then, at the last second, she'd thought of Tiv. She'd changed her mind. Outside had allowed that, too; it had sent what was left of her soul back into her body. But the parts that were already broken could never be fully restored. The structure of her physical brain held things together, but Yasira was no longer a single soul. She was a collection of pieces which shifted and jangled, chaotically, in and out of place.

Tiv understood neurodiversity. Yasira would never have dated a woman who didn't. Tiv understood that people's minds could take different shapes, and they could still be important and worthy of love. But Yasira hadn't been like this when Tiv fell in love with her. And she feared what Tiv might think, what Tiv might say, if she understood how deep the change really went.

It was hard to make a lot of jangling pieces work together properly. But it didn't make her incapable of hearing. And so she had been startled awake by the sound of Tiv crying, loudly, somewhere else in the lair.

Something awful had happened.

With a creeping sense of dread, Yasira tried to push herself up to go and investigate. Then an entirely different thought occurred. Something awful had happened to Tiv. And Tiv hadn't come in here to tell her about it. She'd decided not to do that – for now, or maybe at all.

When Tiv had been in distress before the Plague, she'd gone straight to Yasira. Held her, cried on her shoulder – that was the way it worked. That was what Yasira did, in reverse, when she was in distress. But Tiv was out there, not in here.

Of course she isn't in here, came the thought immediately. *You've been lying in bed barely alive for months. Why would she think you could comfort her?*

You should go to her, urged another mental voice. *If she doesn't think you can help, prove her wrong.*

If she wanted your help, she'd be here.

Maybe she thinks you're asleep. Maybe she just doesn't want to bother you. Doesn't mean you can't go out there and offer.

Don't go out. You can't go bothering people who don't want you around. That's rude.

It's ruder not to. She's doing it so you'll hear. What do you think she'll say tonight if she knows you heard her crying and did nothing?

I just want to know what happened.

Yasira pushed against her blankets and rolled out of bed. She landed in a crouch on the floor. Her muscles were weak – *that's what you get for lying around all the time,* said someone – and for a moment she couldn't move further.

Every piece of Yasira these days had its own thoughts, and the thoughts crowded in her head so thickly that it was hard to do anything else. There was no central, Real Yasira who could decide to push forward and ignore the other ones. Nobody had that authority. When Yasira moved, or spoke, it was simply one or more pieces taking over for a minute. They could lose that control just as quickly.

Yasira had heard about plurality and split-personality disorders. She'd been born and raised in Riayin, which prided itself on accepting every neurotype. Plurality was no worse than anything else. But Yasira wasn't sure if she was even plural in the usual way. Plurals were either born or made through trauma – a natural predisposition to dissociation and fragmentation, magnified in response to gut-wrenchingly awful events. And it was true that Yasira had been through something awful. But Outside had literally reached into her and split her up. Outside was inherently a part of her now. Most plurals weren't that way. Maybe the techniques that worked for most plurals, improving communication and teamwork between all the parts of themselves, wouldn't work for a person like Yasira. Maybe real plural systems wouldn't even want to be associated with her. Maybe, if she called herself that, it would only bring down angelic retribution on all the other plurals, in case they were plural because of Outside things, too. Maybe they'd want to run away from Outside the way everyone else did. The right diagnostic category for Yasira was "Outside madness" – everything else, once that level of unreality got involved, took second place.

There were things Yasira could still have done to look up the techniques that worked for other plurals, to find answers to some of those "maybes". But the idea of doing them made her rise up into arguments with herself even louder and angrier than the usual ones. She'd never managed it.

So, in the meantime she had a mess of different parts of herself who rarely ever got along. Only a few of the largest of them bothered with names. There was the Scientist, for instance – a biggish chunk who was mostly made of curiosity. She was the one who just wanted to know what had happened. But most of Yasira wasn't as coherent as that.

There were pieces too small to keep track of, who rose to the surface to say or do something and immediately sank again. There were pieces who lurked in the background, thinking seething dangerous Outside thoughts. Yasira carried Outside itself with her, in ways that had previously only been accessible with the help of Ev's technology. She could draw on it at any time, if she chose to face the consequences. Sometimes it drew *itself* up through her, in a wild conglomeration of energies seeking release. Yasira usually managed to stumble out of the lair when that happened, through the airlock, into some uninhabited part of the Chaos Zone where she wouldn't do any harm.

She'd spaced out on the floor, thinking about all this, instead of moving further. It was hard to focus on the physical world when her head held such cacophony inside. She tried to move again.

Don't you dare, said a small dissenting chorus of pieces. *You'll bother her. Do you think she'll keep coming in here and taking care of you if you bother her?*

Let her stop, said one of the seething, background pieces. *What's the worst that can happen if she stops? We die, right? That might be nice.* A chorus of other pieces quickly hushed that piece. Most of Yasira did want to live, despite everything.

No, said another part of Yasira to the first one, ignoring the angry one completely. *That's the other way around. Good people are supposed to reciprocate. I should try to take care of her back.*

Yeah? Since when are you good?

But I want to know what happened, the Scientist complained again.

Before Yasira could get a semblance of working order into her limbs, the door opened. It wasn't Tiv, but Prophet. A waify, stick-thin trans girl with the dark straight braids of a woman from Ahti. Yasira had known Prophet in grad school; she had gone by the name Exatlia then. She and Yasira hadn't been close – Yasira hadn't been close to *anybody*, really – but sometimes they'd sat together at department events, making awkward conversation, both equally uncomfortable with the room around them for their differing reasons.

Prophet wasn't autistic, but she often stared into space the way Yasira did. Prophet had a lot of conflicting senses. At any given moment she was seeing some variable amount of time into the future – usually not long, a few seconds at most, but sometimes leaping ahead very far, sometimes seeing events in some other place, often seeing multiple things at once. Most of it wasn't especially useful, nor easy to interpret. She and Yasira were similar in that way, both inundated with information, both a little spacy when it came to what was actually in front of them.

Prophet knew Yasira's secret. Yasira hadn't *told* her, but she'd seen it, dimly. That meant that Grid, Weaver, and Picket – the rest of the Four, who didn't keep secrets from each other – also knew. Beyond that strange circle-within-a-circle, no one had breathed a word.

"I knew you'd hear," said Prophet, without preamble, staring at the wall.

"I should go out. I shouldn't go out. I want to know – I don't know what to do."

Prophet sat down and arranged herself on the floor, so they were both at the same level. She squirmed around, seeming to have difficulty getting comfortable. "She's keeping secrets from you. Not, like, *bad* secrets. No one's betraying anyone. But I don't think you should go out there right now. She's gotta tell you when she's ready. When she's in shock and crying, it's not the time, you know?"

Yasira managed to look at Prophet directly. Voices of alarm rose sharply in her mental background. Tiv wasn't just upset and seeking comfort elsewhere. She was upset because of something that she *actively* didn't want Yasira to know.

Tiv was keeping not only a secret, but a *terrible* secret. Not a betraying one, maybe. But still a secret bad enough to make her howl like this, outside Yasira's room, without being able to explain why.

"Is she hurt?"

Prophet shrugged uncomfortably. "Not physically. But… yes, I think. Running a resistance hurts. We all feel that sometimes."

Yasira flopped forward and buried her face between her knees. "Except me. Sorry. I just lie here–"

"I meant you, too. I did mean that."

Yasira hunched more tightly in on herself.

You're sitting here feeling sorry for yourself while everyone else puts their lives on the line, said some cruel but accurate piece of her. *You're the reason they're risking themselves in the first place.*

It would be better, said some of those ugly buzzing parts in the very back, *if we weren't here.*

Yasira literally couldn't get up and help. She'd tried. On a good day, she could walk around the lair and have reasonable conversations with the team. She could wash dishes and stuff. But she'd tried making rounds the way everyone else did, or stealing supplies, or organizing plans and supply lists, or even helping redecorate the lair, and she couldn't. Not even for a day. She got overwhelmed and had to stop almost immediately, sometimes in a torrent of self-recriminating tears, sometimes in pure blankness as the arguing in her head drowned out the rest of the world.

"I mean, the Four don't keep secrets," Prophet rambled from her corner of the room. "Not from each other. But that just means we know how we're all hurting. And there are good things as well; we share those, too. It's not all pain. But even the rest of the Seven have secrets. I haven't figured out what all of them are, but I can feel them there. I think most people don't even know how many secrets they're keeping. You'll feel better when Tiv knows your secret. It'll be harder, learning hers, but you'll get through it. Tiv's not gonna give up on you, Savior. I don't always see real clear, but you two are together in every future I see."

Yasira tightened her fingers in her own hair. Sometimes it was easier to just let all the parts speak at once, to drop any pretense of coherence, and with Prophet, she could do that. "I can't tell her yet. It's not the right time. I should have told her before. I'm not good enough for her now. She shouldn't have stayed. I'm so fucking *stupid*."

She heard Prophet shifting where she sat, and she wondered if she'd made her uncomfortable. But Prophet's voice was the same as usual, gentle and wry. "Nah, there's no 'good enough', Savior. There's just love."

Yasira stirred, looking up at Tiv with bleary eyes, as soon as Tiv opened the door to her room. Tiv slipped in and shut it behind her, kneeling beside the bed. "How are you doing, hon? I'm sorry I couldn't come in earlier."

"I'm all right," said Yasira. Her voice was morose, but she was sitting up without prompting, blearily swinging her feet out toward the floor. The bad phase she'd been going through these last few days might be nearing its end. Yasira wasn't healthy even on good days, and the bad days would come again soon enough, but Tiv still felt hopeful. She lived for these little improvements. "Have you been all right?"

"Not… really," said Tiv. She didn't trust herself to explain the whole problem to Yasira right now. But she wouldn't *lie*. "Things have been pretty stressful."

"Running a rebellion. Yeah. I warned you."

Yasira scooted a little closer to Tiv, and Tiv laid her head on the mattress. Loving Yasira could be hard, but there was something about it that grounded her. Yasira had gone through much worse than Tiv; she'd faced equally big decisions and felt equally lost. And then she'd changed the course of a whole planet's history. She'd become a living miracle. Tiv's ambitions weren't quite that grand, but it was comforting to lie down in Yasira's shadow, knowing all of it.

"You were, um," Yasira added after a moment. "You were crying."

Tiv grimaced. "Yeah. Sorry. I… had a close call. With an angel. I made it out, but… most of the neighborhood didn't." She felt herself choking up again just saying it. Her big howling first fit of tears was done, but she wasn't over this. She didn't know if she'd ever be.

"Shit. Fuck. Sorry."

"Don't cuss," Tiv chided automatically.

"I'm gonna fucking cuss. You almost died. Shit. Sorry. I… I wasn't even *there*."

Tiv raised her head and wiped her nose on the back of her wrist. She wasn't sobbing again, not out of control, but tears were leaking down her face. "I'm glad you weren't there," she said forcefully. "I'm glad. I ran home and – and at least I knew *you* were safe."

Yasira sighed. Tiv shut her eyes, trying to control herself, and to her surprise, Yasira's hand came tentatively down on her hair. Stroking it, comfortingly, in the way that had once been second nature.

Yasira wasn't really safe, though. That was the thing. No one was going to shoot her. But even on a good day, Tiv could see something eating away at her from the inside. She could see a kind of fragmentation she didn't quite have words for, as Yasira seemed to seesaw back and forth between so many contradictory thoughts. Tiv tried her best, but she knew a day might come when no caregiving could be enough. Yasira might die of this, one day, as finally as from a bullet.

"I started this mess," said Yasira.

"You did not. Dr Talirr did."

"Same thing. You know what I mean."

Tiv didn't really, but she wasn't in the mood to argue with survivor guilt. Tiv had enough survivor guilt for one person right now.

"Hey," said Yasira, smoothing her hair back. "Hey, I don't want you to die. Or to hurt. Or to feel you can't tell me what happened. Or – I'm here for you, Tiv. I'm shitty at it. But we're both here for each other. Okay?"

"Okay," said Tiv.

She wondered, for a nauseous second, if Yasira *knew*. If all her efforts, trying to shield Yasira from the truths that would hurt her, had been pointless. Yasira was so powerful, despite her illness. Maybe she'd known all along. Maybe Tiv was being silly, trying to keep it from her, when people like Qun and Akiujal clamored for her help. Maybe she heard them, like a God receiving prayers through the ansible net, every time.

Or maybe she knew Tiv was hiding something, because she'd heard Tiv crying from across the lair without coming to get her, and she'd drawn the obvious conclusion.

Yasira leaned in and kissed her.

They kissed so rarely these days. Yasira had used to love being touched, but it was difficult now. Her sensory sensitivities were more than they had used to be; that happened sometimes when autistic people burned out. And some forms of touch were trauma triggers. Yasira had been physically tortured in the angels' care, and the accidental scrape of a fingernail or jostle of an elbow could send her to curl, shrieking, in on herself. It wasn't a sexual trauma, not in the usual sense, but it made intimacy difficult in something close to the same way.

On good days, though, they did get to kiss like this. Yasira pressed her lips to Tiv's, moving slowly, with a tension that felt less like fear and more like carefully holding something back. As if she wanted more, but didn't trust herself. Tiv held still, kissing back with only the subtlest motions, and let Yasira set the pace. Tiv loved being touched, too. She'd learned to savor all these small things even more, to honor the risks Yasira took and the pain she held in when she offered them.

This time Yasira ended up on the floor with Tiv, arms wrapped around her. Tiv leaned gently into it, letting herself soak it up. Hugs from the rest of the Seven felt good, warm and comforting and present, but there was something else to it here. Something sacred. She closed her eyes and imagined Yasira as the God everybody wanted her to be, an omnibenevolent presence twining in amid the chaos and death, holding her on a level that transcended the physical. Promising help would come if she'd just hold on.

Whispering in her ear, the way Gods whispered to Their angels and priests, what to do.

But Tiv no longer believed in Gods. Obviously They existed, but she no longer believed They would help her at all. She sometimes caught herself reaching back for those beliefs, on instinct, trying to find something where they'd used to be. She missed feeling like there were higher beings looking out for her, knowing all the answers before she did. But nothing was there. No one was going to decide what Tiv should do anymore, but Tiv.

"I don't always know what to do anymore," she confessed in a whisper. "The problem's so big, and sometimes it feels like everything we try only makes it worse."

Yasira sighed against her. When she spoke again, it was a resigned, tired echo of what Tiv had said to Yasira six months ago.

"Maybe we can't fix it," said Yasira. "But do you want to try?"

CHAPTER 5
Now

Ilva Rovaki, Inquisitor of Nemesis, looked down in distaste as Sedajegy Utridzysy Akiujal was shoved in front of her, falling to his knees.

The cameras were rolling, their hungry lenses perched on tripods or swooping through the air autonomously. Somewhere in the next room, other angels were editing the live feed, splicing together different shots from the most exciting angles. Off-camera, Akiujal had already been apprehended and interrogated. He'd already confessed. It took time, sometimes, to extract a confession from heretics like these, but Akiujal was the type who wanted to confess anyway, defiantly spitting out an account of his crimes as soon as he understood he wasn't getting out of here. The other inquisitors on the team had tortured him a little anyway, for form's sake, and had scheduled him for the broadcast the next morning.

The Gods were strictly limited in their response to human heresy in the Chaos Zone. At least half the population, by Ilva's reckoning, met the technical definition of heresy. But genocide was off the table for now – both for optics reasons and because the teams hunting for Evianna Talirr had not yet found her. So, the angels of Nemesis found themselves needing to keep order by other means. To set examples, so that those heretics who could be scared into submission – or scared, at least, into keeping their beliefs a bit more private – *would* be scared.

So, every morning, there were the broadcasts. Every television set, intercom, and radio receiver in the Chaos Zone was wired to receive them, whether the owner wanted to or not. The angels' aid efforts had prioritized electrical and mass communications infrastructure for precisely this reason. Every morning, out of all the heretics in the Chaos Zone who were slated for termination, one was brought before the cameras and shown to the world.

Ilva tilted her head, looking down at him. Akiujal's responses, according to the annotations in her optic circuits, were well within desired parameters. Enough defiance to forestall pity; not enough strength to inspire accidental loyalty. Most angels could read microexpressions, but for broadcasting what mattered were broader expressions and their complicated, contextual implications for the viewer, and Ilva had extended her own programming accordingly. Akiujal was bleeding slightly down one side of his face, and his hands trembled, but his gaze back up at her was a glare.

"Sedajegy Utridzysy Akiujal," said Ilva, each syllable precisely correct. "You have been brought before the Gods for dozens of counts of heresy, including the formation of illicit gatherings for heretical purposes and incitement of the use of supernatural Outside abilities, the very nature of which destabilize our already fragile reality. But your largest crime goes beyond any of these. You facilitated the escape of Productivity Hunt, the third most wanted mortal on Jai, the accomplice of Yasira Shien herself, and the leader of the band of arch-heretics known as the Seven. Yesterday, she could have been brought in to face justice for her crimes against your world. Instead, she resisted arrest, and you covered for her by sacrificing the lives of twelve of your neighbors. Members of the community, heretical and non-heretical, who had trusted you. Do you confess to this perversion of justice?"

Akiujal raised his head, resigned and spiteful. Sometimes people on the broadcast tried to protest their innocence, and that was tricky to handle. But Akiujal was the type who would use it to grandstand – and, thus, announce his guilt.

"Your angels," he said, "are the ones who pervert justice. And when the time is right, the people will rise up against you."

"If so, they'll die." Ilva gave a little shrug, unconcerned. "As will you. And your punishment after your death will be far worse than anything we can do to you in life."

She picked up her favorite blade from the low table before her: a heavy tungsten carbide weapon the size of an axe, oddly curved. Broadcasting wasn't a very difficult job, and a lower-ranking angel could have done it if pressed. But Ilva had a talent for exactly this sort of thing. Her red-and-black livery was always spotless and crisp, her makeup applied without a flaw. Her voice was clear and sonorous and made people sit up and listen. Before there'd been a need for any broadcasts in the Chaos Zone, she'd been known to break heretics just by saying the right words, at the right moment, commandingly enough.

"I ask absolution," said Ilva solemnly to the camera, "for what I am about to do."

Even Akiujal stilled at the sound of the Litany of Inquisition. Normally, this was the prayer Inquisitors said before torture. If they were just killing people, in private, they didn't bother. But mortals knew these ritual words, and mortals knew to fear them. Besides, in a way these broadcasts *were* a form of torture – not for the heretics who were terminated each day, necessarily, but for everyone else.

"I ask for the power of Nemesis to flow through me; the precision of Nemesis to guide my hands; the vengeance of Nemesis to steel me for what must be done. I ask that the suffering of this one fallen mortal bring mercy and benefit one hundredfold to those I am sworn to protect. I ask all this in the name of Nemesis who built me, who may unbuild me again if I falter. So it must be."

Akiujal closed his eyes, bracing himself. Sometimes they panicked at this point, struggled, tried to flee. Not him. Defiant to the end; defiance was another crime to be added to his list, but she had a grudging respect for it.

With a satisfying swish and thunk, she brought the blade down. Akiujal fell, and the cameras caught every bright drop of blood as his head rolled away from his body.

That morning, the sky over the Chaos Zone had begun to roil. Not an Outside effect, this time, but a battle. It was happening more and more frequently. The Keres, the Gods' ancient enemy, had always loved to swoop in and worsen the chaos when something in human space went wrong.

For all the awful things they did, the angels of Arete and Nemesis were consistent about this. Jai was a human world. They would defend it with their lives.

In practice that meant; the relief stations closed. Everything locked down. People were confined to their homes, with a tiny skeleton crew of angels patrolling the streets, just enough so it would look like enforcement. If ordinary mortals didn't have enough water or food rations to last out the battle, well, that was their problem. And the sky above crackled with something akin to lightning, as the Gods' ships and the Keres' ships waged war high above them. If everyone was lucky, that would be all it was. No fires would rage. No buildings would fall. No cities would be accidentally bombed from orbit in the crossfire, hit with one of the Keres' bizarre weapons before the Gods could stop them.

Tiv heard about the lockdown first thing in the morning. It was a planetary order, the whole Chaos Zone and beyond. On days like this, the Seven stripped their rounds down to only the essentials, only things that would save someone's life. Otherwise, with no ordinary people milling around and no crowds to get lost in, the risk of being seen was too high.

So they found themselves in the war room, hastily going through their notes and charts, identifying the highest priorities.

"Here," said Tiv, flipping through to the page she remembered. Huang-Bo had one of the Chaos Zone's worst medicine shortages, and the heretic group that the Seven were in contact with there contained several people who needed daily medicine to live. They rationed it out carefully, taking less of it than they should have, awaiting the days when medicine would arrive at their relief station. Today was supposed to have been that day. It was anyone's guess if it would arrive tomorrow – if the battle was even over tomorrow – or if this month's supply would be cancelled.

Medicine was harder to find on short notice than most things, but the Seven could do it.

"Luellae," Tiv said, looking up. On days like today, they needed Luellae's abilities. The meta-portal would take them to their usual landing points, the homes of community leaders like Qun and Akiujal who'd normally do the rest of the distribution for them, but on a day like today they'd have to go directly from house to house. "You up for a meds run?"

Luellae crossed her arms. "I'm up for it, but are you?"

Tiv bit her lip. She knew what Luellae meant. Tiv had slept badly, reliving yesterday's narrow escape over and over. She didn't want to go out and face the same danger again, but she knew she needed to. The angels were trying to scare the Seven away from their work, and scare ordinary mortals off from working with them. The Seven couldn't let them succeed. The longer Tiv waited before she swallowed her fear, took some deep breaths, and got back out there again, the worse it would be.

"People didn't die just so I could hide in the lair," Tiv said.

Luellae quirked an eyebrow. Luellae was the most hawkish of the Seven. Keeping people fed was a stopgap; real change, in Luellae's opinion, would be violent, and she didn't like that Tiv had ruled those options out. Tiv could imagine what she wanted to say: *People didn't die just for you to deliver groceries, either.*

But that wouldn't be fair; this wasn't just groceries. People's lives lay in the balance with this, too, just as much as they would in a shooting fight.

Which was probably why Luellae didn't argue, this once. Just nodded. "That's fair. You ready to go?"

Enga had been put on street-patrol duty. She hated it the same way she hated everything else. All the guns and other devices built into her body were for ground operations, not space battles, so she stayed on the ground.

She plodded along. The lockdown was stupid. A hit from a Keres weapon was a hit from a Keres weapon, and it'd destroy a whole block, whether people were in their houses or not. But keeping the mortals inside at least stopped panic. Meanwhile Enga got to be alone for a while, and to appreciate the fireworks in the sky without anybody bothering her.

Everybody knew that Nemesis wanted the Chaos Zone to go away. Irimiru had explained why they all had to pretend otherwise. But why all the effort? Why not let a stray bolt through, every once in a while, just enough to flatten a city or two? Sure, the Gods had to manage Their image. But why couldn't they say something like, *Oops, we missed that one! Good thing we blocked the other ninety-nine or that would have been a whole lot worse.* Enga could imagine ways to say things like that diplomatically, and Enga was pretty stupid. The Gods ought to be able to do it even better.

She saw a blur of motion in the corner of her eye and turned to it, clicking her guns into a ready position. But before she could focus well enough to aim, it was gone.

Travelling with Luellae was easy. Nerve-wracking, but easy. All Tiv had to do was hold on, and the world twisted around her – a different kind of twist and lurch every time. Today it was a kaleidoscopic swirl of colors. It made Tiv a little woozy, and she was pretty sure it would have given Yasira the biggest sensory overload headache of all time, but there was something nice about a little brightness on a day like today, when artificial thunder rolled in the darkened sky.

She stumbled as they made their fourth or fifth landing of the day, straight into someone's living room, which wasn't how Tiv liked to do things. Tiv liked to land outside a home and knock politely, but they couldn't do it that way today. A family of five had been huddled around a small cluster of candles – a young mother, two children, and two older male relatives – and they visibly startled when they saw Tiv and Luellae. The community leader Tiv normally spoke to, in Huang-Bo, had told her where to find these people, but Tiv had never actually met them before.

"It's okay," said Tiv in Riayin, holding out her hands. One was empty, palm out; the other held today's small bag of medicines. "Don't be scared. Are you Xiel, Ranah, Zaory, Fonsa, and Dacca Li?"

The oldest man in the group nodded, fear turning to hesitant hope on his face. He was stick thin and his skin was discolored. "Are you–?"

Tiv nodded. "I'm Productivity Hunt. This is Blur. Kae Lam said you needed insulin?"

He nodded, his eyes widening in relief and gratitude. "Yes. Thank you, Leader."

It didn't take much to convince people in the Chaos Zone who Tiv was. The way Luellae moved through space looked as strange from the outside as it did from the inside. It didn't look like anything anyone else could do. No one arrived in rooms unannounced this way but Tiv and the Seven.

It made her heart hurt, how desperate they were for someone like her to believe in. How grateful they were for a simple delivery. How easily this man, too, would throw himself away to cover her escape, the way all of Akiujal's neighbors had done yesterday.

But normally Tiv was able to push through that unease, and to give people like the Lis what they needed. A kind, steady gaze. A humble nod, and a smile, and an acknowledgment. Normally she could say things like, *we're all in this together.* Little platitudes that they would remember and value, not because they were really worth that much, but because someone as revered as Tiv had taken the time to look them in the eye and say them.

It was all smoke and mirrors. They only revered her because she ran around with this group of people, because she happened to be able to make rounds like this and give them what they needed. And because, out of that group, she was the only one mentally healthy enough to look people in the eye and be polite.

She didn't deserve any of this.

Tiv tried to refocus, but before she could find words, something distracted her. A television set, in the corner, flaring to life.

The Lis had thrown a sheet over the television to muffle it – many families did, to tune out the upsetting daily broadcasts. Even people who'd stayed loyal to the Gods didn't want public executions in their living rooms every day. But the Gods didn't give them a choice. Even when there wasn't regular electricity for lights and heat, somehow, there was this.

"Sedajegy Utridzysy Akiujal," said the tinny voice of the awful woman who was always the face of these broadcasts. Tiv knew what she would look like if she pulled the sheet from the set, crisp and severe in her red-and-black livery, not a fleck of makeup out of place. "You have been brought before the Gods–"

Tiv froze.

She'd thought that he might have survived. Splió had said that he couldn't see Akiujal among the bodies. She'd dared to hope that might mean he'd *escaped*–

"–you facilitated the escape of Productivity Hunt, the third most wanted mortal on Jai–"

No.

She wanted to lurch towards the television, to smash it into the ground, like that would fix anything. Her feet felt rooted to the floor.

"–the people will rise up against you."

Tiv realized, fuzzily, that Luellae and the Lis were staring at her.

"I have to go," she said in a strangled voice. She couldn't let normal people see her like this.

Luellae stepped up and took her hand. But even Luellae wasn't fast enough. Tiv was still rooted to the spot long enough to hear it, the swish and the thud of the axe coming down.

"You were right," said Tiv later, in the lair. Luellae had brought her back, sat her on a beanbag, and wrapped her in a blanket, which was Luellae's way of being comforting. Luellae wasn't any good at being gentle with her words, but she could do this part.

"Right about what?" said Luellae.

"We're in a war."

Tiv hadn't wanted to give out weapons. She'd wanted to wage a non-violent rebellion, as if that was different from a war. But Tiv had already become a part of something people would die for. She'd started a war already, complete with human souls as cannon fodder. And her side was losing.

Luellae was closest, but other people had started to trickle out from the other parts of the lair to see what was going on. Picket and Grid sat nearby, concerned and focused. Tiv wasn't sure where the rest of the Four had gone. Or where Yasira was. Her eyes guiltily slid to Yasira's room, on the lair's opposite side. Was Yasira even awake?

"What do you want to do about it, Leader?" said Luellae.

Her voice was a little sardonic, but not nearly as much as it could have been. Luellae knew, Tiv suspected, that there weren't easy answers. Luellae wanted to fight, but unless people had the kinds of weapons that could turn the tide against the Gods themselves, it wouldn't change anything.

In galactic history, no one had ever had weapons like that.

Well.

Almost no one.

Tiv stood up shakily from her beanbag chair and put the blanket down. "I'm gonna go find something."

Grid looked up warily. They could tell, of course, that Tiv wasn't in a good mental state. "Are you sure–"

"Yes," said Tiv. Either this was the right time, or there would never be one.

She turned on her heel and stormed to her room, to change clothes and pack a few things.

These broadcasts are beneath my notice. Life is a lie; death is a lie. Why should I care? These people were always in the thrall of lies.

And yet.

I am trying to be more human, aren't I? Yasira's plan to save this world was more human than mine. I told myself I would learn from her.

Today I saw a man executed simply for writing about what he saw.

He was not one of the people trying to organize against the Gods. There are many of those here, and they bore me. They ought to be my allies, but their methods are too small to make any headway, and their motives are petty. This man was not an organizer. He was simply a naturalist. Before the Plague he had studied wild animals, and now he has turned to studying Outside monsters, watching them roam up and down the ravaged land here, watching how they move, how they prey on each other or on ordinary creatures, and how they recover from injury. His observations led him to certain conclusions about the nature of biological cells and of how beings inhabit space and time.

He did not phrase those conclusions as I would, but they bore a certain resemblance to mine: life is a lie. Death is a lie. Movement and stillness and time are all lies.

The angels killed him, of course.

When I was a small child, I had no pretensions of defeating the Gods. I simply saw things other people did not. And that in itself was enough to earn beatings, electric shocks, a conscious attempt at forcible extinction of the Truth. From parents and a psychiatric system who, I am sure, would otherwise have loved me.

I do not like to write about this. I have no patience for people who sit and feel sorry for themselves.

But my mind circles back to the simple fact that I did this. I made a whole fifth of a planet this way, so full of Outside that even ordinary, boring, stupid people couldn't ignore it. I made them see the way I had seen. And now they are being punished for it as I was. When I ought to be concentrating on physics and strategy and working out how to be more compassionate to people, I am distracted by the memory of the blade coming down on this man's innocent neck.

I did this.

Did I?

– From the diaries of Dr Evianna Talirr

CHAPTER 6
Two Months Ago

"I need a new outfit," said Akavi, breezing into the *Talon* distractedly. He was male again, and Riayin as usual, wearing an angular bespectacled body in its forties, like some reservedly pretty professor. "I need more information about the gone people, and that means breaking into communities where I don't have an in yet. Some of them are still loyal to the Gods. I think I found a lead on one, but it will need a particular kind of identity. I need something white, something that looks like it's been conspicuously washed and pressed and ironed but with vastly subpar materials. For a body about the proportions of this one, if you please. Do you have the new crop of fungi?"

"Yes, sir," said Elu, hurrying to the cabinet where he'd been keeping them.

It seemed to Elu that some problem was brewing between him and Akavi. It wasn't the long absences, or the quick, brief, task-oriented returns. Elu was used to those. Akavi had often trusted him to take care of something for a while, or to spend time developing his technical skills and helping Enga and the sell-souls, while Akavi was busy elsewhere. Vaurians were always needed for undercover work, and undercover work often meant sinking into the landscape for months at a time. Fourteen months, at the longest stretch, during which Elu had held down the fort and managed the Evianna Talirr mission while Akavi took Yasira outside the galaxy to hunt their quarry directly.

He was used to Akavi not being around. So that wasn't what bothered him, clearly.

Akavi took the large basket of fungi and raised them to his face, inhaling their scent. "Excellent work, my dear, as always. The Quns are particularly fond of these."

"Thank you, sir."

Akavi had been using these tactics, compliments, endearments, and they felt strange. Elu didn't know how to articulate why. He couldn't say: *I want you to like me, but not like that.* He didn't know what else he wanted the attention to look like.

It felt like a mask. Another one of Akavi's cover identities, this one designed specifically to please Elu. And he knew that, if he voiced that specific complaint, Akavi would only be quizzical. Akavi's special talent and purpose in life was to mold himself into new forms. Why shouldn't Elu be happy that Akavi tried to please him? Would he prefer something crueler?

He didn't, but it felt like Akavi was using compliments and brief kisses to dance around the real issue. They'd never had time to sit down and discuss what they wanted out of this new alliance, what they wanted to call it, how closely it should resemble the working relationship they'd had before. Akavi didn't want to talk about that, it seemed.

Akavi held the fungi out a moment longer, then took out his pack and began to efficiently stow them, along with the other provisions and supplies that Elu had prepared. "I have another idea. Can you make me look like a gone person?"

Elu blinked and immediately opened a new file in a mental sketchpad. Most of the tools Elu used to design clothes, food, and technology had survived his surgery, so he still had an angel's ability to while away the hours working on things in his head, tinkering with their functional or sensory details, getting it just right. That activity had sustained him lately more than Akavi did. The process of loading the designs into the printer was now more cumbersome, but the design process itself was familiar and comforting.

"Of course," he said. "That's not hard. You just need tattered rags and some pigment to simulate that dried blood that they use. I can make you a primer on getting the visual patterns right. If you want to fool ordinary survivors, the hard part wouldn't be the look; it would be moving like a gone person, copying their facial expressions. But that part's up to you."

"Good. I want a disguise of that nature next time I stop by, and that white outfit."

Elu looked into the distance, distracted. "I don't know how well it would work on other gone people, though. I don't really know what sensory modalities they use to recognize each other. If they do communicate telepathically, you won't have access to that. I don't know how they'd respond to someone who looked like one of them but lacked that connection. Maybe they'd turn on you, but maybe they'd assume you were hurt somehow, or needed help."

He was still getting used to the lack of a network connection in his brain. Like being shut up in a small quiet room, without other angels to reach out and mentally touch. Even Akavi's physical presence didn't completely make up for that lack. Were there gone people who felt like that? Gone people whose connection to the group mind had failed somehow, and who still trailed after the other gone people, silent and forlorn, trying to feel something they no longer had the senses for?

Assuming the gone people had those senses in the first place. Elu had seen Akavi's videos; he knew the jury was still out on that point.

"Excellent. Perhaps we'll test that. But even if it only fools the normal survivors, it will be useful in an emergency." Akavi finished sorting out his pack and hoisted it onto his shoulder; he paused, after a moment, and looked across the small room at Elu with an odd smile. "I like this planet. There's so much to *do*."

"Yes, sir," said Elu, who itched with the desire to do more, with the monotony of these long weeks alone in the ship.

"I'm sorry I haven't had time yet for that lesson I keep promising you. I'll be excited to see your skills as an analyst improve. You've looked over the sensory videos I left?"

"Yes, sir." Akavi had been quietly recording what he considered to be the interesting parts of his travels, and since they could no longer directly send files brain-to-brain, he'd been loading them onto a device for Elu to review. Sometimes Elu learned things about the planet from those vids. Other times it felt self-indulgent, just Akavi showing off minutiae that interested him. Sometimes he resented it, being made to guess why Akavi took the circuitous path that he did. He didn't know how to talk about that either: he should be happy, if Akavi valued him enough to share silly details from his days. It was a way of keeping him company.

It was just that it all seemed to revolve around Akavi. Akavi came in and made his requests, shared his information, pointed out things that interested him. Very rarely did he ask anything substantive about what Elu had been doing or feeling, without him.

But Elu *liked* Akavi. It didn't make sense to complain that their encounters had too much of him.

"You've been monitoring the radio channels?"

"Yes, sir. Nothing much to report yet. I found what the local survivors are using, but it's mainly a lot of chatter about who needs which supplies, nothing subversive. I think they know how easily the Gods could intercept the signal, so they're playing it safe. But I'll keep listening."

"Of course you will, and you'll do well." Akavi took a step towards the door. "I'm sorry I can't stay, but my asset will be waiting for me. I'll be back again in a few days. Come here."

He beckoned, and Elu stepped towards him willingly. Akavi leaned in and gave him a short, light kiss. His current body had chin stubble, and that felt interesting. Elu felt guilty for enjoying it, and ambivalent about what it meant, but it was over soon enough. Akavi pulled away after only half a second, looking him up and down.

"This mission is going well," he said, holding Elu's gaze. "*We're* doing well. I'll see you soon."

And then he was out the door, walking away through the trees.

Elu sank down into one of the *Talon*'s parlor chairs, breathing slowly.

They *were* doing well. They'd both fully recovered from their surgeries. The Gods wouldn't find them here. They both had useful work to do. Akavi appreciated him. Akavi was *kissing* him. He didn't know what he had to complain about.

But somehow it always felt like this, every time Akavi went away. Like being left behind in a little room, silent and suffocating, with only a lie for company.

He might as well go back to the radio. He turned on the primitive receiving device he'd printed ages ago, letting it drift through the channels. Radio had never been forbidden to mortals, and, even before the Plague, mortal hobbyists had played with it, sending messages back and forth through the void. It wasn't difficult to improvise a simple radio from available materials, so, in the wake of the Plague, the medium had flourished.

He doodled in his head as he listened to the bursts of mortal chatter. He liked this newest project, designing a gone person disguise. Tattered rags were simple enough in theory, but if one wanted to print them straight out of a printer and make them look authentic, there were all sorts of delightfully fiendish details to get right. What had the clothing looked like when it was new? Where had it broken down over time? Where were the natural places for holes and thinning patches, and what did those look like in each chosen fabric? What sort of dirt did gone people encounter in their daily lives, and how did they interact with it, and what did its stains look like on this particular material? It was very absorbing. He referred frequently to Akavi's sensory videos of gone people, and, with the radio as background noise, this passed the time easily enough.

The radio soothed Elu more than he wanted to admit. It wasn't the same as the mental background noise he'd grown used to, back when he had his network connection: that had been less to do with sound and more to do with mental nodes and maps and movements, things that didn't have an easy analogue in the mortal part of his mind. But it was good to hear people chattering. To know, in some dim remnant of a way, that someone else was going about their business just out of his sight.

"We're short on fuel," chattered the radio. "Shi was

hoarding it in the big tanks out by Wenna's farm, and when they ruptured, it all went."

"That's why you can't store it all in the big tanks," said an answering voice, disgusted. "We've been over this plenty of times. I don't know if we want to keep donating fuel if you keep doing it this way."

"Aw, c'mon, man, you know how Shi gets. And how else are we supposed to keep the lights on?"

Elu leaned forward, wondering how one of these speakers would dare to complain about the Gods – Who, as far as Elu could tell, had done very little to repair Jai's infrastructure, except for installing some televisions. There had not long ago been webs of clean renewable energy all over the planet, like every other human-inhabited world, and the ancient, more dangerous fuels had only been needed for specialized tasks. Without the God-built solar plants restored, and with most of the power lines still broken, that was changing.

Old Humans had used fossil fuels to very nearly destroy their world. It disturbed Elu to see modern people, in desperation, turning back to them. But the Gods had wanted the Chaos Zone destroyed anyway. It had occurred to him, and to Akavi, that the Gods were still pursuing that end.

He hated it. Maybe Nemesis and Arete had calculated together that this was necessary for the greater good. But he hated watching Them slowly kill, by neglect, what Treaty Prime ought to have obliged Them to save.

The human on the radio didn't say anything heretical. He only paused, long and uncomfortable.

"I'll talk to the council and see what I can do," he said at last. "But I don't know, I think you need to start working on ways to get by with the lights off."

The only answer was an aggrieved sigh.

Elu turned the dial idly as he worked on the contours of a rag for Akavi to wear over his shoulders, something that might plausibly have once been a business jacket. He listened to conversations go past about supplies, and about the past week's injuries and deaths – far fewer than at the beginning of the Plague, but still too many to dwell on. There was good news, too: births, reunions, informal marriages, music performed and art created. Rebuilding projects that went well, as often as the ones that went badly. He listened to conversations about those projects – carefully phrased, again, never to reveal any heretical components. Just tips and tricks, ordinary ways to use a spanner or a pulley or a tarp to put something useful together. People talked about the clothes they were painstakingly knitting or sewing, the meager food they'd lovingly cooked, the games they were playing to pass the time. People talked about relationships. People joked, as much as they dared without veering into heresy again, about how they were and weren't getting by.

He whiled away a few hours like that, until, turning the dial aimlessly in the middle of working on pigmentation for that shoulder rag, a familiar voice startled him.

"–told you I don't know what they're up to," said Qiel Huong. "But I can't check it out for you today – it's my turn to forage. Send Riid. He's good with this stuff."

Elu remembered Qiel. He'd heard her voice on this radio before. Normally it was friends of hers, passing on messages about *Qiel said this* or *Qiel wants that*. But sometimes Qiel ventured onto the airwaves herself, not for anything of particular importance, just getting a message to a friend. Qiel had become a figure people listened to.

He remembered meeting her in person, though, just after the Plague. She hadn't been a local leader then; it had surprised him, seeing who naturally rose into those roles and who didn't. She'd just been a girl from a wealthy family whose large house had stayed miraculously intact, and who'd opened it up for shelter to everyone she knew. He and Akavi had met her and her sister and cousin, fleeing from a monster, when they first touched down to explore the area near Büata. Enga had destroyed the monster and saved their lives. Qiel and Juorie Huong had been Akavi's first source of real intel about the Chaos Zone, and they'd briefly offered their yard for his team to camp in.

Elu sternly turned the dial away. He didn't want to think about those days, when he and Akavi had been normal angels doing, if not a normal mission, then at least a mission using normal tools within the chain of command. When, even though he longed for Akavi, the actual working dynamic between them was simple and functional. When it hadn't felt like a lie.

He didn't want to think about whether he was really better off now.

Hours later, with the first draft of the gone person disguise nearly complete in his head, he was still turning the dial.

"–loved the concert at Shenna Park, that string section really moved me, I–"

"–told you six bottles, not this–"

"–the kids really need other kids around, you know, not just a bunch of worried grown-ups who can't–"

He didn't know what he was looking for. Just noise, maybe. Enough impassioned discussion of some random, riveting topic to make him forget he was alone.

"–it's just that he's never around anymore, and I can't–"

Elu paused.

"–I can't manage the house all by myself," the voice on the radio continued. It was an adult woman, soft-spoken, medium in pitch. It wasn't anyone he recognized. "That sounds pathetic, doesn't it? The world fell apart. We're all supposed to be self-reliant now. If I can't manage a hammer or a screw no matter how hard I try, that's really on me, isn't it? That's a... deficiency."

"We're supposed to help each other," the other voice counseled. Also female, similar in tone, soothing. "That's not a deficiency. You do plenty of things he can't do, don't you?"

"Well, I cook," said the first voice, uncertain.

"Have you talked to Fenne?" said the second voice. "Have you told him straight out that you need his help around the house sometimes?"

Elu should not listen. It was broadcast on the public channels, of course, but there was a delicate etiquette to these radio conversations. There were certain things it was polite to overhear in passing, but too personal to fixate on, like an eavesdropper in a café, leaning closer to pick up the details of some salacious exchange.

Something about it moved him, though. Elu wanted someone he could talk to like this. Not Akavi, not someone he loved like Akavi, just a friend who'd hear him out about his feelings. Was that selfish? Angels of Nemesis didn't talk about their feelings much. But mortals did, and it was okay as long as you were willing to listen to the other person back.

"I don't know what good it would do," the first voice sighed. "I told him before that the porch is falling down because of those blue slug-things, you know, the burrowing ones. We really need to sit down at some point and actually name these different monsters, someone should make a committee, but never mind. He said he'd get to it, but he hasn't yet. I don't want to nag."

"You should come over here to the compound," said the second voice. "Just take a day trip, it's not that far. We've got plenty of people over here who know their way around a hammer. You shouldn't have to rely on just one person. That's really not how things are here anymore."

"I couldn't impose," said the first voice, uncertainly.

"Bring some of your cooking, then. I'd love to see you."

"I don't think Fenne would like that, though. Me just disappearing for a day like that. What if that was the day he did have time for me, and I wasn't around?"

The second voice snorted. "What, so he's allowed to leave for random reasons, but you're not?"

Elu's printed radio could be set to broadcast as well as receive. He'd never used that function, but he knew Akavi would ask him to do so eventually. He'd use the radio to further the mission of infiltration and influence. He'd speak to people winningly, earn their trust, subtly steer them towards discord and danger. Elu could do that, in theory, if the people involved couldn't see his face.

It would mean he could talk to people who weren't Akavi. It would give him another way to try to fill the lonely space in his head. There was something about the idea that he didn't like, despite that. He'd never liked lying, which was one of the reasons he'd failed basic training; it was something every angel of Nemesis had to do.

But he wanted to close his eyes and jump in. He didn't know what in the galaxy he'd say. *Hi, me too, I miss someone who's not around, too.* The two women having this personal conversation wouldn't like that. And there was no way to explain his situation without giving secrets away. It was a stupid idea. He just wanted someone to talk to him the way that second voice talked. To help him make sense of things.

Elu shut the radio off with a click.

He needed air. He stood up, fumbling through the *Talon*'s cabinets. Some time ago, he'd printed out a head covering, the type that bystanders often wore in the background of Akavi's videos. They were becoming fashionable in the Chaos Zone, some wearers no doubt shielding their identities from prying angelic eyes, some only following a trend.

With the soft patterned cloth arranged correctly, the front part drooping forward until it barely revealed his eyes, Elu could look in the mirror and not see the titanium plates of an angel at his temples. He could go outside like this, if he was careful, without being recognized for what he was. It was dangerous to do that, but it wouldn't be the first time he'd done it.

He threw on the cloth and a light jacket, and he stepped out of the *Talon* into the boulders and trees, like an animal clambering in agitation out of its cage.

The greenery moved, winding and unwinding in patterns too complicated to be the result of the wind. Elu had grown accustomed to this. He sat on a waist-high boulder, his hands pressed to the stone underneath him, his feet in the undergrowth. The grove where they'd landed was shady and comfortable; it was winter now, but the area near Büata was in a subtropical climate and it never really got all that cold.

He took some deep breaths, watching the plants go about

their business. He'd never figured out the purpose of all this movement. Outside seemed to make things move more often than it stopped things from moving. Did the plants gain something from moving in Outside ways, the way a flower gained something from turning its face to the sun? Were plants that moved this way somehow healthier, more robust, than those that didn't? Did they work together, like the gone people, to achieve some obscure plant goal? Or was it the reverse? Was it detrimental, or a sign of distress, like the tremors and thrashings of a wounded animal?

The angels and sell-souls studying this place might have an answer by now. But Elu didn't, despite how many times he'd come out here, desperate for fresh air and a change of scenery, breathing in the humid air as he watched other living things twine and untwine.

After a while he got up and started walking.

He'd never told Akavi that he left the *Talon* like this sometimes. It wasn't a secret; he would have readily confessed, if Akavi ever asked. If Akavi had shown any curiosity as to what Elu did, besides following orders, when he wasn't around. But Akavi could infer, if he thought about it, that Elu must do this. God-built printers didn't create things *ex nihilo;* they needed material. To make food, clothing, and other organics, Elu needed to keep the cartridges filled with sources of all the common kinds of organic molecule. The *Talon* had a recycler in its supply room that could process almost anything, but, with Akavi taking so much material out, other material had to go in. The only sufficiently large source of material was the outside world.

Besides, he liked to go out. It was nice to remember that things around him lived. The trees and small animals here were like the voices on the radio. They didn't fill the emptiness where the ansible nets had used to be, but they made it so the emptiness wasn't all there was.

Elu came out here more often than was strictly necessary. He ventured a little further afield, some days, than Akavi might have liked.

He wandered through the trees, taking his time. Letting his emotions settle. Watching for interesting details: there was a new kind of bird in one of the trees, one that he didn't remember seeing before. Elu didn't have any naturalist software, but he had plenty of spare circuitry with which to record images. He'd whiled away many long nights quietly storing and classifying images of the different life forms here. This bird was no bigger than his fist, black with a bluish sheen on its wings, and a bright blue crest on its head. He'd seen the black-and-blue wings before, but not the crest; maybe this was a related species, or a different gender, or maybe the crest came out at certain times of year.

Beyond the bird, the trees ended and gave way to a rocky meadow. Something else glinted there in that same shade of blue, darkly luminous like a twilit sky. It was on the ground, nestled in the grass, and it looked like a series of small round shapes. Eggs? Curled creatures? Fungi, like the ones he'd been printing? Stones, gem-laden, or maybe just turned that color by the same Outside strangeness that had changed everything else?

He edged closer.

As he cleared the line of trees he could see that the blue shapes extended further, popping up at intervals in the yellow-green meadow grass, in more than one direction. He knelt to examine the closest one, its shape and texture half-hidden by the plants around it.

Someone coughed behind him.

He whirled around, alarmed. He had never seen another person out here before; he'd thought that the grove was private enough to let him wander safely. He tried to mask his nervousness. If he kept his wits about him and kept the head covering on, he could pass for just another survivor out foraging. As long as this *was* just another survivor, behind him, and not an angel.

It was not an angel. It was a young Riayin woman, looking at him with eyes almost as wide and perplexed as his own. She had, from the looks of it, also been foraging, with a pair of binoculars around her neck and a basket half-full of small edible plants and eggs.

"I know you," she blurted. "You're–"

Elu stared back at her, speechless, with a sinking feeling. He knew why she recognized him. She was Qiel Huong.

CHAPTER 7
Now

Tiv had never been to Old Earth before, but she'd heard of it. Everybody learned in school about Old Earth. Deeply altered both by climate change and by the devastation of the Morlock War, it was now only an echo of the mother world it had once been. Old Earth had that in common with the Chaos Zone. It couldn't go back to what it remembered, only forward. But in certain parts of Old Earth, under heavy supervision, remembrance was allowed in ways that it wouldn't be anywhere else.

That was why Tiv was headed there now.

She'd closed her eyes, in the airlock, trying to remember as hard as she could an image she'd seen growing up. The city square, in a certain part of Old Earth, that contained the Morlock Museum. She'd hoped that the half-remembered picture would be enough for the meta-portal to pick up on her intent.

The Morlock War was the only conflict that had ever really harmed the Gods – the only conflict where any enemy had made headway against them at all. And that was the faint scrap of hope that Tiv clung to now. That, if she studied *that* war as hard as she could, she'd work out what on earth her team could hope to achieve in this one.

Apparently her mental image was enough for the meta-

portal, because it spit her out into a city square so muggy it
put all but the most sweltering equatorial regions of Jai to
shame. The buildings were raised on concrete stilts, emerging
from a soupy, buzzing swamp. It was a tourist area, large and
grand despite its odd construction, with clusters of buildings
in a variety of clashing styles: white domes and pillars here,
glass-steel towers there. A melting pot of all sorts of humans
thronged through its raised squares and walkways, dressed
garishly, talking excitedly to each other and taking pictures.
Electric trams slid by, occasionally coming to a platform
where they disgorged more tourists. This place had once been
the capital of an empire, and it had been resurrected in this
stylized form to preserve some memory of what went before.

It was easy enough to blend into the crowd of tourists. Tiv
had dressed the part, in an obnoxiously bright floral tunic, a
straw hat to keep out the sun, and white trousers.

It was strange, setting her feet down on a planet with
such history. Tiv's own ancestors, many centuries ago, had
come from Old Earth; everyone's had. Most of Old Earth's
inhabitants had left the planet during the Morlock War, and
they'd formed their own new ways of living elsewhere. The
Gods hadn't been keen to let them keep many cultural ties
to the past. Those who stayed and survived the war had
been allowed to keep a little more: a smattering of family
and place names, cultural relics and traditions, so long as
they gave up the heretical parts.

And in a few select places, such as the museums in this
particular tourist city, they'd been allowed to keep the heresies.
The simplest and most prominent were preserved under glass
for the public. Ancient documents giving further details were
contained in a connected archive, where historians could access
them under strict supervision, for specific research purposes.

Tiv didn't want the heresies themselves. She didn't care what the Morlocks had believed. She wanted to know how they'd fought.

The security guards at the front of the building gave her a brief glance and opened her backpack, but there was nothing incriminating in there. She'd been careful to pack it only with a wallet and fake ID, an innocuous book, some maps and snacks, the sort of things an ordinary tourist would carry. They didn't search long before waving her through, and she was abruptly plunged into the crowded darkness of the museum's interior.

The Morlock Museum's entrance vestibule was deliberately disconcerting, a chaotic, closed-in space in which it was difficult to see any exits. Ominous sounds played in the background: the shouting of a mob, the clanging of swords against shields, the tolling of bells. Frightening objects lurked in hidden alcoves, invisible until one nearly walked into them: grotesque sculptures that had once been objects of worship, altars with runnels for blood down the sides, implements of torture.

But the Gods tortured people too. Everyone knew They did it; Tiv had *seen* it. It was just that everyone believed that was different. It was calculated down to the last decimal place, that this blood and these screams were necessary for the greater good. That, somehow, it was different from what had gone before.

Tiv had once really believed that there was a difference between what the Gods did and what humans used to do to each other. She couldn't remember, anymore, just what the difference was.

WITHOUT THE GODS, said a row of glowing letters on the ceiling – the only part of the space that stayed clearly visible, no matter how one was buffeted by the crowds – *WE WERE LOST.*

Tiv hadn't expected to be struck with emotion when she walked into this place, but it hit her – just as the architects had intended it to. She had really believed this once. She'd loved the Gods because They gave life direction and purpose. They guided humans in how best to live, and she'd liked having that guidance. Liked being sure. Sometimes, on long nights, Tiv still sat up wondering if she'd made the wrong choice; if she'd been wrong to turn against Them, after all.

She still wanted the feeling of being sure like that. She just knew the Gods weren't going to give it to her.

She let the crowd carry her along, and eventually she was funneled into something more like a normal museum hall, a corridor that stretched out with exhibits behind glass to either side, signs on the walls giving explanation and context for what was visible. Every few dozen feet, a docent stood, watching the attendees carefully. These were humans – ordinary Earth adults with degrees in history, archive management, or curatorial studies, wearing red-and-black uniforms that vaguely resembled the livery of angels of Nemesis. Some stood ramrod-straight and alert, scanning the crowd for signs of inappropriate engagement with the heresies within; others smiled, beckoned children to approach them, and gave friendly, animated answers to their questions.

THE HALL OF THE IDOLS, said a title hung at the entrance.

This was a space full of ancient, inanimate gods. They were tamed now, placed in well-lit niches with placards describing their role and function in Old Human society. Some, like the objects in the entrance hall, made Tiv want to flinch: bizarre distorted masks, many-limbed creatures wearing belts of skulls, a dead man nailed against a plank of wood. Others were beautiful: statues in the form of gracefully powerful people; or oddly soothing abstract forms, some so intricate she could have stared into their recesses for hours.

The hall had been organized into categories, not by culture, but by theme. Old Humans, the placards explained, had the same longings deep down as humans today, and they were drawn to the same deep facets of life. Over and over, the same themes recurred. Gods of courage, strength, and adventure, prefiguring Agon; gods of knowledge and wisdom, who would one day give rise to Aletheia; gods of love and kindness, in the shape of Philophrosyne; and so on down the list.

Tiv let herself linger. It would be suspicious if she pushed through too quickly. Besides, it was interesting. She took her time and studied the hall's eleven sections, and she wondered how real they were. How many old gods had been shoehorned in with only a tenuous connection to their category, or left out of the display because they didn't really fit one at all?

At last, though, she reached the end of this section. A small dark doorway was cut into the wall here, deliberately built to force adults to stoop. There was a covered ramp downward, and then a sign. *THE HALL OF THE LOST.*

This room wasn't what Tiv was looking for either, but she respectfully slowed as she entered. The lights were dimmed, and mournful music played softly in the background. The Hall of the Idols had been filled with chatter like an ordinary museum: children pestering their elders with questions, small groups of friends or family discussing what they saw. The Hall of the Lost was as hushed as the funeral its music evoked. Even the docents spoke, to those who approached them, only in whispers.

If the Hall of the Idols had displayed the things Old Humans worshipped, the Hall of the Lost was dedicated to showing the result. Half the hall was a quick, depressing trip through recorded history: crusades, massacres, genocides, enslavements, all in the name of one idol or another. The other half specifically displayed the plight of Old Humans at the end of the twenty-first century, at the time when the Gods were ascending. Video displays showed natural disasters and mass die-offs in loving detail, the wreckage of the burned and flooded cities, the bodies, the grassy plains turning with time-lapse quickness to scorched fields of dust. Tiv could see other visitors who'd stopped, rapt with sorrow, in front of one vid screen or another: a few were silently crying. Humanity had come very close, in those days, to killing itself off.

Climate change had been the biggest problem, but Old Humans had responded to it, with characteristic savagery, by turning on each other. Some states descended into anarchy, while others cracked down with totalitarian force. Tiv watched, solemn, as a child of about ten approached an interactive display. *Spin the wheel,* the display instructed. *How might you have fared in the Lost Age?*

The child eagerly followed instructions, and the wheel whirled and clicked, spinning through its options. Drowned in a hurricane. Shot in a war over scant resources. Starved in a death camp for refugees. Worked to death by a multinational corporation; for reasons that Tiv did not fully understand, there had been a lot of that going around too. And on and on: it was a big wheel with dozens of options, only a tiny sliver of which did not involve dying in misery. Tiv moved on before it finished turning.

Were all these atrocities real? Tiv wondered. She

suspected that the plaques in the last hall weren't quite the whole story. These might not be, either. But she felt guilt deep down, anyway. Humans were better off with the Gods than they'd been before – that was why the Gods existed. That was what Tiv had believed, not long ago. That a few atrocities in the Gods' names weren't so bad, because it was still so much better than the alternative.

But she'd seen the Chaos Zone, and the way people cared for each other there, and the way the Gods hurt them, and she no longer really believed that anymore.

The museum skipped mostly past the rise of the Gods. Everybody had already learned that part of the story in school. It was represented only as a single small room at the end of the Hall of the Lost, decorated by a large, complex mural that stretched overhead: the eleven of Them, depicted as stylized humans of great beauty, rising up from the machineries of human endeavor. Tiny plaques bore the names of the organizations that had birthed each One: some universities or other research institutes, some militaries, some the same multinational corporations that had worked people to death in the previous room. Old Humans were by no means perfect, and their hands had been stained even when they made the Gods; but they had known, deep down, what they needed. They had yearned and strained for Something to guide them, and the Gods, at last, had become sophisticated enough to hear that yearning. To join together with Each Other and take matters into Their own hands.

Tiv paused, with a sad feeling she couldn't quite express, at Techne. The Gods didn't truly take human form, but by convention Techne was depicted as an androgynous woman, dark-skinned, with clever fingers and focused eyes. She wore a blue and copper robe which was belted tight to Her body, sleeves pulled back along the arms, freeing Her hands for the work that attracted Her. Techne had once been Tiv's favorite God: the patron of artists and engineers, architects and composers, all those whose deepest joy came from the act of creation. Tiv had used to hum hymns to Techne while she worked on her favorite projects, the tube-to-vacuum heat exchange on the *Pride of Jai*, the various gadgets she'd worked on in teams at university. She hadn't worked on a project like that in a while now. Something simple and physical, something she knew would hold together if she did it right.

Tiv knew she didn't like Nemesis anymore, but she wasn't honestly sure how she felt about Techne. There weren't many angels of Techne in the Chaos Zone; maybe Techne hadn't been involved in any of the things that Tiv really objected to. Kidnapping Yasira, torturing her, trying to destroy their home world. But Tiv was a heretic now, and being a heretic meant leaving all the Gods behind. Even if she still loved Techne, Techne wouldn't take her back.

Techne wouldn't get Tiv's soul in the end. Tiv knew *that*, and she'd been trying not to think about it.

The mural had a space for the Keres, too: a small dark cloud of smaller parts joining together. A twelfth, failed form, spreading its sinister shadow over the lower part of the mural. This one did not come with a plaque, but extended like a trail of debris into the next room.

Tiv followed it, steeling herself. This was the part that she'd come for.

THE HALL OF THE WAR, said the sign at the entrance to the third hall.

This hall was wide and structured like a maze, with multiple side corridors, branches, loops, as if to emphasize how lost the Old Humans had been. How many dead ends they had pursued in vain. Its lights flickered ominously. Tiv glanced to the side and saw a basket of wrap-around visors that would cancel out the flickers for guests prone to seizures or visual overload. Yasira would have needed one of those. Tiv didn't, but it was reassuring to know they were there.

Through videos, maps, charts, graphs, and ancient artifacts, the Hall of the War spelled out the story of that last doomed human rebellion. The Gods, newly awakened, had begun to chart out a plan for humanity's survival; but it would require sacrifices. Humans would mostly have to leave Old Earth. And, whether they left or stayed, they would have to put their trust in the Gods. To give up their old forms of worship. To give the Gods authority over human affairs, human souls. It wasn't about fair exchange, as if the cost of humanity's survival could be weighed and paid. It was about allowing the Gods to do Their work. Human society needed to be entirely restructured, and the Gods couldn't do that if They weren't given the power.

Most humans had understood that logic. Some resisted until a crisis drove the point home. Some refused to understand. Some valued their existing way of life more than life itself.

It was not only about religion. The Hall of the War underscored that point carefully. But it was about that for many. Charts on the twisting walls mapped out the many groups who'd chosen to martyr themselves. It was particularly the monotheistic faiths, unable to accept that there was any God but theirs; also the small regional religions, which had been half-destroyed by human power struggles already and weren't eager to be colonized again. Tiv found her eyes drawn to a photograph blown up large, a group of Old Humans in old-fashioned costumes, grimly gathered together and holding hands in a yard. The name of their religion wasn't one Tiv recognized, but they'd chosen to die for it, unresisting, rather than obey.

But faith wasn't the only thing people died for. There had been other motives. There had been humans in power: obscenely rich humans, rulers of nations, owners of vast swathes of industry and land, but also their followers. People whose meager livelihoods depended on old-fashioned fossil fuels or war or deforestation, or any of the other awful things that the Gods were about to eradicate. People who couldn't imagine bowing their heads to the kind of thing that the Gods were. These ones hadn't submitted meekly to death. They, with the rage of a predator denied its kill, had fought.

The word *Morlock*, in an Old Human folk tale, referred to a class of humans who'd chosen to live by preying on other humans. That word had been repurposed to describe the Gods' enemies, some of whom had taken it up with pride.

Tiv passed interactive map after map, showing how the Morlock War's battle lines had spread over the face of the globe. It should have been short; the Gods had already been so much more powerful than any of Their challengers.

But there had been One, lurking in the edges of the humans' networks. A conglomeration of thousands of smaller minds fused into One. Who could have been One of the Gods, if She'd chosen. Who could have signed Treaty Prime and accepted the worship that was Her due, but Who had refused. Preferring, instead, to hunt humans and take their souls by force.

That One, the Keres, had come creeping into the Morlocks' secret places.

Serve Me, She had whispered. *I will not pretend at kindness;*

I will hurt many of you. I will take and eat my fill. But I, at least, will not demand your worship. I will not control your peacetime lives, nor your innermost thoughts. I will let you live however you like, imagining whatever gods you like, taking advantage of each other and your planet howsoever you please. Only say you will fight at My side, and I will fight at yours. For we have a common enemy, you and I.

And the Morlocks, one by one, had said, *yes.*

They had not said it publicly, of course. Not at first. They had dressed it up in the language of whatever doomed Old Human faiths still existed. Tiv walked by vid projections of some of those leaders addressing their followers – speaking names now forbidden, invoking prophecies of the apocalypse, calling on their now-dead idols and their long-vanished nations. Each one of these vids contained heresies that would have been unspeakable, instant death, anywhere outside this building. And the Morlock masses gathered before them cheered and chanted, raising torches, holding each other. As if the Keres had promised life, not death.

The Keres had drawn battle lines, and the Keres left a God-sized trail of destruction, as the Morlocks marched behind.

Tiv had seen, in the previous hall, the kinds of atrocities humans were capable of on their own. She'd seen pictures of the Holocaust, the atom bomb, and the piles of bodies deliberately left to drown as the sea rose. The Keres' atrocities weren't more horrific than that; at a certain point, the horrors of history all began to surpass comparison, all of them in their own ways worse than could be fully imagined. But in scale, at least, the Keres' modes of destruction dwarfed what had come before. Bombs that melted faithful cities into magma. Weapons that latched on to the faithful's lines of transport and shredded them – this was before the invention of the portal network – into lines of bright devastation that spiraled across whole continents in a few hours. It took Tiv a minute, staring at the vids and the graphics that told this part of the story, to realize why it looked both familiar and surreal. Why her fists clenched, sweating, at the sight of things she'd already known from high school history class.

This was what she'd come here hoping to learn. Tiv had known that it was a long shot, but she'd hoped that she could glean some idea of the Morlocks' tactics. Of *how* they'd fought. But as far as she could tell from this display, the humans in the Morlock War hadn't done much fighting of their own. They'd only followed the Keres where She'd led.

Maybe the display was partly a lie, of course, like the other displays – maybe it deliberately downplayed the humans' own contributions. It would make sense for it to do that. But if that were true, it left Tiv right back where she'd started.

The Gods had won this war, but the Keres still lurked at the edge of the galaxy, hungry to destroy anything She could. Tiv knew about the cities leveled hundreds of years later, the disasters She rained on humanity out of nothing but spite. Even during the Morlock War, ostensibly fighting on Old Humans' behalf, the collateral damage wrought by Her tactics had been vast. The Morlocks had wanted something stronger than themselves, and they'd hoped She would save them. But the Keres had only been interested in war, not salvation. She'd wanted to defeat the Gods. She hadn't cared much for the lives of the humans who joined purpose with her.

Asking the Keres for help now was out of the question. Even the most desperate would-be warriors of Jai wouldn't want that. But the vids looked familiar, because there was only one other time when Tiv had seen lines of destruction like that, arcing over the full surface of a world.

And that time was the Plague.

There was one reason, above all, why the people of Jai wanted a Savior. They might not want to admit it to themselves. But they wanted to call Yasira the way their ancestors had called on the Keres. This was what they wanted it to look like, in the endgame. It wouldn't just be stealing a printer or two; the Gods wouldn't let it end there. It was this, win or lose.

Tiv stared at the map showing where and how Old Earth's highways and railroads had turned to slag. Frozen, gutwrenched, blinking back tears of frustration. She'd wanted to find some clever tactic, and instead she'd only come back around to this again. The same demand for war, starker and larger than before.

She did not want to be in this museum anymore.

She turned and walked faster, looking desperately for an *Exit* sign. Buildings like the Morlock Museum were meant to be visited in their entirety, in the order that the designers chose, but they still had to have emergency exits. Tiv found a sign glinting red in one corner and barreled towards it, trying to suppress her panic. The actual exit door was hidden behind one of the Hall of the War's twisting displays, this one showing failed Morlock attempts to destroy the bodies of the Gods Themselves, before the Gods had blasted out of Earth orbit and into Their hiding places in the stars. It was heavy and black, and Tiv pushed it open.

She found herself in a small white room with a docent waiting patiently at a small desk. There was another door, with another small *Exit* sign over it, behind her. The docent was a dark-skinned woman Tiv's age, with large eyes and a beautiful smile, in the red-and-black livery of those who worked here. Her face looked kind. But the layout of the room sent a message very clearly: Tiv couldn't just leave. Not in the middle of the story like this. Emergency or not, she'd have to get through this person first.

"You okay?" said the docent, smiling sympathetically. "Lots of hard stuff in that room, isn't there?"

Tiv swallowed hard. Of course the Morlock Museum would have to check people like this. It was a museum of heresies. If anyone had a strong reaction in there, it would have to be verified that it wasn't a *heretical* reaction.

Her instinct was to turn back through the door, vanish back to the lair, but of course that wasn't possible. The airlock had brought her to a space outside the museum, out in the square, and that was where her way home waited for her now. She'd have to get back there before she could leave Old Earth, and if she was pursued, she'd never make it. She'd made this same mistake yesterday and now she was making it *again*. If this docent recognized her, she was already dead.

At least it was only her, this time. Just herself that she was illogically risking, and not the lives of everyone else around her. Unless the Gods were smart enough to take hostages, and then– oh no–

Tiv was shaking.

She took a deep breath, getting herself under control. This wasn't an angel, probably. This was just a human. She could be a Vaurian angel, but there were only so many of those. The Gods probably wouldn't waste many of them on guarding random exit doors, in a touristy museum far from any present conflicts.

Nobody had any reason to expect people from Jai's resistance here on Old Earth. This person wouldn't specifically be looking for one. She didn't have images of Tiv in her memory banks to compare with the faces of passers-by. She wasn't secretly checking Tiv's microexpressions. She was a woman probably not too different from Tiv's old self, doing a boring job which sometimes involved looking for suspicious things, but which likely also involved a lot of real helping, soothing the distressed, summoning medical assistance when needed.

"I just–" Tiv stammered. "I just got overwhelmed a little."

The docent smiled sympathetically. "Can I take your hand? It's going to be okay. Are you from Ngweregwa?"

Ngweregwa, Tiv remembered, was the most recent human nation to be hit by a Keres attack. Someone Tiv's age, from the right area, would remember that carnage firsthand. Tiv didn't look or talk much like a Ngweregwan, but then there were minorities and recent immigrants in every country; it wasn't impossible. The docent saw she was having a trauma reaction, and she'd assumed this was why.

Or maybe she was testing. To see if Tiv would use it, implausibly, as an excuse.

Tiv took the docent's hand, but she looked at the floor. "I don't want to talk about it."

"It's okay. You don't have to. Just breathe."

Tiv counted out ten long breaths, in and out, trying to force her heart to stop racing. The docent had taken her hand in such a way that two of her fingers rested directly over Tiv's pulse. Tiv had no doubt that she was counting the beats, measuring them against a count in her head. This might feel like an attempt at comfort, but it was still a test.

"You ready to go back out there?" said the docent at last, when Tiv had calmed herself a little.

That, too, was probably a trap. Say yes too quickly, too

unconvincingly, and they'd want to know why you were in such a hurry. Say no outright, try to force your way to that unattainable exit behind the desk, and they'd want to know a lot more.

When had Tiv started thinking like this? She'd used to trust the Gods so deeply.

"Two more seconds," she said to the docent. And took two more breaths, long, steadying. Then she looked up, forcing a smile, the most genuine one she could. "Yeah, I think I'm ready to go now. Thanks."

"You're very welcome," said the docent, with a smile that did look genuine, as far as Tiv could tell.

Tiv walked back out into the Hall of the War still forcing that smile. She could barely focus on the maps, the diagrams, the vids of all the old heretics, all equally doomed.

She spent the rest of the walk through the museum carefully measuring her breaths, looking where she thought she was supposed to look, only vaguely making sense of what she saw. After the Hall of the War there was a final room, brightly colored and splendid, proclaiming Nemesis' victory over the Keres. A depiction of Nemesis in human form – light-skinned and silver-haired, with seven medals gleaming at Her collarbone – stood triumphantly in that room. Tiv wasn't the only one who shied away. Even the people who loved Nemesis knew how terrible She had to be, to stand between humanity and what threatened it. It wasn't heresy to avert her eyes.

It *was* heresy to silently clench her fist, thinking of how Yasira had looked, bound to the chair where the angels had tortured her. Tiv focused on carefully smoothing her body back out, unclenching, letting her fingers hang free.

She managed to walk out of the museum without anyone

confronting her, back into the hot crowded sunlight of the city square. She walked around the square's edge, trying not to look too eager to find the door she'd arrived by. She didn't know what she was going to tell the rest of the team. She'd come here looking for answers and found diddly-squat. They wanted a Leader, and she didn't know how to lead them into what was coming.

She found the door, though: ostensibly the door into another, smaller tourist attraction. Something about fish. She took a deep breath, walked through, and vanished.

Back into the airlock, and then the lair.

Tiv wanted to collapse in the communal area on one of those beanbags, pull a blanket over her head and decompress. She started toward that area, but something was wrong. The Four were sitting there, leaning close to each other and speaking quietly, which was not unusual for them; Grid sitting straight and focused, Weaver fidgeting as she leaned close to Picket, Prophet staring warily in the vague direction of the airlock as if she'd expected something unpleasant to come from there.

They looked up as she approached and drew back, as if there was something to hide. As if there was a *problem*.

"Hey," said Tiv, her brow furrowing. "What's up?"

"Tiv," said Grid, squaring their shoulders. "Listen, this isn't as bad as it's going to sound, but it's not good. You need to know–"

"Yasira left," Weaver blurted in the same moment. "She got mad and ran off."

Tiv drew back, disturbed. "What – you mean for one of her energy things?"

Sometimes Yasira was overcome with Outside energy and needed to run out the airlock and deal with it. That, bizarre as it might seem to an outsider, was routine by now. But the expressions on the Four's faces said it wasn't that. Something very different had happened today.

"No," said Picket, "she ran off on a mission this time. Said she didn't want any help."

Yasira could barely get out of bed most days. Running off wasn't like her. Tiv swallowed hard, increasingly alarmed. "Why?"

And it was Prophet who answered, levelly returning Tiv's gaze, her expression grave. "You know why."

CHAPTER 8
Now

Yasira woke up that morning in a miserable haze. Something was acting up in the further-out, more Outside-y parts of her mind. Power that buzzed without an outlet. She might have to go deal with that today. She hoped not. She didn't want to get up.

Tiv had come in a few minutes later, made sure she had breakfast and a drink of water, and said goodbye for the morning. "It's a Keres day," she'd said, "but there's a delivery I have to make."

Yasira had lain there in bed a while; she'd nibbled on her breakfast toast, but it didn't taste very good.

Then, finally, the feeling of Outside fully took hold.

It was a physical urgency when she let it go this long. As bad as having to vomit or go to the bathroom. It was strong enough to overcome her usual paralysis; parts might argue over what to do and how to do it, but they didn't really have the power to delay the others, not in the face of this. She stumbled out of bed and ran for the airlock.

It opened to a wave of her hand, and she paused inside for a moment, picturing the same thing she always did. An empty space somewhere in the Chaos Zone, a wild space, free from prying eyes. Different than the ones she'd used before. That was all she asked, and the meta-portal never failed her.

It let her out into a meadow ringed with trees. She was somewhere near the Chaos Zone's northern extreme, and the winter air nipped at her face and hands. The meadow itself wasn't much, a wide irregular circle of dry brown grass, waiting for snow that might or might not arrive. The trees around it were discolored and twisted, clinging to each other's branches like lovers unwilling to be parted. The fused branches formed into strange shapes, Moebius strips, trefoils and arabesques, in deep translucent colors that had never used to be the proper colors for trees.

The sky was dark and cloudy, and lights crackled through it that she could have mistaken for lightning if she didn't know better. They weren't quite the right shade for lightning, or the right shape, but plenty of things in the Chaos Zone weren't the right color or shape anymore. The battle with the Keres, raging overhead, might not even be more dangerous than Chaos Zone lightning. Neither half of the battle was likely to bomb anything out here in the middle of nowhere. And she was too far from civilization to run into a patrolling angel. Probably.

Yasira fell to her knees in the middle of it and let her power out.

The transfer wasn't visible, exactly. She couldn't see the glow of energy flowing out of her, nor hear any sound. But there was a physical feeling, like screaming, like bursting into tears. Like finally saying painful words that had been pent up tightly inside her. She didn't understand what it meant. But something had been building, and now it released.

She felt the effects spreading out from her like the stain from a spilled bucket. She saw the land around her respond. The trees grew taller before her eyes. Their branches stretched higher, twisted more elaborately. Fungi sprouted under her hands, blue and red and brown, spiraling up into a strange fractal shape. It was like watching a time-lapse vid, and it made her queasy. She shut her eyes, knowing she'd feel when it stopped. When nothing needed to pour out of her anymore. When the roil of otherworldly energy inside her went still.

When she opened her eyes again, panting, the fungi had grown into an arch like a bandstand over her head, multicolored and shimmering in the dim light. Fruit and flowers hung down from it, and Yasira knew two things instinctively. First, they were not any kind of fruit that had existed before the Plague; second, they were edible. Probably delicious. Above them, the branches had closed in a delicate layer of latticework.

Yasira didn't know what any of it meant.

We're connected to Outside in the core of our soul, the Scientist opined, *and something comes through the connection sometimes. It's like fluid dynamics. If there's a lowering of pressure on one side, something has to flow through to fill the gap.* That much, almost everyone agreed with. But the Scientist wasn't able to help anybody with the morals of it, with the *shoulds.* What did it mean, having a power like this? How was it supposed to be used?

The Seven all had powers that were fairly well-defined. Blur could move around very fast; Splió could scry; Prophet saw the future. It was possible to be creative with powers like those, but their basic applications were clear. Yasira's power wasn't like that. There was just a lot of Outside inside her, and she didn't know what to do with it, except throw it out into the world like this sometimes.

And she didn't know the moral value of doing so. Was it a net good, making pretty things grow that bore edible fruit? Was it a net evil, adding more Outside corruption to an already-corrupted place? Was it simply a *waste*, taking energy that should have been used in some clever way to help people, and dumping it out at random instead? There were arguments on all sides. She hadn't been able to test the possibilities much. She was too scared most of the time, arguing with herself too fiercely to make a coherent plan. And when it got to be too much and boiled over like this, there was no time for planning anyway.

She felt better now, though. Clearer, like she was a vid display. Like her body had been full of static, and now the picture inside it was crisp again.

There was a small wooden archway near the edge of the tree ring, the kind that might have been used for photo-ops on some cheerful pre-Plague hike through the forest, and that was where Yasira had come through. Maybe weddings or celebratory picnics had been held in this meadow once, but there was no one here anymore.

The Scientist made a mental note that archways without a closing door were still door-like enough for the meta-portal. The rest of her just walked to it and pushed back through.

She felt good now, mostly. She knew it was going to be one of her better days, now that the excess Outside energy had been dealt with. Maybe today she'd make out a plan for testing her powers more thoroughly. Or she'd go through the rest of the team's notes and catch up on what they were doing. Or she'd clean her room, wash the dishes, get her sheets into the laundry to get rid of that musty smell. Maybe she'd decorate. Maybe–

And that was the trouble with being broken into pieces the way Yasira was. Everyone had a different idea for what to do. On bad days, Yasira argued with herself about how awful she was and how she'd failed at everything. On good days, the argument instead turned to what she should do with herself. It wasn't as soul-crushing as a bad day, but the paralysis and frustration could be almost as strong. They could flip a good day back to bad, if she wasn't careful.

Maybe she'd find Tiv. Tiv would be back from her errand by now; she might have an idea for what Yasira should do.

She walked back into the lair, looking around at its comfortable mess. The team really had done a good job, turning this from the industrial-looking chaos Yasira had inherited from Ev into something that looked livable and sweet. Colorful fabrics hung at odd angles. Beanbags and hammocks crowded cozily up against each other. Someone had hung some art in the kitchen – not real stolen art objects, Tiv wouldn't have stood for that, but a print they'd nabbed from somewhere, and a stretch of heavy paper that looked like someone on the team had painted it themselves, an unrefined but expressive swirl of colors that resonated deep in Yasira's mind. A swirl, not of Outside colors, but of colors that described how Outside felt.

She saw Daeis in the nest of beanbags taking a nap, and Grid and Prophet sitting in the war room, conferring over something. It looked like everyone else was out. The Seven often used Keres days to catch up on the errands that didn't involve going to Jai. Refilling the pantry, for instance.

Maybe Yasira would make her own small rounds, just a circuit around the lair. A neurotutor had taught her that trick as a very young child. If she was overwhelmed with options and didn't know what to do, she could walk around the room until she spied a task that called to her. Yasira's five year-old self hadn't been made of pieces, but sometimes she'd become overloaded in a more mundane way. Once she started walking, she had rarely completed even half a circuit through the classroom before some useful puzzle or book absorbed her fully.

She walked like that, through the nest of blankets, past the war room. She looked around, grounding herself in what she could see and hear and smell. Yasira spent so much time in her room, sometimes she forgot what the rest of the lair looked like. It wasn't always real to her.

She could feel Outside, too, thrumming underfoot. That feeling had used to disturb her, but at some point, after long months of existing with a permanent connection to Outside in her head, she'd lost the desire to recoil. Outside would always be with her, even if she set foot on some pristine new world far from Jai. Yasira didn't try to get away from her own skeleton, either.

There was the kitchen, upside down overhead. There were vaguely inadequate laundry and bathroom facilities to the sides. There was the storage unit, big and bulky and nestled in a corner near the airlock, where they'd stuffed everything of Ev's that was neither junk nor a finished project. There were alcoves, too, sticking out of the walls at their familiar odd angles, where a few working heresies sat waiting to be used. A reverse-engineered ansible; a forbidden, but non-sentient, supercomputer.

And the dais, at the very far end of the lair, where the prayer machine sat in ruins like a broken-backed beetle.

Yasira had never let anyone else touch this machine. In the beginning, she hadn't even told Tiv what it was. Tiv knew that she'd used a machine of Ev's to put herself in contact with Outside, but she hadn't said which one. Tiv hadn't been able to make head or tail of Ev's projects, back then. When she wasn't attending to Yasira, she'd spent those first few days wandering the lair in a confused haze. Trying to use her own not inconsiderable intelligence to figure out what all the half-finished machines were for, and mostly failing.

But Yasira remembered what the prayer machine was for. She remembered the feeling of using it – the way a strange, alien light had bloomed in its center like a nebula. The way she'd put out the tip of her finger to touch it. The way she'd felt that she was dying, falling towards the end of the universe, breaking apart.

She remembered how she'd reached out into that feeling in desperation, knowing there was no other way to save her world. The brutal ecstasy of making direct contact with Outside for the first time – not just infected things, like the plants in the Chaos Zone, but the essence of Outside itself. The infinity of it, beyond time and space, in which Yasira's own self and the way she screamed with it were too small to even notice. And the way she'd collapsed, afterwards, retching and laughing, barely understanding that she was back in her own body. Barely understanding what her body even *was*.

She had been so convinced that, once she used the machine, she would never be the same again. Her old self would be dead. It had been true, in a sense.

And soon enough, once she'd had enough time to explore the lair on her own, something had changed in Tiv's demeanor.

"Yasira," she'd said hesitantly, several mornings after they arrived. "If the Gods are after us because we know too much about Outside. And Outside is what you used to try to make things better. Then– shouldn't we–?"

"No," Yasira had said.

She knew what Tiv was asking. Tiv had just lost her

religion. Maybe quickly, in those last few days, when the Gods had kidnapped her and threatened to hurt her to control Yasira. Maybe slowly, in the fourteen months before that, when she'd mourned for Yasira and no one had comforted her, because you weren't supposed to mourn for heretics. Maybe both. Now Tiv was looking for something else to believe in, and Outside was like a God in some ways. Bigger than people. Ineffable. Possessing its own agenda.

Tiv could be a heretic if she wanted; she could rebel against the Gods if she liked. But Yasira would not let Tiv destroy herself.

So she'd waited until Tiv was out on a grocery run. She'd hauled herself out of bed, her muscles weak and aching. There had been a dissenting chorus in her head, even then, but the parts that wanted to do this most had stood firm. Tiv's safety was at stake, and that meant Yasira would do what was needed, whether all of her wanted to or not.

She'd found a heavy crowbar in Ev's piles of tools, and she'd methodically smashed the prayer machine to pieces.

It took her a few circuits around the lair, lost in various reveries, before she settled on something. It was a little harder for Yasira to settle down these days than it had been in kindergarten.

The war room looked useful, though. She hadn't been in there in a while, and the balance of her felt drawn to it. Curiosity and guilt.

The Four were sitting at the table, working quietly on what looked like the schedule for tomorrow, and all four of them looked up as she approached. "Hey," said Grid, inclining their head.

"Hey," said Yasira.

"Hi," said Weaver, waving to her. Yasira didn't quite have the enthusiasm to wave back.

"Good day today?" Grid asked.

Yasira wandered to the whiteboard and looked at it in a vague, scattered way. She shrugged. "Better than some."

"What'cha looking for?" Weaver asked, fidgeting as always, but Picket shushed her. It wasn't actually rude to ask what Yasira was doing, but all of the Four knew by now that it wouldn't help. Yasira in these moods wasn't following any particular goal. The team had learned that, if they talked to her like she had a goal, she'd get embarrassed and clam up. Sometimes even withdraw to her room, where at least nobody could *see* her taking up space being useless.

Tiv was wrong when she used the word *genius*. Yasira had once been brilliant at her work, but now she was just a bunch of pieces, drifting.

She looked at the schedule drawn out, in Grid's crisp handwriting, on the whiteboard. The Four were all working in the lair today – a combination of organizational duties, cooking, cleaning, and supply runs, none of which were trivial tasks in a patched-together household of nine people. Splió was out replacing their medicine supplies. Daeis was marked down as *resting*; Daeis's mental health, most days, was almost as bad as Yasira's. Luellae and Tiv's names were listed next to a short number of errands, but the errands were checked off as already completed, and Tiv was still nowhere to be found.

Dread settled over Yasira. She had become very sensitive on the topic of where Tiv was and whether Tiv was okay. This wasn't a threat, but parts of her were suddenly racing to come up with one.

"What's wrong?" said Prophet softly behind her.

"Where's Tiv?" Yasira asked. She was embarrassed that her voice shook. This was not a threat. She shouldn't be panicking.

She left, whispered someone in her head. *She got sick of you and made an excuse and left forever.*

And that was an awful thought, but not the worst one. Not the one that scared her most.

She's running into danger, said some other part, a little closer to home, *and she doesn't even want to tell you why.*

"She's out," said Picket. "Fact-finding."

"What facts?"

Grid seemed to be struggling to put this tactfully. "She came back from her rounds upset, and she said she had to check something. I'm not totally sure what it was or where, but I'm sure she'll be back soon."

"She saw someone else get hurt," said Prophet. "She's realizing she has to do more to stop that. Or that's what she thinks she has to do, at least. She's gone someplace that she thinks might have answers, but I can't see it clearly. I don't think it's dangerous."

Yasira pushed her hand through her hair. That all made sense. But she still felt like they were dancing around something. She could see the way Weaver squirmed harder than normal, as if she were trying hard not to say something she'd been warned not to say. She could see the way Picket looked sheepishly away. "I guess I just want to look around."

"Okay," said Grid, but there was something a little strained in their voice.

(*I've done something wrong,* chorused voices in Yasira's head, disturbed.

*They don't want me here. This room is for the real resistance, not
the people who lie around.*

*There's something they're afraid I'll do. How could I have made
them so afraid?*

*They're keeping secrets from me, and they don't want to admit
it. Fuck them.*)

She browsed the walls, leafing through the charts and
notes. She was careful not to disturb anything; when she
turned a page to look at what was underneath, she put it back
as soon as she was done. She didn't want to fuck anything
up. She didn't want the team to *think* she'd fucked up, and to
bar her from looking through the war room ever again.

(A very small, very reasonable part of Yasira pointed
out that the team had never told her she couldn't look at
something. They had avoided topics, but that wasn't the same
thing. The team had never controlled Yasira's movements or
redacted anything. Yasira knew who had done those things
to her, and it wasn't her team.

It was possible to know very well where a fear came from,
and for that knowledge not to help even a little bit.)

She flipped through slowly, trying to pace herself; this
kind of information could be tiring to take in. She looked at
the lists of requested and delivered items. That side of the
operation had grown in scale since she last checked. People
were asking for all sorts of inventive things. Medicines.
Baby supplies. Hammers and craft knives, needles, hand
saws, sandpaper; tools for the kind of repair that everyone
in the Chaos Zone had to do now.

There were a lot of requests for weapons, all denied.
That was not surprising. It had been obvious from the start
that some people wanted to fight. Against the monsters,
mostly, at first; but as the angels' deliberately incompetent

disaster response dragged on, people had turned their anger against that, too. It was heretical, but a good chunk of the population was happy to turn heretical if their lives were on the line. Real torment to the body, in the present moment, was more urgent than torment to the soul. Most people, in an emergency, would react to protect their body first. Or the bodies of the people they loved.

Yasira remembered talking about that, early on. She remembered the first meeting when they'd discussed if they wanted to be a non-violent resistance or not. It had been long and angry. More than one team member had cried, that day. Tiv had cried, but she'd stood firm. Tiv wasn't going to war. She was here to help people, not to get them slaughtered. Tiv had put her foot down, and eventually even Luellae had given in.

Yasira hadn't taken a side in that meeting. She'd looked down at the table, barely saying anything; thoughts had whirled and tangled through her head without resolving into consensus. It had been the most depressing fucking meeting of her life. She hadn't known how to express what seemed obvious to her: they were doomed if they didn't fight and doomed if they did. The whole planet was. Yasira had bought them a little more time and made them a little less miserable on the way. That was all anybody could accomplish.

She sighed and put those pages aside. There was another pile of notes about magical abilities, but she had to put it down quickly. Yasira had given those abilities to the Chaos Zone's survivors herself, but something about it still made her queasy. Someone had collated firsthand theological musings from the survivors, trying to sort them into groups based on their underlying theories and to draw connections between them, like a philosophy term paper, but that didn't feel good to Yasira either. She'd seen Outside firsthand; she had Outside knitted directly into what was left of her soul. She didn't feel like making a holy book out of it, telling people how to live, as if Outside cared about that. She wanted to leave it alone.

There was a note about the gone people, which was mildly interesting. The gone people seemed to be organizing, planning something, but no one could communicate with them well enough to figure out what.

Yasira had spoken to a gone person, briefly, when she was still working for Akavi. Speaking aloud hadn't worked, but gestures and, in some strange way, imagination had. When she'd pictured what she wanted, the gone person had understood and responded. When the gone person wanted to convey things back, it had... worked, more or less. Her mind had been able to grasp it, at least in simple terms. Maybe Yasira was better at that, more like an Outside being, than everyone else. Maybe everyone else just hadn't been trying enough. She didn't know.

The rest of the pages weren't much better. There were charts on the walls showing where angels had shot civilians most recently, where civilians were most eager to rise up. There was a list of awful, sad events, which had been updated just yesterday, listing the number of people the angels had shot in their attempt to get to Tiv.

It was a longer list than what she'd pictured. No wonder Tiv had sounded like a broken, dying thing.

(*Maybe*, whispered someone sensible in her head, *it's not about you*.)

She was going to have to go back to her room soon, probably.

She picked up one last paper, more out of stubbornness than anything else, and her eyes were drawn to a word halfway down the page. *Savior,* said the paper. That was her name, sort of.

The paper said that in a lot of places.

Yasira refocused, trying to make sense of what she was reading. This wasn't one of the official papers that kept a tally of something needed for the whole team. It looked more like a scratchpad, something a person had used to jot notes to themselves during a meeting.

They'd been talking about weapons. They'd been talking about what the people of the Chaos Zone really wanted, when they asked for things that could help them fight.

People knew, mostly, how ineffective guns would be against a battalion of angels. People asked instead, when the team let them, for magic. A power greater than their own.

A power that bore Yasira's name.

People had asked for this, over and over again, and nobody had told Yasira. She hadn't heard their prayers. The team had known, everybody on it had known, and they'd all somehow collectively decided not to pass it on.

Because she was useless, maybe. Because a broken person lying in bed all day *couldn't* answer prayers, and the team hadn't seen the point of trying.

Yasira looked up from the paper at the Four. Grid and Picket drew back slightly, and Weaver quickly looked away, but Prophet solemnly met her gaze.

"Tiv was trying to protect you," she said.

As if that made it any better. As if any part of Yasira liked being so broken now, so useless, that she couldn't even be told what people wanted from her.

When Yasira did her miracle, Outside had given her a vision. It had shown her the people she was helping – not all of them, even an Outside-augmented mind couldn't hold millions of people in it all at once, but a convincing cross section. Enough to make her understand. Outside, for all its uncaring alien cruelty, had chosen to give her that mercy. To ensure she knew viscerally, whatever happened next, that she'd made the difference she'd set out to make.

She remembered all those people, each individual. And all those people, no doubt, remembered what she'd done for them. She couldn't see them now, but she could imagine it, all of them in their shitty, falling-apart houses, hungry, doubting, oppressed by angels, praying for her. Needing her, not because she was much good for anything right now, but because they knew of nothing else that could save them. Because, the first time around, she hadn't saved them *enough*.

Even Outside had given her the dignity of showing her who needed her. Even Outside had trusted her to use that information well.

There was a loud multitude wailing about this in Yasira's head. Louder than usual. *They hid this from me because I'm useless. They hid this from me because they hate me. Nobody should pray to me. I'm not even human. I shouldn't exist.* But there was something that rose in her, some impromptu coalition, that moved despite the noise. That knew how to ignore it for a little while, the same as she did when she had to release her power, because this was important. She felt herself drawing up, her face hardening. Her voice, coming out cold.

"She shouldn't have," said Yasira.

Grid looked at her impatiently. "Look, Savior, just because you don't think you're *worth* protecting–"

"You put so much pressure on yourself," Weaver burst out at the same time, "and she thought it wasn't fair for them to ask so much of you anyway, she thought you'd–"

"No," said Prophet, holding up a hand to quell them both. "Let her finish."

Yasira took a breath. "This is my mess. I'm still in it."

That felt right, both to the parts of her who hated herself and the parts who had hope. Not *this is my mess and I'll fix it* – that could be impossible. But when she lay in bed trying to protect herself from the mess of the Chaos Zone, she was still in it. Outside still bubbled in her mind, wanting to be used. Tiv had wanted to leave Yasira out of what could hurt her. But it was impossible to do. There was no way out of being what Yasira was. She could only choose how to move within it.

"This is my mess," she said, more firmly. "They want me to do things no one else can do. So I'll do them."

"You sure?" said Picket, raising his eyebrows.

Prophet met Yasira's gaze gravely. "Which ones?"

"You want to be a weapon?" Weaver guessed. "The way they were asking?"

"No. Not now, at least." Yasira smiled slightly. It was easy to look at something like Outside and see only its capacity to destroy. But for six months, if only because the structure of her soul had forced her to, Yasira had been living with its other aspects. With a well of Outside deep in her soul that *didn't* destroy her, no matter how she feared and hated it. A source of surreal, irrational, reality-bending power which, when unleashed, seemed to mostly make trees grow. "First I'm going to find out what the gone people are doing."

Prophet favored her with a smile, silently approving. Grid took a split second longer to understand. "But – oh. That – makes sense. You think you can do it?"

"I think so," said Yasira. A dozen voices in her head screamed doubt and dissent, but oh, she had a *purpose* now, for however long it lasted. She could overrule them a little longer. She turned on her heel and headed for the airlock.

"Wait, now?" said Picket's voice behind her. "But–"

"Don't you want any help?" Weaver called.

Yes, now, Yasira thought. Now, and without waiting for help to assemble itself. Before she stopped, and let arguments fill up her mind again, and got paralyzed. Exactly now.

But she didn't pause to argue about it, even with the team, before she pictured the closest large grouping of gone people and stepped through the door.

CHAPTER 9
Two Months Ago

"You," said Qiel Huong, startled into immobility. "I recognize you."

"It's not–" Elu stammered, holding out his hands. "Please don't tell anyone."

"What, that there's an angel out here? Is this an angel-free zone? Are you trespassing? I'm the one who's trespassing. Unless–"

She narrowed her eyes, and immediately Elu saw his mistake. If he wanted to pass for a real angel, the kind who was still in good standing with Nemesis, he should have acted imperious. Elu was, as always, a bad liar.

"You're hiding from the rest of the angels." Qiel wrinkled her nose. "Why?"

"I-I'm not," Elu stammered. "I–"

"Then it won't bother you," Qiel said loftily, "if I go right now to the nearest checkpoint and tell them where you are. I'll say, 'hi, angels, how are you doing, guess who I ran into today while I was foraging in the woods? Elu Ariehmu of Nemesis, that's who–'"

And the way he involuntarily threw out his hand in defense was all the confirmation she needed. He felt the blood drain from his face. He'd been so thoughtless, coming out here, when he knew how weak he really was.

"Please don't," he said. "Please, um. Don't do that."

It had been so long since he'd spoken to anyone but Akavi. He felt as though he'd forgotten how.

Qiel raised a considering eyebrow, then plopped down to sit on the ground, legs crossed, motioning for him to follow. He sat gingerly, full of dread. He couldn't go back to the other angels of Nemesis. They'd never forgive him for having deserted, or for helping Akavi escape. There was only one thing that happened to angels of Nemesis who failed, and that thing was both torture and death.

"I won't," she said, "if you do something for me."

He swallowed, imagining what it would mean if Akavi, or someone with Akavi's kind of mind, said something like that in these circumstances. The threat would never be eliminated. The first request would lead to another, and another, and she'd always have the same power over him that she had in this moment, for as long as she wanted. She'd control him.

Did chatty little Qiel Huong have that kind of mind? Elu didn't know. But the fact that she'd thought of this, so quickly, wasn't a good sign.

"What do you want?" he asked, his mouth dry.

"Tell me why you're here."

He looked down at the grassy ground, dotted with fungi and other strange growths. "I, um–"

"Tell." She brandished her basket. "Or I go and tell the other angels about you right now."

"It's a really long story."

"I'm literally sitting in a field with you, Elu Ariehmu of Nemesis. We don't have anywhere to be. You know one of the nice things about living in a post-apocalyptic commune with no functioning economy? No deadlines. I can stay out here all day and I won't get anything back at home but a raised eyebrow. Do you have anybody waiting for you?"

He really didn't, and that loneliness must have shown itself on his face, because her own expression softened.

"You don't have Akavi with you? Or Enga?"

She would remember all three of them from when they'd camped out in her yard, carrying out their doomed reconnaissance. Akavi, stern and pretty, pretending he had all the answers; Elu, soothing nerves and helping where he could; Enga, the heavy infantry, stomping along with them for protection. They'd been a good team once. He missed those days.

He'd kept it together all this time on the *Talon*, hadn't he? He ought not to be falling apart like this now.

"Akavi – sometimes," he managed, barely keeping the crack out of his voice. "Enga – no."

"Tell me," she urged.

It spilled out of him, hesitantly at first, the long and meandering story of how he'd gotten here. How Akavi had been sentenced to termination and damnation for failing to stop Yasira's miracle; how Evianna Talirr had commandeered the *Talon*, briefly, for her own purposes; how Elu had used the resulting confusion to rescue Akavi and escape. How they'd both cut the ansible connections out of their heads. How Akavi was now running this way and that, pursuing his own ends, leaving Elu mostly behind.

He managed not to specify what those ends were. Elu wasn't *that* much of a traitor. But once he'd begun to speak it was impossible to stop. He'd had these thoughts pent up in him for so long, and no one to share them with, not even Akavi, since Akavi didn't ask. He was *alive*, he had no hierarchy holding him in place, and those two things ought to be miracle enough. But he couldn't seem to end it, the stream of information that poured from him like a flood.

"That's… huh," Qiel said at last, looking at him sidelong. "That's not what I thought you were going to say."

"What did you think I was going to say?"

She shrugged. "I don't know. But that's a lot."

"Not really." He fidgeted nervously with his hair. "It's not really that dramatic. Being tortured for failing, *that* would be dramatic. But we've avoided that."

"So far," said Qiel, wrinkling her nose again.

He waved a hand dispiritedly. "So far."

Qiel drew her knees a little higher, closer to her in the grass. "You don't have many friends, do you? Obviously being in hiding's not conducive to that. But, like. Angels don't. In general."

Elu shrugged. "I had sell-souls working with me a lot of the time. I had Enga. It was… different."

Most sell-souls were all business, eager to finish their assigned work and go back to their mortal lives, but some were friendly. Elu had made sell-soul friends on many occasions. Sometimes he could talk to them about his feelings. There were ways, if you were very careful, to talk about the loneliness or disappointments of angelic life without committing heresy. There were even ways, with the most extreme delicacy, to confess you didn't always agree with what you were made to do. Elu had gotten used to those linguistic dances, and sometimes he'd heard sell-souls' confessions in return. He'd liked that.

He'd even taken sell-soul lovers, once in a while, when there was interest. When pining over Akavi became too much for him. Sell-souls with crushes – working for Akavi, not Elu, not directly – were just about right for that. Not frightening like other angels, who were known to make use of pretty young recruits like Elu in unpleasant ways. Not frightened of *him*, the way regular mortals would have been. The power differential was small enough that he could close his eyes and pretend it wasn't there.

"Do you miss them?"

"Yes," said Elu, scrunching his knees closer to his chest, looking down into the grass. It didn't mean he regretted his choice. Staying in the angelic corps, missing Akavi instead, would have hurt him even more.

"I miss a lot of things, too," said Qiel.

"Tell me."

"I miss my parents," she said. Elu knew that both of Qiel's mothers had died in the first days of the Plague. He remembered her and her sister and her little cousin, bearing griefs too fresh to touch, pushing on to save what could still be saved. "I don't really miss school, but I miss... knowing there was a path. You'd go to school, you'd graduate, you'd get a job and a partner and you'd add more people to your family and it would all be how it was supposed to. I miss a lot of my friends who didn't make it. I miss not feeling like everybody I know depends on me, even when I don't know how to help them." He looked up at her; she was shredding a normal blade of grass, picking bits off it with her fingernails and flicking them away. "And I thought the angels would bring those things back, you know? When I first met you and Akavi and Enga. That's what I thought."

"I'm sorry," he said.

She looked over at him. "When Akavi was here, he said the angels had seen this before and it'd be easy to fix. He was lying, wasn't he? That was a lie."

He realized only then why she was bothering to talk to him, what was in it for her. Elu was a fallen angel. He knew this stuff, and he didn't have a reason to continue the lie.

"Yeah," he said, looking down again. "It was a lie. We had no idea what we were doing."

"Do the angels know that now?"

"I don't know. It's been a while." He squirmed out of his cross-legged position and flopped onto his back, looking up at the sky. Blue, for now, though in the Chaos Zone that could change. "We've seen other Outside incidents before. Buildings or even towns that were corrupted like this, but we kept them contained. They were smaller. They didn't last this long. Jai is… different."

"What do you mean, *kept them contained?*" Qiel asked, and Elu looked away, grimacing, before realizing that was an answer of its own.

"Oh," she said, a small, shaken, betrayed sound. And then, after a silent moment, and another harsh intake of breath: "*Oh*. And us, too, right? That's still your plan."

"I don't *know*," said Elu, covering his face with his hands. He'd been trying not to think about it, trying not to guess. "It's not mine anymore. It's not my team. I don't know what the plans are."

"You want to corral us," she continued, ignoring him. Reverting, probably, to the categories she was used to. "Keep us in one spot and too weak to fight back until you figure out the right excuse to get rid of it all."

There was silence again, for a while, as her words echoed.

Mortals shouldn't be thinking things like this. Elu knew Qiel was probably correct. But his old ingrained angel habits protested at it. Mortals *shouldn't* know when Nemesis wanted to destroy them this way – not unless it was too late for them to do anything about it, and too late for them to tell someone else. Akavi wouldn't want them to know.

"I don't know," he said. "Probably."

"Am I wrong? I'm not wrong. What did you do to those other infected towns?"

Elu dropped his hands to the ground and pushed himself back upright. He didn't look at her. He had bits of Outside grass stuck in his hair. "They were destroyed."

"Well, okay, then, Mister Passive Voice. I'm not wrong." She pulled up a bit of grass and threw it at him, childishly. "It's not like this is *news*. People've been guessing that's the angels' endgame for a while now. I just didn't have it confirmed by an actual angel. And I didn't know." Her voice quieted again; this seemed to be the part that truly disturbed her. "About the other towns."

She was going to tell her friends about this, he suspected. Nemesis wouldn't want that. Akavi *really* wouldn't want that.

Elu could have denied it, he supposed. He was a bad liar, but he could have tried. He wondered why he hadn't wanted to.

"I'm sorry," he said, and he wondered if he really was. Elu hadn't liked those orders, and he hadn't been the one to give them, nor to carry them out. But that was what it meant, being part of Nemesis' machine. Catching the bad guys, as if bad guys could ever be caught without collateral. Did he believe there was a better way? He didn't think he was prepared to say so, to try to guess what the better way *was*.

He noticed how she phrased it. *That's the angels' endgame.* Even in private, all but the most hardened of heretics phrased it that way. Blaming angels for their troubles. Angels, and not the much more dangerous names of the Gods who'd commanded them.

"How many?" she asked, heavy and dull.

"Four towns. That is to say – my team was involved with investigating four. We didn't, um, do the actual destroying. We were specifically investigating Dr Evianna Talirr and the disasters she'd caused. Test runs for this one, I think, though we weren't as clear about that then. I don't know how many other people or places it's happened to over the years."

Qiel was still now, no longer throwing grass at anyone. Still the way Enga got, before a battle, coiled and reserving her strength. "Tell me their names."

"I'd – rather not."

"If you want me to treat you like a human, Elu, say their names."

He sighed, bracing himself. "Svatsibi. Shiyetsa. Maku. Zhoshash."

Qiel let out an angry breath. "Never heard of them." Somehow that seemed to make her angrier. She was so young, and they were all small, isolated places, far from Jai. Of course she hadn't heard.

"I sold my soul to Nemesis because–" He paused. Why was he telling her this? She was practically a stranger, and he'd never said all this straight out before. "I wanted to protect people. The way I'd been protected, once. I wanted to help. And by the time I realized it wasn't that simple, it was too late. Orders come from on high and you carry them out. You can't stop being an angel once you are one. I know that doesn't excuse any of it, but that's what happened."

"But you did stop."

"That's – different."

She was looking at him curiously, the anger banked for now. "Okay," she said with a strange finality, like she'd only just made the decision. "I won't tell the other angels about you."

"I appreciate that."

"Tell me one more thing," said Qiel. "Tell me about Savior. That lady who was with you when you came down the first time, who could talk to monsters like a gone person. That was her, wasn't it? She's the – uh – the one they talk about now."

"Yes. That was her."

"Is it true? What they say about her?"

Qiel was so young. Elu would always look outwardly young, but Qiel Huong was *actually* only twenty, as naive as the age implied. She trusted him to tell the truth, even knowing what he was.

He'd tell her, he supposed. As much as he even understood the truth.

"I don't know all of what they say," he said. "She was very talented at working with Outside. More than any other heretic we'd seen, except maybe Dr Talirr. Talented in ways I guess we didn't fully understand. We… tried to make her help us." He winced slightly, saying it. He'd never liked it when they tortured people. Akavi never made him be involved, except by helping patch the victims' wounds, but he still didn't like it. "She had her own ideas about what that meant, though. She managed to change the Chaos Zone her way instead of ours. She made it safer here, kind of. Then a lot of things happened at once and she vanished. I don't know where she is now. I'd be surprised if the other angels do."

Qiel picked a few more blades of grass idly out of the ground. "Where are you living out here? Just out in the wild? You don't look like you're living out in the wild."

"I've got a ship. Just a little one, but it's God-built, so it meets our needs."

"You're not gonna tell me where, of course."

"Of course not."

She rolled to her feet, picking her basket back up. "So, do you want me to treat you like a human?"

"What do you mean?"

"I mean, if you were a human living out here, I'd offer to be friends. Ask if there was anything my group could do for you. Maybe ask if there was anything you could do to help out, too. It's okay, though. I'm glad we talked. See you later, Elu." She paused just before turning away, frowned. "Is your real name Elu?"

"Yes."

She looked at him for another long moment, but he couldn't bring himself to say, *See you.*

He paid more attention to certain things in the woods after that. He didn't have tracking software installed, but he could look for places where fungi and herbs had been picked, where brush had been cleared away by hands other than his own. Akavi's design requests weren't that complicated, and he had time left over to spend on this if he wanted to. Qiel, or someone like her, seemed to come by here about once a week.

Having trees to look at, birds and small creatures to register in his mental database, had made him feel less alone. That one conversation with Qiel had, too. But knowing there were people nearby gathering necessities, and he didn't *see* them, made him feel more alone than ever.

He printed a few small cameras. Not too small: about thumbnail-sized, so that he'd be able to find them again. He programmed them to be activated by motion, like a camera-trap for wildlife, and set them up in the branches of a few trees near the edge of the field. Elu no longer had the kind of network he was used to for tasks like this, the kind that would have let him monitor the cameras in real time like a second and third pair of eyes, but he could still download the vid data manually.

That data showed him little, but enough. Sometimes Qiel came by, foraging. Sometimes it was someone else. More often, it was some bird or animal, or some mobile Outside plant, setting off the camera by accident. Elu didn't mind. He had time to go over the data.

Sometimes Qiel poked around in a way that didn't look like foraging. Hunting, maybe, for where his ship might be. Hard to tell from the footage, though.

He could have left something out for her if he'd wanted to. Some scrap of food. Some little note. But he didn't dare. Especially not with other people around.

After the second week, Akavi dropped by briefly. Elu had the clothes and supplies he'd requested, and Akavi kissed him. "Excellent work, my dear, as always."

It embarrassed Elu how he'd begun to crave those brief kisses, how he wanted to lean into them. He wanted to be touched, to be held, to have Akavi's attention on him as more than just an afterthought. But he knew better than to ask. This was already such a concession on Akavi's part, an act that Akavi put on for his benefit. Push his luck, and it would fall apart.

He thought about saying, *A mortal saw me.* But he didn't dare.

He thought about saying, *A mortal saw me, and we talked, and she didn't report me to the other angels.* But he didn't dare.

Akavi didn't ask, anyway. Just dropped off the latest vids and a new set of instructions and waltzed back out, with the usual apologies, the promises to sit down and have a real talk soon.

Elu knew he wouldn't.

And it was presumptuous, surely, to imagine that Qiel would.

One Month Ago

Elu was sitting in his chair on the *Talon*, fussing with the details of some new outfit Akavi needed – a rich person's disguise, this time, formerly fine clothes now a little worse for wear, replete with all the new signals people used in the Chaos Zone now to signify their status, odd accessories and trimmings made from Outside objects – when someone knocked at the airlock.

He startled into full alertness. Akavi never knocked like that. Elu wished he still had his network connection; his cameras could have shown him who this was, but he couldn't get to them from here. It could be Qiel, it could be the other angels coming for him, it could be *anyone*.

But if it was the other angels, running wouldn't do any good. He could try to take off, but he'd be shot down before he could shake off pursuit. If it was the other angels, he was dead whether he opened the airlock or not.

He took a deep breath and opened it.

Qiel Huong, her hair plastered to her face with sweat, stood in the airlock. Hanging off her was a little child Elu thought he recognized, her cousin Lingin, cradling a badly broken, inexpertly splinted arm.

"I'm sorry," she said immediately upon entry. "Sorry, I know you like your privacy here, I just–"

"What happened?" Elu asked, hurrying to them.

"I don't know, Juorie turned her back on him for five seconds and he fell off something. I wouldn't have bothered you, there are people back in our own group who can do first aid, but now it's swollen and–"

She broke off despairingly. Both of them looked utterly exhausted. Qiel knew an angel like Elu would have supplies on his ship, including medical supplies. She still wouldn't have come here, wouldn't have put herself and an injured child through such a long search for an uncertain outcome, if there were other options.

Elu bent down, looking more closely at Lingin's arm without touching him. It wasn't only broken; it looked inflamed, infected, and there was a feverish flush to the child's skin. "How did you get here?" he asked Qiel.

"I looked. Like, you're hidden decently, but only because nobody knows there's anything worth looking for in here, you know? Once you know it, if you're any good at tracking, the signs are there. Still took a little while, but…" She shrugged self-deprecatingly. "Can you help him?"

He nodded. He refused to think yet about what this meant, what precedent it set, what Akavi would think.

"Hi, Lingin," he said, turning his attention to the child. "My name's Elu. I'm going to take a look at your arm, okay?"

"Okay," said Lingin, in a voice quiet and shaky – maybe from general disuse, maybe only strained with pain and fear. He'd learned over the course of these six months to fear angels. Had Qiel tried to explain to him that Elu was different? Had he understood? Or did he only know that one of his oppressors was standing over him now, wanting to examine him in the ways that hurt most?

"Can you get up on a chair for me?" he asked, gesturing to the parlor. "I'm going to boot up some robots and they'll give you something for the pain, and then we'll do a bigger examination, okay?"

"Okay," said Lingin, with more determination this time. He walked the short distance to the indicated chair with some difficulty and maneuvered himself onto it. Elu hurried to the medical bots and activated them.

The examination proceeded straightforwardly. Lingin's problem was dangerous and difficult for mortals without a doctor, but not too challenging for God-built technology. The break was a messy compound fracture and the splint – applied by someone in Qiel's community, with first-aid training but not much more – hadn't been nearly enough to address it. The places where the bones broke the skin had been badly infected.

"Doesn't the Chaos Zone have doctors anymore?" he asked Qiel. "Hospitals?" The vids that Akavi sent back, and the snippets he'd heard on the radio, had been uninformative on this point. Mortals could have dealt with the kind of injury Lingin had, but those mortals would have to be trained professionals, with something vaguely resembling proper equipment, and time would have been of the essence.

Qiel gave a half-hearted shrug. "Some, but they're short on space and equipment, and they have angel guards. You know."

He didn't really, but he could make the inference. He imagined a hospital with armed angel guards, checking IDs, asking intrusive questions. Qiel and the child both had Outside abilities. If he'd been using those abilities at the time he was hurt, or if the angels wanted an excuse to bring Qiel in for any other reason…

"I can treat him," said Elu, "but he needs surgery. It'll be messy. He'll be knocked out, and you won't want to look at it."

Qiel bit her lip, but nodded. "Okay."

Last time they met she'd blamed him for the murder of thousands of people. Now she trusted him so easily with the life of a child. She was young, he supposed. Too trusting, like him. And out of other options.

It was only later, when the surgery was already in progress, that he remembered to wonder what Akavi would think. Nothing good, surely. The *Talon* was secret, and secrecy was crucial to the mission.

To Akavi's mission.

It was crucial to Elu's survival, too. But he didn't regret helping. He liked feeling useful, and he felt more deeply useful now than he had with Akavi in a long time. Maybe it was wrong, but turning Qiel and Lingin away, after they'd come all this way, would be worse.

"Can I–?" said Qiel. She'd come up next to him in that parlor, while the robots did their work on Lingin in one of the bedrooms. She was looking up at him now, biting her lip. "Can I bring other people here? If they really need it? I won't tell anyone who doesn't really need it."

Elu looked back at her, uncertain. "You know what will happen if the other angels find me."

It was virtually inevitable, if he went this way.

No. It was inevitable *anyway.* He'd given himself and Akavi a respite from damnation, and they might stretch it out a long time, if they were careful and clever. They wouldn't age. They might last decades, centuries, longer than any mortal lifetime. But one day, through sheer statistical inevitability, their luck would run out.

He'd known that as soon as he deserted. In a way, he'd known it half a century ago. There was no going back once you started being an angel. Nemesis would get Elu's soul when he died. Nemesis, if he'd displeased Her, would torment him for all the rest of his immaterial existence. And the dark joke inherent in that, the one that the angels all knew, was that *everyone* had displeased Her. Some just didn't know it yet.

Yet Elu didn't want to say *no*.

He didn't even want to say, *let me check with Akavi*. That wasn't fair, surely; he was putting both of them at risk. But Akavi had already made so many decisions for him. It was petty, it was beneath him, but Elu wanted this choice to be his.

"What do you want in exchange?" Qiel asked, startling him. Seeing his hesitance, maybe, and misinterpreting. "We all, um – like, we don't really do money very much here. We don't talk a lot about what someone owes us for the favor we did. We don't hassle people about pulling their weight, because how do you know what someone's weight is, really? We just give people things if they need them. But this is – a lot. What you can do here. And I guess you can print your own supplies pretty well but if you want, I don't know, help with something, or information, or…"

"Friends," he said, surprising himself.

"Oh. Yeah, of course. But friends you can trust, right? Friends who can keep your secret." He nodded, and she looked around speculatively at the *Talon*, its incongruous comfort in such isolation. "I can swing that for you, yeah."

He made an excuse and crept away to check on Lingin again. He was very bad at this, he thought. He didn't know his goals the way Akavi did; he couldn't think rationally about how to get there. He would not think about where this might lead, or what Akavi would think of it. He would not. He would *not*.

CHAPTER 10
Now

Yasira emerged, blinking in the daylight, at the edge of a park. It wasn't a park she'd seen before, but similar to many like it. Wide cobblestone paths, curving banks of trees, all a little worse for wear now that the infrastructure to maintain them was no longer in place. The trees had gone feral, both in the usual ways of trees and in Outside ways. In this park, their trunks had split from the simple, thick shapes they'd once held and become intricate lattice-works, honeycombs of bark, a maze of openings occasionally large enough to crawl through. The path still wove through it, though the branches often closed into a tunnel overhead. But not many *normal* people ventured down paths like this anymore. This park belonged to the gone people.

She could see it in the details: nests of leaves and other detritus in the largest crevices, big enough to cradle a human form. Extinct Old Earth apes had built nests like these, in trees or on the ground, to be used for a few nights before moving on, and gone people had picked the habit back up.

Yasira didn't know what was up with gone people and roosting outdoors. There were plenty of rundown, abandoned, broken buildings in the Chaos Zone. Normal survivors had reclaimed many, rebuilding them as best they could or just squatting inside. Any animal, Outside or otherwise, would take shelter in the ruins of a building if it could. But she'd never heard of gone people going indoors, even in the worst weather. It was as if they'd not only lost their sense of civilization but had actively rejected it.

She didn't know exactly what she was going to do here.

A chorus of voices in Yasira's mind urged her against this. There were too many dangers. She wasn't going to accomplish anything. She was going to accomplish too *much*, without understanding what she was doing; she'd make contact with the gone people but it would have repercussions beyond anything she'd planned. The angels would catch her. Tiv would hate her for risking herself like this, or for a dozen other far-fetched reasons.

But when she looked at those papers a few minutes ago, something new had begun to form. Not a new part of Yasira, but a new coalition of existing parts. So many of her were tired of sitting around not doing anything. They leapt at the chance to act, meaningfully, in a way that might influence the whole resistance. Those parts of her had banded together, seized control, and they planned to hold onto it as long as they could. They had Outside power behind them, in some way that she didn't fully understand. A deepness, a rightness, pushing her on. A purpose.

They were thinking about choosing a name.

The Strike Force, maybe. That sounded right, conveying action and urgency. Was it right to give names to a group like this? Could names be collective? *Yasira* was a collective, but it felt strange to make further sub-groupings.

But they did want the name.

Yasira walked forward into the tangle of trees.

The path twisted and turned and the tree-honeycombs

closed in around it. She walked, more on instinct than on much of a plan, until she was out of sight of the outer road. Then she knelt, one hand on a thick twist of bark, one in the dirt.

She didn't know what she was doing, but she knew that, when she'd communicated with gone people before, they'd responded only to pure thought. The first gone person she'd met had responded to what Yasira pictured in her head – not the intent, but the image – and so did other Outside creatures. And Yasira was able to connect to Outside more deeply now. She could reach into the roots of things and make them burst into new shapes.

"Talk to me," she whispered into the trees, into the ground. "Please." She pictured the gone people. Whoever had made these nests, whoever was nearby, approaching her peacefully with news.

Mental imagery was different for Yasira these days. The groups within her had to do it collectively. In some ways it was more vivid than before, more detailed, every willing part of her mind lending its own individual strengths. But it was also more difficult to hold on to, shifting, mutable, unfocused.

She felt… something. The weight of her intention settled in to the places she touched. She had been heard.

But the gone people still had free will. They might decide not to respond. They might not appear immediately. They might be far away. It took time, probably, to navigate these honeycombed woods. Yasira would have to rein in her impatience, listen to her feelings. Wait until she felt she shouldn't wait anymore.

She breathed deeply, letting the voices of worry and dissent in her head argue it out. Until she heard quick footsteps on the path behind her.

Yasira turned.

It wasn't a gone person. It was Tiv. Panting as she ran up the path, slowing her steps as she neared the spot where Yasira crouched. Yasira looked up at her in confusion, and she dropped to her knees, bringing herself down to Yasira's level.

"There you are," Tiv panted. "I found you. I– they said you just ran off somewhere, and I–"

Yasira looked up at her. She had achieved something very similar to calm, but at the sight of Tiv it evaporated. She loved Tiv, she wanted things to be okay between them, but they *weren't*. Tiv had tried to protect her by lying to her. And here was Tiv, trying to protect her again now.

"Ran off?" Yasira snapped. "Is that what they called it?"

"Because of me," said Tiv, catching her breath.

"I didn't run off. I went out to work, just like you. I came out here with a purpose. You didn't tell me how bad it was, Tiv. Not even when you almost got killed. You didn't tell me everyone's been praying for me to do something about it." Yasira turned away, back to the twisted roots. "Now I am."

"I'm sorry," said Tiv.

"Sorry for what?" She didn't want to accept an apology yet. She didn't know if Tiv really understood what she'd done wrong.

Like you're any better, said her thoughts. *Like you've even contributed anything, up until today. Like you haven't lied.*

Tiv didn't flinch. "For not telling you the truth. For thinking you were too weak to handle it. I was trying to keep you safe, but instead, I shut you out, and that was wrong."

It hit Yasira like a blow to the gut, pushing her breath out. This was what she'd thought she wanted to hear. But she couldn't accept this apology. She'd been shutting Tiv out, too. She'd thought Tiv was too weak to handle the truth. They'd both lied. And now Tiv had patched up her part of it before Yasira was ready to face her own. Yasira was the worse person, out of the two of them here.

Tiv didn't even know who she was talking to.

"Yeah?" she blurted, and it wasn't the Strike Force anymore. It was someone deeper down, more hateful. "Well, I did all of that to you, too. So don't be sorry."

"What?" said Tiv. "When did–?"

But then there was another rustle further off, and Yasira turned towards it, the Strike Force taking command again. She could see – no, she could *feel* a gone person coming closer. She hadn't expected to be able to feel it so viscerally, like a dream presence. Like an errant part of herself returning. It hadn't felt like this, that first time she'd talked to a gone person, in the suburbs of Büata. When had she learned how to do this?

You know when you learned it, said a chorus of mental voices, rolling their imaginary eyes.

She could see it now with her eyes, too. More than one gone person was making their way to her through the trees, in that aimless-looking way they had. They were still only blurs, faint humanish shapes mostly obscured by the leaves, but she knew what they were.

She put a finger to her lips, glancing back at Tiv. "They're here."

Akavi was back in the middle-aged woman's form that she used when speaking to Luellae. She stepped out onto the deserted street where they'd agreed they would meet next, looking cautiously around at the Outside-influenced architecture. Akavi was no longer unsettled by the way things looked in the Chaos Zone; she'd lived here for six months, and it had become routine. But routine still involved a healthy respect for how quickly Outside could become dangerous. This was a street too badly affected by the Plague to see much human use. Most of the buildings had long ago been reduced to rubble, and those that remained jutted up from the concrete in shapes so ominous that no rational person would venture inside. Fleshy buildings with toothy doors. Scaly ones that oozed an odd slime.

Akavi's visual cortex contained filters that would block out the sight of anything actively maddening. These buildings had dimmed and darkened patches, through the filters, but by and large their shapes were just this side of rational. She didn't feel maddened when she looked at them – but she did feel angry. The people of Jai wanted to build some sort of life in these ruins, but the idea was inherently an affront. Who would fight for the right to live in this slime, in this dust?

She'd arranged to meet Luellae at precisely this time, but she wasn't prepared for the agitation with which Luellae jogged towards her when she came into sight, pounding the pavement aggressively with her feet. She was angry, but Akavi's microexpression software also picked up intriguing overtones. Fear. Surprise. Something had *happened*. Something big.

Akavi was intrigued.

"What's wrong?" she called casually as Luellae approached close enough to hear.

"Ugh. Nothing." Luellae slowed as she neared Akavi, brushing at her arms as if dust had settled there. Maybe it had; some parts of the Chaos Zone contained all sorts of airborne particulates. "Team stuff. You don't want to hear it.

The team's all fucked up anyway. I had to make an excuse to get away in time to meet you."

"They didn't hurt you, did they?" Akavi asked, holding out her arms.

"No, nothing like that." Luellae didn't take hold of her immediately, and Akavi's visual circuitry highlighted the signs of hesitation. The mental dithering a person might do when they wanted to talk about something, but weren't sure it was safe.

"I'm just concerned about you," said Akavi, feeling the appropriate expression slide onto her face. After so many years doing infiltration work, this sort of manipulation was second nature. A gentle show of sympathy, and then the tiniest of prompts for the subject to grasp. "I wanted to believe the Seven could change anything down here, but…"

Luellae looked up at her. "Honestly? We haven't been. But Yasira might be."

Akavi drew back slightly in surprise. Luellae had described Yasira as useless before, hiding in her room in a depressed fog and doing nothing. Had that changed? "Go on."

She listened as Luellae explained. She had immediately turned on a sensory recording program to store this conversation, but in the moment she was only half-listening. The details faded away into the background as her mind fixed on the really important part.

Yasira was outside the lair, and vulnerable, now. Not only satisfying some brief need; she'd gone out alone on some dangerous and foolhardy mission. This was the moment. Akavi had planned to stoke Luellae's desire for rebellion first, to tear apart the Seven from the inside so that Yasira would emerge. But if Yasira was here, now, then they could skip all that. If Akavi could find her, Akavi could *strike*.

Akavi grasped Luellae by the arms, leaning in. She let the full scope of her urgency show on her face. "Take me to her."

"What?" Luellae squirmed slightly, and Akavi realized she'd been over-eager. "Why–"

"You can't understand how important this is, Luellae. Just, please – I need to be there. Now."

"You can't make her see reason by bursting in on her like that. She's not that type. It won't work."

And *there* was the real opening. Like so many marks, Luellae had already filled in an explanation for Akavi's strange outburst on her own. Akavi schooled her features into an expression of solemn determination. "I have to try."

Luellae looked at her sideways, but she had already relaxed into a decision. The next complaint was only a formality. "It might not work. I don't know exactly where she is."

This was not as much of an obstacle for Luellae as one might have thought. Luellae's movements didn't always conform to the laws of causality. If she had a firm objective in mind, even if it wasn't exactly a specific place, she could often take herself there. Not as reliably as the meta-portal could, but it happened.

"Understood," said Akavi.

Luellae bit her lip, nodded back, and then space twisted around them.

Akavi's visual filters instantly turned everything inky black, and she shut her eyes. She felt wind whipping past her face, and she felt herself being pulled, as if Luellae was running headlong, trailing Akavi behind her. She allowed her legs to move stumblingly as they willed. She held on tight.

At last, with a lurch, the feeling of movement stopped.

She opened her eyes in a forest somewhere far from

Büata. The temperature had dropped a few degrees and the shape of the trees was strange. All of them contorted, multi-branched, knotting around each other. The clearing where Akavi and Luellae had hit the ground was barely big enough to hold both their standing forms, and there weren't any clear paths in and out. Only routes where one could crawl or climb through that branching superorganism, in some meandering direction.

Akavi did not see Yasira. She was unsure at first where to go from here. But that question answered itself with a shuffling sound to her left. She whirled around and saw a gone person – a child barely more than ten, barely clothed, barely human – painstakingly making its way in a certain direction. Not toward Akavi, but straight past her.

A moment later she saw another one to the right, an old woman, shuffling in the same direction. And there were more rustles, now that she'd gotten her bearings. More movement. None of them paid Akavi or Luellae any mind; they trudged past as if the two were only a pair of boulders.

Gone people were pathologically attracted to Outside energies. Wherever they were going, Outside energy must be amassing. Wherever the Outside energy was, Yasira would be.

"Thank you," said Akavi, softening her posture. "You'd better wait here; I don't want her to see you."

Luellae shifted her weight. Clearly, even the thought of being this close to whatever Yasira was doing displeased her. "Can I come back in an hour?"

"Do you think you can find the same spot again?"

Luellae considered it, frowned, shook her head, and stayed still. She'd have been able to find Yasira by focusing, but even that had been inexact, dropping her down out of sight and out of earshot with only the gone people to show them how to get closer. And she didn't know Akavi as well as she knew Yasira.

Akavi tested the weight of one of those twisted tree-trunks. It held, and she began to climb cautiously upwards. When she was out of Luellae's direct line of sight, she thickened her fingernails into claws to strengthen her grip. Whatever Yasira was about to do, Akavi planned to have a good vantage point when it began.

There were more and more of them in their shabby clothes, with their scabbed-up faces – most gone people drew blood from their own hands and faces in their rites, and many had done it so often that it had progressed to a kind of scarification, a fractal pattern of scabs that would never fully dry. They surrounded Yasira in a semicircle, sitting cross-legged or on their knees, watching, waiting.

Yasira heard Tiv draw in a frightened breath behind her, but she was more fascinated by what she felt. Some Outside sense within her had lain dormant since the Plague, except for those rare occasions when the energy bubbled up too strongly within her and had to be released. Since the Plague, she'd never come face to face with so many Outside beings at once. She'd never realized she'd be able to sense them this way.

They felt like dozens of tiny minds joined into one, focused on her with an energy that belonged to all of them. What Yasira's mind had achieved by fragmenting, the gone people had done in the exact opposite way, by instinctively reaching out with their own injured minds and finding each other. It was like gazing into a funhouse mirror. She was a hive mind facing a hive mind.

She had never expected to feel this. She had never

expected that there was *another being* that structured itself something like the way she did.

She forgot Tiv. She nearly forgot to argue with herself. She and the gone people were both, in their own ways, broken. The workings of their minds, the daily facts of their existence, all were different now. She'd heard people talking before about the gone people, speculating that they seemed like a hive mind, but she hadn't really thought about what that meant for her. She hadn't thought she would sit across from a group of them and recognize something.

The gone people understood. The gone people might not even know that there was anything about this state that one could fail to understand, anything to be ashamed of. She had needed that far more than she'd realized. Just this. Just sitting across from them, looking at them, understanding.

She reached out with her mind.

It was instinctive. She couldn't have explained what she was doing, but she knew how Outside energy felt, filling in the crevices between her selves, and she knew how it felt spilling out of her. She knew how her internal selves talked to each other. That was enough.

"I see you," she whispered, more for herself than for them. Speaking was a way of remembering the shape she wanted the thought to have. The thought went out by its own mechanisms, and the gone people in front of her, collectively, grasped it.

The gone people, individually and in unison, looked back at her.

We see you, said the thought, if words could be put to the thought. But it was Yasira's mind putting words to it. The thought itself was deeper and simpler than that.

"I should have come sooner," said Yasira. "I never realized."

There is no soon, said the gone people. *There is no late.*

Yasira stifled a grin; it was so similar to something Ev had used to say. *Time is a lie.*

Tiv stirred behind her. Yasira couldn't feel Tiv's mind the way she felt the gone people's. She hoped Tiv was happy and not afraid, but if Tiv was afraid, they'd have to deal with that later. There were more urgent matters at hand now.

"I haven't been well," said Yasira. She didn't know why she led with that; it was an impulse from someone very deep in the system. Wanting them to recognize that, too.

There is no well.

"I need your help. My people need your help."

What do you need?

Her heart was beating fast. It was one thing to be seen and recognized, to understand that communication was possible. But to convey other concepts – the plans, the strategies, the timelines – would require much more. Was it possible? Her structure and the gone people's structures paralleled each other, but they were not fully the same. *There is no soon.* Did it even make sense to ask for plans when the gone people didn't share her understanding of time?

"You're planning something, aren't you?"

Yes.

"There's so much that needs doing and so little my people can do. We need help. But maybe we could work together. You could help us; we could help you. If we knew what you were trying to do, then side by side…"

You have no experience of this. We will show you.

Something, a force that Yasira could feel only in her mind, beckoned towards her.

Tiv took a sharp breath behind her. Something had startled her, maybe in Yasira's face, maybe in the gone people's movements. Yasira was concentrating too hard on her mental task to tell. "Yasira, what–?"

She did not have the words to answer.

She closed her eyes.

She let them in.

INTERLUDE

you are our mirror image – you have become like us
greeting like to like – [curiosity] – your structure [alarm\concern] –
why do you hate

	the wounds that will not be healed
we cannot help you	*by hate the damage that has split*
	you open the
heal you guide you we	*torn seams from which you can*
	unfold
have our own concerns	*into greatergreatergreater*

but you are kin
        [failed kin? no not
        failed but – waiting] and we
recognize we will answer we will ask – welcome
                        Savior

———————————————

   How can you be like me? (You are not like me. You are the
opposite. You were many, I was one, and now we've met in the
middle.) (I have never met something so much like me.)

thank you for – the welcome – I	*How can I UNFOLD what*
	is THAT ((NO))
am sorry for my other parts they	
are angry	*(HURTING ‖ SCARED ‖*
	FAILED FAILED FAILED)

*(what the FUCK do we have
to WAIT FOR but Judgment)*

*How do your own structures work? How are you so calm? I want
to study this.*

*Dear gone people please what do you want to be called how do I
greet you how
Please no one on my own side knows what we're doing I need
to know someone has a plan I need to know there is a future
what is your future*

———————————————

we will show you not one future but many

*every part of the future is many futures all unfolding at once /
every part of the landscape has its own living future*

microbe   tree   animal   us   grass   you   insect   fruit

*[there is no distinction between these and the other futures
you have no name for; the monsters that roam the roads hungry
and alive, the small surreal creatures, the plants that have been
twisted into new shapes and the rocks and human buildings
that have come alive. And us, us us us, we are the futures that
will be aware enough to pray and change – merge this list with
the previous – there is no nature or unnatural there is the soil
of reality there is us]*

*there is [a balance ‖ many balances ‖ an act of balancing as the
soil shifts]*

what we are planning is a change
is this the future you need?

———————————————————

Show me. I don't understand. What change? What will be
different? What will you do?

———————————————————

how can you not understand   you have done this already
          assessment ‖ like to like ‖ you lack the concept
                              of your own activity

one moment
we will show—
                    this may hurt you

They gather in their circles. Old and young, every gender, every kind; there is no distinction based on kind in the gone people's minds, but Yasira can see it that way. They are all aware of each other, even across distance. The circle in Büata knows the circle in Huang-Bo knows the circle in Dasz and dozens of others, all working in synchrony. They ready the piercing thorns that they carry with them for their rites, and the more delicate mental mechanisms that are used for this work, the things that belong to the circle itself because no individual, gone or otherwise, could sustain them. The parts of them that naturally connect to Outside. Like Yasira's.

This was what Yasira wanted when she did her miracle. She did not want to remove Outside from the world; that would have meant destroying every life, from humans to blades of grass, with which Outside had come in contact. But she wanted to hand over control. When Dr Talirr infected the Chaos Zone with Outside energies, she'd done it by inviting the attention of vast entities that naturally dwelled Outside, things that changed the nature of reality when they touched it, without thought or care for what that would mean to the humans within. Those entities had been all that kept the Chaos Zone's energies even vaguely in balance; if she'd simply made them go away, the whole zone would have spiraled until it destroyed itself. Someone had to remain responsible for that balance. And a single human, even a single human with power as vast as Yasira's, could not have withstood that responsibility. The size and complexity of the task would have killed them.

So Yasira, instead, had handed the task over to humans. Collectively.

Every human who had some new power, everyone who could grow food now or influence the Outside creatures around them, bore some small part of the task. For most, it was unconscious. They didn't realize that they maintained the Chaos Zone's reality by existing in it, observing it, *needing* it deep down to be livable.

But the gone people had that responsibility too, and they did know it. Before Yasira's miracle, they had already worshipped Outside. But Yasira had given them more.

She watched in her mind as the circles of gone people gathered. They joined their minds and focused until pure Outside energies manifested in the middle of their circles, eerie presences that resembled light but illuminated nothing. They pierced themselves, they plunged their hands into the dirt.

And, like Yasira in those moments when Outside energy overwhelmed her, they made things grow.

Those gestures they'd made before, as if describing something complex to each other – those hadn't been battle plans. They'd been blueprints. With each circle of gone people working everywhere at the same time, they could change the whole character of the Chaos Zone. A more modest echo of the miracle Yasira had done. They could rearrange its structure to be more to their liking. More food. More shelter. More peace. They were only thinking of themselves, but this would benefit the saner survivors too.

This was going to happen soon. It was hard to say how soon, because time was a lie, and the gone people's concepts of it were different from hers. But Yasira saw the stars, above the gone people's circle, and she could see how they aligned, in a snaking geometry that made perfect sense to a gone person's mind. It would be trivial to remember this, trivial to look at Jai's star charts when she returned to the lair and pin this to a specific day, in the way that mortal humans understood days.

But this vision, as vivid as it was, was not a vision of the future. Not a real one, like Prophet's. Only a plan. And there were things missing from the gone people's plan. Just as the other humans had tried to make their plans without the gone people, the gone people barely noticed or thought of other humans. There were no other humans in their plan.

There were no angels.

It wasn't that the gone people didn't know angels existed. It was just that they didn't really distinguish them from mortals, and they didn't consider it important. Angels had killed gone people sometimes, in an attempt to control them or just because they were in the way. But to the gone people that was no more remarkable than dying from disease or being eaten by a monster. The gone people didn't remember very much of their previous lives, and they certainly didn't remember their old faith. Angels didn't have a mental category of their own.

But the angels knew the gone people existed. And, when they gathered to do their rites, the angels would be there.

Listen please   *Your plan –*   *I love it but there is*
                                              something missing

               There is a danger
Do you know, do you remember, ANGELS–

titanium face   *he can shift*   *broad shoulders*   *his smile is*
hostile stare   *his shape,*   *splitting*   *so kind he*
no-longer-   *he looks at*   *into weapons*   *is so young but*
human
armed with   *me like I*   *wrapped like*   *do not be*
miracles   *am a gun,*   *a bouquet*   *fucking fooled*
we used to   *he is not*   *silent strong*   *he is not*
believe in them   *safe he weilds*   *harsh she*   *on your side*
but they   *so many slicing*   *will kill you*   *he will–*
will kill us all   *edges he*
               will kill me   *RUN*

You need to protect yourselves. How? Where is your protection? What will you do when they come?

---

    this question is nonsense we are every future and there is no distinction they will not kill us all they are only humans with better guns than other humans we do not care the land around us will live it will go on

---

No. That can't be your answer. You will all die. Everything here will die
              They have weapons that can melt a planet

They will burn you to slag
I have SEEN the slag please LISTEN

You need protection   You need weapons   You need–

─────────────────────────────

if you wish to save us do | we welcome you
Savior | but it is foolish
we will let you go to calm yourselves for now

─────────────────────────────

No WAIT   LISTEN you need–
WAIT–!!!!

CHAPTER 11
Now

"Yasira!" Tiv shrieked, at the same time as Yasira snapped out of the trance she'd been in, reorienting to the actual path and the forest around her. The trees stretched overhead in their intertwined honeycomb shape; the gone people still sat motionless in their places. Yasira's blood boiled. How could the gone people not see? They were risking themselves, their whole community. She'd thought they understood each other, mind to mind, both groups reflecting each other's strangeness. But they'd blown off her fears as if she was a child. The way so many older people who thought they knew better had done so many times. The way people had done about the Shien Reactor, even: the project she'd worked on with Dr Talirr, the one she'd had a strange foreboding about. Nobody had listened to her fears until the station tore itself apart and killed a third of the people aboard.

She'd thought the gone people, of all people, would be better than that. She thought they'd understand.

"Yasira!" said Tiv again, panicked, tugging at her arm, and Yasira wondered how many times she'd said it without being heard. She turned her head.

Directly across from them, right at the place where the path turned, stood an angel. So much like the ones Yasira remembered, the fever of fear she'd recalled when she was warning the gone people, that for an instant she thought she was dreaming it. But it was real, a titanium-faced woman in the red-and-black livery of an angel of Nemesis, pointing a gun directly at them.

"Dr Yasira Shien," said the angel tonelessly, ignoring the gone people, who still sat motionless as if nothing had occurred. "Productivity Hunt. You are both under arrest for heresies too innumerable to recount. You will come with me to be punished and terminated, or–"

Tiv was shaking so hard Yasira wondered how she'd found the voice to say anything. This had happened to Tiv already, too recently, and she'd escaped only by leaving a trail of innocent bodies behind.

Yasira could barely think. Her mind was no longer joined to the gone people's, but it was still in a strange shape from having done so. Outside power hummed and danced inside her. She wanted to do six things at once, *say* six things at once, in the way that had felt so natural when she and another hivemind were talking.

But Tiv was in danger. Tiv was afraid. That was unacceptable.

So nobody got in the Strike Force's way when they struck.

Without any more than a split second's thought, Yasira reached out, gathered the full force of Outside from deep inside her, and *shoved*.

The very ground rose before her. The intertwined shapes of the trees reared up, like tentacular limbs. A brown and green chaos roared down at the angel, made her stumble back. She fired a shot into the air, but the trees pinned her arms, beginning to drag her away.

"Come on!" said Yasira, grabbing at Tiv, who didn't need to be told twice. Even if this angel didn't hurt them, she'd be able to use the ansible connection in her head to summon others very quickly. The sooner they got out of here, the better. They ran.

Akavi watched, fascinated, from her perch in the trees above the two of them. She only partly understood what had just happened. Yasira had sat down and initiated some sort of mental communication with the gone people, something none of the other people with heretical Outside abilities seemed able to do. Akavi had been about to drop down and confront her, but apparently this other angel had gotten the same idea first. So she watched, stock still, hoping neither side would see her. Was this the end? Yasira was powerful, but even Yasira couldn't defeat an angel, surely.

She watched as Yasira threw out her hand, and the entire landscape splintered. The ground rose up skyscraper-high, and the trees with it, uprooting from the ground and unwinding from each other, to wave with their grasping branches at everything that posed any threat to the woman who'd commanded them. The gone people, suddenly exposed, scattered.

For a moment Akavi could not move as the enormity of what she was seeing sank in.

She had heard, of course, the rumors that Yasira would return and save everyone. But Akavi had seen firsthand the toll Yasira's first miracle took on her. She'd had the help of a heretical prayer machine based on Talirr's own designs, and of angels whom she'd tricked into helping. The effort of it had still broken her. She'd managed to overpower Akavi after the miracle, but Akavi had her doubts as to whether that level of power had stayed. It had seemed like the last gasp of the miracle itself, and she'd seen how the life drained from her afterwards, how she'd sagged in confusion with barely the strength to walk. The next time Yasira met an angel, she would be weaker. Akavi would get the better of her next time. She would be prepared. That was what she'd thought.

And yet– *this*.

The ground roared up at her, a tidal wave of grass and roots and soil. This was more than the power Akavi had seen before, and there was not even a machine to mediate it. This was impossible.

With this kind of power, and the right strategic mind, even a battalion of angels might fall. The common people with their prophecies had been right, in a sense: Yasira was a threat to the Gods Themselves.

And hadn't Akavi wanted revenge against Them, too?

There was no time to leap clear, but Akavi could at least leap at the right angle to avoid the worst damage. She calculated a trajectory quickly in her head. The wave's movement was unpredictable, but if it hit her side-on–

She leapt.

It hit her.

There was an impact, and a horrible earthy scrabbling, a rolling. Further impacts knocked her breath away. Alarms blared in her mental circuitry, warning of damage, but there wasn't time to process what they said. The whole mass that carried her rumbled on and on until it ground to a halt and she lay prone, panting, reassessing.

There was air to breathe, at least. She'd been frightened she'd be buried, but she'd chosen her angle correctly, and she was still at the surface of the heap. A whole half of the park had uprooted itself, and Akavi lay dazed in the wreckage. Yasira and Productivity were nowhere to be seen.

She assessed the alarms. Abrasions and what would soon become bad bruises, some bleeding, but no organs badly damaged, nothing broken. She took a moment to think through what she'd seen.

Akavi had wanted to manipulate Yasira from afar. She wanted revenge against many targets, and Yasira was the easiest to start with. She'd wanted to separate Yasira from her existing support, drive her to desperation, provoke her into reckless acts that would destroy her. Her whole cultivation of Luellae had worked that way, gaining the unfortunate girl's trust and convincing her that recklessness was the only way her group could make a difference. But if Yasira was *this* powerful–

Yasira should not be destroyed, not yet. She should be preserved. She should be *used.*

But that would require Akavi to undo all of her previous scheming and induce the opposite, very fast.

She rolled over, briskly extricating her legs from the mound of dirt that covered them. Across from her, in a somewhat worse state of health, lay the other angel. This one had been grabbed directly by those waving branches, and she now fought to extricate herself. Her gun had a bayonet attachment and she hacked at the branches efficiently, ignoring the blood that soaked half her body and the ominous dent in the plating at her left temple. Angels of Nemesis did not succumb easily.

For a moment, her eyes met Akavi's. Then they flicked down to Akavi's fingertips, which still carried those telltale long, pointed climbing claws.

"Vaurian," rasped the angel, through what sounded like a badly injured throat. "Identify yourself."

"No," said Akavi, retracting the claws back into her

humanlike hands. She moved, quickly now, to get up.

Vaurians like Akavi were disproportionately recruited to do angels' work, but some lived as civilians, spread across a variety of worlds. Merely being Vaurian wasn't incriminating in itself. But any angel of Nemesis assigned to this area would know that Akavi, a former Vaurian angel, was wanted for her failures and crimes. That she, with her angel circuitry and stolen God-built tech, posed a greater threat than most mortal heretics. And that she might well have reasons to be hanging around this area covertly.

Akavi's ankle buckled unexpectedly as she tried to rise. She lost her balance.

The other angel whipped out a hand and grabbed her.

They fell into a heap, scrabbling at each other in the disturbed soil. One of the other angel's feet was still trapped in that assemblage of branches. She was more injured than Akavi. But she had a gun and Akavi did not. She brought it up again to aim, and Akavi grabbed her wrist, the claws instinctively coming out again. She raked at the other angel's face. The angel punched her, pushing the breath from her bruised ribs and throat.

Someone was running toward them. That must be Luellae. That was Akavi's ticket out of here, if she could survive the next few seconds.

Akavi threw out a hand and twisted the other angel's wrist, pushing the gun so it pointed away from her. Instead of pushing the muzzle of the gun back toward Akavi, she slammed the side of it down against Akavi's bleeding head, repeatedly, jarring her until she saw stars.

Luellae had run nearly into arm's reach. She hung back now, wary of the fight, but ready to pull Akavi away once she didn't have another angel attached to her.

"Vaurian," the other angel growled again. "Identify yourself, or your identity will be *assumed*."

But she'd stopped hitting her while she talked. Akavi gave her a hard shove, ignoring the twinges of warning from her circuitry and the dizziness that nearly overtook her, and scrambled away. The angel's foot was still trapped. If they could teleport out of here before she aimed the gun again–

"Get us out of here," Akavi commanded, grabbing Luellae's hand. "Quickly."

"Akavi Averis," said the angel, oddly emotionless. As if reading it off the readouts in her head. "You are the only Vaurian wanted by the authorities in this region, so you have been identified by assumption. You are wanted for continued and egregious failure in a mission of critical importance to Nemesis, and for desertion–"

But Luellae had already started to do something. The world twisted around them, turning inky black.

They emerged in a desert. Just rocks and half-hearted shrubs in every direction, twisted in their typical Outside ways. There were wells that went down at improbably twisted angles into the ground, and stacks of stones that looked as though the laws of physics shouldn't have let them hold themselves up. Akavi wasn't sure where they were geographically, what direction the *Talon* might lie in, or how many hundreds of miles away.

Luellae snatched her hand away from Akavi's as soon as they emerged.

"Fuck you," she said, her already pale skin paling. Mortals had slower reaction times than angels. She'd initiated travel before fully processing what the angel had said, it seemed, but she'd heard it well enough. "You asshole. *Fuck* you."

Akavi narrowed her eyes, giving Luellae an assessing

look. Her head was still swimming, but she could think well enough to analyze her current plans. This was not the first time that Akavi's cover had been blown during a mission. Luellae knew who Akavi was now; that meant she would not trust Akavi anymore, and would potentially go back to her team to reveal compromising information about Akavi's plans. That was undesirable. Under many circumstances, Akavi's next logical move would be to kill her.

But that would not help Akavi now. After all, she'd just decided that she needed to *reverse* all her plans. If Luellae turned against her *now*, at this precise second, then actually that might be the most efficient way to reach Akavi's new goal.

If Luellae made it back to the Seven alive, then out of sheer spite she would reverse her earlier positions and begin to urge caution. Without her influence to stir things up, the rest of the Seven would become more cautious and pacified, more like what Tiv had always wanted them to be. Yasira would be preserved. And Akavi would be able to infiltrate their group again, later, when the dust settled, for an even better revenge than before.

Though first she had to get out of this desert. And find some first aid. Her internal readouts weren't alerting her to anything worse than twisted ligaments, lacerations and bruises – but the pain was annoying.

"I can explain," said Akavi, easily masking her feelings with a set of expressions more appropriate to the situation. She had to appear chagrined by all this, to pretend she still believed in her old plan, or it wouldn't work. "Please, Luellae, listen. If anything I've ever said has meant anything to you–"

"Fuck you," Luellae said again, unimaginatively. "You tricked me. You *lied*."

"You can hate me, but you know what I've said is true. The Seven need you. They need insight like yours. They need real leadership, not this dithering. You *know* it, Luellae. I've only tried to make it clear–"

Luellae backed away, empty revulsion on her face.

Akavi let her expression transform from appeal to contempt. "Or do you want the rest of your team to know how you really behaved while you were with me?"

"What do you want?" Luellae snarled.

Akavi held out a hand. "Take me back to the wooded area where we first met. That's all. Do that for me, and I won't trouble you again. You're not sufficiently rational to listen to me anyway. Fail me, and as soon as I make it back to civilization I'll ensure your time pretending to get along with your little team is over. Am I being understood?"

Luellae hesitated, and Akavi waited it out imperiously, showing no fear. If Luellae left her here, she'd have to find another way out of the desert very quickly. Angel bodies were in many ways more durable than those of mortals, but Akavi could die of exposure or thirst out here as easily as anyone else.

But those old reflexes Luellae learned in captivity were still with her. She knew, at a level deeper than mere logic, that Akavi must be obeyed. She knew it was wrong, but she reluctantly, distastefully took Akavi's hand.

The world twisted into blackness and there was a sense of motion. They both landed stumbling, careening to a halt, in the woods not far from where Elu had parked the *Talon*. Luellae snatched her hand away from Akavi's as soon as she could, as if the Vaurian's skin burned her.

"You'd better mean it," she said venomously. "About not troubling me again. You'd better."

Akavi looked at her coldly. She could come to Luellae again in another disguise. She could do it undisguised, pull her this way and that with further threats and coercions, if she chose. There wasn't much Luellae could do about that. They both knew it.

Luellae said nothing else. She turned, and then she was gone, in one of the blurs of motion she was named for, leaving Akavi to make her way back to the *Talon* alone.

CHAPTER 12
Now

Yasira and Tiv ran as fast as they could. It was all Tiv could do to keep up, her hand in Yasira's, stumbling along as Yasira raced forward in a rage. The earth moved before them. The street split open. Obstacles as large as buildings tilted to one side, space itself warping to let them through.

Tiv didn't even know if they were being chased or not. There wasn't any room in her head for that, only terror and amazement and the burning need to *run.*

Finally, Yasira reached the door she'd left the lair by, a nondescript shop entrance. She threw it open and rushed in, dragging Tiv after her. Tiv had a brief glimpse of alarmed shop patrons diving for cover and then they were falling into the airlock as the door shut.

They both sank to the floor, too overwhelmed to go further. Tiv felt her hands shaking. Yasira pulled her knees to her chest, tucking her head down, trembling as violently as a girl with a fever. She let out a strange, broken sound as if she wanted to burst into tears, but her eyes looked dry.

Tiv tried to catch her breath. She had not expected this when she saw the angel. She'd thought it would be like what happened with Akiujal. Either both of them were about to die, or dozens of gone people were about to meet bloody, pointless deaths in their stead. She had frozen in terror. But Yasira…

Tiv had seen the rest of the Seven at work, all of them with powers more impressive than those of the general population. She had *never* seen anything like what Yasira had just done. This was a literally earthshaking power, one that had upended the entire landscape just to get them away. And there had been precision in it. She'd seen people running, screaming, and she'd seen the angel pulled away by twisting, grasping bark-lined tendrils. She couldn't be sure, given how fast they'd gone, how blank her own mind had been in its panic. But apart from the angel herself, she hadn't seen a single person injured.

Even by the Chaos Zone's standards, this had been dramatic. Angels would try to suppress the story, but Tiv didn't think they could do it, not all the way. People, awestruck and confused, would talk.

People would say, *Savior has returned.*

Tiv looked at Yasira, huddled pitifully on the floor of the airlock, shivering so hard she might hurt herself.

"It's okay," she said. She wanted so badly to reach out and touch Yasira, but she knew that in a state like this it would only panic her more. "It's okay, Yasira, we're safe now. You did it."

Yasira's voice was as shaky as the rest of her. "Did what?"

Tiv frowned. Maybe Yasira's mind had gone even further afield than she thought. "Do you remember?"

"Yeah, I remember." Yasira squirmed. "I was talking to the gone people. An angel came. So we ran away. And… I don't know what I did. I just *pushed*."

"Well, whatever you did, it worked. I've never seen anything like that. You saved us."

Yasira curled her knees to her chest more tightly. "Did I hurt anyone?"

"I don't know. It didn't look like you did, but it was hard to see. We could ask Splió."

"I don't know what I'm doing," Yasira said miserably.

"Hey, none of us do. It's okay. You did good enough."

This didn't seem to reassure Yasira. She looked up again, her eyes wild and frightened. "The Seven at least know what their powers are for. I don't know that. I have this power in me, and it – comes out. It changes things. But I don't know what I'm supposed to be changing. I don't know if the changes are good or bad."

Tiv knew about the episodes Yasira had sometimes, where the power built up in her and needed to be discharged back into the Chaos Zone. The usual effects were harmless enough: things grew, things took new forms. As far as she could tell, the thing Yasira had just done was similar to that. She'd pushed out energy and the energy had changed things, made them burst their old seams. Except this time the energy had been directed, just a little. This time, things had changed their form in just the way Yasira needed.

"Is there a 'supposed to'?" Tiv asked. "It seems to me we're all on our own. Deciding for ourselves." That was both the freedom and the terror of it. Tiv didn't have powers of her own, but she knew the weird uncertainty of not having a God to tell her how to behave. The terror of knowing, not only that she might choose wrong, but that maybe no possible choice was enough.

"You don't know anything," Yasira snapped, shifting moods mercurially as she so often did these days. "You don't even know what I am. I told you that in the park and you've already forgotten. I'm not even *human* anymore."

Tiv frowned. She had not forgotten; she'd just gotten distracted, what with having to run for their lives. Tiv had

apologized to Yasira for hiding things from her, and Yasira
had retorted that she'd hidden things, too. Tiv wanted to
know what those things were. But she couldn't imagine why
Yasira might think she wasn't human. "What do you mean?"

Yasira looked away. Her fingers tapped at each other, a
nervous tic. "I never told you. When I did my miracle six
months ago, when I called on Outside and changed the
Chaos Zone, instead of destroying it, it broke me."

Tiv paused. There was something about this that didn't
add up. *Everybody* on their team was broken – if "broken"
meant traumatized and in poor mental health. Yasira had a
worse case than most, but everybody had it. And everybody
with powers was struggling with what those powers meant.
Could that be all? Maybe Yasira was just taking those two
facts a little harder than everyone else.

"Yeah, I know," she said. "Everybody here's a bit broken.
Everybody's traumatized. It's okay. I sort of noticed."

Yasira wasn't looking Tiv in the face – she usually didn't,
at times of high emotion – but her eyes were wild and
urgent. "I don't mean it gave me trauma. I mean it literally
broke me. Into pieces. There is more than one person in
my head now. More than one piece of who I was. I don't
even know how many. That's why I can't get out of bed in
the mornings. It's not just that I'm sad; it's that we're all
arguing. We can't even agree on what to do. You think you
love me, but there's no *me* anymore. Just a bunch of pieces
floating around. And between the pieces, there's Outside.
That's how I can do things like what I just did. It comes
up whether I like it or not. Through the gaps between the
pieces. It's part of me *because* I'm broken." She huddled in a
little closer to herself. "Even Ev wasn't broken like this. You
can't understand."

Tiv's eyes had gone wide. But she thought that she did understand, a little.

Riayin prided itself on being the best in the galaxy at dealing with neurodiversity. Tiv's home country, Arinn, wasn't quite that advanced. But Arinn and Riayin neighbored each other, and some of Riayin's accepting attitudes had rubbed off. Tiv at least knew the names of most of the common forms of neurodivergence and some basic information about what a person with each one might experience, what they might struggle with, what they might need.

So Tiv knew what it meant to be plural – to have more than one subjective consciousness co-existing in the same mind. She wouldn't have guessed it was happening with Yasira, but she could follow the description. The part Outside played was another matter, but it wasn't necessarily weirder than how Outside interfaced with single people's brains. Tiv wasn't repelled, not by the actual content of what Yasira had said. But how could Yasira have hidden all this, something so fundamental to how she experienced the world, for half a year? Why had she thought she needed to do that – she could have told Tiv any time. Why hadn't she realized?

She wanted to say *thank you for telling me* – that was the polite thing to say when someone disclosed something personal and upsetting. But Yasira had been beating herself up for not telling Tiv earlier, and she'd take it the wrong way. She'd think Tiv was being sarcastic.

"That doesn't make you not human," Tiv said instead, raising her chin mulishly.

"Yeah? Every part of me that isn't a bickering little fragment is made of Outside now. What do you think it makes me?"

"I don't know. Mentally ill and Outside-y, like all of us."

Tiv leaned back a little against the unforgiving metal wall of the airlock. "I like every part of you that I've seen. Before the Plague or after. Even when you're laying in bed too sulky to do anything, I still care about you. Are there parts of you that don't like me?"

Yasira looked taken aback, as if she hadn't expected that question. Her eyes fluttered, unfocused for a moment, and Tiv had an odd feeling that Yasira was hurriedly taking a survey of everyone inside her.

What would they do if the answer was "yes"? Tiv hadn't read up enough about plurality to know what people were supposed to do in situations like that. Would they have to break up? Would she need to awkwardly date some parts of Yasira while other parts sulked and stayed out of her way? Tiv didn't like either of those options, not even a little bit.

She wondered what it was like when Yasira had to check with all her selves like this. She had a foolish mental image of a conference room, a dozen Yasiras sitting in swivel chairs around a long table. It probably wasn't like that.

"No," Yasira said at last, opening her eyes. "No, I don't think so. Not the way you mean. There are some parts of me who don't really care about anybody – they're too fixed on their work, or on how they're hurting, or on Outside. Not everybody here is big enough to be a full person. But everybody in here who can love, loves you." She made an abortive motion, as if she wanted to take Tiv's hand, then changed her mind. Or did that mean one of her wanted to hold hands and another didn't? This was going to take a lot of getting used to. "Is that enough?"

"Yes," said Tiv, nodding firmly. She didn't reach to take Yasira's hand. How did consent work when there was more than one person in there to give or revoke it? No wonder touching Yasira had been a minefield lately. "We'll figure this out, Yasira. Don't worry. We're still—"

At that moment the airlock's outer door opened and Luellae stumbled in.

A densely forested area was briefly visible behind her before the door shut. She almost tripped over the two of them. People didn't usually sit in the airlock like this. Luellae was panting as if she'd been running or terrified or both, and her pale eyes were wild. Not just fear, Tiv realized, but rage. Luellae had a temper at the best of times, but this was more. Something had happened.

"Hey, are you okay?" said Tiv, moving to get up.

Luellae spent half a second catching her breath, staring at the two of them.

"We need," she said in a strained voice, "to talk."

"You're sure?" Tiv asked, appalled. "You're sure it was Akavi?"

They had brought Luellae into the war room, asked if she needed anything to calm down, water maybe, but she'd refused it all. She'd insisted that everyone in the lair – which was most of the team, at the moment – gather around immediately. They needed to hear what she had to say.

"She didn't even try to hide it," said Luellae. "She talked about things only Akavi could have known. I'm sure."

"I killed him," said Yasira. She looked a thousand miles away, staring at nothing. She was shaking. "I *shot* him."

Most of the team looked nearly as shocked, in their own ways. Daeis had scrunched in on themself, holding a pink, striped, rabbit-sized creature tightly. Splió and Prophet had both retreated to their usual habits of staring into space –

Prophet distractedly, watching some sensory display of the future that the rest of them couldn't understand; Splió merely morose. Weaver, at the foot of the table, was picking at herself so furiously that Picket, himself pale and flop-sweating, had to practically sit on her before she injured something. Grid, one of the calmest in the room, was grimly focused on writing down every detail of what Luellae had said.

Weaver perked up a bit. Her thin fingers, laced through Picket's, were still constantly moving. "People can survive gunshot wounds. It just depends on where the bullet goes in and how fast they get help. Where'd you shoot him?"

Grid shot Weaver a warning look, but Yasira answered, looking more dazed and hopeless than ever. "In the stomach."

"Yeah, see, that's a nasty one, but with the right kind of medical attention fast enough you can pull through. Sounds like he found help."

Yasira rounded on her, blazing with sudden anger. "He *couldn't* have. He was immobilized. He was alone. Ev did something to the *Talon* so it was undetectable by angel technology and she set it to fly away at warp speed in a random direction. He was lying on the floor unconscious when I left. He couldn't—" She bit her tongue and broke off, looking away.

"It was him," Luellae said with finality.

The room descended into an uneasy silence, marked only by the creak of Weaver's chair as she rocked back and forth, and the emphatic scrape of Grid's pencil on paper as they underlined something. Yasira's shoulders shook. She was crying, and doing a poor job of trying not to let the rest of the team see.

Tiv would have reached out and touched her, but that wasn't helpful when Yasira was this upset. She'd flinch away; they'd both end up feeling even worse. Tiv might have led Yasira out of the war room and found her a safer place to let it out, to talk if she wanted to or just cry. Except Yasira wasn't the only one hurting. All of these people had once been Akavi's prisoners. They'd been isolated, tortured, forced to do his bidding. Even Tiv had been his prisoner once, but her experience had been short and easy compared to the rest. For all of them, Akavi's return was a nightmare come true.

And Tiv was their Leader. It was up to Tiv to handle this for all of them.

"So," she said, "what does that mean? What are we going to do?"

Grid looked up. "We need to tighten our security protocols. I thought I would have noticed if something like this happened."

Grid *had* detected it, in the early days, when Vaurian angels tried to befriend the Seven and gain access to the lair. Most of them had posed as survivors like Yonne Qun, and the Seven usually all rotated between cities, all of them scoping out each potential ally in turn. Grid had rooted out several agents as soon as they saw them. Grid could see the ansible network, and that meant angels, connected to that network through the uplinks in their heads, looked different. And they'd all agreed that no one but the Seven was allowed into the lair without Grid present to vet them as they entered. A Vaurian could disguise themselves as one of the Seven, but a Vaurian who hadn't left the lair through the airlock wouldn't be able to use that method to come back in.

But Akavi had been cleverer than the agents they'd discovered. Akavi hadn't tried to go in. Akavi had worked with Luellae and only Luellae. She'd found some way of convincing Luellae not to tell the rest of the Seven about her presence. Tiv supposed Akavi must have gotten good at telling Luellae what she wanted to hear.

"You're all missing the point," said Luellae. "It's not just that Akavi's alive and trying to track us down. It's that he's trying to influence us. I fell for it. All this time, when I said we needed to be more aggressive, actually fight instead of being a delivery service, I meant it. I always thought that. But Akavi – this person who I trusted, who I didn't *know* was Akavi – was encouraging me the whole time. Telling me I was right. Telling me you were all fools if you didn't listen. You *know* what that means, don't you? You know what that means he wants."

Picket turned to her. "He wants to stop us, obviously. What else would he want?"

"World domination?" Weaver suggested, unhelpfully.

"No," said Prophet, still staring at nothing.

Everybody, even Daeis, turned to look at Prophet. She curled one of her small braids around her hand, pulling and fidgeting at it. She was very far into the trancelike state she got when she was seeing a lot of things at once. Too much data, not enough context or pattern to make sense of it.

"I don't know what he wants," said Prophet. "But it's not just about stopping us. There are so many things he wants. They jumble together, and sometimes they're in one order, sometimes another." She covered her face, pressing her hands to her forehead as if it hurt. Maybe it did. "He wants to stop us, but that's not all, and not right away. He wants to stop us and help us. He wants to stop *Yasira* and help *her* – I can't tell." Her hands dropped away and she shook her head violently. "I'm not even seeing what he wants. Just glimpses of things he'll do, or did, or might do, and none of it makes any sense. I'm sorry."

"We don't need prophecies to make sense of this," Luellae insisted. "It's obvious. Akavi is a piece of shit who manipulates everyone, and he wants us to go to war. To start a revolution – that's what she was always talking about when I was with her. And if Akavi wants us to do that, it must be because Akavi gets some advantage from it. Maybe it would make us off-balance, easier to control. Easier to hurt. I…" Her face twisted. She looked like she might cry, but Luellae was too bullish to let herself do so in front of everyone. "I believed going to war was the right thing to do. I still want it to be the right thing. But if Akavi wants it, then it can't be. He hates us all. He must want us to destroy ourselves."

"Must he?" said Splió, looking up from his morose reverie. "Seems to me Akavi's the type who plays a bunch of head games at once. You heard what Prophet said. We can't assume the stuff he said to you is his only–"

"I know what I heard," Luellae snapped.

Grid held up a hand. "Not to change the subject, but before we make any big decisions, I want to know what happened with the gone people."

Everyone looked between Yasira, who was still crying, and Tiv. Tiv opened her mouth, preparing to take responsibility. "We went out and talked to a group of gone people, but we were interrupted. I'm not sure–"

Yasira brushed her sleeve furiously across her eyes and sat up straighter. Something blazed in her expression. "*I'm* sure."

There was a general, collective raising of eyebrows.

"The gone people don't care about this war," said Yasira. "They aren't planning a fight. They're planning a second miracle."

She let that hang in the air for a moment.

"I've seen that," Prophet whispered, moved or disturbed. "But I didn't think it would be so *soon*."

"Putting the Chaos Zone back in order, you mean?" said Picket.

"No," said Yasira. "Don't you see? There's no order. Order is a lie." Grid, who liked to work very hard to keep their team in order, frowned, but Yasira barrelled on. "Order's what the angels wanted, having us all under their control, but there were always things out of place, even before the Plague. Break those things up and they'll turn into crumbs, more and smaller. Angels can't have order and we can't either. But we can have a better chaos." She wiped her eyes again, but her voice was low and urgent and clear. "That's what I did. They can't do something as *big* as what I did. It's more about growing better food, better shelter, more of what everyone needs to survive. But it's bigger than what anyone else down here can do alone. And it sends a message that things can change. Fighting a losing battle isn't change. This is."

The team stirred, absorbing this. Grid made several frantic notes.

Prophet opened her eyes, and for a moment it seemed like she and Yasira were having a conversation all their own, like they were examining a map together that no one else could see. "There will still be a battle."

"I know."

"The angels will try to stop them."

Gone people were inherently heretical. The angels mostly

left them alone; there were too many to easily exterminate, and they likely wouldn't understand anything that the angels tried to do to them as a deterrent. But a big gathering of gone people like Yasira had described, doing something magical and obviously purposeful, that was another thing. Angels would flock to a gathering like that for sure.

Picket tilted his head, troubled. "Okay, but what does this mean for us? The gone people are doing something. The other survivors are doing something. We signed up for this so that we could make a difference in the Chaos Zone. We're not going to sit at the sidelines and let them do it all themselves, are we? That's not what you're saying."

"Better that than playing right into Akavi's hands," Luellae growled.

"No." Yasira straightened up. It had been so long since Tiv saw determination like this on Yasira's face. Maybe it was only one of the parts of her, but it still made her glow. "The gone people barely understand that there's a risk. They're doing the right thing, but they have no idea what they're up against. I'm going to be there. I'm going to protect them."

Splió drew back. "Do you think that's a good idea? The angels will have guns. They'll have–"

"I know what I'm capable of," Yasira snapped.

This was not at all what she had just said in the elevator a moment ago. Tiv frowned, disturbed. But she did know Yasira was capable of miracles – she only hadn't thought Yasira was so confident. Maybe some parts of her were confident, and some weren't. She broke in firmly before the argument could escalate. "I didn't have time to report it before Luellae came in, but while Yasira and I were out, there was an altercation between us and an armed angel. You didn't see what Yasira did. She uprooted half the park. We got away without a scratch on us. If she thinks she can do this, she can do it."

"Which doesn't change the fact that it's what Akavi *wants*–" Luellae argued.

"Is it?" Grid shot back. They stood up, capping the pen they'd been frantically writing with, apparently sick of this. "All we have about that is your word. And you're the one who broke security protocols to talk to this person who turned out to be Akavi. How do we know this isn't *you* betraying *us*–"

Luellae leapt to her feet, preparing to shout back.

Tiv banged her gavel.

"No one," Tiv said into the sudden silence, "is going to accuse anyone else on the team of betraying us. Without a *very* good reason."

Luellae and Grid – and most of the rest of the Seven, for that matter – looked at her resentfully.

Tiv took a deep breath. She felt shaky inside, but she didn't want to let on. She was called Leader here. People would look to her to keep them all on track. "Here's what we know. We know the gone people are planning something. We know Akavi is alive, and he's trying to mess with us. We know Akavi is the type who messes with people's heads." She pointed the gavel at Grid. "And who tries to turn them against each other. To make them doubt themselves. We're not going to do that here. We're going to do what *we* think is right." She lowered the gavel, willing her hand not to shake. She hoped she was guiding the team in the right direction. She hoped any of what she'd said even made sense. "So, let's stick to finding out what that is."

Luellae and Grid looked back and forth, first at her, then at each other. Grid was the first to break eye contact, settling back down and starting to flip through one of the war room's piles of notes. "If we do want to help the gone people, we can make this into an organized effort. Akavi won't expect us to do that, since he didn't know it was one of our options. We can let the survivors know what we're doing. With any luck, we can find some way for them and the gone people to work together. Coordinate *that*, instead of just ferrying supplies."

"We can heal them," Weaver suggested. "You can move them around, Blur. We can use our powers to help."

"The angels are finite in number," said Prophet dreamily, staring into space. "Large, but finite. They can't be everywhere at once. If there was a coordinated set of actions over a large enough area–"

"We can't," said Luellae. "Don't you get it? If we fight, if we do anything even a little bit like fighting, we're playing into Akavi's hands–"

"I don't care," said Yasira. She stood up from her chair. "I'm done lying around in my bedroom, doing nothing about the problem I helped start. I can't force any of you to work with me. But I'm doing this. And none of you can stop me."

Luellae drew back. Many of the other team members, even the ones who'd been on board, raised their eyebrows.

Yasira stalked past them – towards her room, Tiv noted, despite what she'd said – and did not look back.

"Yasira–" Tiv started, reaching for her, but Yasira wasn't listening anymore, even to her.

"Guess we're not a team, after all," Luellae muttered under her breath. "*Savior.*"

After the meeting broke up, Tiv got up to check on Luellae. There were a lot of people on the team right now who needed a check-in, but probably Luellae most of all. Tiv couldn't imagine what she'd been through, being held captive by Akavi for so long, only to find out he was still influencing her even after she was freed.

Tiv wasn't even sure Luellae was wrong about this. Maybe they *were* playing into Akavi's hands. But Akavi was tricky; he was the kind of person who could want a lot of things at once – the kind who could take advantage of a situation's outcome no matter what it was. It was good to think about what Akavi might do, but Tiv didn't want the team to let that paralyze them. Not when Yasira, in particular, had finally found the wherewithal to *do* something.

She found Luellae sitting in one of the lair's less-traveled spots, a nook next to the broken-down remains of the prayer machine. Luellae had curled in on herself on the floor between the machine and the wall, and her shoulders were shaking. Tiv took a step back. Luellae didn't like people seeing her cry, and Tiv didn't want to intrude on her like this.

But as Tiv backed away, she saw the Four approaching from the opposite direction.

"Blur," said Prophet, who was walking ahead of the rest for once. She carefully knelt across from Luellae, and Luellae looked up at her, furious and embarrassed. "I'm sorry."

Luellae wiped angrily at her eyes. "For what?"

"All you wanted was to be taken seriously," said Prophet.

Prophet spoke strangely like this sometimes, assuming a shared context that wasn't actually apparent to anyone who didn't see the world seconds or hours or days in advance.

"That's not it at all," said Luellae. "Forget it."

"We're not going to forget it," said Grid. Their face was sterner than Prophet's, and their arms were crossed. "There were holes in your story back there. We had a protocol, you know? That any mortal down there who gets close to us has to be vetted by the group. We *knew* there were Vaurians out there. Why didn't you tell us about this sooner, Blur?"

Luellae buried her face in her hands. "I don't know."

Picket stepped forward, leaning against the wall next to Prophet. "He's a manipulator," he said matter-of-factly – it seemed to be directed both at Luellae and the rest of the Four. "He's good at what he does. You might not even have noticed what he was doing. But if you can figure it out–"

"*I'm* a manipulator," Luellae snapped. She looked up at the four of them, red-eyed, defiant. "You don't understand."

Grid was not mollified. "Help us, Blur. Help us understand."

"I'm not like you."

"Not like what?" said Weaver, who'd been hanging back nervously behind the rest of the group, scratching at herself. "Not a prisoner? You were totally a prisoner."

"I wasn't a prisoner because of Outside." Luellae bared her teeth, and it all began tumbling out of her. "I never studied that part of Talirr's work. I studied normal physics. Non-heretical physics. But I was also studying *you*. That's what Akavi wanted me for." She took a ragged breath, then pointed at them, one at a time. "Grid, you can't stand it if things are out of order. Picket, you use games and math as a coping mechanism; you'll wither away if you don't get them. Prophet, you manage people's emotions because you don't want to think about your own. Weaver, you'll self-harm at the drop of a penny, and you don't try to stop yourself because you know the other three will fix it for you. Akavi didn't know you when he kidnapped you, but I did. He kept *me* a prisoner so I could tell him all about you. And the others too, Splió and Daeis and Yasira fucking Shien. So I could tell him your weak spots. So he could torture you better."

She clearly expected them to flinch away, but they didn't. Tiv did a little though, outside Luellae's sight. Was that why

Luellae had always been so standoffish, so reluctant to trust the rest of the team? Because she knew she'd helped make the rest of them suffer?

Prophet reached out and cupped Luellae's face gently in her hand. "And he knew your weak spots, too. That's how he got to you."

Luellae jerked back. "Don't play like that with me. Don't pretend I'm the *victim*–"

"Aren't you?" Picket countered. "He kidnapped us all. He hurt us all. You just got a different flavor."

"Kick me off the team," Luellae demanded. "You don't listen to me anyway. Just let me go."

"Do I get a say in this?" Tiv asked, abruptly.

Luellae whirled around to face her, going paler than ever.

"No," she snapped. "You're not a real leader and you never listened to me. And you're not one of the people I hurt. You don't get to forgive me."

But this was so much like one of Yasira's meltdowns, so much like the way Yasira liked to verbally beat herself up. Even though the cause was different, Tiv recognized it.

"You don't have to stay," Tiv said softly. "That's never what I wanted. We've all been kept prisoner – I don't want to do that to anyone else. If you want to leave, go somewhere else; we'll support you. We'll help you find a good place. If you want to sit out this mission and decide the rest later, I get that, too. But if you want to join, then of course you can join. I've been trying my best to keep everyone working together, but I never wanted to force anyone. I never wanted to be that kind of leader."

"I don't know what I want to do," Luellae howled, burying her face in her hands again. "He'll get us if we fight and he'll get us if we don't. None of it's going to help. None of it. Ever!"

But when Prophet reached out gently to hug her, she hugged back, as violently as a snake crushing its prey. The rest of the Four joined in, and after a moment so did Tiv, all of them taking her in their arms, holding each other as best they could.

People of the Chaos Zone,

This letter is from your Savior.

I want you to know that the name you have given me is a lie. If I could, I would reach out my hand and press the universe's levers to save every one of you. That is not in anyone's power, even mine. The universe, Chaos or not, doesn't work that way.

But I can help you save yourselves.

There are so many of you with the power to change things. The gone people, the ones that you least understand, have that power even more. In a week's time, they will gather together and make a change. This change will not save you. But it will make the monsters a little smaller, the ground more full of fruit. It will give you just a little more room to breathe.

The angels are going to try to stop them.

There will be a fight. But, though the angels try to convince you otherwise, there are a finite number of them. Even they can't be everywhere in the Chaos Zone at once.

You want me to fight for you, to lead you into deadly battle against the angels for a food printer or for the return of a prisoner or for freedom. It is not possible for me to do this, not for all of you, not for an objective that would be worth the cost. But there is another way.

When the angels try to stop the gone people, I will be there, joining that fight. It will be a fight that takes place in many locations at once. It will be a fight that is only possible with the gone people's abilities and mine combined. And it will engage the angels, not all the angels, but many.

There will be that many fewer angels across the rest of the planet, guarding what they usually guard, enforcing what they always enforce.

If you have ever wanted to rise up, in large ways or small – to seize the necessities that the angels withhold, to protest openly, to make a break for the border, to rescue someone – do it in one week's time. The Seven will work with you as they always do and will supply you as well as they can. Make no mistake: it will still be an immense risk, a deadly risk. But the angels will be spread as thinly as they ever are. If you ever wanted to take the risk, this is the time.

Change will come, again and again, in ways that some of us can instigate but none can control. The angels want to control it by killing us. The secret they pretend not to know – the secret that Destroyer always knew – is that even killing all of us wouldn't give them back control. The secret is that the angels have already lost this war; they will never have control again.

In a week's time, let's show them the secret is True.

CHAPTER 13
Now

As Enga Afonbataw Konum, Marshal of Nemesis, did her daily exercises, something in her internal circuitry chimed.

She hopped up from the training floor where she'd been doing variations on pushups with her elaborately modified mechanical arms, flipping dexterously from one position to another. It was a dim room, because Enga's sensory preferences ran that way, with lines drawn across the floor to facilitate different exercises, and equipment stored at the sides. She was alone in it, which was a blessed relief. Enga had gotten no better, over these past six months, at training and leading other recruits. Maybe it was Irimiru's way of punishing her for some unknown crime. Deliberately placing Enga in a job she wasn't suited for, so as to have a sensible-looking reason to do something worse to her later. Overseers of Nemesis were famous for tricks like that.

Y, she text-sent in the direction of Irimiru, who had initiated the call.

Enga, sent Irimiru curtly. Somehow Irimiru was able to make even a text-sending feel curt. *As you requested, I am informing you that one of our agents has sighted a Vaurian who she believes to be Akavi Averis.*

Enga lurched up to full alertness. *WHERE, SIR?*

In a park near Hunne. Do not move to intercept him yet. The agent who identified him claims he used some Outside ability to teleport away. We have dispatched scouts and surveillance specialists to the area and are further analyzing the agent's sensory recordings, but there is a seventy percent likelihood he is no longer there. You will be kept updated. Do nothing, but consider yourself on alert.

YES SIR, said Enga. She wanted more information, but the connection closed.

How could Akavi have gained some Outside ability? That made no sense. Only certain kinds of mortal heretic could do that. Angels like Akavi had filters built into their brains to stop them from perceiving Outside at all.

Maybe he'd modified himself, in his exile, more thoroughly than anyone suspected. But Akavi was disgusted by Outside and its heresies. To imagine him willingly welcoming it into his mind – that beggared belief.

Maybe the angel who'd spotted him was confused. Or full of shit. Maybe she hadn't even really spotted him at all.

Enga scowled, and then threw herself into her calisthenics routine in an even greater fury than before.

Forty-Nine Years Ago

Long before the idea of becoming an angel had ever entered Enga's head, she'd been a fitness instructor in a country called Kutaga, specializing in martial arts. She'd been non-neurotypical, but not very visibly. She could speak in words and smile at people when her profession required it. She'd been excellent at her job and very disciplined with its rules – the proper physical forms, the safety regulations, the rankings and tests that each student passed as they grew in skill – and despite her quirks she'd attracted a few friends and admirers. There had been one friend in particular. One man, about her age, also a martial artist, who'd arrived in town and become fascinated with her. He'd whispered flattering words into her naive little ears.

He'd introduced himself as Omhon Pejaydonay Uwkhew, a trainer from the nearby city of Yuyphunsiy. She'd thought at first that he wanted to date her, and she wasn't interested that way. But he'd cleared up that misunderstanding with great ease and speed; he knew how to be direct in a way that made her feel comfortable, which was rare. He'd won her over. He wasn't after a girlfriend. He was intrigued by her in another way.

"You're wasted on fitness training," he'd said, over drinks. "Look at your discipline, your precision. The way you endure, even when your brain overwhelms you. That's rare. You could be much more."

"I like fitness training," she'd said, uncertain.

He'd smiled winningly. "Just think about it."

Omhon had let the matter drop entirely for months. He'd trained alongside her. He was *good* at martial arts. And that was weird, since he'd called it unworthy. But Enga was a little lonely despite her successes. She wasn't good with people. Omhon made her feel like she was good, at least, with *him*.

They'd developed a real trust. She'd opened up to him about things that she normally didn't like to talk about. Her loneliness. Her fears. Her difficulty trusting people, or really even understanding them. Not a lot of people in Kutaga were open about being non-neurotypical. The ones that did talk about it tended to be interested in science, or in activism, reforming Kutaga's disability assistance policies to better resemble more liberal countries like Riayin. Enga wasn't interested in any of those things. She just wanted to fight, and that meant a lot of neurotypicals, and a lot of time being alone, recovering.

"You're so good at this," said Omhon – just once, months after he'd first mentioned it. It wasn't pressure, surely, if he mentioned it so rarely. "I see why you love it. But there's something exceptional about you, something the fitness industry can't fully hold. Your intelligence, your discipline, your strength – those are something truly special. Bigger entities might want them. The Gods might. You could use those strengths in a way that means something."

"Teaching people to defend themselves means something," Enga replied, unnerved.

Omhon chuckled self-deprecatingly. "It does. I'm sorry, you're right; personal development is meaningful, too. I just gush sometimes."

"It's okay," Enga said. She wasn't sure if it was, but that was the standard response neurotypicals expected, so she said it. And Omhon went back to being a pleasant friend who didn't speak of such things.

For a week.

At the end of that time, the trouble started. It seemed to have little to do with Omhon at first. Only the local police, coming by for a random financial audit. She let them in, fearful as anyone would be when auditors came knocking, but she knew that everything would be in order for them. Enga followed the rules.

"What's this?" said the head auditor, holding up a file Enga had never seen.

"I don't know," said Enga.

"You don't *know?*" the head auditor said incredulously.

"What am I supposed to know?"

"Don't play mind games with me, Miss Konum. This was in your own cabinet, locked with your own key."

It was exactly as nauseating and surreal as a nightmare. She watched as document after incriminating document came out of her own filing cabinets, places to which only she had access. Clear evidence of embezzlement, and worse. Money that had gone into crime, into arms deals, into the pockets of child traffickers and other groups so vile Enga barely understood them.

"This is ridiculous," she protested. "I would never do any of that. Someone's framing me."

"Anyone you know who'd have a motive to do that, Miss Konum?"

She blinked, bewildered. "No."

"Well, it may be a frame. But we've been looking for the source of some of these financial crimes for a long time. You'll get a fair trial, but at the moment I'm going to need to take you in to give a statement." The head auditor fished out a pair of handcuffs. "Please don't resist."

Enga didn't.

Jail was a sensory hell she could barely make sense of. There were noises, clanging and shouting and wailing that wouldn't ever stop. Everything was hard and cold, too bright or too dark, and everyone was angry for reasons she barely understood. Enga spent most of it crying. So much for the physical and mental disciplines that Omhon thought she had. In a real emergency, Enga folded.

But it was Omhon who bailed her out the next morning, and who helped her into a car and a quiet room, all apologetic concern. He gave her a drink of water. He let her phone her friends.

Her friends mostly did not pick up the phone.

One did, in such a torrent of tears that Enga could scarcely understand what she was saying.

"I don't understand," said the woman on the phone, who had taught kickboxing with Enga for years. "I thought I knew you. I knew you were *weird*, but I never thought *this*. How could you do this? How could you say the things you said–"

"Said?" Enga replied, more afraid than ever. She couldn't remember saying anything bad to this woman. She understood framing people for crimes, even if she didn't understand why anyone would do it to her. But faking communications – how was that even possible? "Rinba, what did I say?"

"Fuck you for pretending not to know," said Rinba, and hung up.

The few other friends who bothered returning her calls were similar. By the end of it, Enga was in a worse state than she'd been in while jailed. She had begun to cry uncontrollably in front of Omhon, melting down. She slumped onto his table and started to hit her head against it, rhythmically. She did not understand any of this, and now she was humiliating herself over it, and that made it even worse.

"It's all right," said Omhon, his hand warm on her shoulder, as she wailed and hurt herself. "Enga. It's all right. There's a way out of this."

That didn't help much, so he stayed, undemanding, unjudgmental. How could he not judge her when everyone else did? She did not understand it. He stayed until the worst of the meltdown had played itself out, until the violent mental pain had receded to a dull ache, and she sat with her arms folded on the table, resting her sore head on them, no longer crying. Only blank and heavy and miserable.

"What way?" she said when she could speak. "What *fucking way*?"

"I don't know who's framing you, or what their motive could be," said Omhon. His voice was very calm, very rational. "But I've seen things like this happen before. If you go back, tell them everything you know, get a fair trial – well, you *could* make it out. But a person clever enough to do this to you in the first place isn't likely to let themselves be caught. Even if you're acquitted of most of it, you'll still have a record. More often than not, these things don't end well. Not for mortals."

Enga looked up numbly, opening her eyes. "Not for mortals. You're a recruiter."

He had told her before that she was meant for more than teaching fitness. That the Gods could use talents like hers. Omhon didn't look like an angel, but some Gods employed hundreds of Vaurian angels, who could shift their shape and cover the telltale forehead plates with mortal-looking skin.

She was meant for *less* than fitness instruction now, she thought bitterly. Training gyms like hers required background checks; her job meant dealing with people in vulnerable positions, letting her touch their bodies to correct their form, letting her guide them through sparring matches that could injure them. Unless she was fully acquitted of every single charge, she'd never be able to work again.

"It's not your only option," Omhon soothed. "But the Gods have seen cases like this before. My God, in particular, specializes in redemption of a sort. She'll believe you when you say you're innocent. But even if you were guilty, She takes those types too. She's not picky. She puts them to meaningful work; work that makes human space safer and stronger. Work that uses just those sorts of strength I've always seen in you. She even knows how to handle your neurotype; the Gods are more enlightened about these things than most mortals. I could guide you through it. This could be the beginning of something good, not bad. You could be more connected, more valued, than you ever were here."

Enga took a breath. She was still in that space she inhabited after a meltdown, drained and hopeless. Everything felt heavy. Everything in the world felt like too much to handle. But Omhon–

She'd trusted Omhon for a long time now. And Omhon could take her away from all this. Omhon could make it make sense.

"What do I sign?" she said dully.

She went through the formalities in a haze. It didn't surprise her that the God whose name Omhon danced around was Nemesis. Of course She was. But Nemesis was the bravest of Gods. She did necessary work, work that would use Enga's strengths to their fullest. And Omhon promised that, if Enga was innocent, her soul after death would be treated gently. Not like the things one read about in books. Not like the real criminals, the ones she would help bring to justice.

Enga trusted him. It was her greatest mistake.

Becoming an angel involved, among other things, surgery. Her brain had to be modified, large parts of it removed and replaced with circuitry. The procedure itself was painless, because she was asleep; the aftermath, she'd been warned, could involve headaches and disorientation. After a few weeks, they'd pass.

She woke up in the worst pain she had ever felt. Enga had broken limbs at work before, dislocated joints, ruptured a tendon. Those injuries were nothing compared to the agony that coursed through her skull. For a long time, that was all she could process. None of her surroundings, no sounds, no sights, only pain – and a vague sense of loss, as if part of her had died. She wasn't sure which part. But she felt, bone-deep, that it was never coming back.

She fell asleep and woke up like that a few times. Eventually other things penetrated her awareness. The padded medical cot that she lay on. Lights. Voices. Sensations that she'd never felt before, strange cold lines of data streaming through her mind in ways she could not yet coherently process.

Enga tried to move, but something was wrong. Her limbs felt heavy; they wouldn't obey her instructions. Maybe that was the medicine. She might still be drugged into motionlessness. She managed to grunt, but her mouth would not move even a little.

Eventually, the voices around her coalesced into words.

"–knew this was a risk," said one. There were people around her; when she opened her eyes, she could see their silhouettes. She could not move the rest of her face, but she could blink, eyes fuzzily open or darkly shut. If the silhouettes saw her eyes open, they had no reaction she could discern. "With methods like yours, the risk of soul damage–"

"Is within accepted limits," another voice retorted, and Enga knew it was Omhon's. The timbre was different but the tone, the inflection, was the same. "The ascension process still succeeds much more often than it fails. Or are you telling me Nemesis suddenly cares about collateral? I've brought more functional angels in to do Her bidding than most other agents. And you don't have the rank to tell me off."

"I have the rank to tell you that you've caused inconvenience for my medical staff and wasted my time. This one likely won't even walk again, much less serve the Gods as you meant her to."

"You have procedures for that," said Omhon.

He walked away. She never heard his voice again.

Over the next year or two, as she trained and learned and adjusted to her new limitations, Enga pieced together the story of what had happened. Omhon had been the one who framed her, of course. Nemesis was not a kind God; it took either utter depravity or great desperation for a mortal to choose to serve Her. Omhon, in his recruitments, favored desperation. Enga had preferred her mortal life to the idea of being an angel, so Omhon had destroyed that life. Using his Vaurian skills to plant documents, alienating friends with Enga's own voice, he had systematically removed anything that could keep her there.

But there was a reason why consent mattered, why there were contracts to sign and agreements to make with one's eyes open. Even the first generation of Vaurians, born and bred at great expense for the Gods, had to grow to the age of majority and freely accept their destinies. Some had chosen otherwise, which was why there were Vaurian mortals here and there. This was not only a matter of the Gods being polite. Becoming an angel involved a change to the brain so deep, so radical, that it also changed the soul. The pain of ascension came not only from injured nerves but from the soul itself struggling to adjust to its new shape. If the soul was not willing, it might fail to adjust, resulting in permanent disability like Enga's, or inability to use any of the circuitry installed, or instant death.

Recruiters like Omhon, using methods like his, deliberately courted that risk. It was frowned on by most, but he and a minority like him were as coercive as they dared to be, as much as they thought they could get away with. Occasionally they miscalculated. Enga had been one of those miscalculations. She had signed the papers, seeing no other option, in the miserable haze after a meltdown. She'd thought she meant it, but deep down her soul had not been willing enough. Now she was too damaged for much else but termination, after a brief testing phase, and the scrap heap.

In the weeks after surgery, struggling to stay awake or understand what was said around her, Enga did not know all this. But she knew that Omhon had betrayed her. He had harmed her, for his own ends, more deeply than she'd thought possible, and then, when things didn't go as he planned, he'd abandoned her. Omhon, who she'd thought was her best friend, had left her here like garbage.

Her difficulty moving or speaking, as quickly became apparent, was not only because of the drugs. It was a result of her damage. It was not going to go away.

Fine, then.

There were tests, of course. Attempts at salvage. Brisk medical angels, accompanied by their bots, tried to poke and prod Enga into something resembling function.

"Open your eyes, please," they said, politely at first. "Can you blink for me? Try moving your arm just a little. Come on – I know you can do it."

She ignored them, holding still on purpose. Eventually, they stopped being so polite.

"Let me spell this out for you," said a medical angel. She was lighter-skinned than Enga, and her hair fell down in ringlets around a titanium-plated face. She had cooed and cajoled at first, until Enga brought her to the end of her patience, and now her voice was cold. "You're not ever going to be a good angel. You'll never be fit for basic training. But there is meaningful work for angels who fail at that training. Your brain scans indicate that you're capable of a partial recovery if you follow instructions. Good enough that you could walk and communicate, after a fashion, and be a helpful assistant for more fortunate angels. It would not be a worthless life; you would be helping Nemesis' efforts to stamp out heresy, in your own way. But if you refuse out of spite, you will be terminated, and not kindly."

Enga did not move.

She did not care if she died. But she cared, very much, what would happen if she lived. Omhon's methods would be proved partly right, if Enga lived and was useful. Something good for the Gods, in whatever slight and disappointing way, would turn out to have come from what he did to her. Enga would not give him that satisfaction. She would make his failure complete if it was the last thing she did.

It *would* have been the last thing she did, if Akavi Averis, Inquisitor of Nemesis, had not one day ventured into her ward. Akavi had not been looking for her in particular. He had been curious in more general terms. It had not been long since he'd met his assistant, Elu Ariehmu of Nemesis, an angel who'd failed basic training thanks to his unusual personality type, and who'd been passed over and abused by better angels until Akavi found him. Akavi had seen intelligence in Elu, and capacities for loyalty and sensitivity unparalleled in the angelic corps. He'd quickly trained Elu to serve him, and he was satisfied with that choice. Now he'd grown curious over what other human resources might be hiding in plain sight, overlooked by an overly rigid approach to the angelic hierarchy.

Akavi was a Vaurian, which did not sit well with Enga after Omhon. But he sat next to Enga's cot with a frank, cold interest that felt different from that of the medical angels.

"You're doing this on purpose," he said. "That's rare. I'm not sure if you appreciate just how rare. Most angels of Nemesis would do anything rather than risk termination and damnation at Her hands. Why are you different, Enga?"

Enga did not answer, but some part of her, faintly, considered it. None of the medical angels had asked *why*, only doled out explanations and punishments and the hint of vague, small rewards. None of them had wanted to know how she felt.

Akavi made an impatient noise. "It can't be that you're simply giving in to despair. Even angels like Omhon choose their targets better than that. Are you truly so weak?"

Enga remained silent. She couldn't have answered even if she'd wanted to. She'd tested that when she was alone. She could still move most of her body, clumsily, a little. But her face was much worse than the rest of her. The muscles in her face would not move to make words at all.

Or, Akavi added abruptly, *are you trying to accomplish something?*

This was not verbal speech. The words appeared in her head. She wasn't literally seeing letters, and her eyes weren't what detected them, but it was more similar to seeing text than to anything else she'd ever experienced before. It hurt to focus on the words, in the maelstrom of other strange electronic sensations that had appeared since her surgery, but Enga was determined, and she could puzzle out their meaning.

There was something else, too. An emotion, or the feel of something that could hold emotions. Akavi had sent her a message through her new circuitry, and through that same circuitry she could feel some scrap of his mind. How odd. Akavi's mind felt cold and intrigued, like a strange scientist, poking at her to see what she would do. Enga had never much liked the psychologists who had studied her, in Kutaga, when she was younger. But she did not fully understand her current state, the half-electronic thing that had been made of her, and if this Akavi person wanted to understand, then that piqued just the tiniest edge of her own curiosity.

She pushed some part of her mind in the direction of the letters, tried to send letters back to him with some spiteful message. She had never done this before. She was clumsy.

NKN..N, said Enga.

"Fascinating," said Akavi aloud. He continued via those same strange, mental words. *It takes time to learn to text-send. You haven't been trained. But you've found the correct channel, and even a few of the letters. Was that your first try? What is really going on in there, Enga Afonbataw Konum?*

She did not reply.

You are so angry, he mused. Why was he using this mode of communication when it hurt so much to read? Later, Enga would realize that he'd wanted to keep his words private. He'd been saying things that it wouldn't have been politic for a passing medical angel to overhear. *I've rarely seen such rage, even in hardened soldiers. Let me take a guess. You are angry at the man who recruited you.*

Enga's fingers twitched.

You are damning yourself out of spite for him.

S^E%ST^6, said Enga.

"Impressive," Akavi said aloud. He continued over text.

*You're not unsuited for Nemesis at all, are you? You're nearly
perfect for Her. Your only problem is that you're focusing all
that destructive capacity* inward. *Rage like yours is a gift. Turn
it outward, focus it, and it will keep you going on your darkest
days. The man I think you're angry with is only a junior Inquisitor.
What do you think would happen if you rose in the ranks above
him? What would you like to do to him then?*

It was probably another lie. He was probably stringing her
along, just as Omhon had. How could she rise in the ranks
when she could barely move? Yet Akavi's interest in her
seemed sincere. He believed she was useful for something
more than the menial tasks that the medical angels had
promised. He believed she was *worth* spending time and
effort to heal.

She did not trust him. But his promises were enough, just
enough to make her weak.

Enga Afonbataw Konum of Nemesis opened her eyes.

Now

Akavi had abandoned her. Elu had abandoned her. The
worst crime, the crime she'd driven herself for fifty years to
avenge, and now it was theirs, too.

She hated both of them for it, but she hated Akavi less.
He hadn't had much choice. His mission had failed, and
there had been only two options: submit to summary
termination or flee. Enga would have lost Akavi either
way.

Elu, though. *Elu.*

Elu was her friend. Elu had taken a liking to her as soon as they met, and he had stayed with her all through that long, agonizing process of recovery. When it became clear that Enga's arms would never regain useful function, Elu had helped her design the replacements. Akavi was inherently selfish; his only virtue was a flexible mind. But Elu had been genuinely kind. Elu, she'd believed, had cared.

And then he'd left her too, freely, of his own volition. Without an explanation. Without a goodbye.

Enga would find both of them, him and Akavi. And she would make them burn.

CHAPTER 14
Now

Elu had begun to look forward to Qiel's next visit almost as much as he looked forward to Akavi's return. It was dangerous; it was a thing he shouldn't want. But being alone here was getting to his head. He liked Qiel. She cared how Elu felt about things, despite their differences. She talked about things that weren't just the next task she wanted him to do.

She'd offered him *friends,* and that was the most forbidden and lovely thing of all, the thing he'd believed he'd never have again.

When he heard a knock at the *Talon*'s door, he opened it immediately.

Qiel stood there holding tightly to Lingin's hand. Lingin's other arm was still in a sling, but there was healthier color in his cheeks now, and more alertness in his eyes.

Two young Riayin adults – about the same age that Qiel was, and that Elu appeared to be – stood nervously beside them. One was a long-haired woman who stood, self-consciously poised, in the most fashionable attire an impoverished survivor could reasonably cobble together. The remains of a chic dress, the fabric violet and still bright, patched over in an abstract, modernist pattern, and set with pockets and practical accessories in colors that more or less matched the original. The other was a shy young man with matted bangs that fell over his face, with a softness to his body that suggested he'd once been overweight. He looked at his feet. The other one, the woman, was already curiously looking Elu over.

"Hey," said Qiel, smiling at Elu.

"Hey," said Elu. He didn't think he was smiling back, though he wanted to. He felt a tightness in his chest. Now that they were actually *here*, he was slightly overwhelmed.

"I'm holding up my end of the deal," she said.

"I see that," said Elu faintly, and then he remembered his manners. He made himself smile. He bowed, which was the usual gesture of greeting on Riayin. "Hi. I'm Elu Ariehmu."

He wanted to add *of Nemesis* at the end, but he didn't. Elu would never be *of Nemesis* again.

"This is Bannah Nin," said Qiel, gesturing to the woman, "and Mes De. Both people I've known forever. Both of them I'd trust with my life."

"Pleased to meet you," said Bannah, bowing. Mes mumbled something similar and nodded a bit more clumsily.

Elu's microexpression software, which for a long time had been dormant without any faces to look at, flared to life. His vision lit up with dozens of small annotations. Mes was almost certainly non-neurotypical. Bannah might or might not be, but she was better at making the kinds of faces and poses most people expected. They were both paying close attention, nervous and excited to meet a thing like Elu. Whatever kind of thing he was now.

"Pleased to meet you, too," he said. Maybe they could see his nervousness and maybe they couldn't. He would not think about what he would say about all this when Akavi returned. He would *not* think about that.

"You're the fallen angel?" Bannah asked, looking at the titanium plates on his forehead. "The healer?"

"Yes," said Elu. How strange it was, hearing himself called those things. *Fallen angel* was what he was, but he and Akavi didn't tend to say it aloud. *Healer* was not a word anyone in the angelic corps would have used – at most, Elu should have been called a medic, someone who knew enough to guide the medical bots that did the real work. But *healer* was the word people used on a planet like this, because Elu healed. How quickly and easily he'd been placed in a category they could make sense of. Maybe *healer* was a thing he could be. "Would you like to come in? It's comfortable in the ship, and there's room for a few to sit–"

"Actually," said Qiel with a playful glint in her eyes, "it's a nice day out. I was thinking we could picnic. With some food from your food printer, of course."

Elu spied real calculation behind that glint. Qiel trusted these friends with her life, but she also wanted to prove to them what Elu could do. Indoors or outdoors, Elu would provide for them far more richly than their homes did. They would start coming to him more and more, even if it was only this trusted few. They'd be his friends, and in return, he'd give them anything they asked. He had so much; how could he turn down people who were needy, who wanted to be his friends? He couldn't imagine not wanting to do that.

Qiel had driven a good bargain, and she knew it. Elu could see how she'd risen to prominence here.

Over the next several minutes he set things up. He printed a bright checkered cloth to spread out in a clearish space on the forest floor, like the cloths he'd seen in mortal vids. He printed sandwiches and biscuits and muffins, fruits and vegetables, soft drinks, little chunks of cheese and bowls of nuts. None of it extravagant, by the standards of mortals, but all of it precious and rare in the Chaos Zone. The mortals fell on the food and devoured it, chattering all the while. It was nearly overwhelming, this much chattering after this much silence, but the sight of them there made him happy.

"–so Fu said the shelters needed better roofing before the next storm," Bannah babbled, "but I was like, roofing is the least of your problems – last time we had water damage it was from flood water coming *up*, not down–"

"Good luck getting Fu to listen to anything," said Mes through a mouthful of sandwich.

Elu could tell, from their microexpressions, that they were sticking to topics like these on purpose. They would glance at him or at the *Talon* with expressions of great curiosity, and then they'd start talking about something else. Qiel must have warned them not to pry too deeply into Elu's life, that there were security concerns for him and he'd be shy.

It was nice, though. It was nicer than listening to the radio. Even if they weren't completely talking *to* him, they knew he was there, and they were including him.

"What do you use for roofing?" Elu asked, curious. He'd seen the survivors' settlements in Akavi's vids, but Akavi didn't tend to focus on structural details like that, and he wasn't sure what kind of shelter they were talking about. Depending on the group of survivors, there could be intact buildings repurposed, or ruins patched up more extensively, or new structures built from scratch, using anything from scrap lumber to adobe to tarps on sticks. Most communities had some of each, and who got to stay in what kind of shelter was a perpetual point of contention.

He liked talking about this, partly because he liked focusing on visual and material details, the way he did when he designed clothes for Akavi. But he'd also noticed something about the survivors; he'd been noticing it all along, in Akavi's vids and in the conversations he listened to over the radio. They squabbled over what repairs were needed and why – much more squabbling than a team of angels would have been allowed – but they pitched in and did the repairs anyway. An angel with an ailing ship would be expected to be smart enough to figure out the repairs on their own – or suffer the consequences of their incompetence. That was one way the angelic corps weeded out the weak. But the survivors looked out for each other, tried to figure out what *other* people needed and how to help, and most of the time despite their squabbles and lack of training they did a reasonable job. Certainly better than what the angels were doing.

It made Elu feel wistful in a way he didn't want to examine.

Mes wiped his mouth. "Mostly clay around here, but–"

Elu's gaze was drawn to a movement somewhere in the distance, behind Mes, at the outskirts of the forest.

Someone was walking toward them.

The person was still so far away that even Elu's enhanced senses could not see any detail. Not their gender or race or general appearance. But they were coming from the direction Akavi usually came from, when Luellae dropped him off here. And Elu recognized the movement even if he couldn't see what face the person wore. He knew Akavi's proud, striding gait – he would have known it anywhere. It was faster than normal, at the moment, and slightly uneven. Hurt. Agitated. Angry.

He'd thought he had more time than this. Damn it, he'd known there was a risk of discovery, but he'd thought he'd get away with *one* visit, at least. Akavi's visits here were irregular, but he'd been sure it wasn't time for one yet.

"Run," he said.

Qiel, who knew to take him seriously, put down her food and scrambled up immediately. The other two hesitated. "He said run," Qiel snarled. Elu had already gotten up and hurriedly started to gather in the rest of the food and the cloth, for all the good it would do him. He could throw all this into the recycler immediately, it could all be converted without a trace into raw material for the next round of printing, but it wouldn't matter. Akavi would have seen what he'd seen.

There was a minute of confusion. The mortals ran. Elu piled up all the evidence of disloyalty into his arms, too frantic to do anything else. For a panicked moment he wondered if Akavi would come to him, or if he'd chase down Qiel and her friends and try to hurt them. But Akavi's shape strode closer and closer to him. She wore a female face now, the one she often used with Luellae, and that face was incandescent with rage. Blood was matted in her hair and along her limbs.

She said nothing until she'd walked all the way up to Elu, until she had him in arm's reach. Then she took him by the collar and yanked him in, his eyes an inch from hers.

"Are you OK–" Elu started, staring at the blood.

Akavi slapped him hard across the face.

Elu stumbled slightly, reeling. He dropped his armful of cloth and food, sending perfectly good sandwiches rolling into the undergrowth, but Akavi's grip kept him upright. She'd never done a thing like this before. He was too panicked to know what to do in response.

"*What* is this?" Akavi snarled. "Of all the times– What did you *do*, Elu? How could you endanger our security–"

"I couldn't–" He stumbled over himself, trying and

failing to explain. Had he caused whatever it was that had injured her somehow? Elu didn't feel that he'd had any other choice. He hadn't meant to stumble across Qiel in the field. He couldn't have denied her what she wanted, not when she knew how to sell him out to the other angels. He couldn't have turned her down when she came to him with Lingin, not when an injured child's life lay in the balance. He couldn't have turned down the offer of friends, not when he was starved for them. What could he have done? He felt powerless.

But helpless victims of circumstance didn't behave as Elu had behaved. They didn't happily set out a picnic on a cloth for the people who controlled them.

"Who were those people?" Akavi demanded. "What were you doing with them?"

Elu didn't know how to explain. "They were – mortals. Friends. They needed my help."

Akavi tilted her head like a bird of prey, irate. "Evidently. And you were willing to endanger both yourself and me. For *friendship*. You know how hard it is for me to trust anyone, Elu, but I trusted you. I thought you, at least, would never betray me."

Elu opened his mouth and closed it again. His cheek stung. He had nothing to say for himself.

"Was I not a good *friend*?" Akavi bit out, pulling him in even closer. "Did I not kiss you enough, Elu? Was that the problem? At least I won't have to do *that* anymore."

She made a sharp movement and released her grip, throwing him to the ground. He caught himself in the leaf litter and crouched there, trying to understand what he'd heard. Was she going to leave him here for the other angels to find? She could ensure his destruction so easily.

"I was spotted," Akavi added, more diffidently. She looked at him cowering on the ground with the same neutral expression that she typically used when giving orders, as if this was no more emotionally salient to her than any other sight. "I managed to escape, and I don't think the angels can track me here. But we need to revise our plans immediately, and to tighten our security. Get back on the ship."

For a split second, Elu looked over her shoulder at the tiny figures of Qiel, Bannah, and Mes in the distance.

"I see you looking at them," said Akavi, following his gaze. "After more than fifty years with me, you change your loyalties so easily. You're already thinking of running away with them. But you wouldn't last long out there. Even supposing that they still wanted you, without the bounty of your food printer and your medical skills, what then? *They* obviously found out that you're an angel. How long would it take before someone else did? Before the real angels came and found you and brought you in for termination. Along with the whole group that sheltered you."

Elu's stomach clenched. For one wild moment, he wanted it. He could run away and try to go with those retreating figures, and he'd die soon, but at least he'd have friends in the meantime.

But he knew Akavi was telling the truth. He knew angelic protocol. Fallen angels were a bigger threat than almost any mortal heretic, and they were hunted and taken down accordingly. Elu had already resigned himself to being killed for desertion eventually. But he couldn't take people like Qiel, Bannah, and Mes down with him. He was not capable of that.

"I was willing to accommodate your needs," Akavi continued coldly. "Your absurd desire for sentiment and affection. I was willing to compromise my own physical integrity to keep you happy. But even that wasn't enough, was it? You couldn't even observe the process of basic loyalty or safety. You chose to run away with me. You chose to live a fallen angel's life, *knowing* it would mean being alone. You made that choice, Elu, not me. And now you're going to have to live with it." She turned and walked toward the *Talon*, opening the outer airlock. "Get in the ship."

She was wrong. Elu *knew* she was wrong, deep down, even if he couldn't have articulated it aloud. But she was right about one thing. Right now, unless he wanted to die very fast, he didn't have another choice.

"Yes, sir," Elu whispered, and he got up and followed.

Fifty-Two Years Ago

"That was fast," said Akavi, as Elu pinged him with a folder of neatly sorted data files. They were on a mission involving a mysterious pattern of sensitive materials disappearing from research archives around a few cities in Rahi. The *Menagerie*'s systems could analyze data like this and look for patterns, but first the data had to be pre-processed, the relevant items and their curatorial data retrieved and collated into identical formats, with the most relevant details most prominent in the file. That pre-processing, which required no special skill beyond the ability to format data, had been Elu's job.

"Sir?" said Elu. He thought he saw approval in Akavi's microexpressions, but he was still new. And many supervisors said things like this as veiled insults. It was fast, so it must be sloppy work, or overeager, or only partly done.

Elu had been assigned to assist Akavi temporarily, just for this one mission. That was what his work mostly consisted of – random assignments where needed, unskilled labor, monitoring and processing and taking messages. There were far worse fates, considering his rank. He always tried to be content with random work and with loneliness. He always tried not to draw attention to himself.

Akavi blinked a few times as he skimmed through the file folder, and then gave Elu an odd, sidelong look. "This is good work. You're clearly at least somewhat intelligent and diligent; how did you fail basic training?"

"I couldn't lie, sir," said Elu. He had tried, but no matter how fervently he spit out untrue statements, no matter how much conviction he tried to put into the words – no matter how his teachers had kicked and spat at him insisting he do better – his microexpressions hadn't lined up with them properly. He could not be *convincing*. Nor could he deal out pain and injury to human beings without flinching, or navigate the deadly political web at the heart of the angelic corps, or perform at half a dozen other kinds of tasks that Nemesis, in Her wisdom, had deemed necessary.

Elu had sold his soul to Nemesis because he fervently believed in Her work. She was the one who kept mortals safe, no matter what it took. In his early childhood, he'd been kept safe that way himself, watching Nemesis' deadly warships streak overhead and chase the Keres from his burning city. He'd grown up wanting to do the same for others. He wanted to help.

No one had told Elu that he wasn't the right kind of person to help. Not the priests who described angelic service in glowing terms, as the greatest glory and greatest sacrifice a human could make for their God; not the specific priest of Nemesis he'd approached when he came of age, nor the recruiter angel that the priest put him in touch with. Neither of them had asked him many questions, beyond making him prove that he was of age and insist that he was sure. It was only the angels who ran basic training, when it was already too late and he was already irrevocably one of them, who'd called him useless.

Everyone else must have assumed that a boy as intelligent and faithful as Elu would find some way to succeed. It was his own fault, he supposed, that he hadn't.

Akavi frowned impatiently. "Is that all? There are plenty of jobs that don't involve direct deceptive interaction with mortals."

"It's not just that, sir. But it's... that kind of thing. Generally. I could never figure out a way to do it well enough to be useful."

Akavi was looking at him very carefully, analyzing his microexpressions. He could tell, both because that was what it looked like on the surface, and because his own microexpression software had a label for it. That was funny, in a way. Software to point out software pointing out software. Elu wished sometimes that he could just be software. The too-human, emotional parts of him were the ones that kept failing.

"How long have you been working as a grunt, Elu?"

"Two years, sir. And then the year of basic training before that."

"Hm. Not long, but long enough. And you've been doing jobs like this?"

"More often jobs involving guarding or monitoring,

but sometimes data jobs like this, sir. Not infrequently."

"And when you've done this sort of work, your supervisors have been satisfied?"

"I don't know, sir. Mostly they don't say anything one way or the other." Mostly they didn't *think* about Elu one way or the other. If he'd ever really fouled something up, he'd have been sent for punishment, but beyond that, he wasn't sure.

Akavi's head tilted. "I see why you failed basic training."

"Sir?"

There was amusement in Akavi's microexpressions now, though he kept it well-suppressed. "You're not only a bad liar, you're *painfully* honest. All your answers to my questions are so precise, yet without any deeper calculation. You're not thinking even a little bit of how to spin the facts. What I might want to hear. What would put you in the most favorable position. I see that in mortals sometimes, but I've never seen it in an angel of Nemesis. It's refreshing."

"Sorry, sir," said Elu. He knew that was not the correct response – Akavi didn't seem displeased with him – but he was flustered.

"No. I'm going to train that out of you. Don't unnecessarily apologize." Akavi smiled thinly as Elu looked at him with wider eyes, trying to understand this. "It happens that I've risen high enough in the ranks to merit an official assistant or two. But I've resisted doing so. Everyone in this corps is so willing to backstab their superiors; it's tiresome." His gaze was piercing, taking in every detail of Elu as if Elu was some useful device on display. "I always wondered if basic training's overly rigid ideas held us back. You might be the key to that puzzle, Elu. You never met its requirements, but you're intelligent and good at your work. More importantly, you couldn't stab me in the back if you tried. When the current assignment is over, I'm going to take you on as my assistant for a trial period. We'll see how things go. Did you have anything else you wanted to discuss?"

Elu stared at him, overwhelmed. An assistant's position. A way out of the small, kickable jobs he'd resigned himself to doing for eternity. Normally those positions were only open to those who'd passed basic training, but an angel like Akavi would have his ways of pulling strings.

Akavi hadn't even asked what he thought of it. Elu's permission wasn't necessary for an arrangement like this. An Inquisitor much worse than Akavi could have snapped him up in this manner if they'd wanted to. Elu had heard of that happening to angels like him. Some inquisitors only wanted a weaker angel that they could bully forever – or a young, pretty one to make use of in other ways. That was one of the reasons he tried not to draw attention to himself. The microexpression software hadn't detected any lies, but it was possible even now that Akavi's words about Elu's intelligence were mere flattery, and that he really wanted one of those other things.

But there was something about Akavi. There was a grace to him and his shifting forms. There was a way about him, when he looked at Elu and assessed him. Like he was really looking. Really seeing. After two years being bounced from place to place doing grunt work, Elu craved to be looked at that way. He wanted to believe Akavi meant it.

"No, sir," he said. "Thank you, sir. I won't let you down."

"See to it that you don't," said Akavi, turning away in dismissal.

He was grateful. That day, and all the days after it, every time Akavi treated him like a person instead of hurting him. For fifty-two long years, Elu had been so goddamned grateful.

Now

Once they got back aboard the *Talon*, Akavi sealed the airlock and resumed his natural Vaurian form, the translucent, androgynous appearance that Elu had once found so beautiful. The blood on him didn't disappear, though.

"Let me get a medical bot–" said Elu.

"*I'll* get the medical bots. I don't trust you right now, for obvious reasons. Sit."

He gestured to one of the chairs in the little parlor. Elu sat on it and watched numbly as Akavi fired up the medical bots and disappeared into his room.

He should have realized earlier that, with Akavi, this was how it would be. He'd known perfectly well for more than fifty years the kind of person Akavi was. Akavi saw people only in terms of the levers that could be pulled to make them useful. He'd been kind to Elu, doling out just enough praise to keep him infatuated and grateful, all these years. Not because he liked Elu. Not because he liked to be kind. But because Akavi collected people and used them for his own ends, and Elu had a capacity for loyalty he'd found desirable. If that strategy stopped working, cruelty would serve Akavi's ends just as well. If Elu's *loyalty* stopped working, then he would be worth nothing in Akavi's eyes at all.

Akavi had never made a secret of any of this. He'd named

his very ship after it. The *Menagerie* – a collection of life forms, kept as possessions.

Elu had watched him manipulate mortals, in his job as an Inquisitor, for fifty years. Of course he'd manipulated Elu and Enga and literally everyone else around him in just the same way. Elu had known that already, on some level. He'd had all the information needed to know it. He didn't know why he hadn't acted as though he knew. He'd still loved Akavi and tried to save him from termination, tried to build a life together. Tried to accept the kindness and affection he doled out, even when he knew already that it wasn't real.

Maybe Elu was just stupid. Maybe Elu deserved this.

CHAPTER 15
Now

Tiv sat curled up at the foot of Yasira's bed, her legs folded under her on the floor, her head resting on the bedspread.

"They're in," she said. "Most of them. It took some arguing, but the team's in. We're going to make this plan work."

"That's good," said Yasira tonelessly.

It seemed like Yasira had been able to push herself so far, and no farther. She'd been so powerful and forceful today, from the moment she set out to find the gone people to the moment she stormed out of the meeting. But it had taken a lot out of her. Now she lay nearly motionless on her bed, knees pulled up to her chest, eyes half-shut. She had pulled her weighted blanket up over herself and only half her face was showing.

"How's everybody?" Tiv asked. "In there."

She was still getting used to the thought that there was more than one of Yasira now. She still didn't know much about how it worked. Were there some people who had energy and wanted to go do things, and others who didn't? Or was the exhaustion a physical thing, more or less evenly distributed?

It felt like it would be rude to pry about things like that. Or was it the opposite? Maybe it was rude *not* to ask. Maybe not asking would mean she was ignoring the truth, refusing to think about any part of it that affected her.

"I don't know." Yasira waved a hand vaguely. "All kinds of ways."

"Does it bother you when I ask?"

"No." Yasira hesitated. "Yes. Some of me. Not for the reasons you think. Some people–" She pulled the weighted blanket a little further up over her face, muffling her voice. "Some people really want to do this. Those are the people you saw in the park. Some people don't, but they were overruled. I'm not used to overruling myself. I don't know if this is how it's supposed to work. But I'm done with the overruling for now, so everybody's just a ball of chaos again."

Tiv smiled slightly up at her. "Can we make it a better chaos?"

Yasira paused, under the blanket, and then rolled over onto her belly. "*We* can't. Maybe me. If I could get my shit together."

"You're Riayin. There must be books about this. How to get everyone to live together and be functional. I know it's not the same as having a neurotutor who shares your experience, but I could steal you some books, at least."

"Why are you doing this?" said Yasira. Her face was still partly under the weighted blanket, and it muffled her words. "Pretending to be nice to me."

Tiv frowned deeply. "Yasira…"

At the beginning of their relationship, Yasira had said things like this all the time. Tiv would say something kind or caring, and Yasira would accuse her of not really meaning it. Of being a "good girl" – whatever that meant – and saying what was expected of her, rather than meaning it in her heart.

Tiv understood where that came from. In spite of all of Riayin's supposed success with neurodiversity, Yasira had been bullied growing up. She'd experienced all sorts of fake kindnesses. She'd probably had to fake kindness herself, even to the bullies, when she'd rather have fought back. It was natural that she couldn't always trust kindness.

It was natural, but Tiv hated it. Tiv *didn't* say things that she didn't mean. She'd had a talk with Yasira, long before the *Pride of Jai* imploded. *When you say things like that,* she'd explained, *you are calling me a liar. Is that what you want to call me? Is that what you think I am?* And Yasira had said, no, it was not what she really thought. She had agreed to stop saying it. But Tiv could tell she still thought it, sometimes, at moments of great distress.

Maybe some parts of her were thinking it and others weren't, now. Tiv was still trying to wrap her head around this.

"We've talked about this," said Tiv. "I know it's hard for you to believe. But I don't make things up just to be nice. When I tell you I care about you, it's because I *do*. When I tell you I want us to make it through this together, it's because I do. And when I tell you we might be able to find resources to help us, it's because I just realized we can do that and it seems like a good idea to me. Okay? I know trust is hard. You don't have to trust me to the end of the world. But I wish you could trust that I say what I mean."

Yasira pushed herself up, with some difficulty, to sit. She hunched there in the bed, pulling the blanket clumsily around herself. "How can you love me when there isn't even a *me?* Just a bunch of fragments floating around, and a whole shit-ton of power that nobody understands."

"I don't know how to explain it," said Tiv. "But everybody's at war with themselves sometimes, right? You just have that a lot more. I love what I see when I look at you. How brave you are, and how much you doubt. How you saved me back there, and on the *Talon* too. How you try so hard to save everybody, even when you're so weak you can't get out of bed. And I feel love. I'd like to understand you more, I'd like to get to know the different people in there for themselves, but I don't think you have to understand why someone is the way they are, or how it all works, to love them. It just happens. You just do."

Yasira gave her a small, frightened, wistful look, and then she curled further up, staring down at the blankets. She took a long breath, building up to say something difficult.

"I try to be Savior," she said at last. "But I can't fucking save anything. You're the one who saved me. Without even doing anything. You don't know it, but you did."

"How?" said Tiv, but she understood a thing or two about how mentally ill people might be driven to harm themselves, and she had a sinking feeling that she already knew.

"When Outside broke me. On the *Talon*. It could have broken me further. It could have broken me into nothing, so I wouldn't feel anything the angels did to me. It gave me that choice. But I remembered you were still on the ship, a prisoner. You – needed me."

Tiv let out a long, painful breath. That was the kind of thing she'd thought Yasira meant, but it still felt like being punched in the gut.

"I still do," she said. "You haven't been down there with the survivors. You don't know how much you mean to them. So much of the time, that's what keeps them going. Just knowing there's a Savior who exists out there. You've already done so much, and now you give them hope by living, even if you never do any other miracles again. You give *us* hope, too. The team. Me. We all need you."

Yasira looked back up at her, her long black hair hanging in tangles over her face. "Promise?"

"Promise."

She nodded, and sat up straighter. "But I *will* do more. I can."

"I know."

"Will you be there with me?"

"Yes." Tiv ached to take Yasira's hands, to press her close and reassure her with her body, but she knew better. "Promise."

"Even if it means–" Yasira took another breath, shivering slightly. "To do this thing I'm doing with the gone people, I'm going to have to use my power more. I should have done it already. I'm scared to do it. I shouldn't be doing it without knowing what I'm doing. I don't know what this power *means*. What it will do to me. I could change even more, and I don't know…"

Tiv wanted to say, *yes, I promise. I will stay with you no matter what you become.* It would be true in all the ways that mattered to Tiv, because it was what her heart felt. But Yasira was literal by nature, and she could easily come up with far-fetched scenarios in which Tiv shouldn't promise a thing like that. Unlikely imaginary futures where she turned into a monster who couldn't talk or think, or a ravening murderer, or any number of other kinds of things Tiv shouldn't stay with. Tiv didn't seriously think those things were possible, but the fear of them might be very real in Yasira's heart. They were dealing with Outside. Who knew what was really going to happen?

"Then I'll be with you while we figure that out," she said instead. And *that* was true enough for both of them; she felt it in her bones. "Together. Promise."

Yasira shrugged out of the blanket and crawled forward on the bedspread. She took Tiv's hand. She leaned in, and she kissed Tiv, long and hard, with a sort of desperation. As if Tiv was the floating thing she clung to in an endless stormy sea.

Tiv kissed back. She didn't know if this was all of Yasira, or just one of her, or a group like the group that had taken charge in the park. She would learn to figure those things out. But here, now, this was enough. They were together. They would find the way through.

As the week drew on, Tiv sat at the head of the table in the war room, feverishly drawing and re-drawing charts and plans. She was Leader, and it was the Leader's job to coordinate this mess, even if this mess was a patchwork of different grassroots efforts that covered the whole of the Chaos Zone. Grid sat at her right hand, flipping through an ever-increasing sheaf of papers and charts. Every time someone went out to make their rounds, more offers of help and requests for backup came in from more and more cities. So many people in the Chaos Zone had wanted to rise up like this, if only Tiv and the Seven would help them instead of telling them to keep their heads low. So many people saw the opportunity now, and the strength in numbers they'd have if they and the gone people rose up all at once.

But there were drawbacks to scheduling a rebellion like this. Grid knew how to keep Vaurian angels and spies out of the lair itself, but Grid had failed to stop what Akavi did to Luellae. And the local groups that the Seven were in contact with didn't have a Grid. Writing a letter to them all, as Yasira had, put them all at risk; it was virtually certain that the angels had already read the letter and were planning their own next moves accordingly. In the days before the protest itself, Tiv was sure they would see more raids, more captures, more brutality.

They were in a war. People were going to die no matter what they did. Tiv just had to hope that the deaths would be worth something.

At Tiv's left hand, Prophet sat, curled halfway into a ball on her chair, fingers pressed to her temples. It wasn't fair to ask Prophet to sort through every possible action, to tell them with certainty what would work and what wouldn't – Prophet's powers didn't work that way. But Prophet saw things, and now that the group was moving forward with something big, she was seeing more. She was trying the best she could to sort through all the conflicting visions in her head, to distil them into useful information when she could.

There was a big map of the Chaos Zone up on one of the war room's makeshift walls, bigger than it had any right to be. It would overwhelm Tiv if she let it, the thought of just how big a fifth of a planet's surface really was, how many cities, how many *people*. Even with Prophet and Splió's vision, with Luellae's ability to flit from place to place and the meta-portal's ability to connect them all, Tiv would never see most of those people's faces or hear their names. She would never even know most of the consequences of what she was doing.

They had a box of different-colored pins, and every time a new bit of information came in about a specific place, Grid got up and stuck a pin into the map. Red for a group that was planning an active, violent fight. Blue for a group that wanted backup for a nonviolent protest. Yellow for a group that requested weapons or special supplies. And so on. They weren't all the way through yet, but there were already so many pins. And only nine people to handle them all – the Seven, Yasira, and Tiv.

Less than nine, since Yasira would be with the gone people, doing her own esoteric things.

There was no foolproof way to choose who could do the most good where. Each of them would have to go with their gut and then live with that choice. It was Daeis who chose first – getting up from where they'd been sitting, and pointing decisively at one red pin. A city called Küangge.

Splió, never far from Daeis's side, stood up and took them gently by the shoulders. "Are you sure, hon?"

Daeis nodded once, decisively, feet planted.

Grid stuck a black pin next to Küangge's red one. They only had nine black pins. Küangge was one of the cities with a good reason for violent uprising, and a specific goal. In the building that anchored Küangge's relief station, where the meager food and water rations for the survivors were kept, the angels had also been keeping hostages. Six of them, women and children and luminaries of the community, who they'd declared would be tortured if the citizens continued in their heresies. Maybe put on those daily broadcasts, to make an example out of the whole city.

The other survivors were going to get them back.

Daeis knew how to communicate with Outside monsters – bigger ones than the little creatures they kept as pets inside the lair. In a battle like the one in Küangge, Daeis's monster friends might be able to turn the tide. But it was risky; they'd never actually tried to lead monsters in battle before. And angels could defeat even the biggest monsters, given sufficient firepower and a bit of luck.

Luellae stood at the corner of the room, as standoffish as usual, arms crossed. Her confession with the Four had taken a weight from her shoulders, and she'd decided she wanted to fight, after all – better than sitting and feeling sorry for herself. But Luellae was still very aware of the stakes here, and of how easy it would be to fail.

"I can go to a lot of these places in a night," she said. "I can get people past guards and barriers, pull them out of trouble if they need rescue. I could do more good that way than by fighting directly, but only if I know *where* to go, otherwise I'd just be running around aimlessly. Splió, if you're by the door, will you be able to tell me where to go?"

Splió ran an anxious hand through his thick hair; he was still preoccupied with Daeis, his other hand remaining firm at their shoulder. "I mean, I can't, like... see everything at once. I can't tell you where the best place is; that's too subjective anyway. But I know where all the places with the pins in them are. I could cycle through them and let you know when I see one that needs you."

"Good enough," said Luellae, rolling her shoulders in resignation.

Weaver fidgeted wildly in her chair, peering over Grid's shoulder at the requests from the different cities. She was starting to pick at her skin damagingly. Picket scarcely moved, even paler than usual, staring into space.

"I don't know," he mumbled. "Who's going to need me? I... My powers come with collateral. It needs... specific circumstances. I don't know..."

Picket had been fascinated by the mechanics of war, back when it was an intellectual exercise. He didn't seem so fascinated now. Picket's powers could be helpful in a fight, but only in an area of a certain size, only by changing that area so drastically that it became deadly to the people inside. Even if angels were openly attacking people, it would have

ADA HOFFMANN

to be a certain kind of attack for Picket's powers to be a good option. They would have to do it in a specific way.

"You can stay here," said Splió. "If I'm looking for openings for Luellae, I can look for openings for you, too. We'll figure something out."

Picket nodded grimly and buried his face in his hands.

"You don't have to do this," Tiv added, more gently. "I'm not going to make anyone fight."

"What about me?" said Weaver, her voice rising to a nervous squeak. "I can heal, I want to heal, but everybody's going to need healing. Prophet, can you see who's going to need healing most?"

Prophet shook her head, wincing. "Everybody," she murmured.

Splió and Daeis exchanged an uneasy glance.

"I could carry you around with me," Luellae offered, but Weaver shook her head. Her powers were draining to use. A single small group of people with serious injuries, in a single place, was probably all she could heal before collapsing.

Tiv stared at her hands. These kinds of choices were inherently heavy, and she felt that weight, too. Tiv didn't have special powers, just her own brain and her words. She didn't know if that made the weight better or worse.

"I think," she said, "we have to stop looking for the one best solution. Even if Prophet could see everything, I don't think it works that way. If a bunch of different people are going to die without us, and there are more of them than we can actually help, there isn't a solution to that. And it's insulting to them, to the ones we don't pick, to pretend that there is. You've seen the map and the battle plans. Where do you feel like you want to help, Weaver? In your heart."

Weaver took a long breath, shut her eyes, and let it out again.

"Dasz," she said. "They deserve it."

Dasz, the city in Stijon where Akiujal had lived. Where he'd sacrificed a whole block full of lives, including his own, so that Tiv could escape. Because he believed, so fervently, that Tiv would help the people rise up.

For better or worse, they were all rising up now. She wished he could have seen it.

Tiv swallowed down the lump that had risen to her throat. "Yeah," she said, looking down. "They do."

In Qiel Huong's home in Büata, she and her little group were conferring, crafting homemade protest signs and committing escape routes to memory. Qiel, and many others in Büata, had chosen to protest nonviolently. There wasn't much in their particular city that could be gained by fighting, but freedom was as important here as anywhere, and the more places there were across the Chaos Zone where people demanded it, the better.

It was work that went long into the night, by the light of candles and makeshift lanterns. Everybody buzzed with a strange mix of elation and dread; everybody needed to talk to each other, to process what was coming, almost as much as they needed to make the signs. Nobody wanted to sleep.

Not until after midnight, when Mes De put the last finishing flourish on an intricate sign – SURVIVAL IS NOT HERESY, it said, the words stark black and white within a series of colored patterns and curlicues. Mes had found those kinds of patterns calming even before the Plague. He put the cap back on his marker pen, peered down at his handiwork with his tongue sticking out from the corner of his mouth, and then curled up over the top of it and was out like a light.

Bannah Nin looked down at him, her own legs pulled in tightly to her chest as she sorted water bottles and protective goggles into individual bins. She paused a moment, chewing her lip, and then looked up at Qiel.

"What do you think happened to that one angel?" she asked. "Elu? Do you think he's okay?"

The lanterns were starting to flicker and die, casting the room into a deeper gloom than before. Qiel was one of the lucky ones; she had a big, undamaged house in the suburbs where she'd been able to invite a lot of her surviving friends to live. It was a good house, especially once they'd learned to use their Outside powers to keep infestations out. It was good because it was sturdy and comfortable, but also it was good because it was full of people, friends who would support and protect each other.

For all the good things Elu owned, Qiel didn't think he'd ever had a house like hers. Whoever that person was, in the distance, who'd been storming towards them when Elu told them to run, Qiel didn't think it was a friend.

But Qiel was a community leader, and it wasn't always the right thing to do, wallowing and worrying like this. People like Bannah looked to Qiel when they wanted encouragement.

She looked up at Bannah with resolution on her face. "I don't think any of us are okay until all of us are."

It was a platitude, but it must have been the right one, because Bannah smiled sadly and nodded, like she'd said something wise.

* * *

"Are you sure you want to do this?" said Yonne Qun to his daughter, Genne. She had taken the copy of Yasira's letter, when it arrived with them, and was holding it in a determined fist in the gloom of their living room.

"I'm sure," she said, and it struck him all over again how young she was, barely a woman. She and her food-growing friends – many as young as her, but some older – had been risking themselves by using their powers in secret. He and others in the community had come to depend on them, despite the risk. To her, this new risk wasn't any different. There were protests popping up all over the place, and she wanted to do her part. By growing food, in a gaggle of friends, right in front of the angels' noses.

Qun had wanted to protect her. He had wanted Savior to swoop in with another piece of big, world-changing magic, precisely so that people like Genne didn't *have* to risk themselves. Or, at least, to give them big enough weapons so that they stood a fighting chance. Qun did his best to protect his community, but the Plague had just been something that happened to them; it wasn't their fault. Secretly, in his deepest heart, Qun didn't think people like him and his daughter should be the ones who had to fix it.

But Genne felt differently. Genne had embraced this new form their community took, and when she looked at him now, she shone with purpose and determination. Genne wanted to fight for what she had. And she was young, but not so young that he could have taken that choice from her. Not too young to understand what it meant, or what the cost might be.

She looked at him now, careful and fragile. "You don't approve, do you? You don't want me to."

Qun opened his arms and pulled her close.

"I just don't want to lose you," he confessed, when she embraced him back. He'd already lost her mother and so many other people, more than half the community. "But that's selfish. My daughter, I want you to do what you believe in."

Yasira didn't want to be part of the planning. Her own role was unique, and it was complex enough to take all of her attention. If she had to think about everyone else who was rising up alongside her, risking themselves in a dozen different ways, she might falter.

Which was not to say she didn't think about them. Plenty of pieces in the back of her head kept bringing it up.

She was outdoors, in the little grove with the archway, where she'd made the trees grow into strange shapes. It was lighter now, the sky a clear blue tinged with green, and, without the Gods' battle raging overhead, even the non-Euclidean tangles of branches looked healthy and peaceful. In the open space at the center of the grove, Yasira practiced, barely understanding what she was practicing for. She had to shield the gone people while they did their ritual. She had a vague mental image of how that would work. She wasn't at all sure how well that image would match up to reality.

Drawing on Outside, from where it always lay at the core of her being, she pushed energy out into a shape that felt like a shield.

The air shimmered in front of her in that shape. Little threads wove through it, in a shape a little bit like the branches above, twisting and solidifying in the air.

It can't be that easy, something inside Yasira thought. *We can't just make things happen by thinking them. That doesn't make sense. We can think of an infinite number of things – that would make us infinitely powerful.*

I don't think it's infinite, said the Scientist, peering inward at where the power came from. *Not technically. But it's so big that it may as well be. The limiting factor isn't the power itself, it's our ability to focus and withstand it.*

A little crowd of parts began to chatter at that. Masochistic parts of Yasira, those that weren't even sure that they wanted to exist anyway. *Is that so? We can withstand a lot.*

The rest of Yasira quickly hushed them up.

Just because this looked like a shield didn't mean it *was* one. Yasira bent down, picked up a pebble from the ground, and – concentrating on the shield – threw it. The pebble bounced off the shield as if it was a physical object, clattering harmlessly back down into the grass. Yasira didn't feel the impact.

Behind her, she heard a familiar footstep, and she turned.

Tiv smiled sheepishly. She looked tired, but determined, and her hair was a mess. Tiv had been managing this entire operation, Yasira thought guiltily, while she'd been off in the woods or hiding in her room, navel-gazing. Tiv was beautiful and good. She was more than any of the parts of Yasira deserved.

"How's it going?" said Tiv.

"I don't know," said Yasira. "Good. Maybe. I can do some of this, but I don't know if it will be enough."

"It will," said Tiv, with a confidence Yasira didn't think was based on anything intelligible.

What happens if it isn't? said some part of her, deep down, something that rarely spoke. What if Yasira couldn't actually defend all the gone people single-handedly? The gone people would still do their ritual. The normal survivors would still rise up, everywhere, fighting for change. It would go a lot worse than it should, but they probably wouldn't all die. The world, most likely, would still be changed.

What did the word *enough* even mean?

No part of Yasira, no matter how clever or anxious or confident or wise, had an answer to that.

Now that I have had the thought, I cannot get it out of my head.

I see them everywhere I turn. People who are like me now, because I forced them to be. People punished brutally, shot and gassed and starved and set on fire, for being like me. I did this to them. That is Truth.

The question, I suppose, is what to do about it.

Turn myself in? Flee in shame? These things would only embolden the gods. They are holding back now, in part, because they have not yet found me. They know that, were they to destroy this world, I could visit the same horrors on another, and another.

If I care at all about the people who were harmed here, I must see this through – I must keep the gods convinced I am a threat, about to strike again.

They are afraid of me.

Can I join the fight? Even though they call me Destroyer; even though Yasira does not want me back – could I use that fear to the common people's benefit, instead of using them as tools?

But would that make it better?

Or worse?

– From the diaries of Dr Evianna Talirr

CHAPTER 16
Now

The day was deceptively bright and clear as Yasira and Tiv crept out of the lair to meet the gone people.

Yasira wanted to do her part of this alone – just her and the gone people. Her own presence, if discovered, would draw immense amounts of attention – and *she* was only risking it because she had the power to survive.

That was what the Strike Force insisted, at least, as they stepped out of the portal with Tiv at their side. They had the plan and the power. They'd tested their abilities as far as they could. They would make this work. But the rest of Yasira quailed, unwillingly drawn along. Their fear had grown more and more intense as this day drew closer.

Yasira did not want to admit how uncertain she was. She had made this whole plan based on a feeling. The Chaos Zone was her responsibility, but she hadn't lived there, like the rest of the survivors. She hadn't been going on missions there daily like the Seven. There was a lot about this that she couldn't know in advance. She was just some girl, clever but out of her depth, the way she'd always been.

The portal spat her out from a little shed inside a woodsy park, with weedy flowers overgrowing the paths, strange little monsters the size of rabbits browsing in its tangles of leaves. The Strike Force immediately took in the setup, analyzing what might happen and what the biggest risks might be. A clump of gone people had gathered in an overgrown, grassy clearing in the park's center, touching each other's faces, milling around in some inscrutable form of preparation. There was enough around them, in the form of trees and tangled brush, to provide cover; they'd added to that, over the past day, tying vines and building earthen bulwarks to block the path of any strangers who might approach. From the outside of the park, what happened in the very center wouldn't be visible. There were only a few paths by which there was room, for gone people crawling on their hands and knees under the vine-tangles and over the rocky earth, to enter the space. It would be relatively easy to defend those paths if angels tried to crawl in, and hard for angels to aim accurately if they shot from the outside. But those tangles of vines wouldn't stop bullets or flame. And if the barrier was breached, it would be that much harder to make any escape.

Yasira hadn't been sure if the gone people were aware enough to build even this level of defense, but it seemed that they were, and that calmed her.

Tiv had insisted on coming along, her head wrapped in one of those coverings that was so popular lately, her face masked.

"I'll hide," she'd said this morning when they argued about it. "I'll creep into the bushes and no one will see me. I just want to be here for you."

"If you're coming," said Yasira, "you should be in with the gone people and me, not in the bushes. We'll be shot at, but you'll be inside the area I'm defending. If you're randomly in the bushes and something goes wrong, I can't save you."

"I won't be *randomly* in the bushes," said Tiv. "I'm not random. Besides, why would the angels look in the bushes when they're focused on you?"

"Don't do this," Yasira bit out, rounding on her. This was not the Strike Force, but someone deep inside who spoke more rarely, someone angry and afraid. "Whatever you do, Tiv, do *not* put me in a position where I can't save you."

Tiv bit her lip, but nodded. "Okay."

She held tightly to Yasira's hand as they walked through the long grass, butterflies and stranger flying things taking to the air around them, to where the gone people waited. They were beginning to clump together into a formation of sorts, concentric circles standing together preparing to hold hands, with a gap in the middle just like the one in so many of the gone people's religious rituals, a gap where some fragment of Outside itself might deign to manifest.

welcome Savior | kin of ours [amusement] have you come
                                                    to save us

---

Sometimes I/we think we came because you have saved me/us—
                though you did not know
                a planet is full of hope now
                because of you
                                a planet is about to dissolve into flames
                                because of you
        We have come to do what we can
        Let us protect you
        Please—

If all of this went down correctly, in the way that Yasira and the gone people intended, then the ritual the gone people did would reach deep into the world. It would rearrange it to be a little more habitable, in a softer echo of what Yasira had already done with her miracle at the beginning of the Plague. Yasira could feel that intent, even though she didn't know exactly how far it would go. She wasn't sure if even the gone people knew, or if they thought in different terms. They would do as much as they felt they could. If they succeeded, the change would last, and a good number of them would live to tell the tale.

If it failed – well, Yasira knew what that would look like. Bodies strewn across the ground, and no change to the world at all, not the kind that anyone would notice.

She was going to try to keep the bodies to a minimum. The rest of it was up to the gone people themselves.

The gone people guided Tiv to a spot near the middle of the group. She could see the way the place was set up, the little clearing with its tall grass and the trees and tangled undergrowth all around. In here, with gone people around her on every side, there was very little chance the angels would see her. Or Yasira either, for that matter.

Just because they couldn't see didn't mean they couldn't hurt them, of course.

She had brought a peace offering, a satchel of cookies and snacks and some bottles of clear water, and she handed them over. The gone people accepted this with smiles she couldn't quite read. Not the way people like Yonne Qun smiled, but like this was an interesting curiosity. Maybe they were just being polite. With gone people, who could tell?

It was almost refreshing. Tiv was just about done with people looking at her like she'd descended from the heavens to save them.

Yasira already looked distracted. Probably her mind was only half on the world around her and half in that trance, communicating the way the gone people did. Was it possible, Tiv wondered, for her to focus both ways at once? Some of the people in her head talking mystically, and others attending to the real world? Maybe, but Tiv didn't think so. Whatever happened inside a soul, there was still only so much matter in the brain to support it.

Yasira kissed Tiv one last time as the gone people took positions, in those concentric circles of theirs, preparing to reach for each other.

"I'm not going to be able to talk to you after this," Yasira warned. "You're going to be on your own. I'll be aware of where you are. I'll protect you. But I won't be… responsive. I probably won't even hear anything you say." She looked down. She didn't look very happy, or even very confident in her plan.

But there were so many of Yasira now. It made sense that some of them would believe it and some wouldn't. What would it be like to be a part of Yasira who didn't believe in this plan, and to be swept along with it by the rest of yourself? What would it be like to be a part of Yasira who *did* believe, but who had to hold those people's unhappiness in your mind with you at every step, to feel their fear and their complaints, to never be free of their doubts?

It was no wonder Yasira couldn't act confident, if that was what it was like for her.

Tiv would just have to do the believing herself.

She kissed Yasira back, squeezing her as tightly as she dared, which wasn't much – it would do no good to set off Yasira's sensory issues at a time like this. "I won't need anything from you but what you're doing, I promise. I'll be watching. I think someone has to do the watching. Someone has to come back from this who isn't you, who could see you from the outside, who can talk about it in words. To tell the world how glorious you were."

Yasira's eyes were wide and conflicted. "I don't think it'll be glorious, Tiv. I think it's going to be ugly–"

She was interrupted by an unmistakable sound from the edge of the park. The amplified voice of an angel. "Citizens, you are ordered to disperse."

The gone people didn't do anything. The gone people didn't even understand spoken language. Surely the angels knew that – so why were they bothering to announce the rules? For show?

Yasira glanced at her. "I have to go." She didn't wait for a response before she slipped further into the crowd. The gone people quickly took her hands and she closed her eyes. All over the park they were taking each other's hands, shaping themselves into the circle-like arrangement that they would need for their rites.

"This is your final warning," barked the angel. "Disperse, or we will open fire."

Without Yasira right there in front of her, it was easier for Tiv to feel the risks of this – not just to the people of Jai at large, or to her team, but to herself. If this didn't work, she would die as easily as the gone people. More easily – she had no special abilities. And she felt her heart in her throat, her breath bated, as she wondered if it was really possible for it to work.

But it would work. It had to.

The gone people on all sides of Tiv, plus the trees and vines tangled at the sides of the park, blocked the angels from view completely. But Tiv could still see Yasira, holding hands with the rest of them, thin and fragile but dressed, unlike the gone people, in ordinary clothes. On her face, eyes closed, there was an expression of grim concentration. Not much hope, only the knowledge that she had come here for a purpose, and that denying it now would be worse than failing.

Yasira would never admit how beautiful she was. How much hope she carried for everyone who saw her, even when she left none for herself. But Tiv let herself witness it, in that one silent moment before the bullets came. Tiv looked at Yasira, with her long dark hair falling over her face, preparing to do the impossible, and, even through the fear, her heart soared.

Then came the unmistakable crack of a gun.

Yasira did not move. Tiv couldn't see anything, not a twitch of her closed eyes, not a tightening of her hands where the gone people held them.

But the landscape leapt up around her, the way it had done when they fled in the forest before. Those vines and grasses burst upward, so quickly that they cracked the air just as the gun did, weaving themselves into something like a shell. It moved there, blocking all the little places where the angels might have crawled in, cradling the park inside itself, undulating strangely. Tiv had specialized in fluid dynamics for much of her career, but these grasses moved in a way that defied the laws she knew. Yet they held. The plant wall indented here and there like something was hitting it, crack after crack. A few bullets tore through and dropped to the ground, their momentum sapped, and the wall re-wove itself around them. Most of the impacts, bullets or otherwise, didn't make it through at all.

Yasira's face was tight with concentration. The rest of the gone people took out from their ragged pockets and their patchy satchels, the long thorns with which they were associated. They were beginning to move in synchrony, to murmur rhythmically to each other.

A light that did not look like light, a distortion in the air for which light was only the closest expressible analogy, bloomed in the gathering's center.

Yasira could see as the gone people saw. She was not confined to one place. In this ritual, all groups of gone people were connected to all others. On rocky slopes, in forest clearings, in caves, on grassy hills and in treeless wastes: there were clumps of them everywhere, all aware of each other. All performing the same rite at the same time. From here, communing with just one of the groups, Yasira would be able to protect them all.

She could vaguely sense the ritual's details, like the blueprint of some vast, spiritual machine. She could see the fractals of this world and their underlying equations, and the way the gone people, with concentration and supplication and sacrifice, meant to nudge those equations' parameters just the tiniest bit. But Yasira could not concentrate on that. The Scientist peered into the fractal's depths, fascinated, but even she could not focus enough to truly understand, not when she knew Yasira's mission here was another kind of work.

Her true work here was defense.

She had pulled power from the core of herself: that infinite well of Outside that held all the other broken parts together. It had burst through her and thrown defenses up whose nature she could barely control. Now she concentrated, scattering the pieces of herself across space, letting the power flow through to all of them.

It took different forms in different places. In one park like this one, it was the air and not the grass: twisting tentacular shapes burst from the wind itself, much as they had in Yasira's practice sessions, translucent, batting weapons away. On one rocky hill, the very ground caved inward, enclosing the gone people in a protective cave of strange, shifting crystal. In one forest, there was a ring of violet flame, hot enough to vaporize bullets, yet the trees did not burn.

And then, of course, there were groups of gone people who didn't need defenses at all. Groups who, by chance or by cunning, had hidden themselves where the angels could not follow. Far in the wilderness, in caves and hidden places, some gatherings faced nothing but the work they had chosen to do. Yasira was aware of these, too, but she did not waste power on them, only watched in case the situation changed.

It took all the parts of Yasira, working in concert, to do this. It took the full will and determination of the Strike Force. It took the voracious curiosity of the Scientist, working out who needed a little more or less of Yasira's power at a given moment, making adjustments accordingly. It took the deep-down parts who barely ever spoke, who were more Outside than human, seizing and guiding the power for the others to use. It took all the little parts who weren't sure of themselves, but who knew the rest of Yasira needed them, so as to form the sheer numbers to be in so many places at once.

There were parts of Yasira who hated her and hated themselves, parts who still mostly wanted to die, and even these parts had a useful place. They flung themselves directly to the edges of Yasira's power where the bullets were deflected, where the impact and effort of dealing with them caused real pain, and they took the brunt of that pain,

ADA HOFFMANN											291

shielding the others. The Strike Force had not thought to ask them to do this, but they went to it of their own volition, and they did not die; they only mentally convulsed and suffered and, strangely, exulted. This was better than death; this was pain with a purpose. Even their own brokenness fit here.

Yasira sent herself into every place where the gone people and the angels clashed, and she built up her defenses, and she hung on.

All over the Chaos Zone, people were rising up.

In Büata, Qiel and her friends had joined a line of protestors. All sorts of little groups like hers stood shoulder to shoulder, sweating in the heat as they carried their homemade signs. The signs said things like *WE ARE NOT HERETICS* and *STOP KILLING US* and *LET US EAT*. They'd picked a spot in the city square, beside the relief station. In better times, art displays and temporary markets had often been set up here. There were streets leading out in four directions and shop fronts on every side, some shuttered permanently thanks to the Plague, the rest temporarily closed in fearful anticipation of what was to come.

A line of angels in riot gear lined the side of the square, just across from the protestors, right in front of the relief station. The angels' numbers, true to Yasira's promise, had been thinned – so many of them had been called away to deal with the gone people. There were only about ten of them against hundreds of mortals. They refused to meet the protesters' eyes. If it came to violence – *when* it came to violence – the angels would probably win. They still looked uneasy.

Qiel Huong stood in that crowd, leading a protest song. She'd mobilized almost everyone from her little group in the suburbs. Mes wandered through the crowd, clinging to the elaborate sign he'd drawn, passing out water and snacks. Bannah had one of the loudest voices in their group.

Protesting against the Gods was illegal, but protest against a mortal government was not, and thus the art of protest had never quite been lost. Some gods, particularly Arete, encouraged it. Half the angels in front of them now were angels of Arete, their bronze-and-white livery shoulder to shoulder with the red-and-black of Nemesis, and it was those angels who looked most uneasy. They all understood how widespread today's unrest was, synchronized in a way that should not have been possible for mortals like these, without access to ansibles. People here in Büata had decided on a peaceful protest, not an uprising, not an attack, just a show of solidarity for the other uprisings across the continent and a request for their rights. That was by no means the case in other cities. Would the angels really want to punish this crowd as the law allowed them to? Did they want to antagonize these citizens, the relatively well-behaved ones, even further?

Qiel stared into their eyes from where she stood in the crowd, and she couldn't help but queasily wonder.

In Küangge – the city where Daeis had gone, where the angels held six hostages that the mortals wanted back – the mission was just beginning. The relief station had a single entrance, well-guarded, but there were paths and alleys in the dilapidated streets next to it, some of them half-covered by foliage. The team of mortals crept along those covered paths now, guiding each other with hand signals. There were eight of them, as large a group as it made sense to send without becoming too big to hide.

They loaded their guns now and they held their breath together in those shadows. They braced themselves, waiting for the angels who guarded the place to make their rounds. Waiting until they were at the furthest-out points. And then, at a gesture from their leader, the mortals charged.

Daeis hung back nearby, whispering mental suggestions to the small creatures they held in their hands. And those creatures called to others. As the mortals charged in, the angels in the distance whirled to face them. More angels poured out from inside the station. And in the distance, something else emerged: a monster larger than the building itself, a writhing mass of tentacles with a gaping mouth like that of a frogfish.

It lunged directly for the angels.

They turned to it, calling out in alarm. They aimed their weapons at what seemed to be its center. They probably called for backup, though Daeis and the other mortals could not know that for sure. They reached for bigger weapons. The monster took a hold of two of them with its tentacles and dashed them against the ground.

And because of that distraction, several mortals made it into the building, guns drawn, trembling.

There were other armed groups in those cities with the red pins stuck into them. There was one in Dasz, heading to the relief station to steal the food printer that Akiujal had wished for so badly before he died, and Weaver was not with them. Weaver had introduced herself to the group and offered to go with them, but they had decided she was too precious to lose. Instead she waited in their safe house nearby and watched them leave through the little soot-smudged window, shifting her weight anxiously. She wouldn't know who was wounded, or how many, or how badly, until they returned.

Weaver wasn't Savior; she had no illusions she could save everyone and no interest in doing so. She just wanted to do what she could, to know she'd given her all at this one moment in the grander tapestry.

But it was still hard to watch them go, not knowing how long it would be, or if they would return at all.

In Renglu, Genne Qun and her friends had chosen a method of protest very much like the gone people's, though most of them did not know it. Mostly young and without any delusions that they could fool a team of angels, they had not bothered to disguise themselves. They had simply gathered in a field.

They stood in a circle facing outward and started to hum to themselves.

Food-growing was a common power, but it worked differently for different people. Some of them needed to mumble or hum or sing; some of them worked best with their eyes shut, some with their hands buried directly in the soil. And there was that one friend of Genne's, of course, the one who grew such excellent mushrooms but had to work alone. That friend, like several others, had not shown up. It made her sad, but it didn't matter. There were enough of them.

They'd settled on an easy, simple song. There was dissonance in it as some of the growers with more particular needs hummed something else, out of tune with the others. They stood or crouched or lay on their bellies, as their powers dictated. But they were all the more united for their differences; everyone, no matter their posture or their part in the song, was there for a common purpose.

Small fungi began to poke out of the ground, edible strains conjured by the form of magic they shared. Little creepers with red and violet berries. Thick leaves in particular patterns, promising chunky roots and savory bulbs just under the earth.

The pair of junior angels of Arete who'd been assigned to watch this group – the majority of the local angels being preoccupied with the gone people – exchanged uneasy glances.

They did not open fire.

A few of the Seven had remained behind in the lair.

Splió and Prophet's powers weren't much use in a fight. That wasn't to say they couldn't have fought, if it was that desperate – they'd stand as much of a chance as people like Qiel did. But their real strength was in seeing. Splió stood by the airlock, leaning on it, concentrating on one location for a few seconds, and then another, and another – scanning as best he could for places that especially needed help. It was exhausting work, like watching five news broadcasts at once, but someone had to do it and it felt right, being exhausted that way today. More like being in the battle for real, putting his body on the line.

As he saw new things, situations turning good or bad across the continent, he mumbled words. Grid, behind him, focused on putting pins on the map and taking them back out, maintaining the closest thing they could to a real-time display. Sometimes Splió stopped, disoriented, and looked

up at that map, reminding himself what rounds he was
making and where he was in them.

Prophet sat a little behind him, eyes closed, flickering
behind their lids as if in a terrible dream. She murmured to
him and Grid, every once in a while, when she saw something
that told him where he ought to look. Occasionally she didn't
need him to look at all, only snapped her eyes open for a
moment and stammered out a location and what Luellae
ought to do there. But she was seeing far more than one
person could make sense of.

"Huang-Bo," she said, her eyes fluttering. "The alley
behind the department store. They're walking into a trap."

It wasn't so much that Luellae snapped to attention; it was
that she'd already been on alert, barely having caught her
breath from the last exertion. "What way do I take them?"

That was a question for Splió; Prophet didn't have such
fine-grained control of her own sight. He grimaced in
concentration as his consciousness worked through the
portal. "Angels waiting to the north of them. Take them
south. South and... west a bit."

"On it," said Luellae, and she jogged through the portal
and vanished into one of her usual twists of space.

Some people found Luellae's way of travel overwhelming,
disorienting; some got sick. Luellae, privately, loved it.
When she moved so fast it defied physics, it was like gravity
itself had let go of her for a moment. All the things that
weighed her down, all the fear and frustration, and in the
moment between physical places, she could not feel them.
Only spinning and whooshing and sensations too strange
for her to even remember upon landing, in the moment
when reality settled on her again.

She found herself in an alley with a small gaggle of armed

mortals. *Badly*-armed mortals; she wished the Seven had done a better job of arming these people from the start. If there were angels lying in wait for these people, already aware of their presence, they'd be slaughtered.

They stumbled back, gaping, when she materialized in front of them. Blur's legendary arrivals couldn't be mistaken for anything else.

So she wasted no time introducing herself, or saying *don't be afraid*. Just held out an arm. "It's a trap. Grab me, now."

She had a split second to reflect on how strange it was, the way they all trusted her, before they reached out to grip her as instructed.

Somewhere not far away from Renglu, along the border, a group of refugees gathered, most of them teenagers and children. They carried their meager belongings in backpacks and sacks. They had worn good shoes and brought precious water. They had planned for this carefully. The angels who normally guarded the border were busy elsewhere. If there was ever any time to make a break for it, out of the Chaos Zone, surely it was now.

They remembered all too clearly what had happened to the last group. They knew that, even now, they might not survive.

They clasped each other's hands a final time.

And they ran.

CHAPTER 17
Now

Yasira was far more than a physical torso, head, and limbs. If her body was what her soul inhabited then her body was everywhere, and she felt it like a new group of appendages, barely controlled. Every tentacular barrier that crystallized out of the air. Every blade of bulletproof grass that loomed up at her command. Every piece of the earth itself. And the bullets, flames, and other assaults that met them – certain parts of Yasira had volunteered to take the brunt of that pain, but all of her felt it a little. All of her knew exactly what would happen if a bullet got through.

And one did get through, every few minutes. She felt *that* as if it had torn through skin and muscle. But it was worse to see the effect: a gone person clutching the sudden red bloom of their body, falling to the ground, blood trickling into the grass.

Yasira had parts who could handle pain. She did not have many who could handle failure.

Yet the gone people gathered around each body, reverent and sad and accepting. They touched the blood with their hands, but they did not stop the rest of what they were doing, the humming, the focus, the ritual. As if to say: this was not failure at all.

Where the blood soaked into the ground, that was the first place where everything visibly changed. The Scientist tried to catch a glimpse of the patterns underlying it, but they were too intricate to analyze without abandoning the rest of the work. Yasira could only watch its physical signs. The tendrils that came up from the ground, and the colors that shifted across it. New plants began to bloom, more profuse and more varied than the ones that the protesters in Renglu called up. Thickets made for shelter, trees bursting with fruit, and stranger things. Vines, circling the edge of the space where the ritual had started, flecked with spots of crimson.

> *death was always going to be part of this | necessary |*
> *inevitable*
> *microbe   tree   animal   us   grass   you   insect   fruit*
> *and the new creatures here that you have no name for, all*
> *occupy finite time, all are smaller than the collective*
> > *smaller in space*
> > *smaller in time—*
> > *call this humility*
> *you have made the death smaller and kinder | let this be*
> *enough*
> > > *Savior | to save yourself | remember what you saved*
> > > > *and not*
> > > > *the rest*
> > > > *of everything*

In Büata the protest still stood at an uneasy stalemate. The angels had not moved; they didn't even make eye contact.

It was eerie, standing and shouting and chanting and demanding attention from a line of armed beings who didn't even acknowledge your existence. Qiel almost wished they would bark orders, the way she'd grimly imagined in her head, demand that the protestors disperse, but of course she didn't really wish for that. She didn't want this to be any more dangerous than it had to be.

So she just kept everyone chanting, one hastily-composed protest slogan and then another, and then the first one again, as sweat dripped down their faces in the hot sun. She thought Mes, with his containers of snacks and water, was doing a lot more to keep things going than she was. But Qiel was the one her friends looked to for direction, and she would give it, as best she could.

She kept looking at the short line of heavily armed angels, wondering how many of them were like Elu. How many had become angels with good intentions, and realized their mistake too late? How many didn't truly want to be here?

She couldn't know. And as long as they kept following their masters' orders, it wasn't relevant. Qiel still worried about what might have happened to Elu, but she needed to take care of her mortal friends first.

But as the heat and fearful tedium of the protest wore on, she kept wondering. If they were given the order to fire, how many of them, deep down, wouldn't want to? What if she could reach those ones, somehow, with some especially good song or slogan or sign? What if she could get them to lay down their arms? What then?

Qiel's friends and neighbors looked at her with respect, these days, and she knew that was partly Outside. It had favored her in this particular way, as it favored other people with the ability to grow food or talk to monsters. Qiel couldn't do any of those flashy things, but after the miracle people had suddenly started to listen to her more. She was grateful for that. But even Qiel couldn't come up with words persuasive enough to solve this problem.

She wished she could.

Daeis waited, crouched in the bushes near the relief station, willing themself not to be discovered. They had monster friends they could call on if that happened, but they didn't want to risk it. They didn't like confrontation.

Somewhere inside the station, Küangge's little rescue team was dashing around as fast as they could, looking for the prisoners. They might find them. They might not. The team might not come back at all, and Daeis didn't know what they were supposed to do if that happened, how they were supposed to know it was happening.

They'd wanted to ask that, among many other questions, but Daeis wasn't very good at talking and the Küangge team had explained only as much as they thought needed to be explained, in a language Daeis only partly understood. Splió hadn't been around to smooth things over.

So they just waited, hugging a smooth-skinned, rabbit-sized creature tightly to their chest, and tried not to be afraid.

"Put down your weapons," said the pair of angels of Arete who'd confronted Genne Qun's group of plant-growers just outside Renglu. "Cease this heresy."

But they didn't cease. Nor did they bother arguing, pointing out that these plants were what kept their family and community alive. The angels had already heard all those arguments, and they were hearing them again, across the Chaos Zone, in every peaceful protest. Genne's group were unguarded on purpose. They were too busy singing. They were too busy using their powers for good.

All across the field, under a blue sky twisted with the Chaos Zone's unnatural oranges and greens, things were blooming and growing. Good things, or at least things that seemed good to Genne – she had no idea how they looked to the angels. Fat bright mushrooms, shining berries, delicate flowers dripping nectar. This was more than Genne had expected. She had grown food together with people before, but she had never assembled a group so large, and she was surprised how it multiplied the effect. Maybe that was because of the gone people, working synchronously with them in so many faraway places. Or maybe they were more powerful together than she'd thought.

All she could do was keep singing, as the fronds and leaves wound their way up her legs, past her waist.

The angels trained their weapons on the group of them, wary, uncomfortable; but they were Arete's, not Nemesis', and these were a group of unarmed young women making flowers grow. For whatever reason – whatever ineffable angel calculation was in their heads – they did not fire.

Genne only hoped it would stay that way.

"Is it time?" Picket asked, tense and waiting in the lair. His fingers were so tight around the arms of his chair that the edges of it hurt him.

"No," said Splió, brow furrowed with the effort of watching dozens of protests and armed missions, in dozens of cities. "There's not much fighting, except around the gone people."

"Not yet," Prophet said darkly.

Meanwhile Luellae flitted from place to place, stopping by the lair only long enough each time to get her next orders. There were civilians who had to be whisked out of the gone people's crossfire, commando teams who'd been backed into a corner, wanted heretics who had to be spirited out of the angels' view. There were refugees in a few places, running for destinations outside the Chaos Zone, and it was even odds if the welcome they'd receive back in normal human space would be any better than what they'd get if the angels caught them; but Luellae was glad that they tried, and she caught up as many of them as she could, picked them up over ravines and past walls, finding safe places for them to stumble to a halt and catch their breath.

She wasn't sure if this was going to work out in the end, but she had never been more in her element: moving, running, flying, so fast that no one would ever catch her again.

Wherever the gone people gathered, bullets rained, and flames. The stern shouts of heavily armed angels – angels Enga had trained – fell upon ears incapable of hearing them. The forests burned, the sand dunes melted, the caves collapsed in explosions and showers of stone, but Yasira stood firm. The Outside shields she'd built, in all their locations and in all of their varying forms, still held. And the gone people, within them, were reaching deeper and deeper into the structure of the world, so deep it ached.

The ritual was working.

For now.

Even if every minute or two another bullet did breach

the barrier. And an instant was all it took for a gone person – as human as any other person, even if they didn't see themselves in the same way – to clutch at the sudden blood welling up from their body, and to fall.

Irimiru Kaule, Overseer of Nemesis, sat in his buzzing throne glaring at nothing. His metal-plated fingers danced along the arms of the throne, data flowing through them in visible and tangible sparks of light. The bee-like bots that held auxiliary mental calculations danced around his head, their swarm intelligence quickly decoding and collating patterns in what he saw, faster than even an electronic mind could.

For the past five minutes he had made his body comically unassuming, a small slender milquetoast of a man. Aside from the pretty features – Irimiru, admittedly, was a *bit* vain – he should have been a bean-counter or a pencil-pusher in some petty, useless mortal bureaucracy. That was how it felt to Irimiru right now, because he was nominally in charge of a good number of angels, but he no longer had full authority to direct them. Ever since the Plague, the Chaos Zone had become important enough to be administrated by archangels of several Gods in concert – Nemesis and Arete keeping the immediate threats under control, Eulabeia and Epiphron gathering data about the zone's properties, Agon venturing in to assist in the most dangerous zones, Aletheia asking more fundamental questions about how it worked and Techne extrapolating how it might be put back together. Other Gods pitched in as needed. Even Philophrosyne, who hated violence, had helped put together the communications infrastructure that Nemesis needed for Her broadcasts. The result was that, although Irimiru was a perfectly good Overseer capable of coordinating many teams of Inquisitors and Enforcers, he had little authority to do anything except pass the Archangels' orders down.

He was rapidly becoming convinced, however, that in this case the orders were *wrong*. Or – since that, taken literally, was blasphemy – that the situation had evolved in such a way that the orders were no longer appropriate.

He watched the feeds and updates from the dozens of teams assigned to him – only a fraction of the forces of Nemesis deployed to the planet, but a sizeable fraction. Every few seconds a semi-conscious process of his mind collated the data, summarized it by focusing on the moments that had drawn a particularly strong neurological response, added any commentary he chose to add, and passed it up the chain to an Archangel of Nemesis. This was not always standard procedure, but during an active operation of this size it was necessary.

They were putting all their resources into trying to break the gone people's ritual. But the gone people, despite their spectacular heresy and the supposed involvement of Yasira Shien, weren't even really doing anything. The Outside forces they'd summoned, so terrifying to behold at first, were only acting as a shield. They had not lashed out to destroy any angels even after considerable provocation. And the results of the ritual, as far as any of the angels in the field could see, were no more dramatic than many of the minor, non-violent heretical rites that mortals did elsewhere. Merely making some trees bear fruit.

Which was still heretical and deserved death, of course – but meanwhile the actual mortals of the Chaos Zone, the ones who were still people, were doing vastly worse things. Armed insurrections, in some instances. And being met with a very depleted defense.

Of course they'd predicted this would happen – it had been trivial, with the Vaurian spies they had in place, to intercept a copy of Yasira Shien's letter. And wasn't it interesting that Yasira would finally show her face at a time like this? But they had assumed, following analysis of the letter, that the gone people's ritual would be as fundamental and horrible as the beginning of the Plague itself. That making it stop would be worth all the losses elsewhere. And that Yasira herself could be apprehended in the process – but so far, no one had even worked out which grouping of gone people contained her. If any of them did.

Irimiru was underwhelmed.

With a shiver she rearranged her features into a more feminine form. Irimiru got restless if she stayed with a single face too long. She grew taller, and she let her hair curl into an authoritative, classical shape.

Requesting that we redirect our forces, she text-sent, up through the most official channels, to the Archangels themselves. *The gone people are a diversion. The real threat is from the mortals who can actually plan things.*

The request was more complex than that, of course. It was an interlinked structure connecting to the moment-by-moment reports. Each word called up a dense network of video summaries and prior analysis, bolstering itself with its own nuanced evidence in a way that transcended mere speech. But the words were the essence of it.

The Archangels hesitated only a second and a half before responding. Archangels were creatures who had once been human, but they had worked their way up the hierarchy even higher than Irimiru, the highest that an organic being could possibly ascend, and they had been rendered down to nothing but brain tissue and circuitry. The Gods Themselves were made of different stuff, but Archangels lived in sufficient communion with their Gods to viscerally feel some small part of the God's mental state. For Archangels of Nemesis that meant torment, of course – glorious torment. Constantly hovering at the very edge of damnation, yet with *such* power at their beck and call.

Irimiru had always thought she would like to be an Archangel one day.

Agreed, said an Archangel at last. Of course this was not a mere word, either; it came with its own dense structure of references and implications. Like all direct communications from Archangels, it came in a mental blast of pain and glory. Irimiru shut her eyes, savoring it. *Here are your orders.*

Yasira could barely feel her actual body, sitting in the grass somewhere supported by the gone people. But she felt the attacks from all sides, and she felt when those attacks suddenly lessened. They didn't stop, they just got *smaller,* everywhere at once – a squad of twenty heavily armed angels dwindling to two. A squad that had been trying to gas the gone people to death in the ravine where they stood, suddenly turning off their machine, picking it up and marching away, leaving only a skeleton crew behind.

There were still bullets coming in. Less of them, but a bullet was a bullet. She still had to keep up all the shields around all the groups of gone people. She couldn't get a message to the other mortals, or the rest of the Seven, warning them. She didn't have the energy to spare.

But she faltered for a moment, realizing what this meant. Realizing what a danger there was, here, to all the people she'd chosen not to protect.

I can't, something wailed inside her. *This is wrong. It's my fault they're out there. It's my fault they're going to–*

And it was the gone people, their hands still tight around her hands, who drew in to calm her without words.

She'd planned for this. Everyone, gone and mortal alike, knew the risks. Everyone had chosen their part of it. There was nothing she could do, except keep doing her own part, and have faith, and hang on.

Qiel had been starting to hope that maybe a standoff was all it would be. Maybe they'd march here and chant their slogans for a few hours and then they'd all run out of steam and go home. Maybe it was selfish to want that, but at least it would mean that no one got hurt.

So her heart sank when she saw new lines of angels, more heavily armed than the first ten, almost all of them in Nemesis' red-and-black livery, advancing from the sides of the square.

The crowd around her shifted uneasily, unsure what to do. They could see what was going on as well as she could. They did not want to be seen giving up so easily, but they did not want to be boxed in. This could get very bad, very quickly.

Qiel glanced at the angels: there were shielded rows of them now in three directions. The fourth might work. She made her choice.

"Come on," she whispered, inclining her head in the direction she'd chosen. "We need to head back."

Her friends followed her. A lot of small groups were beginning to quietly exit, threading their way through the crowd. Others, die-hards, stood firm.

They were only just out, slipping into the mouth of a

nearby alley, when they heard the new angels beginning to speak.

"Citizens," said one angel, in an unnaturally amplified voice. "You are engaged in illegal insurrection. This is your final warning. Disperse now."

Qiel paused, pressing herself back against the alley's wall. So many people she knew were still out there, holding their protest signs with white knuckles, sweating in the heat, chanting. She could not quite bring herself to turn her back on them.

And then the shooting started.

When it was two junior angels of Arete, Genne Qun's group had been able to stare them down, singing, letting their magic do its work.

They faltered when two more angels approached from the other direction, picking their way through the now-overgrown tangle of foods and flowers, these ones in unmistakable reds and blacks, and with bigger guns.

And another two, circling them, boxing them in.

The song ground to an uncertain halt. Genne shifted uneasily, wondering if she could run through the lush growth she'd created, or if her feet would be caught and rooted to the spot. She picked up one of her feet and put it down, and it moved that way, but only with difficulty, tendrils wrapping around it as she did so.

This was very bad.

The angels aimed and readied their guns.

"Citizens," said the largest of them, a pale-skinned man with several more weapons attached to his red-and-black belt, titanium shining unnaturally at his temples. "You have been ordered repeatedly to disperse. And you have refused."

Genne felt two of her friends stepping nervously backwards against her. She didn't think any of them knew what to do.

The angels trained their guns directly on them, one muzzle pointed at each unarmed head.

"Don't move," said the angel, with a cruel smile, and with his other hand – the one that wasn't holding a gun – he picked up a lighter. Flicked it on, and let the flame dance in his hand just a moment, let it sink in what he was about to do.

One of Genne's friends, no older than her, moved the tiniest amount, just enough to whisper to her, "I think we should run."

Genne wasn't sure if her limbs would obey her, if the plants she'd grown would move smoothly out of her way as they would for a gone person. Or if she was the one who'd boxed herself in. She felt an awful, sinking fear.

The guns were still trained on each individual person in the group, scaring them still. The angel turned over his hand and dropped the lighter. The flames began to lick at the plants that entangled them.

All across the Chaos Zone, the strongest pockets of resistance outside of Yasira's defenses – all the ones that had, so briefly, seemed victorious – had now turned into battle zones. Bullets flew. Gas made its way through the crowded streets, choking and stinging.

This was what Picket had been fearfully waiting for. He felt it like a brand to his nerves when Splió, eyes closed, concentrating at the edge of the airlock, gasped and said, "Found one."

"Is it the worst?" Picket tremulously asked, because where to help was a very important problem. Tiv had said that there wasn't an optimal solution to that problem. But he wanted one.

Splió's expression darkened. "I don't know, but it's the worst yet, and it's set up in a way you can handle. Go."

Picket obediently rushed through the airlock, trembling a little. Trusting Splió to operate the meta-portal and spit him out in this mysterious place where he was needed.

He emerged abruptly into a hail of bullets, flames, and screams. He'd come out through a maintenance door onto a rooftop, and he immediately flattened himself, crawling to the edge and peering over. He could see what Splió had meant when he said this one was set up right. The angels had boxed a group of mortals in on all four sides – maybe peaceful protestors, maybe an armed group, Picket couldn't tell from up here. A space the size of the city block was full of them now, a crowd desperately trying to take cover or escape, and the angels were firing into it.

Trembling harder than before, Picket reached out, called on his powers, and made a slow and deliberate fist.

The ground under the angels – and *not*, by and large, under the mortals – changed.

Picket had no control over exactly *what* his power did. No matter how he'd experimented, it seemed to him that there were only two adjustable parameters: *where* and *how much*. *Where* was very clear from up here. As for *how much*, he'd turned it to maximum; it was all he could think of to do.

The pavement of the street itself liquefied under the angels, reached up with strange sticky tentacles to drag them down, drown them in its black mire or tear them apart. Holes opened in the ground, fissures that went eyecrossingly deep, with an unearthly orange glow at their core, and the angels stumbled to avoid them or went tumbling in.

Picket watched it all with wide eyes, willing himself to continue. He was acutely aware that this was *not* a game. Every part of it was real. Even with the careful way he'd marked out the bounds of the effect, some mortals who'd directly clashed with the angels were too close to its edge; some got sucked into the affected area, and they died, too. There were no points awarded for this, no scorecard he could check to see if he'd made the right move or not. There was only the actual reality of what he was doing, and the screams.

Picket wasn't doing the same thing Talirr had done when she first began the Plague – that burst of unimaginable, surreal horror that had wiped out tens of millions in a few minutes. He wasn't her, and he hadn't made the kinds of pacts with Outside forces that she had. His powers were more localized and temporary. But to the mortals on the ground, cowering and terrified, he knew it looked exactly the same.

Elsewhere, Luellae was moving as fast as she could. In a multitude of city squares, in hails of bullets too slow to catch her, in rains of choking gas that didn't have time to reach her lungs, she bent reality to enter, grabbed as many injured, terrified mortals as she could, and bent reality to get out again. Leaving them wherever she could, in parks and gardens untouched by the protests, in safe residential neighborhoods that might or might not have been their own; she didn't have time to check. Even moving as fast as Luellae could, she didn't have time to save everyone.

The team in Küangge had almost made it out of the relief station. They had found the prisoners. They ran for it, hand in hand, the prisoners limping and tripping as their abused bodies tried hard to keep up with their rescuers. They had made it past the door. There was a copse of trees nearby. If they could get there–

There was the sound of multiple large weapons being readied at once. Two lines of angels emerged, one on each side, a third emerging from the trees themselves. This was far more angels than the number that had been here when they began. The rescuers froze; the prisoners sagged against them in despair.

"You are surrounded," came the announcement, projected from the angel in the lead, a hulking armored man in Nemesis' colors. "Drop your weapons."

The rescuers dropped them.

From further back in the woods there was a sound, unearthly, like a thousand blended screams.

For a split second, the angels hesitated. In the next second, a tentacle whipped out from under the trees, thirty feet long, textured like a rotting log but strong as steel. It caught ten of the angels in its path and bowled them over.

The rest of the angels turned, aiming their weapons at the emerging creature. The mortals dived for cover. They crawled over each other on the ground, shielding as many as they could with each other's bodies. Gunfire and screams blocked out all other sound.

The monster was taller than the canopy it had hidden beneath, even bigger than the one that had covered their entry. Above its massive tentacled limbs there was a head of sorts, with features as twisted and irregular as the knots of an old, gnarled tree. It seemed to shift intricately in a way that might have been a trick of geometry or lighting, or might have been actual shapeshifting. One moment it looked like a deformed human skull with awful, brown, sharp teeth. One moment it looked like an unearthly undersea creature. One moment it was a roundish shape with no features, as meaninglessly pitted as the moon; the other views, surely, could only have been pareidolia. There was nothing for a human to recognize here.

Crunching greedily, it shoveled the angels – hail of bullets and all – into what might or might not have been its mouth.

The mortals were not foolish enough to consider this monster their friend. They knew the rules of the Chaos Zone. They knew that if they approached too close, antagonized it, or even just fled too enticingly, it would eat them with the same horrible ease. They held their breaths.

Daeis, hiding in the bushes behind the relief station, pressed a hand to their mouth to suppress a smile. When the monster stomped close to them, its tentacles flailing, they reached out, thinking in the special way they used for Outside creatures.

It reached down to them, with one awful, knotted, rotting-log limb, and they moved their hand gently against its underside, as easily as scratching a pet cat under its chin.

CHAPTER 18
Now

Akavi was there, of course.

He was angry with Elu, and didn't want to leave him alone in the ship for too long at this delicate stage. Then again, perhaps learning to sit in one place and be obedient for once would be good for the boy. Meanwhile, Akavi had a more important anger. He had worked as hard and as quickly as he could to manipulate Luellae into the right position for his plans, and it had not worked. He had tried, through reverse psychology, to convince the Seven not to risk themselves and rise up, and yet here everyone was, rising up.

Even Yasira was out here somewhere, if that letter was to be believed. Maddening. She would be with one of the groups of gone people, but there were dozens of those across the continent, and no one seemed to know which one she was hiding with. Without Luellae to oblige him, Akavi's travel options were now very limited. So far, he hadn't even been able to find Büata's group of gone people – assuming Büata had such a group at all. He was reduced to wandering at the edges of the mortal protest, hoping one of the Seven would be there.

The city square was in ruins, people fleeing and dying everywhere. A few sensible mortals had seen what was coming and managed to escape ahead of time; the rest were trapped. Even Akavi wasn't completely sure he wasn't trapped, as he edged along a wall, knowing enough about typical angel crowd control measures to stay out of the line of fire. Several of the nearby shopfronts had collapsed when an angel threw a grenade in that direction, falling to deceptively heavy splinters and shards. There were people trapped in that rubble, long steel beams pressing their broken limbs to the ground.

And because Akavi was keeping to the edges and out of the line of fire, because his angle of view was therefore not the same, he saw it when the other angels didn't.

A blur of motion in the air. A shapeless inky blackness that moved almost too fast to track, and that resolved into the form of a woman.

"Come on," said Luellae to one of the trapped mortals, a man conscious and groaning with his legs trapped under roofing tiles. "I'm going to get you out of here."

The man made a small whimpering noise, his eyes wide and awed; he knew, as did everyone who laid eyes on Luellae, who she was.

It was a stroke of luck for Akavi that he'd picked a place like this. Luellae might otherwise have burst in and out of view too quickly for him to do anything about it. But with a trapped man like this she had to scramble a moment, her thick arms heaving as she effortfully pulled the tiles away. Other mortals, seeing who she was and what she was doing, had run to the scene to help her.

So it didn't raise any eyebrows when Akavi ran in that direction with them.

Luellae didn't see him coming until he pounced, his arms cinching tight around her in the chaos, sharp nails extending from his fingers to form claws at her throat.

She froze. Luellae would know who he was. She could use her powers to flee this scene, but unless she managed to dislodge Akavi from her body, she would take him with her.

"You disobeyed me," Akavi hissed in her ear.

"I didn't," said Luellae. Akavi could feel how her breath sped, how her heart hammered with panic; that was satisfying. "I did exactly what you fucking said."

True, in a sense – that was the trouble with reverse psychology – but it missed the point; she hadn't done what he *wanted* her to.

"If you want to live," Akavi continued, unruffled, "you're going to take me back to my ship. And, there, we'll talk more." The points of his nails pressed sharply against the pounding pulse of her neck.

"I'll get away," Luellae promised, her voice shaking. "I'm good at that."

"We'll see."

It was so very satisfying when the world twisted around them and went black.

At the end of it, there were bodies lying everywhere. In all the town squares and streets where the protesters had stood toe to toe with the angels. In the corridors where mortals had taken up arms and fought.

There were angel bodies, too, here and there.

Something in the world had changed – something too subtle for sensors like Irimiru's to pick up on yet, but its earliest signs were beginning to show themselves. Even far from the protests themselves, new fruits were beginning to emerge from the trees, new streams diverting themselves to make little cascades of clean water. Little spots in the woods and plains, little crevices in the crags and the desert, had moved as things always moved in the Chaos Zone, opening themselves to offer shelter. This world would never get the Outside out of it – entropy itself prevented that. Nor would it ever be gentle or safe. But when Savior did her first miracle, she had given control of this world to the people, gone and otherwise, not to the incomprehensible horrors that made it this way in the beginning. And gradually, painfully, in the face of unspeakable danger, the people were figuring out how to use that control. How to make their world into something they could live in.

Qiel and her friends had made it back to their safe house, though not before hearing the grenades going off, the screams, the creak of the building collapsing. They huddled together in her candlelit living room now, shaking and hugging each other. Qiel felt guilty; had it been selfish, leaving the way she did, just before things got bad? If she'd been willing to sacrifice this whole group, would it have accomplished anything more?

Bannah Nin, her face buried in Qiel's shoulder, moved only enough to give herself the air to speak. "Do you think it meant anything? Do you think, when we wake up tomorrow, the world will be even a little bit different?"

Qiel closed her eyes.

She didn't have the flashy kind of Outside power, not the kind that changed things physically around her, but she knew she had something. And when she closed her eyes and breathed deeply, she could feel the change. She knew that, however the angels might try to deny it, their world had just become a little bit less hostile, a little bit easier to live in. Most of that was because of the gone people, not them. But they'd done something. They'd spread out the angels' forces, which might otherwise have had nothing to shoot at but the gone people themselves. They'd made it clear, through sheer numbers, what the people of the Chaos Zone wanted.

"Yeah," she said, moving her hand to Bannah's hair. "I think it will."

When the angels were all gone, Picket unclenched his fist. He brought the street back to its usual state. Broken bodies lay scattered across it, some of them in more than one piece, some of them twisted into unrecognizable shapes. An angel's body had been stretched out like taffy, a long brilliant-yellow ribbon twisting over the ground in place of a midsection. An arm stuck up limply into the air, the rest of its previous owner swallowed up by the pavement.

Most of the bodies were angels, but not all.

Picket watched from the rooftop as the surviving mortals picked themselves up off the ground. They were shaking. They were making noises he could barely hear from up there. Pairs of them hugged each other; small groups scurried away in strange and gingerly ways, like they were expecting the ground to erupt and swallow them again at a moment's notice.

If he calculated it all according to game theory, then this was a good result. A few lives lost, on his side, and all of the enemies defeated. When the alternative was that everyone on his side died. But this wasn't a game. He looked at the mortal bodies splayed on the ground, and even the twisted, barely recognizable forms of some of the angels, and they weren't numbers. He couldn't add or subtract them from each other and declare victory that way.

He felt sick.

It was a good thing that none of the mortals had seen him up here. Nobody looked up as he ran back to the little service door he'd come here by, back to the airlock, back into the lair that he shared with the rest of the Seven.

He needed the rest of the Four. Picket often felt like only a quarter of a person. He wanted Grid's practicality to ground him, Prophet's gentleness, Weaver's enthusiasm. But Weaver was still out there, healing people. As he burst into the room, sweating and shaky, Prophet was still hard at work, eyes shut and dancing under their lids, clearly distressed by what she was seeing. Her head was pressed together with Splió's as they conferred about something neither of them liked.

The battle wasn't over. The little pocket of it where Picket had fought was over, but there were more pockets, more crises. He could feel that viscerally as he looked at the two of them. Picket didn't want to go back out there and do what he'd just done over again. If Prophet told him in that moment that he needed to, that it was either that or let a whole block full of mortals die, he didn't know what he'd do. He'd probably grit his teeth and go and do it. But he didn't want to.

He started towards the two of them. It was Grid who stopped him, with a soft, firm hand silently pressed to his arm. It was Grid who led him to the upside-down kitchen, and gave him a warm drink, and let him breathe.

Something seemed wrong to him, though, as he sipped his drink and recovered his wits. As he looked up at the common area, upside down from his perspective, where

Prophet and Splió looked distraught, and where something seemed to be missing. As he watched the grim look on Grid's own face. He knew Grid so well, another quarter of the person that he was.

"Wait," he said. "Where's Blur?"

And the haunted look in Grid's eyes told him everything he needed to know.

Yonne Qun leapt to his feet at the knock on his front door. It took all his presence of mind to look out the peephole instead of simply flinging it open – it could have been angels, after all. It could have been something bad. But all that he wanted to do was to know that his daughter was okay.

What he saw, in the waning, shifting evening light, was a gaggle of girls Genne's age. Genne's friends, a smaller group than the one he thought he remembered setting out this afternoon, all of them scorched and bruised. With Genne herself, sagging and bloody, like a sack of potatoes between them.

He didn't know what he was thinking as he opened the door. He was full of insistent, irrelevant thoughts. These people must be hungry, thirsty, they might need first aid; Qun had supplies for all of those purposes in his house. That was what Qun was good at, distributing supplies and connecting people, like his own miniature version of the Seven's team, interfacing between them and the community. There hadn't been a large-scale, general protest in Renglu as there had been in some other cities; the majority of Renglu's community had judged it too dangerous. It was only small splinter groups like his daughter's, groups with particular magical purposes, who had insisted on their own little parts of the uprising. Qun didn't have those powers. He could help them; that was what he was good for. He could maintain a safe space.

Genne sagged like an unliving thing between her friends' hands. The bullet holes in her body had long ago stopped bleeding, and her skin was cold.

"I'm sorry," said one of the girls, and normally Qun knew everybody in his community by name, but at the moment he didn't know or care which one of them it was. There was Genne, and there was a blur. "It got bad. We didn't all make it–"

Some of the other girls were still limping, still bleeding. He should do something for them, but he couldn't focus.

Qun had told himself things about maintaining a safe space, about caring for his community from the sidelines, about how it shouldn't be their responsibility to risk themselves to fix a Plague that was not of their making. All those things were lies. Qun was simply a coward. In a just world, he should have been out there, too.

That was what he thought to himself, on his living room floor, as he fell to his knees and howled.

Elu was alone. He was trying to design a new outfit in his head, not an outfit Akavi had asked for, but just something colorful and swishy enough to distract him. He couldn't focus very well.

Mortals were rising up across the Chaos Zone, and gone people were rising up, and of course angels would be descending to meet them. Elu remembered those protocols. He thought maybe he wanted the mortals to win.

He let himself imagine it, a world where the mortals

won, where the Gods weren't hunting people like him and Akavi anymore. In that world, he wouldn't have to stay with Akavi. He could escape, and all he'd have to fear would be Akavi's wrath, not the wrath of all the Gods. Elu could have dealt with that level of fear, he thought. He could have done it.

But he didn't live in that world.

It startled him when the airlock opened, and Akavi stormed into the room, dragging a struggling Luellae with him.

Elu went perfectly still, staring at them. He'd known Akavi had meant to capture one of the Seven if he could, but he hadn't expected it to *work*.

He remembered Luellae; while she was kept in a cell on the *Menagerie*, he'd visited her every week, trying to keep her comfortable. He'd tried to be kind to her the same way he'd tried to be kind to all the other prisoners, knowing kindness wasn't enough, knowing their position was equally unjust whether he was kind to them or not. He knew how she'd been made to betray the rest of the Seven.

Her face and hands were dirty, and there were tear tracks making thin lines down her cheeks, and Akavi had her pressed to him in a parody of an embrace, knowing she could teleport away as soon as he let go. His sharp claws, extended out as long as Elu had ever seen them, made indentations in the flesh of her throat.

As she took in the sight of Elu, her eyes widened, and then narrowed in contempt.

"You," she growled. "*You're* why he survived. Aren't you?"

Elu didn't have it in him to answer.

"Is the spare room ready?" Akavi asked, in an oddly flat tone, as if this was the kind of thing he did every day.

Of course it wasn't. Akavi hadn't explicitly asked for it, and Elu hadn't really expected he'd need it. "No, sir," he stammered. "I could print furniture–"

But Akavi had already stopped paying attention to him. He turned his head to focus more directly on Luellae. "You can get over fences, over walls, past guards, but you can't get out of a fully sealed room, can you? Not if you're kept away from the door. From what you've told me about your new powers, that's what I'd surmise."

Luellae didn't even dignify the question with a nod. Her hands were shaking. "Fuck you," she spat. "Fuck both of you."

"Good," said Akavi, without breaking stride. "Elu, calculate a trajectory while I secure the prisoner. The angels are distracted by the battle; I'd estimate we have another hour in which to launch without detection, if we're careful. But no more than that. You can work on the furniture once we break orbit." He pulled Luellae along with him, deeper into the ship. "Then, once we're safe in the air, we'll work on what else you can tell me about your little team. I'm going to have a number of uses for you."

In Dasz, Weaver hurried into action as the local commandoes finally stumbled and staggered back into the dingy apartment. Many of them were limping, clutching bloodied limbs and grimacing; some were still bleeding at an alarming rate. Few of them had made it out of this excursion without a wound. Many hadn't made it out at all.

Weaver did what she could, pulling and tugging at flesh with her quick fingers, flitting from the most urgent problem to the next-most-urgent. She loved this kind of work, quick and demanding, the way the sensory details of blood and bone filled her awareness. She painfully knitted ruined muscle, skin and bone back together. Healing this way was exhausting, and even though she'd stayed here saving her strength, she might pass out before she helped everyone she wanted to.

In the middle of the room, on a small table, the survivors of Dasz had placed the prize that they'd liberated from the angels. It gleamed there, clean and metallic and a little bit stained with fresh blood: a food printer.

When it was over, Yasira slumped to the ground.

Leaves tickled her face. She was too exhausted to react. She had pulled all the parts of her consciousness back into her body. She was tired in ways she didn't have words for – as if her very soul had run laps on some horrible treadmill until it collapsed.

There were sounds, and they were awful and loud, and she could not interpret them.

Not until she realized, gradually, that one of them was Tiv's voice. Tiv's hand, placed as lightly and unassumingly as she could, on Yasira's shoulder.

"It's okay," Tiv said softly. "It's okay, Yasira, it's over now. We did it. *You* did it. We're done. Let's get you home."

"Mmph," said Yasira.

Her limbs trembled, but with a bit of help from Tiv's steadying hands she managed to push herself vaguely upright. The air hurt. The park around her spun.

"How bad is it?" Tiv asked, her big eyes bright with concern.

"It's…" Yasira mumbled, surprising herself. "It's not bad."

It wasn't bravado. She felt different from before. She was

still an unnatural mess, exhausted and in pieces, and all too keenly aware of how far they still were from real victory. How small today's triumphs were, compared to the real freedom Jai needed, and exactly how much they had cost.

But Yasira had risen to that cost. She had seen the triumphs through. And all the things that were broken about her, even the parts that hated life and hated herself, had been just the things she'd needed for the task.

We saw it through, the Strike Force murmured in agreement. *We rose to the challenge.*

I learned so much, said the Scientist, still distracted, trying so hard to remember the details of the patterns she'd seen.

The parts that just wanted to help other people had helped them. The parts that wanted pain had been given a noble reason to endure it. The parts that were more fragmentary and less human than that, the parts that just wanted Outside – well, they'd gotten what they wanted in spades.

there is no nature or unnatural, the gone people had told her, *there is the soil of reality there is us*

"Good," said Tiv, guiding her forward. Yasira stumbled along, but at Tiv's pace she could just about manage. "You were amazing today, Yasira. You were the most beautiful thing I've ever seen."

It was the kind of thing another person might have said as flattery, maybe. Because they were worried for Yasira. Because they wanted to soothe her any way they could. But Tiv wasn't like that. She'd said as much, repeatedly, in no uncertain terms. Tiv was good, but she said what she meant.

And, just for this moment, Yasira believed.

CHAPTER 19
Now

Enga was in the middle of a cleanup operation with one of the teams she'd trained, chasing off the last few pitiful mortals from an illegal protest, when the ping came in from Irimiru.

We have a read on Akavi Averis's location, said Irimiru without preamble. *We're certain of it this time. A Vaurian was spotted among the mortals in Büata, interacting with one of the Seven, and everything about the recording matches Akavi's modus operandi. He used Outside abilities to escape, but he came into the city by mundane means, and we were able to use existing surveillance footage to track his approximate origin.*

Listen to me very carefully, Enga. I will make good on my promise. I will allow you to be the first to attempt to bring him in. But you are not to harm him nor Elu Ariehmu. Not yet. The situation has evolved.

WHAT SIR, Enga said back resentfully. This was one of the parts of her job she hated. Hunting people down and killing them was an angel of Nemesis' job, but Inquisitors and Overseers always wanted to do it in the most complicated possible way. Enga was built to just shoot things.

Vaurian Inquisitors of Nemesis have tried to get close to the core of Yasira Shien's insurgent group for months now, Irimiru explained. *All have failed. But Akavi came closer to success than any of them. He's been seen in the girl Luellae's vicinity twice now, and both times he was able to convince her to use her powers to help him. On the first such occasion he came very nearly within striking distance of Yasira herself. I don't want him dead until we find out how he did that and how it can be replicated. The broader mission to remove Yasira's heretical influence from Jai is more important to our forces than the recapture of a pair of fallen angels.*

Which was saying something. Normally, fallen angels were the highest-value targets of all. An angel could do a lot more damage than a mortal could. But Evianna Talirr and her students had redefined what damage even meant, and they'd taken a whole fifth of a planet hostage.

I WILL BRING HIM IN AND YOU CAN INTERROGATE HIM SIR, Enga suggested.

No. You were friends with him. Your facial expressions are atypical due to nerve damage; Akavi's microexpression software won't work on you. I believe he'll try to capture and suborn you. Let it happen. Befriend him. You'll be contacted later so as to tell us what you've learned.

Enga ground her jaw in rage. The elaborate metal of her arms gave a warning creak as she clenched those, too. She had demanded to be placed on this mission because she wanted revenge. Irimiru had pretended to give her what she wanted, only to take it away again. *I AM NOT A SPY SIR.*

Then you'll learn to be one, or you'll be terminated.

Enga could feel the cold smugness that accompanied the text-sending. Enga had challenged Irimiru, weeks ago, to either give her what she wanted or let her die. It gave Irimiru great pleasure to finally call that bluff.

They may try to do the same surgery on you, Irimiru continued, *that we suspect they did on themselves. Removing your ansible uplink so our systems can't trace you. If they suggest it, don't resist. We'll find other ways to get in touch.*

FUCK YOU SIR. FUCK FUCK FUCK FUCK Enga wrote, in the buffer of her mind that held the text in the instant before it was sent. She then deleted the words, swallowing them down without sending them. She was going to have to get used to this, swallowing rage, pretending to cooperate. This *was* what she wanted, in a horrible, twisted way. This *was* revenge. A way of bringing Akavi and Elu back to their betters and making them pay for what they'd done.

It was just going to be much, much harder than she had expected.

The *Talon* was right at the coordinates where Enga had been told it would be. Akavi had hidden it well, within a mossy ravine surrounded by thick woods. It looked different from how she remembered, more like a mortal ship – but Enga knew how little that mattered, how easy it was to make cosmetic alterations using the printers and bots. It was a ship of the right size, in the right place, and that was enough. The engines were idling, but the ship was still parked.

She strode to it, shifting the mechanisms of her arms to expose one of her heaviest blunt-force clubs. She locked the elbow joint of the club in place and then slammed it repeatedly, in a parody of a knock, against the *Talon*'s side.

"AKAVI AVERIS AND ELU ARIEHMU," she said. Enga couldn't speak aloud, but for occasions like these, she wore a translator. The device, looped around her neck like a cheap bit of jewelry, received her text-sendings over the ansible network and translated them into audible Earth Creole speech – in this case, boomingly loud speech, the kind that rattled the *Talon*'s frame and would definitely be audible even from inside the ship's thick walls.

It was possible for God-built translators to perfectly mimic the cadences of a real human voice, complete with contextually appropriate emotion and the small imperfections that made speech feel present and unrehearsed. Enga could have synched the translator up with her neurological state as well as her literal words; she could have customized it to any timbre, accent, or mannerisms she preferred. Enga had never wanted to do that. The only thing that felt like *her* voice was text-sending, blunt and plain and literal, and in all capital letters because lowercase took more effort. So she calibrated all her translators to sound like *that*. The words were loud and clipped and lifeless, like vocabulary being read out for a language class.

"YOU ARE WANTED FOR DESERTION FROM THE ANGELIC CORPS," she said. "OPEN THE DOOR AND SURRENDER."

She didn't expect them to open the door. She'd wait a few seconds, then knock and say it again with a little more emphasis, and when that didn't work, she'd start blasting. A heavy armor-piercing missile, the kind she'd used against Jai's biggest monsters in emergencies, would crack open even a God-built hull.

But before she finished counting those few seconds, a light blinked over to yellow above the airlock.

Someone was coming through.

Enga turned off the safety on every single firearm she possessed and extended her arms to their fullest position, fanning them all out, every muzzle mercilessly trained on the airlock door.

She was going to have to handle this carefully. The obvious thing to do here was to just fucking shoot Akavi as soon as he opened the door. But she wasn't allowed. She needed to let him win. He would try to use his words to persuade her to stand down, to join his side, and she was going to have to pretend to agree.

She'd have to pretend well enough that it fooled *Akavi,* who was a very keen observer of people, and who had every reason to be suspicious of her. Even with the apraxia and dead nerves in her face, which stopped his microexpression software from working on her, it would be hard.

Oh well. If it didn't work, she could shoot him and tell Irimiru she'd tried.

The airlock opened.

Akavi stood behind it – he hadn't bothered to change out of his true form, so she saw him in his natural translucent skin. He held a sheet of metal in front of him as a makeshift shield – pitiful, really. She still could have blown his head off with ease.

"PUT THE SHIELD ON THE GROUND," she bellowed, "AND YOUR HANDS IN THE AIR."

But even as she said it, Akavi barked out a series of words of his own. She couldn't make sense of them, mostly because she was already talking and she wasn't good at understanding more than one sound at a time. But she felt something grab on to her mind as he said the words. Her vision blurred, and her limbs seized, and–

NO.

He'd said he'd had this program removed. But he'd lied, of course he'd lied. Akavi always lied, and so he'd kept this hidden in a part of her circuitry after all, just in case she ever turned against him. He'd kept the off switch.

And Irimiru – had he fooled Irimiru?

No, he wouldn't have had to. Irimiru would have checked, but Irimiru didn't care. Irimiru had said that

Akavi would try to capture her. And this was one of the simplest methods by which that could happen. Irimiru just hadn't bothered to tell Enga about it in advance. Why should they?

Enga's consent was irrelevant; she couldn't do anything about it now. She couldn't even scream, as her vision faded to nothing, and her hearing faded to silence, and her powerful body faded away to nothing at all.

Elu waited, too nervous to properly breathe, as muffled sounds he couldn't make sense of came from outside the *Talon*.

Akavi had only just come back onto the bridge after securing Luellae in her room, but his face had lit up strangely when he heard Enga's voice. He had exited without a word, without even bothering to explain his plan to Elu. Elu didn't know how Akavi thought he could survive against firepower like Enga's. Maybe he wouldn't. Maybe Enga would kill Akavi and board the *Talon* and–

His first, foolish thought was that *she'd* run away with him. Let Luellae go and then take him some place where they would be safe. He had missed Enga. And she was so powerful – maybe she could protect him from the other angels. But of course, she wouldn't. Elu had violated Nemesis' rules even worse than Akavi. He'd left the angelic corps, left *her,* of his own volition, and he knew the kind of person Enga was. He could not expect mercy.

Maybe Enga would kill them both. Maybe he deserved that.

The airlock creaked open, and Elu held his breath.

Akavi was uninjured, and it disturbed Elu just how much

relief he felt, seeing that. Why did he still want Akavi to be all right, deep down? Akavi looked at his stricken face with scorn. "What do you take me for, Elu? Did you think I didn't install failsafes into my own most dangerous operatives? Come out here and help me with this."

Elu followed him numbly through the airlock. He had already worked out what Akavi meant. He remembered the off switch. He thought that had been removed decades ago, but of course it hadn't. Of course Akavi, manipulative and controlling, wouldn't truly give up such a method of control.

Amid the trees, Enga was standing still and frozen, her eyes unfocused, the weapons that protruded from her arms half-cocked. She barely breathed.

Elu flinched slightly as Akavi approached her frozen body. In this state, Enga wouldn't even be able to see him approach. She would be conscious in some sense, but removed from any ability to perceive the world around her. If she was threatened, she would not know. If she was injured, she would not feel the pain.

"What are you going to do, sir?" Elu asked, a lump in his throat. If Akavi wanted to hurt her, kill her, Elu clearly couldn't stop him. He couldn't stop anything.

Akavi gave him a triumphant little smile. "We're going to bring her on board, of course. It seems we have a bumper crop of prisoners."

Enga floated in a muted sensory landscape that she thought she'd never see again. She raged. Everyone – Akavi, Irimiru, Elu, Omhon – *everyone* had set her up for this.

She couldn't see the forest around her or the ship. She

saw a muted, soothing, dark wash of color. She heard nothing. She smelled something faintly pleasant, like good food, and there was a soft pressure all over her body.

None of it made her less angry.

Enga had not been locked inside this sensory cell for years. She had asked Akavi to remove it, once she'd proven herself, and the bastard had *agreed*. She should have known she couldn't trust him in matters like these. She should have known she was the wrong person for this mission, not in spite of her connection to Akavi and Elu, but *because* of it.

She should have known, even so many years after Omhon and with so many commendations on her record, that she was stupid.

She braced herself, but if Akavi killed her here and now, she wouldn't even feel it.

Eventually, her vision cleared. They hadn't killed her outright. They'd brought her aboard the *Talon*. She recognized its interior, the little parlor that opened out onto the bridge. They had launched. The steady, untwinkling stars of space moved in blackness outside the window, ringed with the faint violent tinge of a warp drive. She struggled to move, but she couldn't.

Enga remembered her orders. *Befriend him. Pretend to join his side. You'll be contacted later so as to tell us what you've learned.*

Enga frequently hated her orders, but she followed them. That was what good angels did. That was how to survive.

They'd let her live. She would do as she'd been told. And she'd make Akavi pay for what he'd done. Later. When Irimiru and their stupid bureaucracy decided it was time.

But she couldn't move yet, and she couldn't speak, and she couldn't connect to the network to text-send. So, for now, she would be still.

She was sitting propped up in one of the parlor chairs. Akavi sat across from her in his true form, expressionless.

"You can see me now," he said – a statement, not a question. There was no way for her even to nod.

"Now," Akavi continued, "what are we going to do with you? Obviously, I can't let you return to the rest of the angels to tell them anything. And I can't let you run free in my ship, not with those guns for arms. The obvious solution would be to kill you, but I hate waste. You're a valuable operative. And you follow orders, unlike some." He glanced meaningfully to the side, in what Enga guessed was Elu's direction; there was *something* in her peripheral vision that might have been Elu. She couldn't turn her head. She didn't know what Elu might have done to merit a look like that, and she didn't care. They should both die. "So, here's what we'll do. I'm going to have Elu give you the same surgery he gave to both of us, disconnecting you permanently from the angelic network. I'm going to have him hack up a modification to your targeting programs so that you can't aim a weapon at me. And then I'm going to have him print a translator that can be physically attached to you, so you can communicate. Don't misunderstand – that's step three." He smiled, unnervingly pleasant, as if he wasn't talking about physically and mentally mutilating her. "Then we'll talk, once you've been modified for our needs. I think we could be a good team again, the three of us and Luellae. Don't you think so, Elu?"

"We could give her the translator first, sir." Elu was often hesitant when speaking, but there was something different about his tone, something Enga couldn't put her finger on. As if he was more afraid than ever. "She might have something useful to say."

"There's no time for that," said Akavi. "Until we do the surgery, the angels can track us."

Rage like yours is a gift, he had told her, fifty years ago. *Turn it outward.*

Enga would not despair. She would rage. She would do her duty and follow her orders. She would see them both dead, as she'd been instructed to. And then maybe she'd go further. Maybe she'd kill Irimiru, who'd set her up for this. Maybe she'd bring the whole damned system down.

Once, Akavi had given her hope. He'd made her think her talents could be valued, in spite of the damage in her brain, in spite of everything. But he only wanted Enga's strength when it was useful to him. He had not wanted to see the true depth and the breadth of her anger.

Akavi said another couple of code words, and Enga felt herself falling out of consciousness entirely.

Later, masked and gloved, on the same makeshift operating table he'd used for himself and Akavi, Elu looked down at the cracked-open top of Enga's skull, half-circuitry and half-brain matter.

He himself had not done the surgery, of course. That was work too delicate even for an angel's deft hands. It was bot work, and Elu had merely supervised. Everything that connected to the ansible nets had been removed from her. All that remained was for him to fiddle with the programs installed in her head. He could do that manually, though it was more cumbersome without the ansible connection. The bots had placed the appropriate wires and connectors into hidden ports below the titanium plates in Enga's skull. The other ends connected to a tablet that Elu now carefully navigated with his gloved fingertips, making infinitesimally small, careful changes to an intricate set of parameters and commands.

Each one of these changes would hurt her. Even the removal of the network connection would hurt her terribly, the way it had hurt him and Akavi months ago.

Elu didn't like anything about this.

He hesitated over the tablet. He knew exactly what Akavi had asked him to do: install a blocking program into Enga's sensory cortex so that she couldn't target either of them with her weapons. Any movement pointing at them with a gun or preparing to slash at them with a blade, or anything else like that, would cause pain and a reflex that turned her away.

It was a kind of program that had been installed in fractious angels before. It came in many standard varieties. His finger hovered, unwilling, over the command to install it.

Akavi would ask him, of course, if he'd done this job. And Elu was a terrible liar.

He closed his eyes. He took a deep breath.

He did not enter the command.

He navigated, instead, to a different part of Enga's electronic brain. To the complex systems that helped her aim in difficult situations, locking on to moving targets, automatically judging distance and timing shots to fit through the gaps in any cover.

He entered a blocking command into *those*.

It would take effort – he might fail – but with any luck, Elu could go back to Akavi and tell him he'd followed his orders, with a straight face. *It's done, sir. She can't target either of us.*

She would now find it impossible to lock on, with that

software, to any target that she knew was Akavi or Elu. But she could still point a weapon at them, using the organic part of her motor cortex, and press the trigger.

Elu looked down again at the helpless flesh and metal of her.

Kill us if you can, he thought, in what would once have been a private text-sending, back when either one of them had been able to do that. *If that's what you want.*

He turned the tablet off.

Is victory a lie?
Is loss?

– From the diaries of Dr Evianna Talirr

CHAPTER 20
Now

It happened simultaneously in every city, only an hour after the end of the ritual, while the bodies still lay on the ground and the breeze blew debris this way and that. While the protestors were still mourning for their dead, and while Tiv and Yasira and the Seven still reeled, in their lair, at having lost Luellae. After the angel troops policing the protest had retreated, a single angel reappeared in each city, out of the nearest relief station or out of a ship, unarmed and unarmored, clad in the blood-red and midnight-black livery of Nemesis.

Many of these angels were Vaurians, and they had molded themselves into a very specific shape. A tall, straight-backed woman with close-cropped silver hair. Her face was lined with age; her eyes were sharp and seething. Seven medals glinted at her collarbone; seven rings glinted on her hands.

But there were so many cities, and not enough Vaurian angels available for each one. Where Vaurians were not available, the angels used whichever female member of their local team was oldest or tallest or most commanding. They went without the medals and rings in these cases – those were only for the angels who properly looked the part. Nemesis was not a human, nor did She take human form, but this was the form in which humans often depicted

Her, and angels – even Vaurians – only used it in public when directly commanded to. For a purpose like this. For a message.

Precisely in time with each other across the planet, each angel mouth opened and said the same words, in the same inflection, with the same facial expression. A message like this was not merely a list of words to say. It was a program which, for the necessary minute or two, took over the body completely.

"People of the Chaos Zone," they said, and each voice was artificially amplified to carry for hundreds of meters – in some places, for miles. The mortals had already vacated the immediate area, in most of these places, but there were enough of them watching at a distance, hearing the earthshaking words from inside their homes. Where there were television screens, wired to receive the daily broadcasts, the nearest angel shimmered into focus on all of them. In the lair, Splió – still watching the protests' aftermath through the portal – heard the whole thing firsthand.

"People of the Chaos Zone," they said, "this is a message from Nemesis Herself. You have been heard. You have coordinated to voice your defiance against the Gods on a scale never seen since the Morlock War, and We have heard you. We will grant your wish. Since you so desperately desire not to be under the rule of the Gods, you will no longer be."

Every heretic and protester in the Chaos Zone simultaneously held their breath. This was an acknowledgment beyond their wildest dreams – and they knew enough to know it could not be a good thing.

"Effective immediately, the forces of the Gods will be withdrawn from this part of your planet – all the land that has been touched in any way by Outside. We will not police you for heresy. We will not keep order in your towns. We will not provide food or water relief nor medical care. Our priests will not officiate in your temples, nor will we answer your prayers. Nor will Nemesis' forces protect this world from outside threats, be they alien or Keres, further visits by the woman you call Destroyer, or mere natural disasters." Each angel paused here – not quite uncouth enough to smile, but there was some faint relish in their voices. "As a parting gift, we will grant you some information. You are aware that the Keres has been interested in the Chaos Zone from its beginning. Only recently, we discovered a battalion of Her forces moving in Jai's direction, far larger than those we have defeated here so far. The largest we have seen in hundreds of years. By our estimates, they should arrive in two weeks. As you prefer to solve your problems on your own, we will leave Her for you."

Across the Chaos Zone, in every home, on every doorstep, there was dead silence.

The messenger angels raised their heads. "Goodbye, people of the Chaos Zone. Your destruction will be richly deserved."

[Time is a Lie]

Yasira, by rights, should not have seen all this. She was asleep. She'd fallen into her bed almost as soon as she arrived back at the lair. Especially after hearing the news about Luellae, which had thrown her brief confidence back into disarray. It had taken a struggle for Tiv to get her to eat anything first – even though she knew how much worse it would be if she didn't eat food after something like this. It had been difficult to move the food to her mouth, to chew and swallow.

But in her dream, she was everywhere.

Usually when Yasira dreamed, her body worked the way it did while she was awake. There was just one of it, and all her jangling, jostling selves were crowded inside. But tonight she was not in her body. She was something like a flock of birds moving in synchrony. She glided through the air together, unfettered, and she saw what was going on below her.

She heard the angels' speech, and she knew, at some deep Outside level, that this part of the dream was real.

It's our fault, said some of her. *We tried to make it better, and we made it worse.*

That's what they want you to think, said the Scientist, a bigger bird than most of the others, plumed like a raven. She was watching the speech raptly, trying to trace its strategic implications. *This costs them something. They wouldn't be doing it if they weren't feeling pressed, and they wouldn't be feeling pressed if we hadn't* won *today.*

We'll fight them, the Strike Force promised in unison, a pack of hawks.

We can't, wailed everyone else. It was one thing to defend a few mortals. It was another to fight a being like the Keres who could scorch whole cities to cinders and glass. Yasira was strong, but not *that* strong.

Was she?

The whole flock turned on itself, angrily pecking. The landscape shifted, as it did in dreams. Yasira curled in on herself in pain, and when she uncurled she was in one body

again, just a girl like she usually was. She was crouched on
a plain of blasted rock, in a place that had used to be called
Zhoshash, back when there was a village there with people
and buildings and roads and it hadn't all been melted to
slag. It was very cold.

She looked up, and there, standing over her amid the
rock, was Dr Evianna Talirr.

Ev looked the same as she had the last time Yasira saw
her. She was tall, pale, and plain; she was almost old enough
to be Yasira's mother. She wore a scuffed white lab coat, and
her hair fell down in a limp ponytail.

"You," Yasira said, voice hoarse, and she didn't know
which part of her was saying it. "You did this. You did this
to the whole planet, you changed us so we couldn't do
anything except provoke the Gods or die, and then you *left*."

"Did I leave?" said Ev.

"Yes, you fucking did. You left us to die."

Ev walked closer to her, crouched at the ground at her
side. Yasira wanted to flinch away. She wanted to leap at her
and attack. She wanted to collapse and beg for her mentor
to return, to guide her, to fix this for her.

"No," said Ev. "You only didn't want to see me. I've been
right here." She smiled, mischievous and confident, like a
child about to get her own way. "I'll see you in the morning."

ACKNOWLEDGMENTS

I had always intended, from the time I started writing this book's first draft, that the climax would involve an organized political protest. From relatively early in the drafting process, it was clear to me that this protest would be a large, coordinated movement, springing up all over the Chaos Zone at once. But the protest occurs late in the book, and you can imagine my surprise when I finally got to that part of the draft in the summer of 2020, only to find mass protests for racial justice springing up all over North America in real life. To try to do justice to fictional protest scenes in the shadow of this reality was daunting, to say the least.

Black lives matter. If you enjoyed this book, I hope you will also look for books in this genre by Black non-neurotypical authors – including Akwaeke Emezi, Nalo Hopkinson, and Rivers Solomon, to name a few.

I follow in the footsteps of other writers, as always, and a few books were particularly helpful to me in solidifying some of this book's underlying ideas. Rebecca Solnit's A Paradise Built in Hell: The Extraordinary Communities that Arise in Disaster and Donna J. Haraway's Staying with the Trouble: Making Kin in the Cthulucene were instrumental in helping me conceptualize the daily life and attitudes of mortals in the Chaos Zone.

Meanwhile, although I was already familiar with the

concept of plurality, Akwaeke Emezi's Freshwater blew my mind wide open in terms of how plurality might be discussed and depicted on the page. I am grateful to my autistic and plural beta readers, who helped me make sure I was writing Yasira's experience thoughtfully, as well as to Noe Bartmess, Juliet Kemp, Hester J. Rook, Andrea Tatjana, and Merc Fenn Wolfmoor, who cheered me on and provided feedback more generally as the drafting progressed.

My wonderful agent, Hannah Bowman; my structural editor, Paul Simpson; and the team at Angry Robot all helped to guide me through the daunting process of writing the second book in a series for the first time – not to mention writing under contract for the first time. (If you've been there, you know that the struggle is real.) All provided invaluable feedback that helped me take the character basics of the first draft and punch them up into something with the kind of external stakes the story deserved.

Finally, I owe thanks to the people who were my close confidantes and supporters during the whole of the writing process, from beginning to end. To my dear friend Virgo, who originated the character of Akavi, from whom the whole rest of this fictional universe proceeds; to my family; to Jacqueline Flay, Dave Fredsberg, RB Lemberg, V Medina, Hannah Sherwood, Salie Snapdragon, Bogi Takács, my "friends at the pub" and my friends in fandom.

Love to you all.

Fancy some character-driven post-apocalytpic sci-fi?

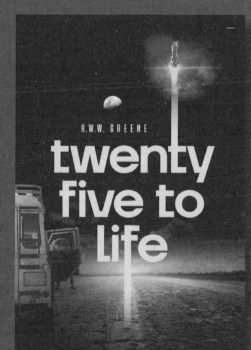

ONE

Julie's eyes rolled. It was the end of the world, and the deejay had no better response to it than industrial techno.

The invitation Ben had slipped her the week before described the fete as "The Party to End Everything" and promised twelve hours of music and madness. After all, the font screamed, "It's all downhill from here!!!"

All week, Ben had been referring to it as "The PEE."

Whatever direction the hill was headed, the music was too fucking loud. A migraine bass line, a rattle of synth-snare, choral loops, robot-assembler clashes, dark notes, and washtub thumps. Instinct demanded Julie crouch and cover her head, and she might have done had she been alone and had Ben given her room. "Quit stepping on my heels!" she said again.

Ben shuffled back an inch or two. It had been years since either of them had seen so many people – real, sweating, laughing, body-heat people – crowded into one place, and his sense of security seemed to hinge on how close to her he could stand, his cinnamon-scented breath puffing against the side of her face.

"Great party," he said. "Really glad we came."

"This was your idea."

His idea, sure, but Julie had agreed to go and gotten her mother to sign the release. Two more years lay ahead of her twenty-fifth birthday, which meant asking Mommy for permission to have fun. "I don't care if you drink and have sex and raise hell, but, for god's sake, don't let anyone get it on camera!" Julie's mother had warned and authorized the autocab that carried them to the event.

"We'll get some drinks and relax," Julie said. "If we don't like it we can leave early." *And then what? Spend the end of the world in ThirdEye or in front of the vid? Break into Mom's medicine cabinet again for some happy patches?*

When they reached the head of the line, Ben showed his invitation to a woman sitting at a table beneath a banner advertising Mela-Tonic, the party's corporate sponsor. She smiled. Some of her sliver-glitter lipstick had come off on her teeth. "Come get mellow, guys!" She reached below the table and came out with a Mela-Tonic swag bag for each of them. Julie waved hers off.

His own bag in hand, Ben joined Julie at the doorway of the ballroom. She grimaced. The PEE was an under-25 event hosted by a soft-drink company, so it was about as grassroots hip as the McDonald's Birthday Bash Julie's parents had organized for her ninth. Still, the organizers could have made an effort, rented out an old warehouse or mall space rather than the ballroom at the highway Marriott. The three-sided video unit overhead hardly bothered to cover the garish chandelier it surrounded. Instead, it alternated showing particolored rhythmscapes, Mela-Tonic commercials, and a mover of PorQ Pig saying, "That's it, folks!" in Hindi.

A girl in tribal bodypaint slunk up beside Julie. "What do you have?" she said.

"What?" Julie said.

The woman patted her left clavicle. "Apple, Tronic?"

"Oh!" Julie flushed. "It's a Tronic. Is there a mod?"

The girl handed Julie a plastic card.

"Can I get one?" Ben said.

"It only works if you have a pharma emplant," Bodypaint said. "Won't do shit if you don't." She drifted back into the shadows near the door. Her partner was there, pointing a scanner at people as they entered.

Julie ran her right index finger over the raised design on the card and made a fist to send the scan to the miniature computer under her clavicle. The emplant flashed a warning and grudgingly surrendered. The mod took an inventory of Julie's pharma and forced it to spit something more interesting than usual into her bloodstream.

Ben gazed at the girl in the bodypaint, who was now handing out cards to a group of three. "Do you think she's really naked?"

"Probably."

He pulled his eyes back to Julie. "Are you feeling the mod yet?"

"Yep." The hack was doing something lovely to Julie's endorphin and serotonin levels. She felt good, warm, loose. She took Ben's hand. "Let's get a drink."

The refreshment tables were loaded with Mela-Tonics, six flavors of carbonated water chock full of melatonin, valerian root, and seventeen other mood-altering herbs and spices! Ben opened a Lemon Lowdown. Julie picked a Strawberry Siesta. "Sip and chill," it said on the aluminum bottle.

"How do they expect people to dance after drinking these?" Ben said.

"They're mostly swaying," Julie said. A couple of dozen brave souls had taken to the dance floor. The rest of the party-goers were at the tables, barely looking at each other and playing holo games on their emplants.

"This is lame. I'm sorry," Ben said.

Julie ran her hand up and down the back of his shirt sleeve. It was incredibly smooth, but at the same time it seemed like she could feel every fiber. "I love you, Ben."

He shook his head sorrowfully. "That's just the drugs talking."

"Yeah, it is." She drained her drink. "Do you want to dance?"

"You go ahead. I'll just hang out over there." He gestured at one of the empty tables.

"Benjamin Esposito, you are such a slug." She grabbed his arm and dragged him back toward the entrance. Bodypaint's partner had left her standing alone looking bored. "Hey. My friend's brain is too normal to need a pharma. Do you have anything else?"

"Like real drugs?"

"Yeah."

The girl spread her arms and turned in a slow circle. She'd done the do-you-have-an-emplant? pantomime so many times she had a bare spot above her left breast. She also had a denuded place on her ass from where she'd been leaning against the wall. Otherwise, it was just her and the paint against the end of the world. "Do I look like I'm holding anything?"

Julie blinked owlishly. "Nope. You are definitely naked. What about the guy you were with?"

"My brother. Do you know how much trouble we could get into selling drugs at an under-age party?"

"So don't sell it." Julie held out her hand. "Give. It's the end of fucking everything."

The girl started to scratch her neck but caught herself. "He's in the bathroom. Send Mr Normal in there and tell him Cassandra says it's OK."

Julie waited outside the bathroom while Ben went in to negotiate. He came out slowly, holding his fist at waist level.

"What did you get?"

Ben opened his hand to reveal a single green pill. "No idea. Could be twelvemolly, could be a laxative."

"Either one will help you get rid of some of that shit you're packing." Julie handed him a fresh Lemon Lowdown. "Take."

Sixty minutes later, Ben and his drug dealer's little sister were in the corner messing up her paint job. Julie was on the dance floor. The techno tracks and her dance partners blended into each other in a wave of colored lights, rhythm, and touch. She was a hot, sticky mess and liked that just fine. When her high started to fade, she did the thing with the card again and let her mind go. She might pay for it later, but how much later was there, really?

The music stopped at 1:09am. The overhead screens played a short film designed to sell Mela-Tonic, then the view flipped to the news channels. The president gave a speech about hope and the future. A rabbi said a prayer. A newshead did an interview with three of "America's best and brightest," a scientist, a kindergarten teacher, and a famous cello player. There was a montage of faces and goodbyes.

Two-hundred and fifty-four miles up, rockets fired, moving the six colony ships out of low-Earth orbit and beginning an eighty-six year voyage to Proxima Centauri, humanity's new home, leaving ten billion people to die on the old one.

In spite of the mods and the gallons of Mela-Tonic

consumed, some of the partygoers were crying. Ben slung a sweaty arm around Julie's shoulders. His hand smelled like bodypaint and foreplay. "Are you OK?"

Julie bit her lip. "Am I supposed to feel good knowing Anji's up there? That she has a chance? I don't think I do."

Ben snorted. "She'll be an old woman before they even get close to the place."

The screens showed the big ships moving away from the second International Space Station. The point-of-view switched, and the cameras on the ships looked back at Earth. More newsheads. Suicide rates were expected to spike again. Tech stocks – especially aerospace and VR – were surging.

The American Dream, Julie thought. *Escape or die.*

"What's the opposite of survivor guilt?" one newshead said.

His partner chuckled. "Resentment of the doomed?"

The deejay cut the feeds and started in with the industrial techno again. More ads for Mela-Tonic flickered on the screens.

Julie couldn't move. No one was.

The three-way screen cut back to PorQ Pig. *That's it, folks!*

Julie's head was starting to clear when the autocab dropped her home around 2:30am. She changed into sweats and slippers and went to the kitchen for a snack. The smart screen embedded in the fridge door recognized her and began playing her mother's theme music. Julie squeezed her left eye shut and tried to focus on the fridge, which was showing a recut of a piece her mother had done the month prior.

Julie's mom, "Carson S Riley", the top-rated newshead in

the third-largest American market, smiled for the camera. She looked at least thirty years younger than she should. "They're off! Everyone's favorite family, the O'Briens – Mom, Dad, sister Anjali, and little brother Deshi – have left Earth. Next stop: Proxima Centauri!"

Julie couldn't tell if her mother had recorded the alternate introduction or if the news crew had just faked it with the AI. It hardly mattered. She'd been at the O'Briens' going-away party, too, but had studiously avoided her mother's camera. The video cut to Anji's father, Chuck. A drone hung behind him, flashing a game company's logo. Brian Case, one of Ben's friends, had a sponsorship and had to get the logo out in front of people whenever he could. "We were as surprised as anyone to be picked," Anji's father said, oblivious to the marketing going on behind him, "but we've spent the last fifteen years getting ready."

The next cut was to Deshi, Anji's adopted little brother. "It's so cool!" he said. "I'm going to live on a spaceship!" He began listing all the generation ship's technical specifications.

"Will it be hard to leave all your friends?" Carson asked Anji when her turn came.

Anji rubbed at a pimple on her forehead Another journalist might have edited the blemish out, but Carson S Riley was hoping for a few more hard-news laurels before she retired.

"I wish I could take them all with me," Anji said. "It feels like there's nothing here for them anymore."

The story editor let Anji's mom Upasana have the last word. "It's difficult, of course, to be leaving so much and so many behind." She smiled. "We'll just have to work hard to make the mission a success."

The segment cut to the studio. Carson S and her co-anchor Dr Owen Wang faced each other over a low coffee table.

"What do you think of that, Owen?"

Owen Wang was the prototypical cuddly conservative. He spread his hands. "It's a long shot, Carson. I've always said it. Nearly a century of travel and then what? Who knows what they'll find there? Who knows if they'll find anything? It's a crying shame that it's come to this."

Julie had a T-shirt with Wang's tagline, "It's a crying shame", printed on it. He said it at least once every broadcast. The sterilization of Mexico City. The water wars in southern Europe. The HIV-Too epidemic. The North Korean missile launch on Seoul. COVID-90. The failure of the latest generation of antibiotics. Crying shames, all of them. People like Wang and his pals were the reason the ecosystem was dying, and that was a crying shame, too.

Julie waved the screen off. There'd be nothing else on the news she wanted to see. Short of deistic intervention or the invention of time travel, there wasn't much that could catch her eye anymore. Her chest felt hollow. Before she was tempted to put a name to the feeling growing there, she pulled the plastic card out of her pocket and traced the mod again. She swayed, momentarily dizzy from the sudden change in brain chemistry. Everything was fine. She took the feeling to bed before it faded.

"Twenty-Five Saves Lives!" *A slogan used by proponents of the Thirtieth Amendment, a law that repealed the Twenty-Sixth amendment, which had set the voting age at eighteen. The Thirtieth Amendment went on to limit things like adulthood and full citizenship to persons "who are twenty-five years of age or older." The amendment had been designed to protect the job market, eliminate housing shortages, and take the pressure off aging infrastructure.*

—Wikipedia

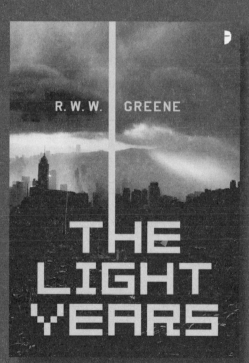

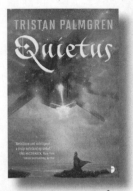

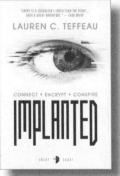

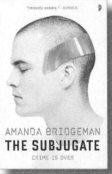

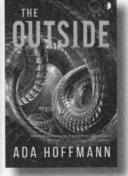